THE PRODIGAL MOTHER

Stephen Edger has been writing crime thrillers since 2010. An avid reader, Stephen writes what he likes to read: fast-paced, suspense thrillers with more than a nod to the darker side of the human psyche. He also writes under the pen name M.A. Hunter.

Stephen was born in the north-east of England, but grew up in London, meaning he is both a northerner and a southerner. By day he works in the financial industry using his insider knowledge to help shape the plots of his books.

He is passionate about reading and writing, and cites Simon Kernick and C.L. Taylor as major influences on his writing style.

www.stephenedger.com

/AuthorStephenEdger

@StephenEdger

ALSO BY STEPHEN EDGER

Snatched
Nowhere To Hide
Then He Was Gone
Little Girl Gone
Till Death Do Us Part
Future Echoes
Look Closer
Blood On Her Hands
What Lies Beneath

The DI Kate Matthews Series
Dead to Me
Dying Day
Cold Heart

THE PRODIGAL MOTHER

Stephen Edger

This novel is entirely a work of fiction. The names, characters and incidents portrayed in it are the work of the author's imagination. Any resemblance to actual persons, living or dead, events or localities is entirely coincidental.

All rights reserved. No part of this publication may be reproduced, stored in a retrieval system, or transmitted, in any form or by any means, electronic, mechanical, photocopying, recording or otherwise, without the prior permission of the author

Copyright © 2022 Stephen Edger

ISBN: 9798421858485

Dedicated to my wife and children whom I love more than life itself.

Chapter 1

Abbie – Now

'I'm so, so sorry, Abbie, but ... your son didn't survive the birth.'

I will never forget the moment the midwife broke the news. I'd already suspected that something wasn't right when I hadn't heard my baby cry, and then the sudden increase in activity behind the curtain they'd erected around my legs during the caesarean section procedure. But to actually hear those words as a mother ... there's nothing can prepare you for it. In the days that followed, my mind and soul sank to some very dark places, and I didn't think I'd ever be able to allow light and hope back into my life.

Mark did what he could to offer words of support and encouragement, but I could see the grief and heartbreak in the tears he held back. He desperately tried not to cry in front of me, and despite his regular protestations that he didn't blame me for what happened to Josh, I've never been able to forgive myself. My body managed to carry him for forty weeks, and then a further ten days, before we were invited in for inducement.

'You're obviously just keeping it too warm and cosy for him that he doesn't want to leave,' the midwife had joked that morning as I'd changed into the hospital robe and anticipated the moment I'd be able to hold my child to my skin for the first time.

We hadn't wanted to know the sex of the baby at the scan, but we'd chosen Josh for if he was a boy, and Clarissa for if she was a girl. And then we'd waited, imagining watching them growing up, taking their first steps, and hearing their first words.

And then my body failed me at the vital moment. Twenty hours of labour pains after the inducement had the midwife worried, and after a consultation, the medical team agreed it would be safest for the baby and me if they attempted delivery via a caesarean. I tried to stay calm, to tell myself that this was perfectly normal, and that thousands of women experience the same agony every year, but deep down, I feared the worst. And then when she broke the news, my gravest fears were confirmed.

'This one looks nice,' Yolanda says to me now, holding up a white baby grow with blue stripes down the sides. 'What is your instinct telling you? Does blue feel right, or does it repulse you?'

I look back at the baby grow, and to be honest I don't feel anything instinctive about it. It's very cute, as are all the new-born clothes we're perusing in the mother and baby shop, but I can't say I'm either drawn or put off by it.

Yolanda has been trying to predict the gender of the baby I've been carrying for eight months all morning, dragging me towards different toys and clothing, but she doesn't really appreciate that I really don't want to know. To consider holding my baby in my arms feels like tempting fate, and I'm not taking any chances this time. I've read every book about pregnancy I can find; I've taken every vitamin and mineral, exercised regularly, eaten the healthiest food I can prepare, and kept my stress levels as low as possible.

'I just don't know,' I finally respond, when she shakes the baby grow insistently.

She returns it to the display, and comes across to join me, placing a warm and gentle hand on my bump. 'I don't know how you can't want to find out what he, she or they is going to be. I had to know,' she says, moving her hand to her own bump. 'But after two boys, I needed to know whether there was any point in hanging on to their old clothes or whether I'd get to buy all the sweet, girly clothes I've craved since my first pregnancy. When we had the 4D scan and they confirmed a daughter, I can't tell you how excited I was. Not that I don't love my sons, but ... boys are disgusting pigs. That probably shouldn't have come as such a surprise after being married to one for ten years, but there you go.'

She rolls her eyes, and laughs. 'Has Mark said what he thinks you're having?'

He's told me he doesn't know, but I overheard him on the phone to his mum, and whether consciously or not, he's referred to "he," and "him," several times. I think he's as keen to avoid jinxing anything for us, which is why he doesn't want to say in front of me, but telling his mum feels almost as dangerous a curse to put on us.

'He says he just hopes they're healthy.'

'Well, yes, that's all that matters to any of us, isn't it?' She pauses and winces, twisting slightly. 'What I do know is that this one likes a good kick when I stand for too long, which tells me we ought to go and find somewhere for a large glass of wine and an all-you-can-eat cheese buffet.'

I raise my eyebrows in stunned surprise.

'Well, a girl can dream, can't she?' she quickly clarifies, batting away my concern. 'That's the first thing I plan to eat once this one arrives. I've missed wine, and Camembert, ooh and Roquefort.'

She's practically drooling as she speaks, a glazed look in her eyes, and sniffing the air, as if she's suddenly been transported to Paris and is eagerly tucking in.

I link my arm through hers. 'You'll just have to settle for a decaffeinated or green tea.'

She scowls at the suggestion. 'Well, I'm having the largest cream cake they've got on the side. I no longer care how much of a whale I become, I'll just blame it on this little one. Cream slice, chocolate éclair, or apple turnover. Hell, maybe I'll have all three!'

I stifle a yawn, as the morning's exertions begin to catch up, and nod that a rest and refreshment will be very welcome.

'I need to use the facilities before refilling my bladder,' I tell her, breaking arms.

'No worries. Why don't I go pay for my bits and pieces, and you go to the ladies, and then we'll meet by the escalator up to the café on the third floor?'

I nod my agreement at the plan, and watch as she moves away in search of a pay point, while I check the overhead signs for any reference to the toilets. Spotting it, I'm about to move off, when I crash in to a slight woman in a faded leather jacket, who's a good foot shorter than me, despite my own lower than average height.

'Oh, I'm sorry,' I quickly say, guilty of having not been looking where I was going.

But when our eyes meet, the terror and anxiety in hers, instantly makes me want to check I haven't injured her in some way.

'Are you hurt?' I ask, my own brow furrowing.

She opens her mouth to speak, before quickly shaking her head, and checking over her shoulder as if she's expecting to see some kind of harrowing figure approaching.

'Are you sure? You seem upset. Do you want me to get you some help?'

Her eyes are screaming yes, but she shakes her head silently again, before pulling away and muttering the word 'Sorry,' in what I can only guess is an Eastern European accent.

I continue to watch as she hustles away, quickly disappearing into the crowd of shoppers milling about in the large department store. I would hurry after her, my concern genuine, but baby is tap-dancing on my bladder, and I think it may burst if I don't get there soon. Checking the sign again, I ease into a cubicle, and close and lock the door behind me. Relief swiftly warms my body.

But these are the times I find hardest. When I'm alone with just my imagination for company, I picture myself in the maternity ward in a month's time, reliving the nightmare. What if my body fails us again? What if the precious life growing inside of me is robbed of their chance of life, because I wasn't built to have children?

I know such thoughts are dangerous, and could become a self-fulfilling prophecy if I'm not careful, but it's difficult to remain positive. When I think back to this time five years ago, I hadn't even considered the prospect that something might go wrong during labour. My pregnancy then had been relatively easy up to that point. I'd only experienced small bouts of morning sickness in the first trimester, no concerns had been identified in either of the scans, or in the numerous blood tests I was forced to endure. Everything had been on course for a safe delivery and a lifetime of happy memories. Until it was snatched away.

'It wasn't your fault; unfortunately sometimes these things just ... happen,' the grief counsellor tried to explain when I shut myself off from the rest of the world and spent all day in pyjamas, practically daring death to come for me so I could be reunited with Josh.

At my lowest point, I actually envied other women who miscarry earlier in their pregnancies. Somehow it felt crueller that I was robbed of my chance to become a mother right at the finish line. But in truth, the pain is horrific no matter when the loss occurs, and no one mother's level of grief is any better or worse than another's. We all experience the bitter pill, and realising this was the moment when I began to try and claw myself back from the brink.

The job at the preschool has helped more than I'd ever realised. When Mark had first suggested the apprenticeship and qualification I'd thought it was just his way of getting me out of the house and earning a salary, but he was right. It's been cathartic helping other children learn and develop, and it has helped me begin to try and forgive myself for what happened to Josh. I may never fully find the absolution I crave, but I'm willing to show our new baby all the love my heart possesses, and protect them until the day I die.

Tearing off tissue, I dab my eyes, and take a deep breath, slowly exhaling, and hoping that my puffy cheeks won't show Yolanda why I really came in here. Exiting the cubicle I wash my hands, straighten my hair in the mirror, and splash some cold water on my face.

When I emerge from the toilets, it isn't Yolanda I spot first, but the woman in the faded leather jacket. She's standing beside a pillar bearing the store directory, and she's biting one of her fingernails. It is clear when she's glancing over, it's me she's looking at. Now that I can see her properly, she is gaunt, her dark hair greasy and ends split. She doesn't look well, and again I want to check on her well-being, but there's something about the way she's standing, and staring that isn't quite right. I spot Yolanda by the escalator and wave as I approach.

'Let's go find those cakes,' I tell her as airily as the fear now coursing through my veins will allow.

We link arms again, and board the escalator, but I keep one eye on the woman at the pillar, and my pulse quickens when I see her peel away and join the escalator several travellers behind. She's following us.

I lean closer to Yolanda so she'll be able to hear me whisper. 'Don't look now, but I think we're being followed?'

Yolanda instantly turns her head, until I tug on her arm.

'She's wearing a faded and crumpled black leather jacket, skinny jeans and a heavy metal t-shirt. I bumped into her outside the toilets, and there was something ... I don't know, just something not right about her.'

There's concern in Yolanda's eyes as she meets my gaze. 'Do you recognise her? A friend of Mark's?'

I shake my head in answer to both questions. 'I've never seen her before in my life.'

We arrive at the third floor, and I hurry us off the escalator, in the direction of the large restaurant area, figuring there's safety in numbers. But Yolanda freezes as we're about to enter, and swiftly turns back towards the escalator.

'W-What are you doing?' I stammer, trying to stop her movement, quickly realising that she is stronger and more determined.

'Let's go find out what your stalker wants,' she says casually.

The woman in the leather jacket looks shocked when she spots us waiting for her at the top of the escalator, and tries to turn her head and body away as she arrives, but Yolanda isn't one to take no for an answer.

'Why are you following me and my friend? We're both heavily pregnant and in no mood for fun and games.'

The girl stops, and stares from me to Yolanda and back again. Her lips tremor as she opens her mouth, but no words emerge.

There are huffs of discontent from other customers as they try to squeeze past us, and so Yolanda steers us away from the escalator and into a quiet corner. 'Well? What do you want?' she tries again.

I start as the girl looks directly at me. 'Y-You lost child, no?'

My eyes narrow at the question. 'That's none of your business.'

'N-No, you need listen. Your child not die. He still alive. I can prove it.'

Chapter 2

Louisa – Five years ago

The smell of burning rubber, the pressure of a crippling weight across her shoulders, the sound of metal splintering, and an intense heat like she'd never experienced: these were the senses that met Louisa as she groggily came to beneath the wreck of the upturned Aston Martin.

'She's pregnant! Please, you've got to get her out of there,' she heard Pete yelling from somewhere out of sight. It was so dark that she couldn't tell whether her eyes were closed or if night had fallen.

'H-Help,' she tried to stay, but the words caught in her throat as the smoke billowed around her.

Sparks flew past her eyes as the chainsaw recommenced its battle with the steel frame of the car, and as she tried to scream, all that emerged was a sob. Tears borne of terror, confusion, and regret. What the hell had happened to the car? One minute she was at home, waiting for Pete to return from his meeting, and the next, barely breathing in this state of confusion. She didn't even remember getting in the car.

'Louisa, it's going to be fine,' Pete's voice called in through the darkness between bursts of the chainsaw. 'The fire brigade are going to cut you out of there, and the ambulance is waiting to take you to hospital.'

She closed her eyes as warm tears swam down her cheeks, stinging where they intercepted the broken skin. What day was it anyway? Her memory of waiting for Pete was definitely a Tuesday. Wasn't it? Pete had gone to the office on Tuesday, so it must have been, but how much more of her memory was missing? If she couldn't recall the accident, or even getting in the car, how many days were now lost amongst the throbbing behind her temples.

'Louisa? Louisa? Can you hear me?'

She didn't recognise the broad Scottish accent, but she coughed and spluttered in acknowledgement.

'Louisa? I'm reaching my arm in to you. Squeeze my hand if you can hear me, and if it feels comfortable to do so.'

It was so hard to see anything, but she opened her left eye and squinted towards where the voice had come, and saw a blue gloved hand appear from the shadow, fingers waggling for touch. She winced as she tried to move her left hand out to greet it, the pressure on her shoulders intensifying, as she gently brushed the tips of the latex.

'That's good, Louisa. I can feel you. My name's Angus, and I'm going to get you out of here, but I need you to do a couple of things for me. Is that alright, Louisa? Touch my hand again if you understand?'

She grimaced as she strained her fingers again.

'Good. Now listen, I need you to stay as still as you can while we do what we need to cut you out. Your health and wellbeing are our top priority, which is why we are moving very slowly. As soon as it is safe to do so, we will get the paramedics to you, and get you out safely. Touch my hand again if you understand.'

She complied, but felt the burden on her shoulders shift, and bend her further forwards, the pressure on her spine immeasurable. She screamed.

'Are you okay? What's happened?' Angus called in, his voice abandoning its previous calm state. 'Boys stop, stop, she's screaming.'

The whir of the circular saw stopped, and the sound of distant sirens filtered through the darkness.

'Louisa? Tell me what's going on in there,' Angus called in, his hand disappearing and replaced by the dim beam of torchlight.

'P-Pain,' she spluttered. 'Sh-Shoulders.'

'Is there something pressing on your shoulders, Louisa? Is that what you're saying?'

'Y-Yes,' she wailed as the pressure turned into a deep burning fissure that jarred the length of her spine. It was as if gravity had targeted all its force on her alone, and was slowly crushing her spirit and body.

The torch beam vanished, and the sound of voices talking hurriedly just out of earshot was followed by the restarting of the circular saw, and as a shower of sparks erupted in her periphery, darkness swallowed Louisa's mind.

***

'Louisa? Open your eyes if you can hear me,' she heard a voice calling, gradually getting louder.

Louisa's body shook and bounced as whatever she was lying on shuddered. It reminded her of being on a rollercoaster, but there wasn't any pain. The pressure from her shoulders was gone, and she felt as light as a cloud.

'Louisa, we're on our way to the hospital, but I need you to open your eyes if you can hear my voice. Please?'

The cloud-like surface continued to jostle her about sideways and back and forth, but she strained to separate her eyelids, and the blurred face of a young woman with short, dark, and spiky hair appeared.

'There we go.' The woman's face temporarily disappeared, as she shouted to the driver. 'Her eyes are open. What's our ETA?'

Louisa didn't hear the bellowed response, as her eyelids began to close and shut out the blinding light of the back of the ambulance.

'Louisa, I need you to keep your eyes open, sweetheart. You've taken a bit of a beating, and we need to keep you awake.'

Louisa forced her eyelids apart again, and saw the young paramedic scrutinising her pupils, running other tests as the ambulance continued to speed towards the hospital.

Louisa gasped as she suddenly realised that what she couldn't feel was her baby, and she quickly moved her hand over the sheet wrapped around her bump, feeling an elasticated belt.

'It's alright,' the paramedic said quickly, 'we're monitoring baby's heartbeat to make sure he or she is okay. Do you know what you're having?'

Louisa shook her head, now conscious of the mask covering her mouth and chin. She moved her hand up to the mask, trying to pull it away, but the paramedic took her hand instead.

'That's just to make sure you and the baby are getting enough oxygen. Unless it's uncomfortable, I really need you to keep the mask in place.'

Louisa nodded her understanding, trying to ignore the voice in her mind, telling her that something was very wrong with her unborn.

'Is everything okay with the baby?' she mumbled behind the mask.

'The heartbeat is good, but we're taking you to the hospital to be safe. They'll do an ultrasound and just ensure no damage was caused by the accident. How is the pain in your legs?'

Louisa tried to focus on any pain receptors, but whatever painkillers they'd given seemed to be doing a great job of blocking them.

'No pain. I just want to know my baby is okay.' The tear sliding down her temple was a surprise, but she made no effort to wipe it away.

'Okay, sweetheart, well we'll know more soon enough. Your husband –'

'Pete? Where's Pete?'

'He's going to meet us at the hospital. He went home to get your notes and bits and pieces, and then he'll join us there. He said you have a private physician overseeing your pregnancy, so he's going to get him over as well. Try not to worry, and just focus on keeping your blood pressure down. It's the best thing you can do for yourself and baby. Okay?'

Louisa blinked in acknowledgement.

***

When she came to again, Louisa found herself inside a private room, cold gel on her bump, and a paddle being moved around it. Turning, the screen the sonographer was viewing was blocked from Louisa's sight, but she saw Pete sitting beside her, holding her hand. Her heart warmed as she met his tearful stare, and he smiled.

'I'm never letting you out of my sight again,' he whispered.

The baby moved inside her, and Louisa erupted with happy tears at the sensation, finally allowing the fears to slowly subside from her mind.

The sonographer glanced over and smiled. 'Baby seems to be intact, but given how far along you are, and because we can't be certain that no damage has been done to the amniotic sac, your physician may decide to bring birth day forward. I'm going to go and have a word with him now, but I don't want you to worry.'

The sonographer stood to leave, before freezing as something caught her attention, and she turned back, unable to keep the obvious panic from her eyes. 'Louisa, I need you to listen to me carefully, are you in any discomfort, or pain?'

Louisa shook her head as her pulse increased with the fear staring back at her. The sonographer didn't wait to explain what was disturbing her, racing from the room in search of her obstetrician.

'W-What's going on?' Louisa asked Pete, beside her, but he was busy staring at something at the foot of the bed, his face ashen.

'Pete? W-What is it? Pete?'

She tried to sit up, but it was too painful to do so, but as she craned her neck, her shoulders aching from the earlier pressure, she saw the red puddle, rapidly spreading from between her legs.

Dr Michelson was hauled into the room seconds later by the sonographer, and he attempted to offer Louisa a reassuring smile, but his face was as pale as Pete's.

And that's when she felt the roaring surge of pain blast out of her abdomen, careering like a rocket until it slammed into her chest and head. It was all she could do not to throw up as excruciating pain squeezed her torso.

'We need to get her to the operating theatre stat,' Dr Michelson shouted, shuffling Pete out of the way, and raising the bar of the trolley she was still lying in.

The sonographer mimicked the action on the right side of the trolley. 'I should call for a porter.'

'There's no time for a porter,' Michelson barked back. 'We need her in theatre immediately.'

Pete's chair scraped across the hard floor as he slowly stood and moved back towards the wall. Louisa stared at him for hope and reassurance, but he couldn't return her gaze; his face paralysed with fear.

'P-Pete, tell me it will be okay?' she wailed as the pain continued to squeeze her in its grip.

But he didn't answer; couldn't answer as he watched Michelson and the sonographer steer the trolley out of the room and into the darkness of the corridor.

Chapter 3

Abbie – Now

I can't process what this woman has just told me, but it's Yolanda who reacts first.

'What did you just say?'

The woman ignores the question, and continues to stare at me, with a look that penetrates any defence mechanism my body is trying to erect. 'He not dead.'

Yolanda shoots out a protective arm, her hand resting on my shoulder, as she twists to block the woman's path to me. 'What kind of mad woman are you?' Yolanda bites back at her. 'You can't just approach a stranger in the street and bowl out with something like that. In case it slipped your attention, we're both *heavily* pregnant.'

Yolanda starts to steer me away, and back in the direction of the restaurant, but I can see this woman in my periphery, bouncing as a puppy might when trying to get her owner's attention.

'Please? You have to listen. I know sound crazy, but is truth. If you just –'

Yolanda's head snaps around so fast it's in danger of breaking away. 'I don't know who you think you are or what con you're trying to instigate, but you're messing with the wrong women. My patience is so thin that if it goes, I won't be to blame for what happens.

We have no money to give you, and if you try and lay a finger on us, I will scream so loud for security that my voice will crack these windows beside us. I don't know who you think my friend is, but you've made a mistake.'

The woman tries to interject, but Yolanda stares her down.

'You've made a mistake. This is my friend's first pregnancy, so whatever poppycock you're trying to spin, it won't wash with us.'

Yolanda's right, or at least she's right to think she is: I've never told her about Josh or the traumatic experience that put my life on freeze for the best part of five years. I didn't deliberately withhold the truth, but when we met at the prenatal class for the first time, she was so full of excitement about being pregnant again that it just didn't feel right to put a dampener on it. And then how could I casually throw into conversation that I too had been pregnant before, only to fall just before the line? I've thought about bringing it up, but there hasn't been the need. My therapist kept telling me I needed to move forward with my life, rather than remaining so preoccupied with the past.

Yolanda gently moves me towards the restaurant and away from the protesting puppy, but I freeze when I hear the woman say the words "St Philomena Birthing Centre". Yolanda tries to move me again, but my feet are planted. The faded leather jacket circles into my path.

'I'm right, no? You lose child there too? My son was taken too. But he didn't die. Please? I tell truth. Your son didn't die.'

My knees go, and it's only because Yolanda still has her arms on me that I don't collapse to the floor. The woman in the faded leather jacket also helps prop me up, and between them they lead me into the restaurant, and to one of the green booths in a quiet area reserved for new mums who want to discreetly breastfeed. There's only one mother in the area, making the most of the quiet time while her baby sleeps in the pram beside her. She looks drawn and exhausted, but she's glowing too: a mother thriving in her new role.

'I'll be fine,' I try to reassure Yolanda, but a chill has gripped my bones, and I can't seem to shake it, even though the climate in the restaurant must be decidedly warm judging by the sheen forming on Yolanda's forehead, beneath her shaved locks.

'I think you should go,' Yolanda glares at the stranger, but the woman looks fragile, as she looks to me for a decision.

'No,' I eventually whisper to Yolanda. 'I want to hear what she has to say.'

Yolanda looks back at me with wide eyes and raised eyebrows. I can understand her confusion.

'Can you give us a minute?' I ask the woman, who shrugs and moves away to the elasticated cordon separating the seating area from the thoroughfare of diners with their trays and purchases.

'What's going on, Abbie?' Yolanda asks, as she sits in the chair across the table from me. 'Do you know this woman?'

I shake my head, my mouth suddenly dry. 'I've never met her before in my life, but ... I don't know, there's just ... something about her that makes me want to hear what she has to say.'

'She looks like trouble,' Yolanda mumbles under her breath firing a quick glare at her, and checking she's still waiting by the cordon.

I don't agree with the conclusion; I'd say she looks more like she's *in* trouble, and I don't know if it's my maternal instinct taking control, or my general need to look after those I perceive in need of my support, but I can't just turn my back on her. Whether she's spinning a lie or not, I can't ignore the fact that I feel I should at least listen to what she has to say.

'And what was all that garbage about you having another baby?' Yolanda asks now, and I can't bring my eyes to meet hers.

'My son was stillborn,' I say quietly, focused on my fingers as they tangle with each other on the table before me. It was years ago, and I never told you because …'

I don't have a legitimate reason that will justify my deceit for the seven months we've known each other, so I don't say anything.

Yolanda's warm hand falls on mine, and she squeezes my fingers gently. 'I'm so sorry, I had no idea.'

Typical Yolanda to offer her apology when I'm the one in the wrong.

'No, I'm the one who's sorry,' I say, daring to meet her gaze, and relieved when I see nothing but empathy in those beautiful black eyes. 'I should have told you, but the time just never seemed … I'm sorry.'

All animosity has vanished from her face as she offers a reassuring smile. 'At least that explains why you're so willing to hear her out. The hospital she mentioned, is that where …?'

I nod, instantly recalling the dark grey building that had given me the shivers the moment we'd arrived. There was no way Mark and I would have chosen to go to a private hospital, but he receives free private medical care through work, and thought he should make the most of the cover for dependents. The moment we arrived, in the middle of a storm, I'd wanted us to abandon the plan and head to the nearest NHS-run, more traditional looking hospital, but he'd told me everything had been set up, and I shouldn't worry because it might affect the delivery. It had looked more like some gothic motel from the outside, but it felt clean once we were in through the doors, and I soon forgot what it looked like when the contractions intensified.

'Are you sure you're alright?' Yolanda asks, drawing me back to the busy restaurant. 'You're pale as a sheet. Do you want me to call someone?'

'No, I'll be fine,' I half-lie. 'I could do with something to drink though.'

Yolanda stands, despite the struggle with her bump. 'I'll get us some tea, you wait here.'

Given she's due sooner than me, I should be the one fetching drinks, but my legs are still tremoring beneath the table, and I'm not sure I could stand even if I wanted to.

'Relax,' Yolanda says, as if reading my mind, 'I'm sure I can find someone to carry my tray back for me. The staff in here are always only too willing to help.' There's a twinkle of mischief in her eyes as she heads away from the table and joins the queue at one of the food stations.

I can see the woman in the faded leather jacket moving left to right, glancing at me every few seconds, as if trying to work out whether she's now permitted to approach. I indicate the second chair at the table, and she hurries across, keeping one eye out in case Yolanda comes haring back.

'Is okay now?' she asks as she sits, and pulls a packet of cigarettes from her pocket.

'Oh you can't smoke in here,' I say, and as she looks around, she suddenly recalls the rules on smoking indoors in the UK, and blushes as she returns the packet to her pocket.

Up close, I believe there is a very beautiful young woman buried beneath the greasy, split hair, and heavily sunken eyes. Her cheeks and neck bear long-healed scars, and the jacket looks at least two sizes too big for her slight frame. But there's a resilience to her as well. I don't doubt that this woman has led a harrowing life, and managed to survive. She's a fighter, and there's something incredibly inspiring about that.

'What's your name?' I ask.

She has another glance around, though I can't be sure if she's checking for Yolanda or some other menace in the shadows.

'Kinga,' she says pressing a hand to her chest.

There's no sign of a wedding ring, but her nails are chewed to the quick, and there is obvious banana-like bruising around her thumb. I have no doubt that this woman has had to fight every day of her life to be here now.

'I'm Abbie,' I acknowledge, and offer an empathetic smile, 'and my friend is called Yolanda. You'll have to forgive her, she only has my best interest at heart. She's a good listener, if you give her the chance.'

Kinga doesn't look convinced, but then I imagine she probably doesn't accept anything at face value anymore, though I can't put my finger on what makes me think this.

'Where are you from?' I ask, before quickly adding, 'your accent isn't local.'

Another look around as if she suspects the mother jostling the pram to buy herself a few minutes more peace is some kind of spy.

'From Chechnya.'

Geography was never my strong suit at school, and it hasn't improved in the intervening years, but I think that's a Russian republic, which would explain her accent and haunted appearance, but I make a mental note to check later.

I don't know what else to say to her. I want her to explain what she meant about Josh still being alive, and what led her to finding me here in the Trafford Centre of all places, but I don't know where to begin.

I don't recall meeting any other parents when I was at the St Philomena Birthing Centre, so I don't believe we have met before, and it disturbs me to think that that kind of information might be readily available online for anyone to find.

'My son die too,' she blurts out, leaning further forwards, resting her elbows on the table, her hands stretched out towards me. 'At hospital. That what they told me.'

I hate myself for thinking it, but I can't see how someone of Kinga's means would have been referred to the private hospital. It wasn't until a month after we were there that I was gobsmacked at the size of the bill for our two-night stay. I remember telling Mark that we could have bought a small car for the price, but he said work paid for most of it. He told me he'd done what he thought was for the best, and that money was no object as far as mine and Josh's health were concerned. I won't deny that I haven't wondered whether things would have been different if I'd been induced at an NHS Hospital, but it doesn't help anyone to spend too long focusing on the what-ifs in life: regret is for those who can't live with the decisions they've made.

I start as Kinga slams her palm on the table top. 'But he didn't die. Not then. I know this because he died this year.'

Chapter 4

Abbie – Now

In my periphery, I can see that Yolanda is nearing the front of the queue, but I can't take my eyes off Kinga.

'How do you know he died this year?' I ask, struggling to keep up.

The pitch of her broken English suggests a woman in her early twenties at most, but the way the dark circles hang beneath her eyes, gives her face a haunted look. I can almost picture her sitting around a campfire late at night reciting horror stories, only hers are true and based on real experiences.

She glances around nervously again, and it's becoming infectious as I too double-check the coast is clear, even though I have no clue who or what she's so afraid of.

'I come to this country as refugee. It maybe six or seven year ago. Chechnya still suffering from bombs that drop decades ago. It is hard life. My parents died during the conflict, and my brother – he still there – he want better life for me, so he arrange for me to come to England. Land of opportunity, he tell me. But I have no passport, so he pay men to bring me here. My brother is – how you say – writer for newspaper.'

'Journalist?' I offer. 'Reporter?'

She snaps her fingers at this. 'Yes. Reporter, like

Clark Kent. He know some people who are not good people. They know people who can get things for right price. My brother he work hard, save money, and pay for my trip, giving men money for me to get flat and clothes when I get here. But these men steal money, and make me … they make me do things I not want to do.'

Her stare drops to her hands on the table, and my imagination floods with terrifying thoughts of the kind of abuse she may have suffered. I'm not ignorant to the horrors suffered by immigrants entering the company illegally. The sort of people that traffic others aren't known for their empathy and humanity.

'My brother want what best for me, but he trust wrong people. I try get message to him, but I know it dangerous. They made me phone him when we first arrive, and tell him that I have flat, and job, and clothes, and that very happy. I wanted to cry and scream, and tell him truth, but they threaten to kill me and him if I do, so I lie to my brother. I wish he with me now, but he want to stay in Chechnya and help others survive.'

I never had any siblings, and there's a part of me envies her idolising her brother. I'm not entirely sure why she's sharing details of her background with me, and I hate myself for daring to question whether this is all part of an act as Yolanda hinted earlier. If her next words are to ask me for money to help her escape the clutches of the people who helped her get into the country, or to help her brother move here, then I'll have to make my excuses and ask her to leave.

Yet, instinctively I want to believe what she's telling me. There is a brutal honesty in her tone that's breaking my heart, and making me realise that my own history – as paralysing as it's been – isn't as bad as some others. I'm still suffering the loss of Josh, but I've never not had a roof over my head, a husband who supports me, or had to question where my next meal is coming from. I've certainly never been forced to perform certain acts for fear of my life, and although Kinga hasn't gone into detail about what she was made to do, I can imagine.

'Men who bring me to England, they lock me in room, and if I not do what they tell me, they beat and not give food. I tried to escape once, and they kick and … rape me.' Her head snaps up, and I see her tearful eyes about to burst the dam.

We both start as something collides with the table. I look up and see Yolanda, but catch Kinga as she looks away and dries her eyes with the sleeve of her jacket. A young man in a green tabard is hovering just behind Yolanda, the tray he's carrying weighed down with two metal pots, cups, saucers, plates, cutlery and a mountain of food. I move my hands from the table, allowing him to slide the tray onto it.

'Is there anything else I can get for you?' he asks, but Yolanda thanks him and sends him on his way.

I have no appetite after what Kinga has told me, but I don't want to belittle Yolanda's efforts. 'It looks delicious,' I mutter, as the words catch in my throat.

She looks from Kinga to me. 'Is everything *okay* here?'

I nod, and she sits.

'Good, well I hope you don't think I'm imposing, but I ordered your new friend some soup and a roll. Is that okay?'

Kinga turns back and looks at Yolanda, before nodding gratefully. I introduce them, and watch as Kinga tears into the granary roll, dipping it into the small bowl of steaming soup.

Yolanda dishes out the cups and saucers for the three of us, and pours from the largest of the metal pots, before passing me a plate with an enormous choux bun.

'I wasn't sure what to get you, so I hope this is okay?'

I thank her as she passes me a fork, and then watch as she tucks into her own choux bun.

'Kinga was just telling me about how she came to be in England,' I explain, leaving out some of the more gruesome detail.

'That how I came to be pregnant,' Kinga picks up when I'm done. 'I not know at first. I just thought I was sick. But then eventually, I become fat, and men realise that there is problem. We don't know who father is, but I tell them I want to keep my baby, and we reach agreement on how I can pay for my stay with them by other means.'

Her eyes dart around the restaurant again, and it's only now that she's fallen silent that I realise her soup and roll are gone.

'I work for them delivering packages. I guess as pregnant lady, I less suspicious to police maybe? I don't know. But then time arrive for baby to come, and they take me to hospital, but doctors there give me drugs, and when I wake, there is no baby. They tell me he die during birth. I not believe it at first, but then they bring me dead baby, and I hold him, and he so cold that my heart break.'

A single tear escapes her eyes and falls silently, blotting in the tired skin of her cheek.

I reach a hand across the table and gently squeeze hers. 'I'm sorry.'

She squeezes my fingers back, and something passes between us: two women bonded by their grief.

'Men say that after baby, I no longer attractive to men who want sex, but they say I still owe them money for my life in England, and so they put me back to work, delivering packages. But without baby, I am arrested couple of years ago, and go to prison for several months. When I get out, I … they give me drugs, until point where I need them as much as they need me. I clean now, but it was long road back.'

Yolanda has been listening quietly, but the little that she has heard has limited her appetite too, and half the choux bun remains uneaten on her plate. I don't think either of us can truly appreciate the journey Kinga has been on, but I still don't know how any of this has anything to do with Josh.

'Just after Christmas, I receive telephone call from doctor. She tell me my son die in fire. I think it some kind of mistake, but tell me boy in fire was five years-old and DNA was ninety-nine per cent match to me.'

My mind is racing at her story. I know how much she would have suffered when the obstetrician or midwife explained that her son had died, and how hard it will have been for her to reach acceptance of that heartbreak. I don't know how I'd react to learn that I'd been lied to for all these years. But there is a pinprick of hope now trying to penetrate my conscious mind.

I pass her one of the paper napkins from the tray as she begins to cry quietly. Yolanda meets my gaze, but I have no words to explain or comfort Kinga. There is no longer any part of me that doubts the story she's told, but I don't know what I can do for her. I don't know whether we still have any contact details for St Philomena's at home, but I'm sure I can ask Mark to check the box in the loft with all of Josh's things to see if there is anything there.

'I'm so sorry, Kinga,' Yolanda says, and I'm relieved to see that she's hung up her cynic's hat as well. 'What you've been through ... I'm so sorry.'

Kinga lowers the paper napkin, and offers a nod of gratitude, and then fixes me with a hard stare. 'This why I am here now, why I find you. They told you your son dead too, but I believe they lie to you. They stole my boy from me and give him to other family. They stole baby from you too.'

My blood runs cold, and my throat fills with bile; I'm not sure I'm going to be able to stop myself from bringing up the few mouthfuls of choux bun.

'I go to address of Philomena Centre, and it all boarded up. No longer in business. Land is listed for sale. I angry, and so break in, wanting to start fire for revenge. But inside there is nothing left to burn. I check every cupboard in every room, looking for anything to find people responsible. That is when I find this ...' She pauses and reaches into the inner pocket of her jacket, slowly extracting a folded piece of paper. She flattens it on the table and slides it across to me.

It is a torn page, with very little detail. At first I can't read what it says as my vision is blurred with tears of my own, but then I see mine and Josh's names, and a large monetary value.

'I think doctors lie to you and sell your baby too,' Kinga says, and it's the last thing I hear before leaning over and retching.

Chapter 5

Louisa – Five years ago

The grunt of the circular saw echoed in her dreamless sleep, the darkness exploding in a shower of tiny, orange sparks, each one catching her attention, before fading to nothing. She wanted to scream out, to beg anyone to pull her from the enclosed space constricting her movement, and yet every time she opened her mouth to wail, the saw would start again, and drown out her cries.

Was this how she was going to die? Trapped in a crumpled car, with the walls slowly squashing her until she was no bigger than at atom?

But then, just as she was ready to give up, something ripped through the darkness, opening the nearest wall like a tin opener; the metal screaming in resistance as the jaws of the spikes tore it apart. A brilliant white light replaced the darkness, and then a tiny hand – so small it couldn't weight more than a feather – reached through the light and gently tugged on her body, until she was free of the constraints and floating towards the light.

Suddenly all her pain was gone too, and as if gravity no longer held her, she floated onwards, being pulled by the baby-like hand.

'Is this heaven …?' she was about to ask, when

suddenly she was plunging. Faster and faster she fell, through nothingness, the hand no longer keeping her up. She plummeted into more darkness, her heart racing so quick that it might burst out of her chest, discarding the rest of her before it was too late.

And then suddenly she gasped, the air being sucked into her lungs to the sound of rumbling thunder. Her eyes flew open, but she couldn't work out of she was still falling or whether she'd landed. Her vision blurred as she tried to fix her concentration on one object, but it was all she could do to keep her focus and vision straight. Was her head spinning, or was someone rolling it around.

She tried to call out for help, but when her mouth opened, no words emerged, as if the receptor between her brain and voice box had been cut. She allowed her eyes to close and tried to collect her other senses.

What can I hear?

A chirping of some sort; regular rhythm. No not chirping, but maybe bleeping? Yes, rhythmic and regular as clockwork: bleep, pause, bleep, pause, bleep. No sound of the circular saw scratching at the car door. No voices nearby, but maybe just about a distant hum, as if they're not too far away, but nothing distinct enough to recognise.

What can I smell?

She inhaled as deeply as she could manage: fresh sheets, but not the smell of the fabric softener she was used to. No, this was different; sterile; free of scent. What else? Burning? No, that's not it. Something metallic? But not in the room, closer than that, as if the smell was trapped inside the membrane of her nostrils.

What can I taste?

Her mouth was so dry, that she needed to peel her tongue from behind her lower teeth, but couldn't generate enough saliva to swallow. She coughed with the strain of the effort, parting her dry, cracked lips. She grimaced at the sour and salty perfume that seemed to fill the dry void. She knew instantly she was thirsty, and couldn't recall the last drink she'd had.

Allowing her head and arms to move next, she tried to see through her fingers and ears. Her head was being supported by something firm and yet soft in equal measure. Her face felt cooler when she pressed her cheek against something, and the same when she twisted her neck to press the other cheek against the same surface. A pillow of some sort she deduced. Next her hands, brushed against her legs, and then ran obstacle-free across the cool and smooth sheet.

I'm in bed.

Relief washed over her as she concluded that whatever had come before was simply a nightmare, one so intense it had completely thrown her off balance. She was at home, and all she'd need to do is reach out to feel the warmth of Pete's hairy chest beside her.

No that's not right.

Her hands reached both edges of the firm mattress, too small to be her own, and with no sign of Pete squashed in beside her. And under second thoughts, these definitely weren't the Egyptian cotton bed sheets, or the memory foam mattress they'd had custom made for their king-size bed.

I'm not at home.

She had no recollection of checking into a hotel, or going to visit a friend. Her head felt heavy enough that she could just be suffering the side-effects of a bender, with an intense hangover waiting to pounce, but she wouldn't go on a bender with her baby due …

She froze.

The baby.

She couldn't feel the baby inside her.

Suddenly moving her hands to her abdomen, the protruding bump was gone, replaced by course bandages that seemed to spiral down past her waist.

Where is my baby?

A flash of memory shattered the darkness behind her eyelids. An ambulance; the cool gel, the sonographer's wand, Pete's ashen face as Dr Michelson appeared in a panic.

'B-Baby …?' she stammered, starting as she felt something warm suddenly pressed against her damp forehead, but without the strength or mobility to fight it off.

'Louisa? Lou?'

Pete's voice. He'd come to her rescue.

'Thank God you're awake. I'll call for the doctor.'

The warmth of his hand vanished, and she moaned for it to be returned. She couldn't let Pete slip away too.

'I'm here, I'm here,' he said, this time pressing his hand against her cheek as a tear robbed her of more vital fluids. 'Can you open your eyes?'

It took all her strength to prise her eyelids apart, but as she did, Pete's handsome face filled her view, and she felt her lips slowly curl up at the edges.

'Everything's going to be okay. You were in an accident. Do you remember? The firemen had to cut you out of the car. Gave us all such a fright.'

The image of the circular saw and shower of sparks permeated her mind once more.

A sound of a chair scraping across a hard tiled floor was followed by Pete's face lowering, but she was able to tilt her head to the side and still look at him.

'You're at the hospital, and while they were examining you … you started to bleed. They were worried about the baby and had to rush you into theatre. Do you remember?'

It was so hard to concentrate on any memory. She could see fragments, but not enough to formulate a timeline of what had happened.

'They asked me for consent to perform surgery to get the baby out safely. I agreed because they said both of your lives were in danger.'

Where's my baby? She wanted to scream, but the words wouldn't get past the swelling lump in her throat.

'They said it would be easiest to give you a spinal tap, so they could operate without causing further damage, and I told them to do whatever was necessary.'

She realised now there's a melancholy to his tone.

'You were pretty out of it. You kept screaming that something was wrong, and that the baby needed you. I'm not going to lie, but it totally freaked me out! So much was going on. Men and women in white coats and masks kept coming and going, so many that I couldn't keep track of them all. There could have been twenty people involved, but just as easily a handful coming back and forth. I don't know.'

He took her hand in his and squeezed it tight. 'I've never been so scared in all my life. I thought I was going to lose you.'

She moved her free hand over the coarse bandage around her middle again. The midwife had discussed the possibility of an emergency caesarean months before when she'd asked for a natural birth. She understood the healing time would be greater, but if it was necessary for the baby, then there was no question of blame.

The breath caught in her throat as her fingertips brushed against the top of her thigh, and her brain now only registered that there was no signal of touch from her legs. She attempted to bend her toes, but it was as if they weren't there anymore.

'I-I can't f-feel my l-legs,' she stammered, barely more than a whisper.

Pete wiped his filling eyes. 'They warned that might happen. The spinal tap numbs everything below the waist so that you don't feel the cut. Apparently you'll have a permanent reminder courtesy of a scar and numbness, I'm sorry, I didn't know what else to do.'

Her own health was the least of her worries, as she glimpsed the tiny hand poking through the brilliant white light from her dream.

'W-What happened ... w-where's our baby ...?'

'I wasn't in the operating theatre – they didn't think it was a good idea due to the potential for complications. You were thirty-six weeks along, but they believe the car accident – the stress and fear – is probably what triggered things to start, and caused the bleeding.'

Pete was always so direct and forthright, why was he now delaying answering her question? Unless ...

'T-Tell me, Pete. Please? W-What happened to our baby?' She barely managed to get the words out before her mind filled with worst case scenarios, and her heart braced itself to be shattered into a thousand tiny shards.

'They've placed him in the prenatal suite to be safe.'

Her mouth dropped. 'He? *He?*'

Pete nodded, a smile finally breaking out across his face. 'Yep, *our* son is in the prenatal suite being monitored.'

Relief flooded her mind, blocking out her surprise at the news. They'd deliberately chosen not to find out the sex of the baby, preferring the prospect of surprise on delivery day. And yet, she'd read every book on predicting the gender of a baby, and in her own mind she'd become convinced that she was having a girl. Not that it bothered her, but learning that she'd delivered a boy was certainly a shock. But Pete looked so happy. He'd got his wish: someone to continue the family name.

'He's four weeks premature,' Pete continued, 'so not as big as they'd like, and so they're just giving him some extra attention to avoid further complications.'

'I-I want to see him.'

Pete wiped his eyes with his hand again. 'Of course, of course, and I'm sure they'll let you go down there in a bit. The doctor said he wanted to have a word first of all, but then I'm sure you visiting the prenatal suite will be top of the priority list.'

He leaned down, and hugged her tightly. 'You did it, Lou. I've never loved you more than I do right now.'

Something flashed at the edges of her memory: Pete red-faced, animated, yelling ... something smashing against the wall behind his head.

But almost as soon as it appeared, it vanished, and she felt the painkillers carrying her like a cloud.

A knock off to the left, had her turning, and taking in the rest of the private room. Brightly painted, white walls, the medical equipment discreetly juxtaposed with modern-looking furniture.

If IKEA made hospital rooms, Louisa thought to herself, finally relaxing into the impending prospect of motherhood, and willing the seconds to pass until she'd be able to see and cherish her baby.

The door to the room opened, and a moment later, Dr Michelson appeared, closing the door quietly behind him, approaching the foot of the bed without so much as a greeting.

His bedside manner certainly left a lot to be desired, but then she'd thought the same the first time they'd met, and Mark had arranged for her to deliver here at St Philomena's.

Pete stood, and stretched his arm out across the bed, shaking Michelson's hand. 'And here's the man we have to thank for making our miracle happen. Dr Michelson, we're forever in your debt.'

He smiled awkwardly, not one prone to accepting praise easily. 'I was just doing my job.'

'Well, we're both hugely grateful that you acted as quickly as you did. Lou can't wait to see him.'

Michelson looked down at her for the first time

since entering the room, a sadness in his eyes. 'As I'm sure any new mother would be. And we'll arrange for Mrs Caulfield to be taken to the prenatal area imminently. But before we do that, I need to talk to you both about something …' he paused and studied the clipboard in his left hand. 'We're concerned about the extent of damage to Mrs Caulfield's spine sustained in the car accident. I don't wish to cause alarm, but you need to be prepared for the prospect that you may never regain full use of your legs.'

Chapter 6

Abbie – Now

'There, there,' Yolanda says, holding my hair back, as I finally finish retching into the bowl, having relocated to the nearest accessible toilet. 'How are you feeling now?'

I sit back on my knees, not particularly comfortable given the extra person I'm carrying, but I'm not yet convinced the retching is over. I'm in a state of confusion, I don't tell her. There is so much improbable about what Kinga said, yet there was enough detail there to support her claims. But to acknowledge that she's telling the truth is to open a door that I barricaded so many years ago, and I'm not sure I have the strength to break through.

'Thank you,' I mouth, knowing it can't have been easy for her to wait here so patiently with me. She's perched on the hinged hand rest, but I can see the strain on her face.

She tears off a piece of tissue and hands it to me, dabbing her own lips with her free hand, and I take the cue to wipe my mouth and blow my nose, before depositing the tissue in the bowl and flushing. Pushing myself up, I take a moment to compose myself and allow the blood to disperse more evenly, before moving to the small basin and washing my hands.

Yolanda transfers herself from her perch to the toilet bowl to sit more comfortably. 'It was quite a story to hear,' she says, and I can see the concern in her eyes via the mirror above the basin.

I meet her stare with my own confusion. 'It would be easy to believe her,' I whisper. 'To allow my imagination to run with the possibility that Josh is still alive out there, maybe living an even better life than I ever could have given him, but I know it can't be true … They showed me his corpse.'

Minutes after the midwife had broken the news about Josh's passing, I'd been wheeled to a dark room, Mark at my side, where a man in a dog collar greeted us, passed on his condolences, and preached that Josh was now with God. Neither Mark nor I have ever been particularly religious, and the priest's words sounded false on my ears. How could he choose to believe in a God capable of such cruelty? To have robbed me of my chance of caring for my son at the last minute was so inhumane.

'They had him in a plastic incubator, his tiny body covered by the softest white sheet. It didn't feel real. How could this bag of bones be the same baby who had been punching and kicking, and dancing inside of me an hour earlier? It made no sense.'

My vision blurs as the memory of that room flashes behind my eyes.

'I wanted to hold him to me … I think there was this part of me that thought if I could just touch him – for him to feel *me* –somehow it would be reversed and he'd come back to life. It was like he'd been born, hadn't been able to find me, and just gave up, but if I could show him I was here, then ...'

I switch off the tap, and tear off a paper towel to dry them and my eyes. I turn back to Yolanda, perching on the rim of the basin. I can see she's doing her best to keep her own feelings at bay, but it can't be easy to have all this laid on her like this.

'They told me it wouldn't be right to hold him, and that it wouldn't be good for either of us. I was allowed to see him from about two metres away, but he didn't look as I'd expected. You see babies online and on television, and they're always so full of life. Kicking, screaming, smiling ... my Josh was none of those things. It was like someone had confused him with a life-like toy doll.'

Yolanda's eyes now fill. 'I'm so sorry you had to go through that.'

'I'm sorry I didn't tell you sooner,' I offer with an apologetic smile.

'You don't need to apologise, Abbie. It's none of my business. I understand, but I'm grateful you feel comfortable talking to me about it now. I wish there was something I could say or do to make it easier for you. I've been lucky to safely deliver two boys, and this little princess is booked in for a caesarean, and will hopefully arrive safe and easy. I know how fortunate I am never to have experienced the heartbreak of miscarriage.'

'It was so devastating that my therapist says I repressed a lot of what followed seeing him in that incubator. I have flashes of shouting and wailing; of Mark having to drag me away. They gave me a sedative to calm me down, and then after a day we were sent on our way. Our house felt so empty when we got home, even though we'd never heard Josh laugh or cry there, his absence was so real. I don't know how many dark days then passed before Mark begged me to go to grief counselling, and for a very long time I didn't see how I would ever be able to get back to any kind of normal life.'

My blood runs cold as I picture the tiny white, wooden coffin being lowered into the ground on that grey, wet morning in October. My Josh was buried that day, and I'm not willing to consider the prospect that the coffin was empty or that we buried someone else's baby.

Yolanda pushes herself up and forwards, and embraces me. 'You are one of the strongest women I know, and I don't doubt how much of a struggle it must have been.'

It feels good to be held, and I welcome her support. When I woke up this morning, I never would have guessed we'd end up crying together in an accessible toilet. We separate and she hands me a fresh paper towel.

'What do you make of Kinga?' I ask now, keen to move past reliving that day again.

'She sounds credible, is my honest answer, but then …' she trails off.

'Then what?'

Her lips part but morph into a pained grimace like she regrets what she is about to say.

'It's okay, Yolanda, I won't be cross. I genuinely don't know what to make of her, and I value your opinion. Please be honest with me.'

She nods, and sighs. 'I was going to say that those of a criminal persuasion are often very believable. Confidence tricksters are so good at what they do because they're able to sound convincing. I'm not saying she's a criminal, but by her own admission she entered the country illegally, has been a prostitute – albeit not of her own volition – and a drug distributor. If all of those parts of the story are true, it should automatically trigger a red flag that the rest of her speech can't be trusted.'

I'm grateful it's not just me with misgivings.

'But I want to believe her for *your* sake,' Yolanda continues. 'Because if she is telling the truth, then that means –'

I lift my hand up to cut her off before she says the words I don't think I can hear anybody else say yet.

'There were things she knew that were convincing,' I say, replaying the conversation in my head. 'She knew about St. Philomena's Birthing Centre; she knew Josh was stillborn; her story sounded so similar to mine in terms of her being shown a baby's corpse too. I guess what I need to understand is how she could know that detail but this be a lie.'

Yolanda is silent for a moment while she considers the rhetorical question.

'Usually, con artists harvest data from social media, and dark web sites. All it would take is an image of you with the hospital sign in the background, or a throwaway comment about your Mark paying for you to go private, or whatever.'

'What about the scrap of paper with mine and Josh's names on it?'

She shrugs. 'It's exactly that: a scrap of paper. Sure it looks like it could have been torn out of a ledger, but something like that could be easily faked. And the sum of money linked to the names could have been anything. A hundred grand is a large sum of money, but it could just as easily be a figure plucked out of the air. What's easier to believe: that there's a conspiracy where doctors at a private hospital are stealing and selling babies to the highest bidder, or that some confidence trickster is trying to get close before stealing from you?'

I appreciate her pragmatism, as it gives me strength in my own conviction that Kinga's admission *can't* be true, as much as I wish it was.

'Speaking of which,' Yolanda comments, checking her watch,' we should be getting back to see if she's still waiting with our stuff at the table. I grabbed our handbags but left the bag of baby clothes and toys with her, so if she's disappeared with it, we'll have our answer.'

She moves towards the door, before stopping and spinning to face me. '*If* Kinga is to be believed then the ramifications are huge! How many other women had their babies stolen and sold to rich benefactors? Kinga, you, who knows how many more? At the very least, it warrants further investigation. Even if the hospital went out of business, there must be records of trustees, or directors that police could follow up with? *If* Kinga is right, then someone needs to be held accountable, and I can't believe that the police wouldn't try and progress things.'

I agree, but it isn't the only questionable element to

Kinga's story. I don't know what troubles me most: the possibility that Kinga is a con artist trying to sink her hooks in me, or that she's telling the truth and I'm being blinded by my own prejudices.

I have a list of questions to ask when we return to the table, but all three chairs at our table are empty. A member of staff in a green tabard is standing a couple of feet away from the table and explains that our friend asked him to wait with our things as she had to get to an appointment.

I apologise profusely for the stain now scarring the brown carpet beneath our feet and for the smell of the disinfectant mixed with vomit that hangs above the table. He doesn't seem too concerned and asks if I'm feeling better. I acknowledge that I am and thank him for guarding our things.

'Everything's still here,' Yolanda says when we're alone again, and she's searched through her shopping bag, 'but she didn't stick around, so make of that what you will.'

'If she was a con artist, wouldn't she stick around?' I counter.

Yolanda shakes her head. 'Not if she's playing the long game. Mark my words: it won't be long until she randomly pops up in your life again. And think about it: if she'd really spent all this time looking for you, why take off when she's only just found you?'

I scoop up my anorak, and spot the scrap of paper on the table where I left it. I discreetly pocket it while Yolanda isn't looking.

'Listen, Abbie, I think we should go to the police and report what happened. It could be that she's known to the police, and they'll be able to keep an eye out for her. I'm happy to go with you and make a statement or whatever.'

I know she's right, but before I make a final judgement, there's someone else I need to discuss it with.

'Thanks, but I want to go home and speak to Mark first. Even though it's highly unlikely that Kinga was telling the truth, he deserves to know as much as me.'

Chapter 7

Abbie – Now

I can hear the low rumble of Mark's voice the moment I'm in through the front door. I wave at Yolanda as the Uber takes her the rest of the way to her house. She offered to stay with me and help me explain the confrontation with Kinga, but I don't think her usual bull-in-a-china-shop routine will help. It isn't always obvious to the outside world, but Mark is sensitive, and I need to approach the subject in a delicate manner.

Closing the door, I can't help yawning widely as the pressure of the day takes its toll. On any normal day, I'd head straight upstairs and spend the next half an hour soaking in the bathtub, but I know my mind won't allow me to rest until I've processed Kinga's claims and discussed them with Mark. Heading to the kitchen, it smells like burned toast, suggesting Mark has been working from home since at least lunchtime. I have a vague recollection of him saying he was planning to finish early today, but if he's talking in the office at the back of the house, then his boss must have had different ideas.

Filling the kettle, I carry it back to the stove and light the gas, wincing as the baby turns and elbows my abdomen. He or she is probably not happy that the only food to pass my lips since breakfast didn't make it past my stomach before being violently ejected over the carpet of the restaurant area. My stomach feels empty, but I have no appetite yet. Grabbing a banana from the bowl beside the stove, I peel and shovel it in, hoping the energy boost will stimulate me as much as the baby.

Resting my hand on the bump, I slowly massage the area, hoping the tiny person inside can feel the love radiating from me. I swear I will protect him or her with every ounce of my soul. Mark and I discussed our previous heartache with the midwife when she talked about birthing plan, and although I insisted on manual intervention in the safety of an NHS hospital, I'm now wondering whether I'd be better off giving birth at home. Nobody would be able to steal my baby and swap them with someone else's child in the confines of my home. But that of course would mean no elective caesarean, and run the risk of my labour failing to deliver baby safely.

A belch rises in my chest and echoes off the kitchen walls as it's expelled from my dry mouth. It's so loud that I laugh involuntarily, and the tension in my tired shoulders eases a fraction. I've just heard how ridiculous Kinga's claim sounds in my own mind. For her version of events to have occurred would require a tremendous amount of planning and collusion to be pulled off. Am I really meant to think that a hospital of medical professionals – all who would have signed up to the Hippocratic Oath – could undertake something so underhand? It's too farfetched.

Kinga clearly believes it happened to her, but even if it did, that doesn't dictate that the same thing happened to me. Given what she said about the people who were minding her – traffickers, pimps, and drug dealers – is it not possible that one of them agreed to sell her baby on the black-market, and made her believe she'd lost it so they could keep the money?

The kettle reaches its crescendo, and I make myself a fruit tea, and Mark a coffee, before carrying his steaming mug through to the back room. The door is closed, so I knock gently, and he opens it a moment later. I'm about to start in on my story, when he points at the earpiece on the side of his face, and continues speaking to whoever is on the other end. I step into the office and rest the mug on the coaster on his desk. The three monitors on the wall all have brightly-coloured numbers and messages, but none of it means anything to me. All I know about Mark's role as a trader is that he starts early, finishes late, and receives a decent bonus for knowing more than the next guy.

I remember watching the film *Wall Street* with him once, and asking if that was what he did, but he gave a vague answer, and I decided not to push further. I'm sure if I started talking about Ofsted requirements at the preschool, his eyes would glaze over as quickly as mine would when he explained the ins and outs of hedge funds, and FX trades.

He leans over and pecks my cheek, covering the microphone with his hand, and whispering, 'I'll be done soon.'

I nod my understanding, and leave the room, closing the door behind me. I need his full attention for when I tell him about Kinga, so it's best to wait until he's finished for the day. Leaving my tea to cool in the kitchen, I head upstairs, and then lower the wooden steps up into the loft. If Mark knew why I was going up here he'd tell me not to, but there's something I need to see to straighten the focus of my mind's eye.

The steps creak as they bear the strain of my mass, but I'm soon in the musty, dry air of the loft space in the roof of our three bed semi. I never come up here, as the loft has always been Mark's area of responsibility. It's jarringly warm, and even with the light on it isn't easy to see what I'm looking for. When we first moved in to the house he insisted we wouldn't become one of those families who hoard stuff they'll never use again, yet the space is littered with old boxes for televisions and other electrical equipment. Our holiday suitcases are immediately to my left as I climb onto the wooden boarding slats on my hands and knees. The first one groans as I crawl across it, but Mark has assured me the boarding is perfectly safe to walk on, and that there's no danger of me falling through the ceiling. For now, I'll remain on all fours to be safe.

Crawling to the far side, I move boxes out of the way as I search for the clear plastic tub containing a small, blue, metal box of treasures. I know it is up here somewhere, but it's been years since I last looked at it, when I agreed with Mark's suggestion to put Josh's things somewhere safe. He said it would help us both get much needed closure, and despite my initial reservations, looking back on it now, I think boxing Josh's few bits and pieces probably was the first step towards recovery. But now I need to see them, and to try and remember more about that truly horrific day.

Sliding a box labelled 'Christmas Lights' out of the

way, my eyes fall on the dusty plastic container, but the bright blue of its innards shines through. Dragging the box to the centre of the loft where the light is strongest, I take a moment to compose my racing mind and pulse, before lifting off the plastic lid, and gently reaching in and lifting the blue box onto my lap. It isn't much bigger than a shoe box, and there's something painfully sad that all of our son's mementoes can be stored in something so small. But then he never had the chance to go to school and paint pictures of trees that were simply blobs on a page. No cities made out of toilet tubes and old washing-up bottles for us to worry about. No examination certificates, nor any photographs of first days of school.

The first item I find is the plain white Babygro that we'd planned to put him in as part of his leaving hospital outfit. Pressing it to my nose, it is soft and gentle as he would have been, so precious, but he never got to wear it, so I can't even pretend that it still smells of him. The only thing we have that he did wear is the small pair of baby mittens that are held within a tiny lace bag. They're almost the only evidence that he ever existed. I feel my eyes warming as they fill as I delicately hold the bag close to my heart. He was wearing these in the incubator, and the image of his tiny, shrivelled body now floods my mind. His skin was so pale, and prune like, in the same way my skin wrinkles when I've spent too much time in the bath. I drop the lace bag back into the box, and clutch at my eyes, struggling to keep the tears at bay.

I know in my heart that it *was* Josh we saw in that incubator, and I'm angry that Kinga would suggest otherwise. The only memory I have of laying eyes on the baby I carried for nine months is that of the incubator, and Kinga's claim feels like she's trying to steal that one memory from me. If there is any truth in what she said, then that would mean I never laid eyes on my baby, and that isn't something I can accept.

Looking up at the roof beams, I blink my eyes several times, taking deep breaths of the dusty air, and gradually calm myself again. Looking back into the box, the glint of the metal tube catches the overhead light, and I extract that next, and unscrew the end, gently patting the tube as the rolled paper certificate slides out. Uncurling the sheet, it's still as raw seeing Josh's name adorning the death certificate as it was the first day we received it. It's not common for the date of birth and death to be identical, but it serves as another reminder that Kinga's claim must be wrong. This is physical evidence that *my* son died that day. Something like this couldn't be faked, and I refuse to accept that there's some big conspiracy that has robbed me of the chance to watch my son grow.

The baby kicks at the sound of Mark calling my name from downstairs. Putting the lid back on the blue box, I grip it tightly as I carry it down the wooden steps, and then down to meet Mark in the kitchen. He's still wearing his earpiece, but is bent over, looking for sustenance in the fridge.

'Hey,' he says, slowly turning, 'what do you fancy for dinner tonight? I was thinking I could whip up my tuna pasta casserole if you fancy something indulgent and –'

He stops as his eyes fall on the blue box in my

hands, and confusion slowly spreads across his face. 'What's going on?'

I open my mouth to speak, ready to recite the speech I've been silently rehearsing since Yolanda and I got in the Uber, but the words won't come. My vision blurs with fresh tears, and then something strange happens. It's as if I'm no longer in control of my thoughts or words. Looking up at the man I love more than anything, I say: 'It's Josh … He's still alive.'

Chapter 8

Louisa – Five years ago

'W-hat did you say?' Louisa stammered, certain more than one of her senses were still playing tricks on her.

Michelson looked down at his notes, the frown settling deeper. 'We won't know for certain until we've carried out further neurological tests, but the brain and CAP MRI carried out when you arrived –'

'The what?' she snapped, her eyes filling as she glared hard at him.

Just say this is some practical joke, she willed silently.

'It's routine for a brain, chest, abdomen, and pelvis MRI to be performed on patients who've experienced the severity of car accident that you were recovering from.'

She still had no memory of getting in the car, let alone what could possibly have caused the accident, but that wasn't top of her list of her questions. She had no recollection of an MRI being performed either, having woken as the sonographer was examining the baby. How long had she been passed out for?

'Given the complications that can arise from labour, particularly an emergency C-section, we had to be sure our work on you wouldn't cause further damage.'

Her eyes snapped to Pete next. Had he known when

she'd woken, but had been too cowardly to tell her, blaming the lack of feeling in her legs on a spinal tap? She studied the white of his cheeks, the dropped lips, and panic rapidly flooding his pupils. If he had known, he was putting on one hell of a good act.

'The MRI results revealed swelling and a possible fracture, and as you were non-responsive, we carried out a full spinal MRI. This confirmed a spinal column fracture, and ultimately damage to the spinal column. It meant that when you were rushed to theatre ...'

She refused to listen to anymore. There had to be some mistake. Focusing her breathing, she concentrated her mind on trying to move any part of her leg. How many times had her brain silently sent signals to ensure her legs and feet appeared to move independently of her conscious mind? She'd been walking since three weeks after her first birthday – a story her mum always told with such pride – how could they have failed her now? She was only thirty-two, and she still had so many ambitions she'd yet to achieve.

She bit down as she willed them to move, but was soon out of breath, opting next to grab a handful of skin, and pinch her nails into it. But she might as well have been squeezing someone else's leg, as not even a hint of pain and warning triggered in her head.

'There has to be some mistake,' she blurted out, cutting off Michelson mid-sentence. 'Do the scans again.'

His eyes brightened momentarily. 'I assure you, there are plenty of further tests that will be carried out in the weeks and months to come to assess the severity of the damage. I already told your father that I'll refer you to the best spinal surgeon in the country. It's possible that your injury may be less limiting than first feared, but I'm no specialist –'

'S-So you could be wrong? About the MRI results. If you're not a spinal specialist, then maybe …'

All she wanted was a slight shrug; something to give her hope. He didn't provide it, instead looking at Pete. 'I'm sure you're both keen to meet your new arrival. I'll contact the neonatal unit, and check they're ready to receive you.'

He nodded at them both, with a thin, awkward smile before disappearing back through the door.

'Holy fucking Christ!' Pete exclaimed under his breath.

It wasn't the reassurance and support she needed.

'H-How do you … feel?' he asked next.

In truth, she wasn't convinced she wasn't still trapped inside the intense dream, though it felt more real, and that terrified her the most.

Doctors make mistakes all the time, she told herself. *Michelson admitted he's no expert. The lack of feeling could still be from the drugs.*

'Louisa?' Pete said next, taking her hand, and kissing the back of it. 'Is there anything you need? Or want? Should I get you a tea from the nurses' station?

Ah yes, the British way of solving all problems: a cup of tea, but that wouldn't heal the fracture in her spine.

'Is there anything you want me to fetch from home if you're going to be in hospital for a bit?'

Pete's searching for any kind of excuse to abandon her and get out of the room clawed at her frustration, but it was probably as great a shock for him too, and knowing Pete's naturally pragmatic approach to life, he probably didn't want to cry in front of her. He'd never been good at sharing his emotions. Even on their wedding day, he'd maintained his stiff upper lip throughout proceedings.

'Maybe your favourite pyjamas, or something to read – perhaps to take your mind off …?'

Did he really think it was that simple? How would cosy pyjamas and a good book help her deal with the sharpest turn in the road she'd ever faced?

An image of her behind the wheel of Pete's Aston Martin fractured into her mind's eye momentarily. It lasted less than a second, but she could see herself thumping her palms against the dark leather of the wheel.

He was glancing at the door like a child desperately trying to make a break for the toilet.

'Just go,' she sighed, allowing her chin to drop, and closing her eyes.

'I-I'll just grab a few bits and pieces that might help,' he said, as he slunk away to the door. 'I'll be back before you realise I'm gone.'

He was practically out of the door, when he turned and raced back, kissing her forehead. 'I love you, Lou, and nothing will ever change that. You hear me? We'll find a way through this. You'll see.'

The tears stung at the back of her eyes, but she kept them closed as she felt him shrink away again. He'd told her before how much he wanted her to give up her job and become a stay at home mum once the baby was born, and now he'd have his wish. What good would she be to anyone without her mobility?

She tried to concentrate on the image of the leather steering wheel again. Had she been driving Pete's car when the accident occurred? That made no sense, as she never drove his car, and yet where else had the splinter of memory come from. But as hard as she tried to expand the glimpse that's all that remained.

It would help to know what day it was to determine where she might have been going. Pete hadn't mentioned the accident when he'd been in here, nor had he questioned her about what happened. It was possible that he was more concerned over her wellbeing than the likely insurance write-off, but that car was his pride and joy. He'd never told her she couldn't drive the vintage Aston Martin, but it was an unsaid rule between them that it was his baby and not to be touched by her. That was why he'd bought her the BMW; so she wouldn't be jealous.

The door to the private room burst open and her mum and dad hurried to her side, her mum's face bearing the stain of tears, and her dad's empathy and concern rolled into a frown.

'Thank God you're alive,' her mum said, always looking for the silver lining.

Judith Kinghorn ran her hands through her daughter's shoulder-length brown hair, flattening it as she went, and trying to brush the fringe to one side. There was a time when being her mother's plaything would have filled Louisa with a sense of warmth and worth, but she'd happily lose all her hair if it meant proving Michelson wrong.

'We'll get you the best doctors,' David Kinghorn

said, his deep baritone conveying the gravity of the situation. Born as World War Two was ending, he'd grown up tough, and had always vowed his own children wouldn't have to experience similar hardship.

'We'll get a second opinion, of course,' he said rubbing a hand over his tanned and wrinkled chin, 'and then we'll see what's what. Science is making great strides all the time, so even if ... if the news is not what we'd hope, we'll find whatever you need to minimise limitations.'

He meant well, and she was grateful for his positivity, even if it felt misplaced.

'How are you feeling, my darling?' her mum asked next. 'I'm sure you're in shock, but if you want to vent or share your pain, I'm here for you. Always.'

Louisa's eyes filled, and unable to speak, she leaned forwards, and allowed her mum to cradle her head.

'There, there, my darling. We're here for you.'

She allowed the tears to fall freely. Tears of frustration for not recalling what had caused the accident; tears of relief that her baby had escaped unharmed; tears of regret for not making better life choices.

When the porter arrived with a wheelchair that had seen better days, the reality of her situation began to sink in. Not only did the impending diagnosis mean the loss of feeling, but she would now find herself confined to a wheelchair, and all she could see was the ball and chain it represented: independence all but stolen away from her.

She didn't fight as her parents pulled back the bed sheets, and lifted her into the chair; she didn't have the emotional or physical strength to resist even if she'd wanted to.

'We'll sort you out a motorised one for when you come home,' her dad whispered into her ear from behind, as he gripped the handles.

She wanted to tell him that money wasn't always the answer, and that his love and support meant much more, but he wouldn't listen.

'Thank you, but I'll escort my daughter to meet her son,' he told the porter dismissively, as Judith held open the door for them both.

Louisa kept her head bowed as she was wheeled along the corridor, the sound of babies' cries echoing off the ever-closing walls and ceiling. It wasn't that any of the nurses or new mothers said anything as they progressed, but the sudden silencing of conversations as she moved past them was louder than their pitying stares.

Why me? Internalising her despondency wouldn't serve any purpose. She wanted to scream and to shout, and to swear vengeance on the God who'd caused the accident, and left her without a future. But the moment they arrived outside the neonatal unit, all anger and bitterness evaporated, as one of the nurses wheeled a small incubator to the window, and the tiny wrinkled ball of skin welcomed her stare. The tufts of hair on his head were darker than she'd anticipated, but not dissimilar to her own. His nose seemed to be pointing up at a slight angle, but she'd never seen a more beautiful baby, and as the warm tears washed the fatigue from her face, she felt her heart slowly mending, and hope returning.

Chapter 9

Abbie – Now

Mark is staring back at me like I've just spoken in tongues. The love that is always in those beautiful brown eyes looks strained and the folds of skin around them shows his obvious concern.

'What did you just say?' he says, barely more than a whisper, but each word laced with trepidation.

I place the blue, metal box on the hob, so I can take both his hands in mine. 'I know it sounds crazy, but Josh is still alive. I've never felt more certain of anything, and I realise how crazy that sounds, and before you ask, I'm not having a nervous breakdown – at least I don't think I am –'

'Slow down, Abbie,' he says, curling his long fingers around my palm, so that he is now the one holding me. 'You're hyperventilating, and whatever's going on can't be good for the baby. Please, come and sit, and we can talk, just you and me.'

He leads me to the stool beside the breakfast bar, and helps me up onto it. I don't know where to begin telling him why I am now ignoring all the doubts I had about Kinga and her claims, but deep down, my heart is refusing to accept that our meeting could be anything but fate trying to correct the course of our lives.

Mark makes sure I'm comfortable, before reaching

for the fruit tea I made fifteen minutes before. He hands it to me, with a smile that promises no judgement.

'Now, why don't you tell me what's got you all flustered,' he sneaks a glance at the blue box, but returns his gaze to me.

I realise now that just bowling out with the announcement about Josh wasn't the best approach. It's sometimes easy to forget just how tough the loss was on Mark as well. I wasn't the only one on the brink, and if anything he had to be doubly strong to pull us both back from the brink. Despite his ruthless job, when he's away from work, he's a totally different person. He's kind and considerate. There isn't a thing he wouldn't do for me or one of his close friends. And he's far more resilient than I am. I really don't think I'd be here today if it wasn't for his reassurance and strength.

But that sensitive nature means he's always looking for the risk in every situation. Again, that's probably what makes him such a successful trader. I can't read his thoughts but if I had to guess, I'd say he's already considering the worst causes for my brash statement. He's probably already trying to remember where he left the number for my counsellor, and whether they make a version of Prozac that pregnant women can take without harming the baby.

There's a part of me wishing I hadn't said anything to him at all, but that wouldn't have been fair on him. He *needs* to know that it's possible we were lied to all those years ago; he needs to know that our son still needs us to fight for him.

I take a deep breath and fix him with a tough stare.

'There was a woman who approached me and Yolanda when we were in John Lewis. I know that what I'm about to relay to you sounds fantastical and that your mind – like mine – will want to reject the story out of hand, but please listen to me before passing judgement.'

I pause, and wait for him to be in the right frame of mind. The skin around his eyes is taut with tension, and his shoulders are hunched. I place my palm on his cheek and gently rub at the late day's stubble. I take several deep breaths, encouraging him to do the same, and the tension in his shoulders eases a fraction.

'The woman told me she was a patient at St. Philomena's too, and also lost her son a number of years ago. At least that's what she was told. However, she said she was contacted by a doctor a few months ago and learned that a child who was a DNA match to her had been discovered. She refused to believe it at first but saw the DNA results and her son hadn't died at St Philomena's but had been raised by a different family.'

He's trying to focus on me, but I can see the subtle twitches of his pupils as his mind races with questions and analyses the risks of what I'm saying. No matter what else I now say, I've already lost his attention.

'I realise how crazy this sounds – it's like something you'd read in a trashy magazine – and I told Yolanda that I didn't believe the woman, but now that I've come home, and being close to Josh's things again ... I don't know, it just ...'

Mark collects my hand from his cheek, and kisses the back of it, before lowering it to my lap, but keeping hold of it. 'Josh is dead, Abbie. I know that isn't easy to hear, and I wish there was a way I could make it not so, but we both know it is.'

I figured this would be Mark's reaction: trying to hold it together for us both, but I'm not giving up on convincing him. If there's any chance that Josh *is* still out there waiting for us, I'm going to need Mark at my side fighting, not restraining me.

'She said she returned to the site of St Philomena's and found mine and Josh's names on a scrap of paper. That was why she got in touch. She didn't find her son until it was too late, and she doesn't want us to make the same mistake.'

The Bluetooth ear piece is flashing, suggesting he's receiving a call.

'It's okay if you need to take that,' I offer, hoping the break will give me time to compose my thoughts before coming for him again.

He checks the display on his mobile and grimaces, but declines the call. 'Work can wait. Right now, we need to talk about this.'

'Who was this woman? Have you ever seen her before?'

I shake my head. 'Not before today. She just approached us out of the blue, but she knew who I was, and she knew all about St Philomena's. If you'd heard her story – what she's been through – you couldn't make up something like that.'

'Did she give you her name? Contact information? Tell me you didn't tell her where we live.'

'No nothing like that. She said her name is Kinga, but she'd gone by the time Yolanda and I came back from the toilets.'

His brow furrows. 'So she turned up, told you Josh is still alive, and then just took off?'

'No, not exactly.'

'Well what exactly?' He takes a breath as he catches the frustration in his tone. 'What else did she say to you?'

'She didn't tell me Josh is definitely alive, but she suggested that the doctors at St Philomena's may have lied to us so they could sell Josh to another family.

He tightens his grip on my hands, but I sense it is more for his benefit than mine. 'Nobody sold Josh. He died, Abbie. We saw ... we saw his body.'

The image of the incubator flashes before my eyes, and the breath catches in my throat as the torrent of angst from that day hits like a wrecking ball.

'We saw what they wanted us to see. Who's to say that was really Josh? We only had their word for it.'

He breaks away from me and moves to the kitchen sink, his eyes on the misted pane of glass, but I don't imagine he's looking at anything specifically, as his neck bends and his shoulders sag.

I hobble off the bar stool, and move behind him, wrapping my arms around his waist awkwardly as the bump gets in the way. 'Don't shut me out, Mark. I realise how crazy it sounds, and I'm not having a mental breakdown. But just think back to that day. What do you remember? I was so heavily drugged that my memories are patchy at best. I remember the midwife breaking the news and me sobbing, but everything else is fits and starts. I don't know how much of my memory has been created by my imagination to plug gaps.'

He doesn't immediately respond, but I stay where I am, enjoying the warmth of us being so close. If I had to choose one place I had to spend the rest of my life, it would be snuggled close to him. I'm just resting my fuzzy head on his back, when he jars.

'I … I remember they wouldn't let us see him for a long time. We were in the birthing theatre, and they had this screen up because they were cutting you open. I remember you were squeezing my hand so tight that I developed pins and needles in my little finger. I kept telling you that everything was going to be okay because you needed to hear it, but my heart was in my mouth. And then when there wasn't a cry, and the staff suddenly seemed panicked … They said there was a complication, and escorted me out of the room. I was placed in our private room and told to wait. What felt like hours, but was probably only minutes later you were wheeled in on a trolley, but they'd given you some kind of sedative, and there was no sign of our baby. I asked the nurse what was happening, and all she would say was that they were working hard and someone would update us in time.

'Then, eventually the midwife came in and broke the news. I couldn't speak. I remember wanting to shout that there had to be some kind of mistake! I knew that babies could be stillborn, but I'd never imagined something like that happening to us. It was something that happened to other more unlucky people. I wanted to see him, to hold him, to give him the kiss of life, but they said we needed to wait and gather our emotions before we'd be allowed to see him. It wasn't until hours later that we were led to that quiet room. And then afterwards, they moved us to a different ward, away from all the living and screaming babies with their blessed parents. Almost as if they didn't want our misfortune infecting anyone else.'

I'd almost forgotten that part, though I'd assumed they'd moved us so we wouldn't have to suffer the trauma of seeing others' unbridled joy.

'And then there was the mix-up when registering his death,' Mark continues, and I freeze.

'What mix-up?'

He slowly turns to face me, and I can see the stain of drying tears on his rosy cheeks. 'The date thing.'

I'm still oblivious to what he's talking about. 'What date thing?'

'Don't you remember? I'm sure I told you at the time. It was painful enough having to go into town to register Josh's birth and death in the same meeting. I went alone because I didn't think you'd cope with it. I remember having to wait an age to be seen, and then the woman – as uptight and emotionless as anyone I've ever met, and with a huge wart on her chin – took me into her office and asked for my paperwork from the hospital. I gave it to her but she dared to argue that there was a mistake with the paperwork and that the hospital had supplied Josh's date of birth as the day before. He was born on 21st May, but the hospital had sent it through as 20th. She got so uppity about it; like I wouldn't know the day my son was born and died. I insisted she phone the hospital, and eventually relented before updating her system.'

He must see the confusion in my face. 'I'm sure I

must have told you about that before, no?'

If he did, I certainly have no recollection of it.

'What if the hospital gave the wrong date because it wasn't Josh's date of death they'd sent?' I ask.

Mark shakes his head. 'I know you want to believe that, but just take a step backwards for a minute. Please? What you're suggesting is some massive conspiracy involving medical professionals acting immorally. And we have no evidence other than a claim made by some stranger.'

I know he's right to doubt, and he's only echoing the very doubts flooding my own mind, but there's one question my soul will not let me ignore: *what if?*

'We have to do something, Mark. I don't think I'll be able to stop thinking about it unless we do.'

His earpiece is flashing again, but he presses his lips against my forehead. 'Very well, once I finish this call, we'll go to the police station and see if there's anyone we can report it to. Okay?'

I nod, grateful that his first thought isn't just to hand me over to the men in white coats. He taps his ear and leaves the room, launching into a conversation with whoever's on the line. I turn back and stare at Josh's blue tin. The thought that my son has been alive and well for five years fills me with hope, but at the same time I'm angry at myself for not fighting to find him sooner.

Chapter 10

Abbie – Now

I never imagined I'd find myself sitting inside an interview room at a police station, like I've seen in hundreds of TV shows. My mind can't process what's going on. It's all so surreal. There's a stale smell and dim gloom, even though there are windows marking out one corner of the room. The clouds beyond the panes of glass are darkening as night draws in, and it adds to the menace clawing at the edges of my psyche.

Why am I feeling so guilty? Is it just the nature of being sat here in a place so commonly associated with crime and punishment? Or is it because my soul feels like it has being squashed under the weight of expectation?

When we arrived, the young officer behind the counter listened intently to what we had to say, before reciting that due to resourcing issues within the modern force, the police are not able to investigate every small crime. Thank God, Mark wasn't in a mood to be dismissed so easily.

He took control, as I cowered behind his arm, grateful that the aggression erupting from his lips wasn't targeted at me. He was careful not to cross a line, and probably placed too much reliance on my vulnerability as a pregnant woman weeks from due date, but I can forgive him for that, because the young officer agreed to ask a colleague to come and take some details from us. She showed us into this room and offered us tea, which we both declined.

It isn't her fault that she probably has to recite those lines a dozen or so times a day when a member of the public feels wronged, but in the eyes of the target-setters, the crime isn't great enough to warrant the time of an overstretched force. It was less that she didn't want to help, but felt she couldn't. She looked relieved when whomever she spoke to on the phone agreed to meet with us.

The feeling of guilt remains. Even though I know I'm not guilty of any crime, it feels like I'm behind enemy lines, and my conscience is replaying every time I've dared to drive over the speed limit, or parked on a yellow line. Mark is sprawled across the two person settee, while I'm perched on the hardback chair to support the bump. Opposite the window there is a compact unit, with two cupboard doors beneath it, a small basin beside it and two more cupboard doors on the wall above it. A small plastic kettle stands unused on the draining board, and a box of supermarket brand tea bags and jar of coffee look uninviting.

There is a pin board on the wall beside the fire door, littered with posters warning of pickpockets, the dangers of alcohol abuse, and offering anonymity for anyone wishing to report any kind of marital abuse. I'm trying to ignore all of the negativity, but the large, bright fonts keep attracting my attention, reminding me that I don't belong somewhere like this.

A short, sharp knock is followed by the fire door

being opened, and a man in a white shirt with black lapels enters, and introduces himself as PS William Brearton. He is stocky built, with thinning white hair, and enough folds of skin around his eyes to place him in his mid to late sixties at best guess. But there is a kindness to his face, and when he smiles at the two of us, I'm instantly transported back to my own childhood when my grandfather would offer me one of his lemon sherbets from a paper bag.

He drags over the second hard backed chair and sits at the pivot of the two of us, so eye contact will be easier. He is carrying a notebook and pen in his hands, but he keeps both closed, while he asks whether we require any refreshment. Mark and I decline again.

'How long have you got to go?' he asks, nodding at the bump, his eyes lighting up when I tell him the due date. 'My daughter's expecting my first grandchild later this year,' he says, his smile widening proudly. 'I still remember the day she was born, and now in no time she's starting a family of her own. The time really des fly by, so be sure to make the most of the early years. You never get them back.'

I resist the sting in the corner of my eyes as I think about all of Josh's first moments that were stolen from me: his first smile, first laugh, first steps.

Brearton opens the notebook, and flicks on the pen. 'If it's okay, can you tell me in your own words what's brought you in today?'

Someone stole our son, I want to scream, but Mark takes control of the situation again.

'My wife was approached by a strange woman while she was out shopping earlier, and was given some disturbing news.'

Brearton writes in his book, but doesn't speak, despite Mark's pause.

'This woman claimed that our dead son is in fact still alive and was taken from us when we were at the St Philomena's Birthing Centre five years ago. Given my wife's current ... state, I'm sure you can appreciate how such a story would be malicious and stressful.'

Brearton meets both of our stares, and nods, but still doesn't speak.

'My wife said this woman claimed to have entered the UK illegally and has been in trouble with the police here, so we were hoping you might be able to look her up and ... I don't know, have a word with her about making such claims?'

I know now that despite Mark's words of comfort when we were at home, he doesn't believe Kinga's story, or my belief that she was telling the truth. My reason for coming to the police station was to try and find out where she lives so I can speak to her again. Whether she was lying with an ulterior motive or not, I need to know for certain; I need to hear her tell me it was all a lie to silence the voice in the back of my head that won't stop screaming that Josh is still alive.

Brearton stops writing when Mark remains silent. He nods at Mark in acknowledgment, and then fixes me with a sympathetic stare that has my eyes stinging again.

'I can understand how distressing that must have been for you. Did the woman give you a name or show you any kind of identification? Driver's licence, passport, anything like that?'

I shake my head. 'She called herself Kinga, but no, I didn't ask for proof.'

'Just *Kinga*? She didn't provide a surname?'

I shake my head again. 'No, I'm sorry.'

'There's no reason for you to apologise, Mrs Friar. Is there anything else you can tell me about her? For instance, how tall was she, did she have any distinguishing marks or tattoos?'

I bring her face to the forefront of my mind, but it's blurred at the edges. I certainly don't recall seeing any tattoos.

'She … she was a bit shorter than me I guess, um … her hair was dark and greasy, like it hadn't been washed in a while. She had bags under her eyes, and she spoke with a foreign accent. Oh and there was a long scar from the edge of her chin down her neck. Does that help?'

'Any idea where the accent originated?'

'I'm not good with accents, but I'd say more Eastern Europe than west. She said she was from Chechnya, but I don't know for certain.'

He writes this down. 'Thank you, Mrs Friar. Can you tell me anymore about what she said regarding her illegal entry into the country?'

'She has a brother,' I exclaim as the memory fires. 'She said her brother paid some men to get her to the UK. She said they were supposed to set her up in a flat and find her a job, but they forced her …' I can't look at Mark as I recall this salient detail for the first time. 'She said they forced her to have sex with men, and then got her hooked on drugs. When she fell pregnant, she said they made her deliver drugs parcels, and after she lost her son, she said she was arrested, and spent some time in prison.'

As the words leave my lips, I can understand why Mark and Brearton have questioning looks about my willingness to believe the tale Kinga told. But they can't feel what I do in my heart.

Brearton flicks off his pen and places it in the notebook as he folds it closed around the pen. 'There's a contradiction there already,' he says without judgement. 'If she did enter the country illegally, and was later arrested, she is unlikely to have been imprisoned in the UK and then released without questions being raised about the legitimacy of her stay here.'

Mark sits up, keen to get on board with Brearton's view about the discrepancies in Kinga's story. 'If this woman did serve time behind bars, she'd have a criminal record, right? Would you be able to look for her on whatever internal police system you have?'

Brearton grimaces painfully. 'You really haven't given me a lot to go on. A name and a vague description aren't as helpful as a surname and address.'

'I'd estimate she was in her late twenties,' I speak up, keen to see whether he can run a search for her. 'Please, can you check for us?'

He opens his mouth to argue against the idea, but must take pity on the pleading in my eyes. He glances back at my bump, and gives a short nod. 'I'll run a check on the name "Kinga" and based on the brief description you provided, but I should caution that she may have given you a false name too, so the chances of me finding anything are pretty remote.'

He excuses himself and asks us to remain in the room.

'You never told me she was a prostitute and druggie,' Mark says quietly.

'I'm sorry. I wasn't trying to keep it from you, it just didn't come up.'

'Had I known, I probably wouldn't have agreed on coming here.' He looks at me, and his eyes have nothing but love in them. 'I understand why you want to believe her story, but I think you need to be prepared for the likelihood that she was just trying her luck. She may have been trying to solicit money and –'

'How did she know about Josh and St Philomena's?'

'I-I don't know. In this day and age, nothing is secret anymore, is it? There's all sorts of transient information on the dark web waiting to be exploited by the kind of criminals who take pleasure in hurting others.' He shuffles along the settee so that he's next to me, and rests his hands around the bump. 'We need to focus on keeping this little one calm and content, and all this stress today isn't good for either of you. I think we just need to chalk this up to experience and focus on building our bright and happy future. Can we agree on that?'

I gently rest my hands on his, and nod. And that's where we remain until PS Brearton returns ten or so minutes later and informs us he couldn't find anyone matching Kinga's description. He tells us not to worry, and that the chances are we won't ever see her again. He hands me a business card with his name and telephone number on, and tells me I should phone immediately if Kinga does approach me again, and despite the little voice in the back of my head, I agree that I'll try not to think about it anymore.

Chapter 11

Louisa – Five years ago

The interior of the building reminded Louisa of a traditional headmaster's office, from one of those period dramas her mum liked to watch on television. The hardwood floor echoed whenever the consultant's secretary would walk across it. Clip-clop-clip-clop as she crossed the room from her desk to the filing cabinet, then clip-clop-clip-clop as she returned to the desk, followed by a sigh of the cushion as she dropped back onto the rickety, wooden chair.

When Dr Michelson had promised he'd put them in touch with the best spinal consultant in the country, this was not what she'd expected; nor the three hour journey down to London to visit these offices in Harley Street. Pete was squashed into the hard, leather tub chair, while she was parked beside him in her chair. She'd wanted to turn around and head home as soon as they arrived and realised there was no lift up to Mr Fitzgerald's second floor office. Surely if he was one of the country's leading experts in spinal injuries, he must be visited by many wheelchair-bound patients. Did they all have to be carried up the stairs by willing partners?

This outer office smelled like an old library, and she'd still yet to get used to the pungent aroma. The low ceiling also gave it a claustrophobic feel, and the small sets of windows allowed little light to penetrate. If Fitzgerald was such a specialist, why couldn't he afford a better working environment, and newer furniture? She wondered whether her parents would have been so willing to foot the bill if they'd come here with them.

Louisa had never liked travelling to London, ever since she'd come on a school trip and had become displaced from her class when the tube doors had closed with her still on the platform. The look of horror on her history teacher's face when the train had pulled away still haunted her to this day. And in the minutes that passed, she'd been torn between waiting to see if someone came back for her, or braving it and just getting on the next tube, praying it would be going to the same place. Thankfully nobody seemed to notice the eleven year-old girl panicking on the platform, and by the time she'd decided to try and find a member of staff, her history teacher was back and quickly apologising for any trauma caused; begging her not to tell her parents.

Pete seemed to be revelling in being here though.

'I feel like I'm going home,' he kept saying in the car, more frequently the nearer they'd got to the city. And then when they'd parked and he got out, inhaling a lungful of the smog and commented how much he'd missed it.

She didn't like to point out that growing up in Uxbridge on the border with Berkshire didn't make him a true Londoner

The truth was she didn't want to come all this way

today. Caleb had been fighting for his life in the neonatal unit for two weeks, and today was the first time she hadn't been to see him since he was born. Did he realise that she wasn't there? Would he be upset not to hear her voice? Louisa's parents had promised they would visit him, but it wouldn't be the same. Caleb needed to hear his mum tell him how great his life would be if he pulled through. Despite intensive care, he still wasn't able to breathe on his own, and seeing the pitying faces of the nurses was like a fresh stab to the heart every day.

Clip-clop-clip-clop.

'I'm sure Mr Fitzgerald won't be much longer,' his secretary said to them, as she pushed the half-rimmed glasses up her nose. 'Can I get you something to drink? We have espresso, latte, and a range of fruit teas.'

Louisa shook her head, but Pete rubbed his hands together as if he'd just been offered ambrosia from the Gods.

'I'll have an espresso, thank you,' he said.

The secretary, with her librarian's cardigan and brunette hair tied in a bun, clip-clopped to a closed door, opened it and disappeared, leaving the two of them alone.

'Let's just go,' Louisa said to him. 'If we hurry, we can be back in Manchester by mid-afternoon, with time to see Caleb.'

Pete leaned across and lifted her hand into his. 'I know you're scared about what Mr Fitzgerald is going to say about your test results, but I'm here to help shoulder the burden.'

'It's not that,' she said, biting her lip, 'but I just

think we should have insisted on a telephone appointment. Was it really necessary for us to come so far for test results? He didn't seem to mind that the tests were carried out in Leeds, so why all this added hassle?'

'Maybe he just wants to meet us. Talking on the phone is a bit impersonal, and maybe he wants to share good news in person.'

Or bad news, she didn't add.

The tests they'd run had been exhausting, and despite asking the doctors and nurses involved for any hint at what their conclusions were, they'd all simply told her she'd have to wait to hear from Mr Fitzgerald. She'd tried not to think about what he would say, and being with Caleb at the hospital had served as a welcome distraction, but that didn't stop the paranoid thoughts coming in the dead of night.

Pete squeezed her hand again. 'I know you're worried about Caleb, but your mum and dad are there, so he isn't alone. And if anything happens, they'll phone straight away.' He raised her hand and kissed the back of it. 'We need to focus on *you* right now. Caleb needs his mum to get better too. Okay?'

She nodded compliantly, as the clip-clop announced the return of Mr Fitzgerald's secretary.

A further ten minutes passed, but it felt like ten times as long, the hands on the wall clock seeming to tick by in slow motion. When Mr Fitzgerald finally opened his door, it felt as though they'd been waiting for an hour.

He was younger than she'd expected. Maybe in his mid-fifties, rather than late sixties, which she'd assumed from the low gravel of his voice on the phone, and his preference for antique furniture. He was wearing a bright red tie, and navy waistcoat over his blue and white striped shirt, making him resemble a tube of toothpaste. His goatee looked tired and in need of a trim, but he smiled broadly as he welcomed them into his office, almost a carbon copy of the waiting room.

'Mr and Mrs Caulfield, I must apologise for my tardiness. I was just checking something on your results with the team who carried out the tests. I hope my secretary offered you refreshments?'

Pete had left his espresso cup in the waiting room, but nodded gratefully.

'And I hope your journey down this morning wasn't too stressful?'

'Some traffic, but not too bad,' Pete responded, and for a moment, it felt to Louisa like this was how the rest of the appointment would play out: the two men talking while the little woman disappeared into the background.

But then Fitzgerald, turned and looked at her directly, offering his hand. 'And how are you, Mrs Caulfield? Is it okay if I call you Louisa?'

Louisa strained a smile as she shook his hand, and nodded.

'Good,' he said, clapping his hands together and moving back around to his side of the enormous oak desk. 'Before we continue, can I check whether there have been any changes you've noticed since the tests were performed last week? Any additional pain, loss of feeling, return of feeling, maybe?'

She'd followed the guidance of the team last week, attempting to move her thighs even a fraction every morning and evening in bed, but there'd been no change that she'd observed.

'No, nothing's changed,' she said, the words tumbling with regret at her body's failure.

'And how is your little lad doing?'

'He …' but the words stuck in her throat, and she couldn't finish the sentence as the tears stung the back of her eyes.

'He's still in the neonatal unit,' Pete confirmed, 'but we're trying to remain positive.'

Fitzgerald nodded empathetically, and then looked away at his monitor for a few seconds, before staring back at Louisa. 'Well the good news is, the team who saw you last week have confirmed a reduction in the swelling around the fracture, which is positive. It's allowed them to get a clearer picture of what's going on through the MRI, and now we have options.'

'Is that good?' Pete asked.

'Options are always good,' Mr Caulfield. The one I'd like to discuss with you both today would involve an operation to try and repair some of the damage to the spinal cord as a result of the fracture. I believe, if we performed the surgery, there's a sixty-five per cent chance that you could regain partial feeling below the waist, Louisa. It won't be an instant recovery, but it could speed up the healing process.'

'Sixty-five per cent sounds good,' Pete acknowledged, looking at his wife.

'There are, of course, risks with any surgery, but the biggest factor you need to consider is the risk of further irreparable damage to the spinal cord. The MRI images suggest that we might be able to make a positive difference, but we won't know for certain until we open you up to look.'

'And if she doesn't have the surgery?'

Fitzgerald's face tautened. 'Then the chances of regaining any feeling is much lower. There are a range of exercises that Louisa can continue to perform to strengthen the surrounding cells, but the odds are much worse.'

'Well then, it's a no-brainer,' Pete declared. 'When can you book her in?'

'Louisa? Are you happy to consent to the surgery?'

She didn't respond at first, seeing the hope in Pete's eyes, but unable to shake the doubt flooding her mind. 'Can you ... How long would I be out of action? I'm assuming there'll be a period of time in hospital?'

'Of course, of course, an operation of this complexity isn't something we'd rush. We'd want the swelling to reduce a little further first, and then we'd get you into one of our private hospitals, and there will be several days where your spine will be restricted from movement while you recover. All in all, we're probably talking ten days in hospital; no more than two weeks.'

Two weeks of being trapped in a hospital bed while Caleb fought for his life just wasn't an option.

'I appreciate it's a big decision, and I'm not expecting your answer today, Louisa, but I should warn you that the longer we delay, the lesser the chance of success.'

She looked down at her hands, fingers knotting,

feeling the weight of Pete's stare.

'I'd like to show you a diagram to explain what the operation will entail,' Fitzgerald continued. 'It might help you make up your –'

The blare of Louisa's ringtone cut him off mid-sentence. She retrieved it from the bag hanging from the handles of the chair, ready to dismiss the call, until she saw it was from her mum's mobile.

'Mum? What's going on? Is everything okay?'

'No my darling, I'm afraid it isn't. How quickly can you get back here?'

Chapter 12

Abbie – Now

I'm grateful when the alarm sounds the end of a virtually sleepless night. I'm sure I must have dozed at some point, but my mind wouldn't let deep sleep take me, focusing instead on the prospect of what Kinga stood to gain from lying to me. She didn't ask for money, didn't steal our items left at the table when Yolanda and I went to the bathroom, and left no future means of contact. I understand Mark's and PS Brearton's conclusions, but I don't want to believe it as much as the prospect that she wasn't lying. Absurd as it is, what if Josh really is out there somewhere, and with a little effort on my part, we could be reunited?

Mark had already left for work when I made it to the breakfast table, but he had left a note telling me not to work too hard, and promising takeaway tonight if I fancy it. Bless him, the last thing he needs is for his heavily pregnant wife to go off the rails. I know he's under pressure with work, and I don't blame him for choosing pragmatism over hope after all these years. If he'd been approached by Kinga instead of me, would I be the one pouring cold water on the prospect?

Sitting in my car in the preschool car park, I can't stop my eyes wandering to the string of children in trousers and jumpers walking to the infant school just up the road. Any one of them could be Josh, and I'd have no clue. There are many times when I've pictured in my mind what he would look like as a growing child, but the image is never as sharp or defined as I'd like. The truth is, I only saw the tiny bundle of skin in the incubator for a matter of minutes, and most of those were spent sobbing, so it's difficult for my imagination to turn that into a boy still at the start of his life journey. What I'm desperately not trying to think about is the prospect that my eyes never saw the infant I carried for so long. If I am to believe Kinga's version of events, then the baby in the incubator wasn't Josh, and that would mean we never met at all, and that's too much for my heart to take.

A boy appears only a stone's throw away from my window and stares straight at me. He's wearing a light grey, woollen jumper with the school's maroon crest emblazoned over his heart. The collar of a maroon t-shirt pokes from beneath the jumper. He looks so smart in dark grey trousers and two straps of a backpack hang over his shoulders. His hair is blonde and wavy much like Mark's was in childhood pictures his mum shows me whenever I visit, and his eyes are a brilliant crystal blue like my own.

My heart skips a beat, and the breath catches in my throat.

He is statuesque, and there's no sign that he is with a parent, and my heart wants to reach out to him and check he is okay. Despite myself, I am willing to believe that fate heard Kinga's message and has delivered a miracle. The boy nods in my direction, and I can't keep my hand shooting up to wave back, as if our souls are somehow talking to each other. But then a stir of colour in my periphery turns into the tall figure of a slim woman with auburn hair, and wrapped in a navy blue anorak. She hurries across the car park and takes the boy's hand as he beams at her. She must have been dropping another child at the preschool and had asked him to wait for her. He was nodding at her, rather than me, and my cheeks burn with embarrassment.

I watch them move away, and press the back of my hand against my eyes as they fill with tears. How easily my intrigue sucked me in, and my imagination held me in its vice-like grip as it painted pictures of a mother and son reunited.

I recognise the mum in the anorak now. She's Kyla's mum, and I know that three year-old Kyla has a brother in the infant's school whom she adores. Now that I come to think of it, there's a three year age gap between Kyla and her brother, so the smart looking boy must be at least six.

Pull yourself together, Abbie, I silently chastise, adjusting the rear-view mirror so I can check my eyeliner hasn't run. I'm relieved it hasn't, and bail out of the car, taking several deep breaths to compose myself, before following the slight incline up to the preschool. I can see Gail and Sally through the window, and wave as Sally spots me, and moves to unlock the door. Breakfast club, for those whose parents can't make the nine o'clock drop-off, is just finishing, and I can see Gail is busying herself putting out crayons and pictures on one of the desks.

'Morning, Sally calls out to me, as she carries a small stack of plates to the large sink in the corner.

'Good day off?'

I don't know where I'd begin to tell her how strange yesterday was, and smile back instead.

'Went to buy a few last bits and bobs for the baby,' I reply. 'How was everything here?'

She lowers the plates into the sink and rinses them, as I hang my coat and bag in the tiny cupboard referred to as the staff room, adjacent to her.

'You know, same old, same old.'

I've worked with Sally for the best part of two years, and she and Gail are both so friendly and welcoming, but away from this place we don't socialise, so it doesn't feel right to mention Kinga or the trip to the police station. Instead, I help Sally clear the jam and remaining plates from the tables, before helping her set up the train track.

'I'll finish this up,' Sally says, wiping her forehead with the sleeve of her jumper, her short, brown bob, bouncing as she continues to lay out the track. 'Can you go and wait by the door, ready for the next arrivals?'

I know she's taking pity on my inability to bend as easily with the bump, but I'm not about to argue as my lower back twinges under the strain of being slightly bent over. I unlock the door, and hook it to the wall, putting on my warmest and brightest smile as the first children arrive with their exhausted and harried parents keen to get on with their day.

I wait patiently as cagoules and hoodies are peeled from gangly arms and hung haphazardly on the pegs just inside the door, and make a point of welcoming every child who enters, even those I'm not directly responsible for. Sally always says that to make the preschool a safe and happy place for those we care for, we need to show the children that we are pleased to see them and make them feel valued. It's my favourite part of the day. Most days here are hard work, being responsible for other people's children is never easy, but watching them grow and learn is so satisfying. I'm so grateful that Gail and Sally took a chance on me when I was at my lowest ebb, and that is why I make an extra effort with the children.

'Danny's got the dentists at ten thirty,' one of the parents tells me as she ushers her son in through the door. 'I'll come and collect him at quarter past, if that's okay?'

Danny is in Sally's group, so I let Danny's mum know that I will pass the message on to Sally, even though more than an hour's notice would have been more beneficial to us. I don't make a fuss, assuring Danny's mum that she just needs to knock on the door when she arrives, as it will be locked for the children's safety.

I'm not sure she's listening as she hurries away, one eye on her watch, and the other putting her mobile to her ear. It's then I catch sight of a boy from within my group, and I wave. Toby stares straight back at me, but make no effort to acknowledge the greeting. He is standing on the driveway leading to the preschool and as I adjust my position I see his dad hurrying up the driveway behind him, but my heart is in my mouth as I see the man grab Toby by the upper arm and pull him back to face him. Toby's father's cheeks redden as he bellows at the boy, although from inside I can't hear what is being shouted. I keep my eyes on the pair of them, more than aware of my duty of care towards Toby, even though he's technically still in his father's care.

Children continue to funnel past me as I try to watch the scene unfolding, desperately wanting to run to Toby, and to remind his father that no child deserves such a tirade, especially at this time of the morning. It's over almost as soon as it's begun, and Toby's dad drags the pale-faced boy to the door, but turns and leaves before I have chance to get through the pool of children struggling to hang coats on the pegs in the doorway.

'Morning, Toby,' I say cheerily instead, trying not to show what I witnessed. 'How are you today?'

He stares up at me, but says nothing, before heading inside and placing his laminated name in the registration box to show he's arrived. I stay by the door until Sally relieves me, and then I make a beeline for Toby as I don't want his day starting in such a sombre manner. Taking him by the hand, I lead him away from the rest of the children to a quiet corner, and ask him if he's okay, reminding him that he can tell me anything in confidence.

He shrugs, and stares at his feet.

'Is everything okay with your dad?' I ask, aware that I don't want to push him too much.

He shrugs again, but doesn't answer the question.

'You can tell me absolutely anything, Toby. You know that don't you? If something is bothering you, or you're upset about something, I'd like it if you told me. It doesn't mean anyone will get into trouble, I just want to make sure that everything is okay. You just ... seem a bit sad today.'

He slowly raises his eyes to mine, and I brace myself for the moment he will reveal all, but he looks away again, before shaking his head. 'I'm fine. Can I go play now?'

I have little choice, and smile warmly. 'Of course you can, but remember I'm always here if you want to talk about anything. Okay?'

He takes off without another word, finding the only vacant table, before settling down to play with the plastic dinosaur toys in the tub on the table.

I know that this morning's exchange with his father could be nothing, and I have to be careful not to leap to conclusions and assumptions about what I witnessed. I won't discuss my concerns with Gail or Sally yet, not until I have something a bit more concrete, but I'll make an effort to watch Toby in the hope he feels confident enough about opening up to me later. It's the least any scared little boy deserves.

Chapter 13

Abbie – Now

It's only when Danny's mum arrives to collect him for the dentist that I even remember the message I should have passed to Sally. I look over and grimace apologetically as Sally tries to cover for my slipup and act as if she knows exactly why Danny's mum is banging on the glass.

Danny's mum looks irate that he isn't at the door with his coat on waiting for her, and I feel like I should go over and apologise to the both of them for my lack of communication, but I can't leave my group unattended, as Gail is already keeping one eye on Sally's as well as her own. Danny's mum huffs as she pulls the sleeves back through on the coat, and then slips Danny's arms in. Sally apologises again as she shows them out, and then relocks the front door.

'Sorry, I meant to say something,' I apologise as Sally breezes past, returning to her group who are sitting on the mat, waiting for her to finish the story she was reading.

'That's okay,' she says, waving away my concern, but I can see she's holding back her frustration at the interruption.

'I really am sorry,' I repeat firmly.

Sally stops, and takes my hand. 'And it really is

okay. Don't worry about it. We'll chalk it up to baby brain. Okay?'

I nod with acceptance because I don't want to cause more of a fuss, but I don't think it has anything to do with the temporary amnesia associated with pregnancy. The truth is, I've been so focused on watching Toby, and trying to get him to speak to me about what happened with his dad that I totally forgot what Danny's mum had said.

I tried to engage with him when he was playing with the dinosaurs, but he refused to answer my questions. Then when he moved to the set of cars, I tried again, challenging him to a race, but he simply shrugged and said he wanted to play on his own. If I can't get him to open up soon, I'm going to have to flag my concern with Gail and Sally. Ultimately, they are the leads at the preschool, and all child welfare concerns need to be recorded with them, as there are standard protocols in place to handle such situations. I would just prefer to be certain about what I witnessed before I start spreading false rumours. For all I know, Toby may have done something very naughty and his father was merely doling out what he deemed to be an appropriate punishment, even if I consider it overly aggressive. If Toby would just open up and tell me what happened, I'd be better placed to make a decision about next steps.

At least this worrying has stopped me thinking about Kinga and her explosive revelation. If Josh is still alive then where would I begin trying to find him? Kinga said St Philomena's is closed down, and I'm not sure I can remember the name of the doctor or midwife, though I suppose we may have a record of them somewhere at home. Could we hire a private detective to dig further? I don't know what they charge, or whether that's even the sort of thing they'd consider. PS Brearton certainly didn't seem interested in investigating the possibility that Kinga was telling the truth.

And if we did somehow manage to locate Josh, how would I prove the truth about what happened? A DNA test would verify that I'm his mother, but what if his new family refused to provide a sample, or denied any such claims on their son? What then?

And how would I begin to explain to a five year-old that the life he's been living has been a lie and that Mark and I are his real parents? I'm thirty, and I can't get my head around it all, let alone a child who probably doesn't yet fully comprehend the difference between right and wrong. And how do I explain that we allowed him to live that lie for five years before we came looking? That kind of acknowledgement could cause irreversible psychological damage on a mind so early in its development. I know that children are resilient, but even so.

A bloodcurdling scream snaps me back to the present. Even though I've been facing my small group of children, I haven't been concentrating on them, but it doesn't take long to identify the cause of the scream, or the wailing tears that have now followed. I hurry over to Bella who is huddled on the floor, her head buried in her knees, and the angel wings on her back sparkling with the light from the overhead halogen bulb.

I crouch down as best I can, eventually making it onto my knees, and shuffle over to her. 'Oh dear, Bella, what's wrong? Why are you crying?'

Her head raises and I see her eyes are red raw with tears, but she thrusts out an arm and points menacingly at one of the boys in the small group that has gathered around us. 'Toby kicked me.'

I turn my head to where Toby is standing, his face balled up with anger.

'She snatched the train off me,' he snaps back defensively.

'No I didn't,' Bella wails back, though I spot the plastic train carriage between her white, sparkly trainers.

'Let's all take a breath, shall we?' I say calmly, keen to diffuse the situation before it escalates further. 'The rest of you can return to playing, but Toby and Bella will stay with me while we talk about what happened.'

I should probably take them to the corner of the room to talk quietly, but I'm still slightly breathless from getting down to the floor that I need a couple of minutes before trying to stand again. Thankfully the group disperses, the memory of the incident already dissipating like a cloud.

I look at Toby, not wanting to be the second adult to chastise him today, but knowing the situation needs to be dealt with swiftly. 'Did you kick Bella, Toby?' I ask, keeping my voice low but firm.

'She took the train I was playing with and –'

I put up a finger to interrupt him. 'We never hit or kick others, do we? You know the rules of preschool.' I turn to look at Bella again. 'Did you snatch the train from Toby, Bella?

'No,' she pouts, but she can't look me in the eye as she says it.

'You also know the preschool rules, and that we don't snatch toys from other children.'

'But he's been playing with the train all day!' she sobs. 'I asked him for a turn and he said no.'

'That's not an excuse to snatch, Bella, and Toby you shouldn't have kicked Bella. What should you have both done to resolve the problem?'

I wait patiently for the pair of them to think through the most appropriate course of action, which would be to find me and tell me about the problem. Neither speaks, and I can feel the onset of pins and needles in my feet. I'm going to have to stand soon.

'I want you to apologise to one another. Bella, say sorry to Toby for snatching the train.'

'Sorry,' she huffs.

'And Toby, you say sorry to Bella for kicking her.'

He glares at Bella and me, but shakes his head. 'No! She shouldn't have taken the train.'

I can't stay where I am, and place my hands on the laminated floor, starting to push myself upwards. 'Toby, you need to say sorry to Bella.'

I'm not expecting him to lunge forward and clatter into my leg while I'm still trying to straighten my knees. I'm already off balance, and suddenly I'm toppling backwards, and only one thought leaps to the forefront of my mind: how can I protect my baby?

In the milliseconds it takes for my top-heavy body to crash to the floor, I do all I can to adjust my position so that the bump will be protected, but I'm not quite quick enough and my shoulders and hip bear the brunt of the impact.

I hear a gasp of shock go up from somewhere near the back of the room, and Gail's ponytail of silver hair is by my side within seconds.

'Oh gosh, Abbie, are you okay? What happened?'

Toby is no longer standing nearby, having reintegrated himself with the rest of the group by the crayons and paper.

'I-I must have slipped,' I say, lying on my back, and taking shallow breaths, my hands involuntarily feeling around the bump for signs of activity.

'Stay on your back for now,' Gail says, alarm ruffling the crow's feet at the corner of her eyes. 'I'll phone for an ambulance.'

The last thing I want is to cause a fuss, and I try to shake my head. 'You don't need to phone for an ambulance. I'm sure I'm fine.'

The panic grows as her usually placid face drops. I don't doubt that her first concern is for my safety, but probably somewhere in the back of her mind she's thinking of the liability implications if harm has come to the baby. Given what happened with Josh all those years ago, on second thoughts, having the doctor check over my baby is a good idea.

Gail rushes to the staff room and collects her mobile, returning to my side and taking my hand in hers. 'Does it hurt anywhere?'

My ego probably suffered the most damage, but I never thought Toby would lash out at me like that. He wasn't always so withdrawn. I remember the first time he arrived, and how shy he seemed until we told him he could play with the apparatus that had been left on the tables. His face lit up, and he played happily with the other children, his imagination shining through. But in truth, these last few months, he has been quieter, more sullen, and less engaged with the other children. Subconsciously I'd put it down to him maturing quicker than some of the others, but having witnessed his father's aggression this morning, I can't help thinking I've missed the signs.

I feel a slight kick from the baby on the opposite side to where I collapsed, and that brings relief that he or she is probably perfectly safe, but I'm not going to take any chances.

'It doesn't hurt, but it might be best to be checked over,' I say, offering a smile of reassurance.

Sally joins us, immediately asking what happened as Gail withdraws to place the call. Had I not been thinking about Kinga and Josh, I would have seen Bella snatch the train, and could have prevented the fallout. What if the distraction has done irreparable damage to my second chance of a family? I'll never forgive myself.

Chapter 14

Louisa – Five years ago

The multi-faith chapel on the ground floor of the hospital was tiny, barely big enough for a handful of people to pray without being overheard. A week ago when Louisa's mum phoned her at Mr Fitzgerald's, she never would have imagined herself being down here. Seven days was a long time when waiting for news about Caleb's progression.

That next forty-eight hours had been the hardest of her life. Pete and her parents had all whispered words of encouragement, and she'd cringed every time they'd said he'd pull through. It was her mum who'd specifically said it wasn't in God's plan to steal Caleb away from them, but for Louisa it was the biggest test of her own faith.

What if they were wrong? What if he didn't pull through?

She'd pictured the moment over and over in her head: the nurses telling her that Caleb was now with the angels; that their prayers had gone unanswered; that there was nothing further they could do.

And how she would hate Pete and her parents for all their false claims about his chances of survival.

She'd held his hand through the protective lining of the incubator, trying to show him how sorry she was that he was facing upheaval so early in his life. Had she not been driving that day, then she wouldn't have had the accident, the amniotic sack wouldn't have punctured, and he wouldn't have been born premature.

It was all her fault.

Caleb was fighting for his life, and she had made herself a ball and chain around Pete's neck all because of the stupid accident.

And that's why she now found herself in the small chapel, searching for answers but uncertain where to start. She still couldn't recall what she was doing in Pete's car in the first place, and hadn't managed to ask him either, as there just hadn't been a convenient moment. He hadn't asked her what had caused the accident, presumably because he didn't want her to think he blamed her for the troubles facing Caleb.

But he must have been thinking it was all her fault too.

If only the black hole in her memory would reveal the dark secret it was hiding she might have found the strength to handle the guilt of knowing she was the one who put Caleb in that incubator. But even the slight glimpses that had returned were now fading as all her emotional strength focused on willing hope to her son.

Applying the brake, she bowed her head before the cross hanging from the wall at the front of the room. It wasn't a traditional crucifix – no figure with nails in his hands and feet here – instead a cross shape made up of stacks of colourful books. In the far left corner of the room, there was a stand holding glass candle jars. One lone jar flickered from the electrical flame inside it. A small label on the money box beneath the candles instructed that a donation would light a jar at random and it would burn for an hour. Beside the candle stand was a small table with leaf-shaped paper where visitors were encouraged to write the names of a lost one and then hang them from the small bonsai tree on the windowsill above the table. On the right of the room, two vacant chairs waited for someone to support.

Facing the cross on the wall, and bowing her head, she tried to find the words to communicate with God, but she didn't know where to begin. The sound of approaching footsteps startled her, and she quickly realised that in that brief moment of quiet reflection, she'd actually fallen asleep. She had no idea how long she'd been out for, but the sky beyond the small window was a shade or two darker than she recalled.

Embarrassed, she was just releasing the brake on the tyres when the new arrival cleared her throat. 'Excuse me, do you have coin for candle?'

The voice belonged to a gaunt woman with hair that would have made Cher envious in the 80s. With splits in the knees of her jeans, she was in her early twenties, and her eyes carried a sadness that spoke to Louisa of loss.

Reaching into her purse, Louisa found a pound coin and offered it to the woman, before locating a second and asking her to light one for her too.

'Do you mind if I sit with you?' the woman asked, and Louisa didn't know how to refuse. The younger woman selected one of the two chairs and carried it towards Louisa, before sitting.

'You lose someone too?' the woman asked.

'Not exactly,' Louisa began, not ready to unburden

her problems on a total stranger. 'My ... My son is in the neonatal unit.'

She didn't know why she'd revealed such a personal detail, but once the words had tumbled from her mouth, she couldn't stop herself.

'It's my fault he's in there. I had a car accident and he was born early. He's fighting, and actually the nurses are really pleased with his progress in the last forty-eight hours. He's now breathing by himself, and it's ... It's like a miracle. That's ... That's why I'm here: to say thank you I suppose, but I don't know how. It's been a while since I prayed properly, and I think I'm out of practice.'

The woman didn't respond, but her head tilted, and it was all the encouragement Louisa needed.

'I'm terrified that he'll blame me for what he's been through,' Louisa said, as her eyes filled with tears. 'Nobody yet knows of the long-term damage that's been caused to him as a result of my actions, and I don't know how to process the guilt I'm feeling. My husband would tell me I shouldn't blame myself, but he isn't the one who put Caleb in the hospital. He isn't the one who left Caleb fighting for his life.'

'I like that name. You chose it?'

Louisa nodded. 'We didn't know if we were going to have a son or a daughter, and we'd discussed names, but when I first saw him in the neonatal unit, it just kind of came to me. It was the weirdest thing.'

'It's a Hebrew name that means *faithful*, or *brave*. Some people from my country think it means *devotion to God*.'

'I've been anything but devoted to God. Maybe if I

had been I wouldn't be in this mess now.'

'Yet here you are, in a place of worship.'

Louisa hadn't thought of it like that. In her true hour of need, her faith was strong enough to bring her back to God, and maybe that was all part of His plan, as her mum had suggested.

'The car accident has meant I may never walk again. I wonder whether God is punishing me for something, but I'm not a bad person. And now my poor son is going to be stuck with a mum who is needier than others. He doesn't deserve that. I don't know how I'm going to give him the support he needs if I can't walk.'

The woman remained silent, and despite herself, Louisa couldn't stop talking.

'A brilliant surgeon has offered to try and help me regain some of the feeling in my legs, but he says the treatment will take a couple of weeks to prepare and recover from. What happens if I agree to have it done, and then Caleb takes a turn for the worse? What if my not being in the neonatal unit makes him think that I've abandoned him, and he loses the will to keep fighting? I have to put his life first, right? But then I'll disappoint my husband, so it's a lose-lose situation.'

She pictured Pete's face in the car as he drove them back from Harley Street. She'd seen him angry before, but this was beyond that. He'd accused her of neglecting her duties as his wife. He'd said if she didn't go through with the surgery and at least try to get some help, then she was practically turning her back on them. She hadn't argued, deciding it was better to remain silent than disappoint him further.

But he was wrong to assume that the surgery

Fitzgerald suggested would solve all their problems. He'd said there was only a sixty-five per cent chance of success, and even then "success" was defined in loose terms. It's not like Fitzgerald was suggesting a full on cure to her paralysis, so was it worth risking being away from Caleb for something that could simply result in her being able to feel more pain?

Why couldn't Pete understand that? Why was he always trying to fix things, rather than listening to her feelings?

'My mother lose arm as result of bomb,' the younger woman said, cutting through Louisa's internal monologue. 'But she still work three jobs to put food on table for family after my father leave home. I never saw my mum's disability. Children don't. Just the love and kindness only a parent can give.'

The words stirred something in Louisa's head, but she couldn't quite see what.

The woman stood. 'I need to go. Have place to be. I will pray for your son.'

'Th-Thank you.'

'Do me a favour, though, okay?'

Louisa wasn't sure how to respond. 'Okay.'

'*When* your son is better, don't blame yourself for what happened. He won't remember the accident, just the love you share. Make him see why God spare him, as not all children are so lucky.'

Louisa didn't have the chance to ask what she meant, as the woman turned on her heel and marched out of the chapel without looking back. Louisa's eyes fell back on the cross on the wall, unable to ignore the feeling that God had spoken to her through the unlikeliest of angels. She'd heard the message loud and clear.

Extracting her mobile from her bag, she located the number for Mr Fitzgerald's secretary. 'Hello? Yes, this is Louisa Caulfield, can you let Mr Fitzgerald know that I'd like to go ahead with the surgery? My son's going to need a strong mother, and I owe him a chance at that.'

Chapter 15

Abbie – Now

The paramedics told me Gail was right to 999, and they quickly reassured me that their equipment detected the baby's pulse, but they would take me to the hospital for an ultrasound to ensure no damage had been sustained.

Gail and Sally were both full of concern for me, with Gail even suggesting the possibility of me starting my maternity leave sooner than anticipated to avoid any further incidents. Mark and I always agreed that I would work as close to due date as possible, allowing me more time to spend with the baby post birth before I had to return to work, so I'm not sure I'm happy with Gail's suggestion. I know she means well and is only suggesting it for my benefit, but if she knew the truth about why I'd ended up on the floor she might not be leaping to such dramatic conclusions.

I told them I must have had a rush of blood from being crouched down with Bella, and that it was that rather than the shove by Toby that caused me to topple. I still don't know what to do about him. It was absolutely wrong of Toby to lash out at Bella and then at me, and I know I should have told the others what really happened, but this is the first time he's done anything like this at preschool, and I want to tackle the problem head-on, rather than handing it over. For all I know, he didn't deliberately clatter in to me. If he was keen to avoid further confrontation, he could easily have been trying to get past and clattered me by accident. My gaze was on the laminate flooring, trying to steady myself as I rose, so I can't say for certain that the collision was premeditated.

I will speak to Gail and Sally when I next see them, and all going well at the hospital, I might go into work a few minutes early tomorrow and chat to them about the best way forwards. The last thing I want is for Toby to think he can get away with using violence on others, but it has to be handled sensitively; more so if he's only copying what he's witnessed behind closed doors.

I am sitting in a wheelchair in the Ultrasound department of the outpatients department, and I desperately need to use the toilet. They gave me a pint of water to drink ahead of the sonogram, but I'm not sure they quite appreciated that there isn't a lot of room for my bladder to hold that volume of liquid at the moment. I've been told I'll be seen as a priority, but there hasn't been any staff come by in some time.

'How long have you got to go?' a woman sitting in the seat closet to me in the waiting room asks.

She can't be much older than twenty if not younger, with a petite figure, and no sign of a bump, unless it's just well-covered by the flowery t-shirt she's swamped in.

'Less than a month,' I tell her, smiling despite my discomfort. 'And you?'

'This is my first scan so should find out for certain today. Well, as certain as they can be, you know. Is this your first?'

In an instant I'm transported back to this very room five years ago when Mark and I were sitting as anxiously as this mother-to-be waiting to hear about Josh's first scan. All parents go through this anxiety: the potential for things to not be quite right or as anticipated is huge, although in most cases everything works out okay in the end. She doesn't appear to have anyone with her, and I'm sensing now that her attempt to engage me is for her own benefit rather than mine. She doesn't deserve to hear about the trauma we suffered with Josh, so I nod instead.

'Terrifying isn't it?' I say with a sympathetic shrug. 'But totally worth it when you see the image of the baby on the little screen.

'I know, right? My mum offered to come with me to help with the nerves, and I wish I hadn't told her I'd be fine.'

I reach out and squeeze her hand. 'I'm sure you have nothing to worry about.'

She takes a deep breath and lets it out slowly, and the tension in her shoulders reduces.

'Abbie Friar,' a woman in scrubs calls out, and I raise my hand.

She smiles when she spots me, rests a paper folder on my lap and moves behind the wheelchair.

'It was nice meeting you,' I say to the younger woman, as I'm wheeled away. 'Try not to worry.'

I wish I could take my own advice. Despite the kick I felt at the preschool and the reassurance offered by the paramedics in the back of the ambulance, my imagination is playing tricks on me. I'm certain I haven't felt any movement since that kick, and now I'm desperately keen to be told that everything is fine. I don't know what I'll do if they tell me the fall has harmed my baby in some way.

'Are you okay to get up on to the bed,' the woman in scrubs asks when she has wheeled me in to the private room.

I wait for her to apply the brake, before shuffling to the edge of the seat, and lifting myself up. She pulls the wheelchair away when my hands and weight are pressed into the bed, before lowering it with the remote, and helping me to get into position on my back.

'The sonographer shouldn't be a moment,' she promises, exiting the room with a smile, and closing the door to.

Maybe I should have told Mark I was coming to the hospital. If there's any new risk to the baby he'd want to know. He deserves to know, but with the pressure he's under at work, I don't want to add to his stress and woes.

Everything will be okay, I remind myself, even if I'm not totally convinced. Surely lightning won't strike twice?

I rest my palms on my work shirt, and gently massage the bump beneath, searching for any sign of reassuring movement.

'Just be safe, and I swear I'll do everything in my power to protect you,' I whisper.

'Mrs Friar?' the sonographer asks as she pushes the door open, startling me.

'Y-Yes,' I stammer, uncertain whether she heard

my whisper.

She comes around the bed, and drops on to the stool beside me, switching on the ultrasound machine between us, and then asking me to raise my work shirt. I wince slightly as she squirts the cool gel on to the bump, and then proceeds to move the handheld device over my skin, her eyes fixed on the screen, searching for signs of life. I can't see the screen, but am barely breathing as she continues to wave the wand over my bump.

Shouldn't I have heard the sound of a heartbeat by now?

Oh God, please no ... not again.

And then relief washes over me as I hear the du-dum, du-dum echoing out of the machine.

The sonographer reaches across and hands me a tissue for my eyes, even though I hadn't realised I was crying.

'I understand you had a fall earlier?' she enquires, still studying the screen.

'Yes, at work,' I confirm. 'I didn't fall very far, and I think the baby was on my other side – away from the floor – but the paramedics thought it best to check everything is okay.'

She turns the screen so that I can see the outline of my baby as she performs a routine of checks. My eyes don't leave the screen, as they try to picture what his or her face will look like. I've never wanted something more than to hold and nurse my baby.

'Well everything looks to be okay,' the sonographer says after several minutes. 'The amniotic sac appears to be intact, which is the most important thing, and she has a strong sounding heartbeat, so there's nothing to …'

She trails off as she sees the blood drain from my face.

'I'm having … a girl?' I ask as my eyes fill again.

She pulls an apologetic face. 'Oh gosh, I'm sorry. You didn't know? Sorry, I usually ask … I thought I had … I'm sorry.'

I'm too stunned for words, but I don't remember feeling this happy and excited in forever.

'You're certain she's … a *she*?'

The sonographer nods, and chuckles. 'There's one obvious omission that makes me pretty certain. Of course, sonographers have been wrong before, but I'm usually pretty accurate. She is a healthy size and shape, and is forward facing at the moment, which is all good. Are you due in the next few weeks?'

I nod, and dab at my eyes.

'Well, in light of the fall, I'd just take a bit of extra care if I were you. Whilst there's no obvious trauma to the infant, situations like this can trigger things to move a bit swifter, so if you feel any twinges, get in touch with your midwife, and don't be shocked if the wheels start turning before your due date.'

She hands me a second tissue to wipe the remaining gel from my belly, before passing me a scrap of paper with a code on should I wish to print copies of the scan pictures. I slide myself from the mattress, too desperate for the toilet to wait for the janitor and the wheelchair. Thanking the sonographer, I leave the room feeling lighter than when I arrived, and once I've emptied my bladder I head to the hospital's main entrance, away from the smokers congregated under the shelter, and dial Mark's number. He answers on the second ring.

'Hi babe, everything okay?'

I take a deep breath. 'Yes, I'm fine. Everything is great. But listen, I'm at the hospital, because I took a tumble at work, and just wanted to check that the baby is okay, and –'

'Oh my God, are you okay?'

'Yes, yes, listen, everything is fine. They did an ultrasound, and aren't concerned.'

'Well that's a relief, but how are *you*? What happened?'

'Um, I don't know really. I was crouched down talking to one of my kids, and must have had a rush of blood and the next thing I knew I was tumbling. But I'm fine. And the baby is healthy and that's the most important thing.'

'Are they keeping you in? Do you want me to fetch you anything?'

'No, they've said I'm fine to leave. I was going to go home, but wondered if you're able to come and collect me?'

'Um … I mean, I can, only I've got a meeting in like ten minutes. I can ask Faye if we can delay it for a couple of hours.'

I can hear the reluctance in his voice, not that I doubt his desire to support me, but I know from experience how awkward his boss Faye can be about family time. Without a partner or children of her own, her working day starts at six and doesn't end until ten.

'No, it's fine, Mark, I can get a taxi home from here. Don't worry about it.'

'No, Abbie, if you need me, then I'll just speak to Faye. Sorry, it shouldn't be a question.'

'Seriously, Mark, I appreciate the offer, but I don't want to make things difficult. I really am okay, and there are loads of taxis around here, so please don't worry. I'd rather you don't piss off Faye and still make it home with the takeaway you promised.'

'Okay, well if you're sure?'

'I am. You'd better get back to work. I love you.'

'I love you too. Bye, sweetie.'

I feel our daughter elbow me in the side as the line disconnects. I could have told him about the sonographer's admission, but we previously agreed we wanted the surprise, and I don't want to spoil that for him. I'll just have to be careful I don't let it slip in the next few weeks. Now that I do know, I can't help gushing at the prospect of meeting my daughter for the first time.

But it's too big a secret to keep to myself, so I pull out my phone and call Yolanda.

Chapter 16

Abbie – Now

'You'll have to forgive the mess,' Yolanda warns me as we pull onto the driveway outside her three storey townhouse. 'I wasn't expecting guests, and the living room looks like a bomb's gone off.'

I'm just grateful that she agreed to collect me from the hospital and bring me back across town. Our house is walking distance from here, and I'm sure a burst of fresh air will do wonders for the cloud surrounding my mind right now. But first, I want to share my baby news with her. I almost blurted it out over the phone, but when she suggested bringing me here for a cuppa and chat, I bit my tongue. I still can't believe the little bundle growing inside me is a daughter. I can't stop thinking about plaiting her hair, going shopping for shoes and handbags, and one day doing each other's nails. I can't believe how vain I sound! Even if she turns out to do none of those things, I can't wait to hold her for the first time.

Yolanda applies the handbrake, and then looks me direct in the eye. 'You're hiding something,' she says quizzically.

I raise my eyebrows. 'What makes you say that?' I ask with false innocence.

She scrunches her nose. 'I don't know. There's …

there's something different about you today. You're *glowing*. Has something happened?'

I casually shrug and open my door, clutching my bump, as I shuffle off the seat, and plant my feet on the paved driveway, silently counting to five before I stand and straighten. Yolanda is already at the front door by the time I sidle over, and we enter.

There are trainers lining one side of the hallway, but it isn't nearly as untidy as she suggested in the car. She shows me through to the living room, apologising again, but where she sees mess, I see a house that's well lived in; I see a home. There are dog toys scattered in the corners of the room, and on the cushioned dog bed in front of the television stand. On the large apothecary table in the centre of the room, is a mug with a half-drunk cup of tea, an open laptop, and a collection of children's colouring pencils and some paper. For a mother of two boys, running her own business, and expecting a third child, I am impressed with how well she has things organised.

'Tea?' she offers when I'm seated in the armchair, 'or maybe something stronger for the shock?'

What I wouldn't give for a cool glass of white wine, sitting on a warm veranda, and just letting all my stress and anxiety disappear for a few hours. But I have avoided temptation for the last year, while Mark and I were trying to conceive, I'm not about to give in so close to the due date. I vowed I'd do whatever it took to keep my baby safe, and I am prepared to live up to that promise no matter what.

'A decaf tea would be great,' I say smiling.

She hovers for a moment, staring at me with a

quizzical look on her face. 'There's definitely something different about you today. Give me two ticks, and I'll make us tea.'

She disappears behind the door, and I replay the sonographer's words in my head: *she has a strong sounding heartbeat.*

I want to pinch myself because it feels like a dream, but I'm definitely awake. I don't want to get carried away because of what happened with Josh, and I tell myself not to picture those future shopping trips, until she arrives and is at home with Mark and me.

'Do you want me to fix you anything to eat?' Yolanda calls from the kitchen.

'Thanks,' I holler back, 'but I ate my packed lunch at the hospital while I was waiting for you to collect me, so I'm fine.'

Yolanda returns to the room a few minutes later with a tray bearing two mugs and a tin of biscuits. She sits on the sofa where the laptop remains open, and I realise now that my calling her interrupted the work she was doing.

'Oh, I'm so sorry,' I say, nodding at the laptop. 'I didn't mean to interrupt your work.'

She closes the laptop, and waves her hand dismissively. 'To be honest, I was in need of a break. Is there anything more depressing than doing someone else's accounts and realising how much wealthier they are than you'll ever be?' She screws up her face when I don't reply, and she realises what she's said. 'Sorry, there are plenty of other things more depressing, I just meant –'

'Forget about it,' I say, smiling. I know she didn't

mean to suggest the stress of her job is comparable to our losing Josh. 'Anyway, the reason I called was because I have some exciting news.'

She lowers her mug and stares at me expectantly.

'I know you've been trying to guess the gender of my baby since we met, and so I thought you might like to know that the sonographer accidentally let it slip when she was performing the ultrasound …'

Yolanda's eyes sparkle with excitement, and she's almost bouncing on the sofa.

'We're also expecting a daughter,' I say as my face breaks into a huge grin.

'I knew it!' she declares triumphantly. 'Your bump is more spread out around your middle like mine, which is often a sign. If it was lower and sticking out like a netball then I'd have said boy. Oh, Abbie, this is so exciting! Just imagine if our girls become good friends like you and me, how perfect would that be?'

My eyes fill with happy tears, and I can't help beaming back at her. 'I hope they become the best of friends!'

'I knew there was something you were holding back from me too. I was going to ask if you'd found out, but you've always been so adamant about keeping it a surprise that I thought you'd shoot me down straight away.'

Her eyes are filling too, and she locates a box of tissues from the window ledge behind her, takes one, and hands me the box so I can take one too.

'What are we like?' she laughs, dabbing her eyes. 'I blame the hormones! What does Mark think about the news?'

I pull a face. 'I haven't told him yet. I don't want to spoil the surprise for *him*. Does that make me bad?'

'No, not at all. If you agreed that you wouldn't find out, then maybe it's best not to say anything. Do you think he'd be cross if he later found out you knew and kept it from him?'

I really can't be sure, but shake my head. 'Maybe I should tell him that I accidentally found out and ask him whether he wants to know.'

Yolanda shrugs at the suggestion. 'Or just pretend and play along on the day. You know, they say ultrasound scans can be misinterpreted. It's unlikely, but she could have got it wrong. Wouldn't it be worse to tell Mark it's a girl, and then a boy arrives?'

It's a fair point, but I'll wait until I see him before deciding what to do.

'What else did the sonographer say? Is everything okay with the baby?'

'Yes, from what she said, though she did warn that the stress of the fall might act as a catalyst and get things moving quicker than expected.'

'What exactly happened? You were a bit vague on the phone.'

I take a sip of tea, but it's still too hot to properly drink, so I return it to the tray, and reach for a shortbread finger from the tin instead.

'That's the thing ... I'm not entirely sure. I was knelt down, separating two of the children in my group after a kicking incident. I was asking the boy – Toby Orville – to apologise to Bella, when he collided into me and I fell.'

Her eyes widen and her mouth drops open. 'You

think he pushed you deliberately?'

It sounds so paranoid hearing the words out loud, so I shrug. 'I honestly don't know. I don't want to think that he deliberately charged at me, but after what I witnessed with his dad, and then his kicking Bella, I …'

This is precisely why I didn't say anything to Gail and Sally, because it sounds insane, but if there is more going on at home, and Toby is struggling to cope with it emotionally, isn't it possible his lashing out was deliberate? I don't want to think badly of him, and I'm not sure a child of three would have the malice aforethought.

'Wait, back up,' Yolanda says, frowning. 'What happened with his dad?'

I explain the aggressive grabbing of Toby's arm and apparent verbal torrent that was unleashed.

'What did your boss say about the incident?'

'I haven't told either of them yet. I need to be certain before I act.'

'Did you ask this Toby about it?'

'I'm not allowed. We have procedures for these types of things, and unless he comes to me to talk about something that's troubling him, I'm not allowed to ask him direct questions about it. If he had said he was upset about being shouted at, I could have asked him what had happened. I tried asking if everything is okay, but he didn't want to talk about it.'

'Can you speak to his dad about what you saw?'

'I don't know him that well, as he tends to drop Toby at the door rather than coming in. It's a bit awkward.'

'What else do you know about him and the family?'

'Not a lot. His name's Chris, and he always arrives in jeans and a flannel shirt. I assume he's some kind of handyman or decorator, because his jeans and boots are always splashed with paint and –'

'Not Chris Orville?' Yolanda interrupts. 'Looks a bit like Tom Cruise, only much taller?'

I picture the blazing cheeks of the man yelling at Toby, and the description is apt. 'Yeah, do you know him?'

'My Tyrese is a plumber and those in the trade tend to know one another. Chris and Tyrese did a couple of jobs together a few years back, but then Chris and his wife moved away from the area. I hadn't realised they were back.'

This puts me in an awkward position. I never should have told Yolanda the family name, because now I'm spreading rumours about a child in my duty of care, and that's a breach of privacy.

'Please, you can't say anything. I shouldn't have told you, and if anyone finds out I could get in a lot of trouble.'

Yolanda shakes her head. 'I won't say a word, I promise, I'm just a bit surprised to be honest. The Chris Orville I know is so laid back that maybe they're not the same person after all. It's not like Orville isn't a pretty common surname, as is Chris, so it's possible there's another general handyman in the area with the same name …'

I know she's trying to reassure me, but it isn't working. I can't stop thinking about her description of him as a taller Tom Cruise, and I'm pretty sure we are both talking about the same guy. That said, if it is the same person, Yolanda might be able to fill in some of the blanks for me, and help me understand what I witnessed this morning.

'If Tyrese and Chris worked together, did you know his wife?'

'I knew of her. If I saw her in the supermarket, we'd make small talk, but that's about it. Lovely lady though from what I gathered. She was one of those who always seemed to have a batch of cookies baking in the oven when Tyrese would call around to collect Chris for a job. Is it okay if I let Tyrese know that Chris is back in town? I won't mention what we discussed.'

I'm pretty sure Yolanda will mention it to Tyrese whether I give my blessing or not, so I nod for both of our sakes, and reach for my tea.

'I really do appreciate you collecting me from the hospital,' I say, keen to change the subject. 'Mark was heading in to a meeting, and I didn't fancy getting a taxi.'

'I was happy to help out. How is everything with Mark? What did he say when you told him about Kinga approaching us yesterday?'

'He agreed that it was very odd, but when I asked him what he could recall about ... the day we lost Josh ... he said there were a couple of things that troubled him. He thought it was odd how we were kept from seeing Josh for a number of hours, and then apparently when he went to register the birth and death, there was some discrepancy with the date. The Registrar put it down to a hospital mix-up, but it was enough of a reason for us to go to the police station last night. But the officer we spoke to wasn't much help, and said without more information about Kinga, there wasn't anything he could pursue.'

'Did Mark agree with us that it was all some lame attempt at a con?'

I want to tell her about the feeling in my soul when I looked through Josh's blue metal tin, but I hold back. 'Yes, he and the police officer said it was probably an attempt to extort money, but she must have panicked after my projectile vomiting.'

Yolanda is nodding. 'Either that or her conscience got the better of her. I don't doubt that she's one troubled girl. Did you see the needle scars on her arms? I noticed it when she rolled up her sleeve to check the time. People like that – and I don't want to sound like a snob, but – they'll do anything to get the funds for their next fix. It's the biggest illness of our time and continues to remain only partially treated. You mark my words: you'll probably never see or hear from her again.'

I smile and nod at Yolanda, even though there is a part of me desperately hoping she's wrong. One thing's for certain: if Kinga does find me again, I'm going to demand proof of her admission before allowing myself to believe it.

Chapter 17

Louisa – Five years ago

'Right then,' Louisa said, staring at Caleb through the side of the transparent crib, 'I suppose I'd better get you changed into your going home outfit.'

He didn't respond, eyes closed, lips slightly apart, lost in a sea of dreams. In the six weeks since his arrival, there had been few times when she'd actually allowed herself to believe that his condition would improve and she'd be in a position to take him home and finally kick-start their new life together. The doctors and nurses seemed pleased with the progress he'd made, and he'd been out of the neonatal unit for three days without any deterioration, so now the only thing keeping him here was the paranoia in Louisa's mind.

Pete appeared at her side, and rested a hand on her shoulder. 'What do you need?'

Louisa recited the list in her head. 'I'd better change his nappy; there should be one in the front zipped pocket. Oh, and the baby wipes, and a nappy sack to put the used one in. His baby grow should be in the main body of the bag if you can get that out too?'

Pete followed her instructions carefully, placing each item on the hospital bed, before holding up the baby-grow. 'It's a bit big isn't it?'

She bit her lip. 'It's fine. It's the one I brought for him to travel home in, so that's what he'll wear.'

'What about the blue one your mum bought yesterday? It's a snugger fit for new-borns.'

Louisa ground her teeth together, trying to quell the rising frustration. 'I said it's fine. Why don't you make yourself useful and pass Caleb down to me. I'm not going to be able to reach up to the crib.'

'Why don't you let me do it then?'

She closed her eyes, silently counting to five. 'Because I *want* to do it. You and my parents have had the chance to change plenty of nappies, and this will be my first. Please? I just want to–'

'Okay, okay,' Pete said, finally picking up on her tone.

He scooped up Caleb, one hand beneath his back, and the other cradling his neck. Caleb stirred but didn't wake as Pete gently rested him on the perfectly pressed sheet. Louisa moved closer to the bed, leaning forward in her wheelchair, and then un-popping the baby-grow he was already wearing. Caleb stirred again, as she extracted his chipolata-sized arm from the sleeve, before repeating the exercise with the other arm. Pete hovered behind her, observing like an umpire, and all Louisa wanted to tell him was to back off and allow her to focus on the task at hand.

'You need to pull some of the top down to get his legs out,' Pete warned. 'These things can be pretty tight.'

Is this what their life was going to be like now: Pete constantly checking she was doing things correctly? Just because she couldn't walk, didn't mean she couldn't think or use her upper body. Fitzgerald had scheduled her surgery for next week, and she was determined to make the most of the next few days with Caleb before she had to leave him in her parents' custody.

Sliding the baby-grow from beneath him, Caleb screwed his face up as his skin made contact with the coolness of the sheet. She didn't want him to wake screaming and crying, as Pete's judgement and criticism was already too much for her to bear. Moving quickly, she peeled off the tabs of his nappy, lifting his legs as she slid it out and pressed a new one in place.

You've got this, she silently reminded herself.

She'd watched the nurses change Caleb many times, although she doubted she'd ever be as slick with the activity.

Pete was already unfastening the poppers on the new baby-grow, and handed it to her. 'You should put his legs in first, and then his arms. Just reverse how you got him out of the other one.'

Yes, I know, Pete, she didn't snap.

On the rare occasions when she'd pictured taking Caleb home, she'd always seen him in this particular baby-grow, which is why she was now so determined to use it, even thought it was at least two sizes too big. In fact it was so big that it probably wouldn't matter which order she manhandled his limbs into it, but she pushed his legs in first, careful not to wake him.

She was just starting to fasten the poppers when she smelled it. Like a bag of rotten fish wafted beneath her nose, she knew instantly why Caleb appeared to be grinning in his sleep.

Pete stepped back, holding a hand beneath his nose. 'Blimey, he definitely takes after his dad, doesn't he?' Pete chuckled.

Why did he have to wait until I'd changed him?

It wasn't Caleb's fault she knew, but his timing was atrocious. Once again she unfastened the poppers, but left his arms in place, pulling on the baby-grow as she extracted Caleb's legs, the smell of his deposit rising, and turning her stomach. Pete was already passing her a fresh nappy, as she peeled off the tabs, and attempted to slide the nappy from her son's bottom without smearing the contents over his legs. And that's when Caleb chose to empty his bladder. Like a tiny sprinkler, urine shot out of him, and it was all Louisa could do to push the nappy back down and limit the impact. But a yellow stain was already spreading out across the once white sheet.

'Oh Jesus,' she said under her breath, feeling a twinge in her shoulder as she continued to lean forward to hold the nappy in place. 'You're going to have to fetch one of the nurses and explain what's happened to the bed,' she told Pete.

'Are you sure? Why don't I help change Caleb, and then–'

'Pete, please,' she snapped, 'just go and find a nurse and explain what happened.'

He didn't argue, and she let out a small sigh when she felt the gust of air as he opened the door and exited the room. Daring to lift the flap of the nappy, she was relieved to see the sprinkler had stopped, and even laughed at the ridiculousness of the situation. Caleb looked rather pleased with himself too.

Confident he was finished, she once again attempted to slide out the used nappy, wiped up the mess on his bottom, and then slipped a new one into place. She worked methodically, determined to have Caleb dressed and ready to go before Pete returned. It was more than just proving to herself that she could change her son; she needed to prove to Pete *and* her parents that she could do it. The accident had stolen her legs but not her humanity.

With the nappy secured, she lifted Caleb's legs, ready to slide them into the baby-grow, when she felt how wet the material was.

'No, no, no,' she whimpered, realising now that the sprinkler had hit more than just the bed sheet. Both legs of the outfit were soaked through.

'No, no, no,' she repeated, fighting against the sting of tears now scratching at the corner of her eyes.

'Is everything okay in here?'

Louisa started at the woman's voice, and tried to blink back the dam. The owner of the voice was dressed in a green nurse's uniform and appeared across the bed.

'I'm Sister Arnott,' she explained, her accent Irish in origin. 'You probably don't remember, but I was on duty the day you were brought in.'

Louisa raised her eyes, and focused on the woman's face. Probably in her early to mid-fifties, she had small, dark eyes, and a nose that pointed up slightly at the end. But there was warmth there too, and when she smiled, the wrinkles at the side of her face gathered together like folded sheets. Louisa didn't recognise her.

'And this must be little Caleb? He's certainly

looking far healthier than when I first met him. I hope you don't mind me stopping by? I just like to say goodbye to all our little ones before they head off to start their new lives.'

'I was just getting him ready to go home but he had a little accident.'

'Don't worry about the sheets. We can get them cleaned up. Do you have a spare baby-grow to change him into?'

The dam burst and the tear splashed against Louisa's cheeks. 'It's just … I bought this one the day I found out I was pregnant, and I always pictured this would be what I took my baby home in. And now it's ruined.'

Sister Arnott nodded without judgement. 'Can I let you in on a little secret?' she said, leaning closer, her voice barely more than a whisper. 'Babies can be little tinkers with our best laid plans. Believe me! I know it's not how you imagined it, but I promise you'll look back on this and laugh one day. Mark my words. And he won't care what he's wearing. Not yet anyway. Wait till he's a teenager, and then you'll miss the fact that you once got to choose his clothes.'

Louisa found herself laughing at her own outburst, embarrassed at her overreaction to the situation.

'Would you like some help, or should I leave you to it?' Sister Arnott asked next.

'There should be a spare baby-grow in the bag behind my chair. A blue one I think. If you could pass that to me, it would be a huge help.'

Sister Arnott disappeared behind the chair, located the baby-grow and passed it to her. With a deep breath,

Louisa carefully removed the old one, and slipped Caleb into the new one, proud that she completed the task without waking him. Sister Arnott helped her strap him into the baby seat, adjusting the small hat on his head.

He looked so perfect that Louisa could feel her heart bulging, but then the paranoia returned to her conscious mind, and she instantly filled with self-doubt.

'What happens if he starts to get sick again?' she asked. 'Do we bring him back here, or take him to a normal hospital?'

Sister Arnott gave her a knowing smile. 'I'm sure Caleb is going to be perfectly fine. I know it was a bit touch and go at the start, but he's doing much better now. That's why the doctor has released him.'

'Yes, but what if being away from these surroundings, things go backwards? Or what if he catches a cold and can't breathe properly again? Or he can't settle in our home? What if …?'

Sister Arnott tilted her head. 'It's perfectly natural to have doubts after what you've been through, but things will be perfectly okay. I promise you, no matter what happens, you'll cope. I think you're far stronger than you give yourself credit for, Louisa.'

'But what if …?'

'You'll deal with it. Try not to let worry spoil things.'

Louisa tried to smile, but she wasn't sure she'd ever stop worrying. A flash of her stumbling towards Pete's car smashed to the front of her mind. She was physically upset about something, yelling back at someone over her shoulder, before yanking open the door, and sliding the seat back so she could fit the bump in behind the wheel. The vision splintered into a thousand tiny shards as quickly as it arrived.

'What a perfect pair the two of you make,' Sister Arnott commented, as Pete returned to the room, with a dazed look on his face.

'I couldn't find anyone,' he said absently, then noticed Sister Arnott. 'Oh you've already reported it.'

Sister Arnott patted Louisa's arm. 'You're going to be a fabulous mother to Caleb. He's very lucky to have found you.'

Louisa's brow instantly furrowed at the line, but Sister Arnott was already on her way, leaving the door open as she returned to her duties.

'Did you hear what she just said?' Louisa asked Pete.

'W-What? What who said?'

'Sister Arnott. It was the strangest thing. She said Caleb was lucky to have found me. What an odd thing to say.'

Pete wasn't really listening, lifting the car seat onto the wheeled frame that meant they'd be able to push Caleb to the car, rather than carry him.

'Are you ready to go?' he asked.

Louisa looked from him to Caleb, and then back again, giving a firm nod. Wheeling herself behind the frame of the makeshift pram, she put her hands on the plastic bar, while Pete moved behind her wheelchair. They stuttered forwards, but Louisa grimaced at the strain of the stretch up to the plastic bar.

'Stop, stop,' she winced when they'd barely made it

to the door. 'I-I can't do this. You're going to have to push him while I manoeuver myself.'

'Are you sure?'

She nodded in defeat; yet another dream torn from her grasp.

Pete pulled the frame away, and proceeded out of the door, leaving Louisa to follow slowly behind. Watching her husband accepting the congratulatory applause offered by the small gathering of nurses who'd come to wish them on her way, she couldn't ignore the feeling of anger that had come with the glimpse of her stumbling towards his car.

Chapter 18

Abbie – Now

I left Yolanda's when she said it was time for her to collect her boys from school, but the short walk home has done nothing to clear the thunderous clouds from my mind. When I try not to think about the incident with Toby and his dad, I hear Kinga's words in my head: *Your child not die. He still alive. I can prove it.*

Prove it how though? All she told us before my projectile vomiting was the story about her own son – for which she offered no proof – and showed us the scrap of paper with mine and Josh's names on it. Hardly enough to stand up in a criminal court, but what if there is more she didn't tell us about? Does she know where Josh is now? Can she show me where he is or who has him? If I saw him with my own eyes, would I know instinctively that it was him?

I stand and begin to pace the kitchen as the strain on my lower back becomes uncomfortable. These thoughts are not helping me relax, and I feel wrung up right now. Is entertaining this possibility causing harm to the baby I'm still growing? Can she sense my inner turmoil? I place both hands beneath the bump as I walk, trying to lift her slightly to ease the strain on my spine, but it offers little support.

Caving, I pull on my anorak, and grab my shoulder

bag and head out, determined to walk in fresh air until my mind settles. I try not to think about Toby and Kinga, wiping them clear whenever a thought about either appears. I think, instead about the future.

I don't want to tempt fate, but since hearing that we're expecting a daughter, I can't help imagining what our future will hold. Will she have Mark's deep-set eyes and almost Latin look, with hair as black as coal? Or will she inherit my family's slightly elongated nose, and wide eyes? Will her hair hang straight like Mark's or frizz up at the slightest moisture like mine? There was a time as a teenager when I would spend hours trying to straighten my hair only for a spit of rain to undo my hard work. I don't bother straightening it anymore, and have become accustomed to the way it curls unrestrained.

The chill breeze whips at my cheeks, but still I march onwards, until I'm close to breathlessness, and realise I've inadvertently walked to the park and playground near the preschool. I hadn't really thought about where I was heading, and I guess on some subconscious level my mind reverted to the default setting of work. Or maybe my subconscious wanted me to collect my car from the car park. In the fuss of falling and being escorted away by the ambulance, I hadn't even thought about the fact my car was still here. Maybe there is more to Sally's theory about the baby brain amnesia.

The car park is full of cars, some departing, others arriving and fighting over the limited number of parking spaces. Trying to drive home right now isn't sensible, as the road is full of parents collecting children from the preschool as well as the infant school up the road. Deciding to rest, I step through the gate and into the playground, locating a wooden bench and gently lowering myself into it.

I spot Bella from preschool on one of the swings being pushed by her mum. I wave, but Bella doesn't see me, instead lost in a world of flying through the air, squealing the higher she goes. I'm envious; how I wish I could experience the unbridled joy of swinging with no consideration of the risks and pressures of life.

The playground is busy, and there are other faces I recognise from preschool, but I stay seated, my ankles swollen and in need of a bag of frozen peas when I do make it home. Perhaps walking so far wasn't such a great idea. It's not exactly helped me forget about Toby and Kinga. At least there's no chance I'll run into Toby and his dad here, as Toby would have been collected just after lunch.

I need to stop thinking about him. The collision was probably just an accident, and it's just my fragile psyche daring to think it could be anything more. Instead, I stare out across the playground, spotting a boy I don't recognise tackling the huge spider-shaped climbing frame. The boy can't be much older than five, but he scales one of the spider's legs as if he's a professional climber, swinging from one bar to the next, using his hands to pull, and his trainers to grip. It's an impressive skill he has, and he is soon halfway up the structure that stands three metres from the ground.

Would Josh be adventurous like Mark and this boy: constantly climbing trees, and treating each strip of grass as a training camp for a battle zone?

I shake the thought from my mind, close my eyes, and try to focus on my breathing. In a month or so, I'll be just like the other parents here: beaming with joy and offering reassuring smiles as I panic at every unconceivable danger that might threaten my child's upbringing.

A shadow falls across my face, and I start as I open my eyes and see the faded leather jacket that first crashed in to me in John Lewis yesterday. I open my mouth to speak, but the breath catches in my throat.

'I sit. Is okay?' Kinga asks, pointing at the space beside me on the bench.

My mind is telling me to stand and leave. Her appearance in this park, so close to my work can't be a coincidence. Has she been waiting nearby, assuming I'd be due to finish my shift about now? Or was she waiting for me at home and followed me here? Both possibilities have my heart racing and pulse increased, but like the beginnings of a nightmare, there is nothing I can do to change what's about to unfold.

I picture PS Brearton as he handed me his business card and urged me to phone immediately if Kinga approached me again. The business card is in my shoulder bag along with my phone. Should I just whip both out and call him? I don't think my ankles are in any state for me to get to the safety of my car. Surely she won't do anything harmful with so many witnesses around? But if she is desperate for money as Yolanda suggested, I can't be sure how far she'll go to get what she wants. Should I just offer her money and hope she goes away? I don't know how much cash I have in my purse – a few notes maybe – will that be enough?

'I sorry,' she says, so close that our elbows are touching.

'W-What for?' I ask, the words sticking in my throat. Why is my mouth suddenly so dry?

'For leaving yesterday. You were sick. Okay now?'

I try to smile, but it's tough when my frown weighs so heavily on the rest of my face. I don't tell her that nausea is starting to flood my body in waves.

She looks over both shoulders, before leaning closer. 'I being watched.'

My eyes widen at the statement, and I too look around behind us, but don't spot a menacing figure in the shadows as expected. The car park behind us is still just a maze of cars coming and going, with parents and children ducking between.

'W-Watched by whom?'

She shuffles lower on the bench. 'Don't know. Could be people from Philomena's, or someone worse.'

I remember what Yolanda said about needle marks on Kinga's arms. Is she high now? Is that what's causing this spark of paranoia? All I know is I want her as far from me and my baby.

'I want to prove you that your son alive,' she says next, and the tug at my heart strings isn't fair. My hormones are all over the place.

'H-How do you know Josh is still alive? Just because your son was, doesn't mean the same for mine.'

Her head slowly turns and she meets my determined stare with a look of confusion. 'You still not believe me? They took your son, Abbie. They sold him to rich family, and he out there now. Living. Breathing. He is your son, do you not want him back?'

'Of course I do!' I snap back, before lowering my voice as one of the parents closest to us turns and looks at us. 'But you have to appreciate that until you approached me yesterday, I had no idea that my son didn't die. How would you feel if some stranger approached you and made such a declaration?'

'I would be grateful,' she sneers between gritted teeth. 'I would give anything to have my boy with me now, but I was too late. You still have chance.'

'If you know where my son is, then let's go to the police together and tell –'

'No! No police.'

I know if Mark was here he'd take this as proof that Kinga is trying to deceive us, but I push the voice of doubt from my mind.

'What is it you want from me?'

'I want help you find your son. That is all.'

'Then you've got to give me something. I *want* to believe what you're saying, Kinga, I *really* do, but you need to convince me that this isn't just a scam.'

'This what I try to do.'

'That scrap of paper you showed to me isn't evidence of what happened. Don't you see? For all I know you wrote our names and the sum on the scrap. It isn't enough, I'm sorry.'

'I have proof in safe place. I will take you to it.'

I don't move. My sixth sense is warning me not to go anywhere alone with this woman, and that I'm safer with these parents and children close enough to hear if

I scream.

'W-Where is this proof?'

'I tell you is in *safe* place.'

'What do you mean? Why don't you have it with you now?'

'People watching. I already say. I not safe.' She stands but remains close enough that I can still hear her. 'I have to go.'

'No, wait,' I say, reaching out to her. 'Please? I want to know where Josh is, but I'm in no condition to go with you now. Let me talk to my husband, and then we'll see. Is that okay? Can my husband come to your safe place?'

She considers the request. 'Just husband; no police.'

'Why are you so afraid of the police? If you share what you know they'll be able to locate Josh quicker.'

She leans down so that I can smell the tar on her breath. 'No police. They send me back to Chechnya.'

I hear Brearton's words in my mind: *If she did enter the country illegally, and was later arrested, she is unlikely to have been imprisoned in the UK and then released without questions being raised about the legitimacy of her stay here.*

I reach in to my handbag and remove a scrap of paper and a pen. 'Let me have your phone number and I will message you once I've spoken to my husband. Is that okay?'

Her eyes narrow, before she reaches for the pen and scribbles a number on the paper. 'You phone me if you want to find son. If no call tonight, I go and you never see me again. Understand?'

She doesn't wait for my answer, skulking away

pulling up the hood of the sweater beneath the leather jacket, and disappearing into the crowd of parents and excitable children.

Chapter 19

Abbie – Now

Arriving in the car park of Apollo Financial Services, I'm relieved to spot Mark's Audi parked in his space, and pull in to a visitor bay. I tried calling him as soon as I'd composed myself after Kinga left the park, but if he saw my calls, he didn't answer them. I know he was supposed to be meeting with his boss Faye, but I had hoped they would have finished up by now.

Coming across town in rush hour traffic wasn't a great idea, and I can feel the stress prickling at my skin, and it's a relief to open the door and allow the cool breeze to blow in and take the edge off. Kinga's appearance at the park and her continued assertion that Josh is still alive has my head all over the place. Mark, Brearton, and Yolanda were all convinced that I wouldn't see or hear from her again, and yet there she was. She'd hunted me down for a second time. I'm not comfortable with the prospect of having a stalker, but *what if* she is telling the truth? It sounds so farfetched, but what kind of mother would I be if I didn't pursue the possibility that my child is still alive?

It also troubles me how Kinga spoke of being watched. How far does her conspiracy stretch? Does she mean the people responsible for stealing our children are still keeping tabs on us? To what end? And if it isn't them, then who? I've never been a fan of mysteries, and the prospect that I'm now living in one is uncomfortable. And it's added stress that my daughter doesn't need. I rest my hand on the bump as I say this, and I'm sure she high fives me back, but in truth it could be any limb. I need to remember not to be so loose with my words when describing her around Mark.

Pushing myself out of the car, I grab my bag from the passenger seat, and slowly straighten, feeling every twinge in my lower back. Despite the pain, I wouldn't swap this experience with anyone. I've waited a long time to be able to hold my own child's hand.

Locking the car, I cross the tarmac to the front entrance of the five storey building. The brickwork shines with a fresh coat of paint, but there's something clinical about the three metre panes of glass that dominate the mouth of the entrance. It looks clean, but almost too clean, as if the building's appearance has been designed to hide all the dirty secrets inside.

The automated swivel door looks precarious, but when the security guard just inside spots my bump, he opens a side door and allows me to enter, sending me to the front desk to identify myself and reason for coming today. The entrance hall bustles with men and women in suits and ties in intimate conversations as they pass in and out of the security barriers. The beeping of the pass scanners and grinding of the metal arm must irritate after a while, and yet the lady in the charcoal suit, white blouse and red neckerchief has a Marsha Brady smile plastered across her face as she hangs up the phone and welcomes me to Apollo

Finance.

'I'm here to see my husband Mark Friar,' I tell her.

She continues to smile as she averts her gaze to the monitor between us and types something into her keyboard. She picks up the phone and types in his extension, but the smile is replaced by a frown when she returns the phone to its receiver.

'There's no answer at his desk, I'm afraid,' she tells me. 'If you want to take a seat over there,' she points towards a pod of stiff, leather sofas beside the swivel door, 'I'll send him an email, and let him know you're waiting for him.'

I thank her and head to the seats, though all four are low down and not practical for someone in my state. I perch on the arm of one of the sofas instead, but I won't be able to stay here long. In fairness, Mark didn't say how long his meeting with Faye would last, and he has no idea I've blazed across town to meet with him. I hope he gets my message and comes down soon.

My gaze wanders from the concourse to the car park, and I'm unprepared for seeing Mark laughing and smiling as he climbs out of a sports car with a woman whose skirt leaves little to the imagination. Her shiny blonde hair is tied in a bun and she looks painfully thin. She too is laughing at whatever my husband has just said, and as they come around to the front of the car she playfully slaps his upper arm. It's like someone has taken my worst nightmare and acted it out in front of me. They come through the swivel door, and Mark's mouth drops open as he spots me perched on the arm of the chair.

'Abbie, what are you ... Is everything okay?' He

glances nervously back at the woman beside him. 'You remember, Faye, don't you?'

I blink several times as I now recognise the hazel-coloured eyes, and plated teeth; I hadn't realised it was her at first. I don't think I've ever seen her so relaxed and happy, though her shoulders are tensing as she reaches out a hand to me, which I feel obliged and slightly nauseous to shake.

'We were just meeting with a client,' Mark quickly explains. 'What are you doing here?'

I don't want to tell him in front of the woman who he's always described as hard work, and with no sentiment for family, so I stay quiet until he takes my hint.

'Faye, do you mind if I just …?'

She looks happy to be relieved of the potential emotional struggle that's about to unfold. 'No worries, I'll see you back upstairs.'

With that she spins and heads for the security barriers, and Mark sits beside me on the sofa.

'Kinga showed up at the park near the preschool,' I bowl out with before he's settled.

'Oh my, did you phone that policeman, what's his name …? Brearton?'

'Not yet. I wanted to speak to you first.'

'Okay, well tell me what she said.'

I explain how I went for a walk and only stopped at the park to catch my breath before I planned to drive my car home, and then I tell him about her wanting to meet later and reveal the conclusive proof that Josh is still alive. He listens, and doesn't interrupt, but the ever-creasing skin beneath his eyes shows that questions are building.

'She wanted you to go with her then?' he asks when I'm done.

I nod. 'But I told her I was in no condition to go with her alone, and asked that you accompany me. She seemed okay with that, but was adamant we weren't to involve the police.'

He raises his eyebrows. 'Of course not, because then they'd arrest her for this con.'

I'm not surprised that this is still his conclusion. He's always been pragmatic, and like a doubting Thomas, he needs to see things with his own eyes to believe. His cynicism makes a good counterweight to my own feelings.

'The fact that she showed up again, and is sticking with the same story could mean she's telling the truth,' I assert. 'I know you don't want to believe Josh is still alive, but I feel it in my heart, and I would never forgive myself if we didn't at least try.'

He looks sceptical. 'I think we need to tell Brearton what happened, and see what he says. You never know, he might have had more luck finding out who this Kinga woman really is, or whether she's tried anything similar with anyone else.'

I know he's right, and that we have to protect ourselves. I wait on the arm of the sofa while he heads upstairs to sign out, and then we drive separately to the police station, talking to each other hands-free. He tells me about his day, and explains that Faye was in a jovial mood because they managed to sign up a new major client as their meeting. I don't tell him how it made me feel watching an attractive woman openly flirting with him, but I hope deep down he realises how it must have looked. Unlike his own cynicism, I want to believe it was nothing more than overt friendliness. I trust my husband more than any person on the planet.

We park and walk the short distance to the police station, but our efforts are in vain when the young PC from the other night informs us that it's PS Brearton's day off, but offers to take an update from us to pass on. Neither Mark, nor I want to repeat our story to another stranger, and Mark simply asks that Brearton phone us when he's next on shift. Instead, we head back outside and Mark leans against my car, while I sit behind the wheel.

'You want us to go and meet her, don't you?' he asks.

'She seemed so resolute that we would feel compelled to believe when she showed us whatever it is she has. Don't we owe it to Josh to look?'

He groans under his breath. 'Not if it endangers the little one you're carrying. All this additional stress and anxiety can't be healthy.'

I know he's right, and I too am concerned about the potential ramifications, but the sonographer said everything is okay with her, and I feel like she deserves to meet her big brother if against the odds he did survive.

'What's the worst that can happen?' I counter. 'We arrange to meet her, and so long as the location doesn't seem dodgy, we listen to what she has to say, view whatever she's got, and then make a decision from there. I have her mobile number now, which we can pass on to Brearton when he calls tomorrow, and then maybe they can ... I don't know ... triangulate her signal or something?'

He snickers at this. 'I'll have to start calling you Miss Marple.'

'I'm serious, Mark. We tried it your way by coming to the police, but they can't help. Maybe if you hear what she has to say, some of your doubt will go. What do you say?'

He looks down at me, and I can see how difficult he's finding all this. 'Call her.'

Chapter 20

Louisa – Five years ago

They hadn't warned her that she would lose her dignity, as well as use of her legs. Watching Pete secure the car seat to the fitted bracket in the back of his new Land Rover, she then had to wait for him to grapple a hand beneath the dead weight of her thighs, and then hoist her up and into the front seat. Subconsciously he pulled the seatbelt around her chest and grunted as he stretched over and plugged it in. She knew he was only trying to help, but the achy groan as he'd hoisted her into the air had done nothing to relieve her embarrassment at being so dependent.

Why oh why did he choose a car as high as a replacement? Did he want her to be ever-reliant on him? Or was this his guarantee that she wouldn't be able to drive his car again?

He'd claimed he'd been seduced by the salesman at the garage, but she wouldn't know as he hadn't invited her to tag along. He'd left her at the hospital visiting Caleb three days ago, and when he'd returned to collect her, he'd already bought the car. They'd agreed he needed to replace the written off Aston Martin, but she hadn't anticipated his decision to be so quickly made and without discussion.

He probably just thought I had enough on my plate

without car complications.

He closes the passenger door with a heavy shove, and she shudders at the loud echo as it connects. Caleb is in the seat directly behind her, so she can't see him. Even lowering the vanity mirror in the sun visor, all she can see is her own face and the headrest.

'Mum's here, Caleb,' she coos, hoping the sound of her voice will settle him in these new surroundings. 'This is your first car ride; I bet you're excited?'

No response, and she desperately wanted to be able to swivel in her chair and check on him, but her movement was restricted. If only Pete had thought to connect the seat behind his, she'd at least be able to touch Caleb.

The car shook as Pete pulled open his own door, and climbed in, slamming it behind him. He inhaled deeply and audibly, and grinned at her. 'It still has that new car smell. Love it!'

'I can't see Caleb,' she said, unable to bite her tongue.

Pete glanced over his shoulder. 'He's fine. I can see him, and I can keep an eye on him via this,' he said tapping a finger against the bottom rim of the rear-view mirror.

'Are you sure he's okay? I can't hear him breathing.'

Pete glanced back at the car seat again. 'He's wiggling his toes, so I'm pretty sure he's okay.'

He was making a pitying face, his eyes almost slanting down at the sides.

'Can't we move him to the other side so I can see him, and he can see me?'

They both knew she meant the royal 'we', as she didn't have the strength or height to move Caleb anywhere.

Pete's face switched from pity to anger in an instant, but he caught himself quickly enough, settling on frustration and an unsatisfied sigh. 'The car seat is attached to a fitted base. The garage fitted it for me. I'm not even sure I'd know how to unclip it and move it to the other seat.' He checked his watch. 'Can it wait until later? We'll only be in the car for twenty or so minutes depending on traffic. I promise I'll keep checking on him, and updating you on what he's doing. I'm sure he's as exhausted as us after the fuss of getting ready to come home for the first time. He isn't crying, which means he's happy. Our little star is cool as a cucumber, taking everything in his stride. You should be pleased.'

I should be pleased? Why, because I caused all the trauma he's suffered so far?

She didn't react to the implication, chewing the inside of her cheek instead. She didn't want to spoil the day by getting into an argument over the placement of the seat, and if the garage had chosen to put it that side without Pete's knowledge then she couldn't hold him responsible. She did her best to try and turn in her seat, but in truth, even if he was on the other seat, he'd still just be out of sight.

She nodded to show Pete that her challenge was over, and lowered her eyes, as he started the engine and slipped the car into reverse. She watched him in her periphery to check he was living up to his promise to look in the mirror, and for the first four or five minutes he did, but then the time between glances grew. He was making no effort to engage her in conversation, leaving her alone with her thoughts, which wasn't where she wanted to be.

'What do you remember about the day of the accident?' she blurted out, without thinking.

His face turned slowly to meet hers, his brow furrowed with confusion. 'I remember it was possibly the scariest day of my life. The accident, the fire brigade having to cut you out of the car, the ride to the hospital, and then them having to rush you into theatre.' He shuddered noisily, as if the memory had been a blast of cold air. 'You should try not to think about it. With Caleb coming home this is a fresh start for all of us.'

She looked away, the words triggering a nerve inside her mind, but she couldn't quite see what or why.

'But I don't understand why I was in your car to begin with,' she pushed, keeping her hands in her lap, knotting her fingers together. 'I have no recollection of that day whatsoever. Was I going somewhere? Was there some reason I was in the Aston Martin?'

She heard him sigh again, louder this time, but he kept his eyes fixed on the road. 'Why does any of that matter now? You can't change what's happened; none of us can.'

'I'm not trying to change the past,' she pleaded, 'I just want to understand how I got here. To this point. I need to understand whether the accident was my fault, or whether someone or something caused me to lose control.'

He rested a hand on her knee. 'There's nothing to be gained from blaming yourself. Yes, I miss the Aston Martin – she was my little baby – but I'm nearly forty, and it was probably impractical to be driving something so small and sporty. If anything, your accident has given me the kick up the arse to get something more practical and akin to a man of my age. Besides, how on earth would we have got a baby seat into the Aston Martin? In the boot maybe.' He laughed uproariously at this, but it sounded false.

'The accident was on a Tuesday, right?'

She caught sight of him rolling his eyes. 'And?'

'Well, were you at work? Did I come and collect the Aston Martin from you there? I – I have this black hole in my memory, and it is killing me not knowing.'

'I wasn't at work, and I'm not really sure why you went out in my car. Maybe I was blocking you in, and it was easier for you to grab my keys than ask me to move it. I don't know, Lou.'

He was probably right, and she was potentially reading far too much into things. Deep down she was certain that she wouldn't just take his car without express permission, but maybe that was more down to her own insecurities than any unwritten rule between them. It felt likely that he'd blocked her in, as he was always parking his car at stupid angles, and maybe she did just lose patience and take it to spite him.

But that still didn't explain how she lost control and wound up in a crumpled heap upside down.

'Maybe I should phone the police,' she said rhetorically.

'Why phone the police to report you've lost your

memory?'

'They must have had to investigate the accident to determine who was to blame.'

'You don't need to worry about the police, Lou. Your dad and I have made all that go away. You just need to focus on getting yourself better. Yes? It's not long until your operation, so you need to keep your mind clear, and your strength up. Let me worry about everything else.'

Pete as pragmatic as ever, but she didn't understand what he meant by him and her dad making it *all go away*. Did that mean she was at fault? Or had they simply handled all matters pertaining to what was ultimately an accident that left one car written off and the driver severely injured? She couldn't remember being breathalysed, but given how far along she was, she wouldn't have been drinking alcohol anyway. Maybe they'd run a blood test at the hospital while she was passed out, and the results had come back as normal.

'Can we change the subject?' Pete asked next. 'I was thinking we should book a holiday after your operation. God knows we could both do with a break away.'

'Caleb's only just arrived; I'm not sure we're allowed to fly anywhere with him yet. He hasn't got a passport for one thing.'

'No, I meant you and me. Your mum has said she's happy to look after him if we want to get a few days of sun somewhere exotic. I'm owed some time off work, and it could aid your recovery too.'

It had been almost a year since their last holiday

abroad, and ordinarily she'd be chomping at the bit to escape the monotony of life, but she wasn't ready to handover Caleb just like that; not after everything they'd been through.

'I-I'm not sure, Pete. Can I think about it?'

'Of course, of course. I picked up some travel brochures for you to peruse. Maybe seeing the glossy pictures of sandy beaches and cocktails by the pool will inspire you.'

She wasn't convinced, but cleared her mind to focus on trying to hear whether Caleb was still breathing.

'He's fine,' Pete added, as if reading her mind. 'His foot is twitching. I reckon he's dreaming about playing football. He could be a future Premier League star, you never know.'

Louisa wasn't sure babies dreamed the same as adults, and given Caleb had never seen a football, she doubted the content of a dream as well, but she didn't like to dampen Pete's enthusiasm.

She felt a wave of relief as their road came into view, but anxiety kicked in as soon as she saw all the cars parked along the side of the road, recognising two of them.

'W-What's going on?' she asked, already fearing the answer.

'Surprise!' Pete exclaimed. 'I know how hard you've been finding all of this, so I thought a small gathering of our closest friends to welcome you both home would cheer you up.'

She forced the smile, as the dread clawed at the edges of her sanity. Parking on the driveway, Pete fetched the collapsible wheelchair from the boot and carried it inside, before returning for her. She could feel every pair of eyes watching as Pete struggled to lift her from her seat and carry her inside. Didn't he realise how humiliating this was? Her cheeks burned as he lowered her into the chair indoors, and then made a play of back ache as he emerged from the house to collect Caleb.

Bunting was hung from every corner of the downstairs, with balloons floating by the ceiling. She wheeled the chair into the lounge-diner, noticing that the table had been moved to the narrowest wall, and was now loaded with sausage rolls, crisps, and sandwiches.

Louisa's mum emerged from the kitchen on cue, an apron tied around her middle. 'Welcome home, sweetheart. How was the drive?'

'Fine,' Louisa lied.

'And where's that cheeky wee grandson of mine? I should warn you that I might smother him with kisses,' she chuckled, as she untied the apron and folded it away.

She clapped her hands together in delight as Pete entered the room, carrying the baby seat, followed by twenty or so others, all trying to squeeze into the room. Hands were patted on Louisa's shoulders, and kisses blown as the throng gathered and chatted until she could only hear a hum rather than distinct words. She couldn't see Caleb as the group gathered around where Pete had placed him on the sofa.

Louisa held her breath and counted to five.

'A picture,' someone shouted out. 'Let's get a picture of mum and son reunited.'

The crowd parted like the red sea, and Pete strode forward, with sleeping Caleb in his arms, presenting him to Louisa on bended knee like he was offering a gift. All eyes were on her again, and she opened her arms to accept her son, but as soon as he was in her grasp, it was as if an alarm had sounded. His tiny face balled up, and his lips parted into a guttural sob.

Louisa rocked her arms gently, blowing tenderly on his face to try and ease his pain, but that only seemed to agitate him further.

'There, there, Caleb. It's okay. It's your Mummy,' she cooed, but his eyelids screwed tighter, and the wail worsened.

Louisa could feel the judgemental eyes assessing her poor parenting skills and craved a hole opening in the ground and swallowing them up.

'Please, Caleb, don't be sad,' she said, still rocking him lightly, and bending over as much as she could to kiss the top of his head.

Pete's hands shot forward from where he was still crouched, and scooped Caleb out of her grasp. Straightening, Pete pressed Caleb's face into his shoulder, and gently patted his back. The crying stopped in an instant.

'Ah he just wanted a cuddle with Daddy,' Pete said carrying Caleb away and into the garden, the majority of the crowd following him.

Louisa didn't follow, the pain in her chest unbearable, and as she spun the wheelchair around, she caught sight of her Mum's pitying gaze.

'Don't worry about it,' she told Louisa. 'He'll get used to you soon enough.'

Her mum meant well, but all Louisa heard was confirmation that she was failing as a mother. Staring at the ground she wheeled herself out of the room and along the hallway until she reached the bathroom. Locking the door behind her, she grabbed a handful of tissue and balled it up, pressing it against her nose and mouth as the hot tears exploded from her eyes.

Chapter 21

Abbie – Now

It's after eight by the time we pull in to the Morrison's supermarket car park, and the sky is a blanket of night cloud, with no stars visible. I's been raining since we got back from the police station, and under normal circumstances I wouldn't have ventured out on such a stormy night. The wipers are thrashing at the downpour on the windscreen, and the road is slick with puddles; I've never been so grateful for the heated seats in Mark's Audi.

'There she is,' I say pointing at the hooded figure standing beside the tall fuel price sign.

A supermarket petrol station seems such an odd place for her to suggest we meet. Surely she isn't hiding her evidence here? At least it's somewhere public, which makes me feel fractionally safer to be meeting her so late. I certainly wouldn't have come if she hadn't agreed to Mark being here too. I haven't been able to concentrate on anything else since the phone call. I forced down a couple of slices of takeaway pizza to satisfy the grumbling bump, but my appetite wasn't there.

Mark pulls over to the kerbside, and is about to lower his window to ask Kinga what happens next, when she passes the window, and opens the rear door, sliding across the leather seats. I shift awkwardly in my chair, so that I can see her and formally introduce her to Mark. She is soaked through, her hair with a dull shine beneath the internal light. She is still wearing the faded leather jacket, which has done little to keep her under garments dry. Her face is free of makeup, but still looks tired, the dark patches beneath her eyes able to give my own bags a run for their money after last night's lack of sleep.

'This is my husband Mark,' I say, and glance up to see him watching her from the rear-view mirror, but he doesn't speak. 'What are we doing here? Where is this evidence?'

'You drive,' she says, glaring back at Mark's reflected eyes, and fastening her seatbelt. 'Is near here. Go to main road.'

'Wait, we're going somewhere else?' I start. 'Where? You said you would give us proof about Josh.'

Her gaze switches to me. 'I had to make sure you not followed, and no police. Is close. I show you.'

I catch Mark looking at me, and I shrug in agreement with the instruction, as I shuffle back around to face the front. He indicates and pulls slowly away from the kerb, the rain's beat on the windscreen sounding like a death march. Mark continues to follow the instructions that she calls from the rear seat. Every now and again she looks over her shoulder between the headrests and out of the rear window. I can't be sure what she's looking for – a tail maybe – but from the wing mirror, I can't see more than the bright white lights of the vehicle behind. I certainly can't make out the colour or brand.

'Follow signs for airport,' Kinga instructs.

We're heading south, away from Cheadle, and further from home. She didn't tell us to bring passports, so I can only assume we're not actually going to the airport; God knows they wouldn't let me board a plane in my condition anyway. Mark continues to obey her instructions, eventually following signs to the Stanley Green Trading Estate in Cheadle Hulme. I can't say I'm familiar with the area, but the industrial estate is as dark and menacing as the night sky as we pull into it. It's probably full of life and thriving during the day, but the shutters are down, and lights switched off as we follow the one way route between the hangars, eventually arriving at the one building with any sign of light on the ground floor. The office window beneath the Apex Self Storage sign has a bright interior, but there are no other cars in the parking bays, aside from a covered scooter, which I can only assume belongs to the guard on duty inside reception.

'Wait minute,' Kinga says, as she unfastens her belt and exits the car, hurrying through the rain and into the reception area.

She disappears behind some frosted glass, and I can only just see her outline, before she hurries back and tells Mark to park, handing us both lanyards marked GUEST.

This is the last place I expected her to bring us, but in hindsight I guess it makes sense that she might rent a storage box to keep whatever evidence she has safe. The collection from the supermarket five miles away seemed a bit overly dramatic, but again it makes sense if she's paranoid about being watched. I don't want to consider the possibility that we've been lured to our deaths, especially as she has signed us in with the security guard, but then I can't be certain what names she gave to him.

Now who's being paranoid?

Mark and I get out of the car, and hurry after Kinga with our hoods pulled up, but instead of heading to reception, she takes us around the back of the building where we find larger metal shutters and loading bays for vans and lorries. She walks up the small staircase to a door marked PRIVATE, and types a code into the small panel beside the door, being careful to shield the number from our view. There is a short, sharp buzz, and then she pulls the door open and leads us into echoed darkness. A moment later there is a fizz and light flickers on high above our heads. I see now we are in a high ceilinged warehouse, and there is a cool breeze blowing at our ankles. Overhead the continued rain can be heard reverberating off the corrugated roof. The whole place smells of damp, but I seem to be the only one who's noticed as Kinga continues to stride across the bare, stone floor towards more shadowy darkness.

She suddenly darts to the left and for a moment I lose sight of her as the light sensors search for her, but then they flash on, and I see she is waiting by a bank of lifts. She grabs the handle of one, heaving it across with some strain, before repeating the process with a pair of horizontal shutters inside the carriage. She beckons us to join her, and the smell of damp and perspiration grows. She pulls both sets of doors back together and the clash of metal on metal echoes loudly inside the box carriage.

We head up to the second floor with none of us speaking, and when the doors are once again dragged open, Kinga takes a moment to get her bearings before pointing for us to follow. The space here is filled with floor to ceiling units, each sealed by one or two sturdy fire doors, and most bearing padlocks. It's a maze, and I'm soon feeling lightheaded as she weaves us left, then right, then straight and once more to the left. We finally stop at box 237, and she covers the padlock with her hand as she twists the dial to unfasten it. She pockets the padlock as she pulls one of the doors open, and enters.

We follow her in, and allow our eyes to adjust to the much dimmer light inside. The floor space can't be much more than three metre squared, but most of it is taken up with an inflatable mattress, sleeping bag and pillow. She doesn't say it, but I realise now why she insisted on all the secrecy.

'This is where you live?' I say without thinking.

Her eyes narrow. 'The guard, he ... he is kind to me. Let me stay here sometimes, so long as gone before six when his shift finish.'

I notice a midsize suitcase propped up against a stack of plastic boxes. I don't like to think that this amounts to her total possessions, but it certainly makes sense given what she told Yolanda and me about her history and how she arrived in the UK.

Instinctively I want to tell her to pack up her things and offer her the chance to stay at our house for a few nights until she's got herself together; she certainly looks like she would benefit from a shower and fresh sheets. But then I remember that she is still a virtual stranger and that this could all be part of whatever trick she is trying to play.

She crosses the room to the plastic boxes, and lifts the lid from the one on top, before skimming through the paper wallets I now see inside. I look to Mark, who offers a confused shrug. Kinga doesn't explain what she is doing, eventually pulling out whatever she was looking for and handing it to me. I glance back at Mark again as he joins me, and I open the wallet to find a newspaper clipping.

'Read,' Kinga encourages.

My eyes dart across the article which is only a few hundred words, detailing the closure of a birthing centre in Hampshire's New Forest, and the impacted parents-to-be who are up in arms about the closure, citing deposits of money that have yet to be returned by the insolvent parent company of the private enterprise. Mark and I exchange glances and then look to Kinga for an explanation.

She rolls her eyes, and shuffles the cut out to the back, revealing a second clipping relating to a different private birthing centre near Hamilton in Scotland. This time the story hints at a trail of deaths left in the wake of the birthing centre, and how criminal proceedings are being sought against the now insolvent parent company, but there's little more on offer.

'This is how they operate,' Kinga says, pointing at the clipping. 'They set up new company and hospital in new area, take money from rich parents who want special treatment –'

My cheeks burn at this slight.

'And then when problems start, they pack up and leave. Company declared bankrupt, and they start again somewhere far away.'

'What does this have to do with us? With Josh?' I question.

'Philomena's was same setup. That why they now out of business. So many companies, so many hospitals.'

A conspiracy involving private healthcare, but I'm still not seeing how this proves that Josh is still alive.

Mark takes the folder from me, and continues to skim through the clippings. 'Where did you get all of this from? There must be dozens of clippings here.'

'Research,' she answers, but there is a tremor in her voice that is less-assured than before.

'You researched all of this?' Mark asks with a disbelieving tone.

'I do lot of reading. I cut out stories. I print from internet.'

'And how exactly do you do that? There's no computer or printer here.'

'I use computers at library,' she snaps back defensively, before reaching into the plastic box again and extracting a second wallet that she hands to me.

I open it and read from a printed sheet this time, the http address in a bar at the top of the page. The online article reveals one mother's anguish at her son's still birth following delivery at a private birthing centre near Carmarthen in Wales. I could almost be reading my own heart-breaking story about Josh. I feel every line of betrayal and regret in the quotation marks.

Mark closes his paper wallet, and thrusts it back towards Kinga. 'There's more to this than you're telling us. I'm not willing to accept that you've managed to connect all these pieces together on your own. It doesn't ring true. Now you'll tell me what's really going on, or we're leaving.'

It's unlike Mark to make such snap decisions, but when Kinga bows her head in defeat, it seems he is right to question her part in all of this.

'Okay, I have source who help me.'

'What source?' he almost shouts.

'I think she inside their operation. She the one who contact me about my son and tell me about the fire that kill him. She also one who tell me to find you and that Josh still alive.'

Chapter 22

Louisa – Five years ago

Louisa pressed the back of her hand to Caleb's forehead, but she couldn't tell if it felt warmer than it had five minutes before, or whether any increased heat was as a result of a raised temperature, or the fact that he hadn't stopped screaming in that time. As she leaned over him in the dimly-lit crib, she could no longer be certain of anything. It had to have been two hours of the pair of them alone in Caleb's room, and still she hadn't managed to get him back to sleep. With nerves frazzled, and no sign of daylight poking through the slightly-parted curtains, she could feel her own tears lurking.

'Please, Caleb,' she pleaded in a voice so high-pitched it was almost only audible to dogs, 'I've changed you, I've offered you milk, and I've winded you. I've held you, I've rocked you, and I've placed you on your back. What more do you want from me?'

If only he could tell her, she'd happily cave to any demand, but at eight-weeks old, he was far from finding his voice. He'd certainly found his lungs though, and this routine had become a nightly ritual. Pete had even taken to wearing earplugs to make it through the night.

Leaning forwards, and pressing her hand to Caleb's

face again, there was only one logical conclusion: he was ill. Maybe he'd picked up an infection from somewhere. Pete was off at work all day in the city, and she was certain he didn't wash his hands the moment he came through the door, despite her asking him to. God only knew what he might have picked up mixing with all the other miscreants. How easy it would have been for him to brush against some germ-carrier and transfer it to Caleb when he got home.

Stroking Caleb's cheeks with her fingernails, she used her free hand to open the search engine on her phone and study the list of symptoms on mumsnet. She'd been certain it was too early to bring him back from the neonatal unit. She'd almost pre-empted that he'd fall ill and she wouldn't be able to cope. Why hadn't they heeded her warning?

Pete said she was just being paranoid, but he didn't have to see how difficult things were when he was at work. Caleb didn't seem to kick up nearly as much fuss when Pete was here; almost as if he was just reserving it especially for her.

Perhaps that's it, she thought now. *Perhaps he just doesn't like me. If he knows that I was the one who put his early life in danger, why would he want to be left alone with me? He's probably terrified I'm going to hurt him again.*

'I'm not a bad person,' she said aloud, for her own benefit as much as his. 'Believe it or not, I can actually be a lot of fun if you'd just get to know me. Before this,' her eyes dropped to the frame of the chair, and she slapped it with both hands, 'before *this* I used to dance. I was a brilliant dancer. I could hear any piece of music and find the right rhythm. I wish you could have seen me, then you'd realise that I'm more than just this chair. And I will be again, Caleb. I promise you. Once I've had Mr Fitzgerald's surgery, my back will grow stronger, and who knows, maybe one day you and I will be able to dance. Would you like that? Would that make you happy?'

Still he wailed, probably having not heard a word of what she'd said.

'Please, Caleb, just stop crying for a few minutes so I can get my shit together. *Please?*'

He'd had her up at midnight for feeding, and then again at two. Then he'd been sick just after four, and she'd just managed to get him back to sleep at six, and had hoped for a few minutes shut eye, but Pete's alarm had woken him and then he'd showered in the en suite. She'd maybe had fifteen minutes of sleep before Caleb had started again. Maybe he could sense how close to the edge she was and his screaming was a warning to her. Like she didn't know how close she was to tumbling into the abyss.

Lowering the side of the crib, she reached in, placing one palm beneath his hot neck and head, and the other beneath his bottom, instantly feeling the bulge. Her eyes widened with relief. He'd messed himself again and that was why he was crying. It was like a light at the end of the tunnel, and she wiped her own eyes, now focusing on the task at hand. Placing him into her lap, she cradled him with one hand, to stop him falling off, as she used her right hand to manoeuver the wheels over to the low changing table Pete had had custom-made for her. With a stack of nappies and packets of baby wipes in the frame on one side, and nappy sacks and clean baby grows in the other, she sanitized her hands, and then lifted Caleb onto the changing mat.

'Why didn't you tell me you'd pooed again, you little monster?' she asked, her voice breezier now that she'd managed to solve the great mystery. 'If you'd told me I'd have changed your nappy sooner.

She wiped more tears from her eyes, and took several deep breaths to compose herself, before quickly stripping him, and slowly unsticking the tabs of the nappy. How she hadn't noticed the pong earlier was beyond her, but she put it down to exhaustion.

'All water under the bridge now,' she added calmly, rolling up the nappy, careful not to allow anything to leak out the sides, and then wiping his warm cheeks clean.

Applying the new nappy and a fresh, cooler baby grow, she lifted him into her arms, resting his tiny head against her shoulder as she'd seen Pete do a dozen times.

'There, there,' she cooed, desperately trying to convince Caleb that everything was calm and sorted now, and he could go back to sleep, and give them both a break.

Yet, rather than settling and drifting off – as he would have done for Pete – his shoulders began to jostle as his sobbing grew louder once again.

'No, no, no, Caleb, it's okay now. Mummy has changed you, and you're not due any more food for at least an hour.'

Winding, she told herself, ticking off the mental

checklist.

Holding him still against her left shoulder, she gently rubbed her right hand over his back, drawing circle shapes ten times, before gently patting his back to release any trapped wind. That had to be it, but if anything the motion seemed to be making his sobbing worse again.

The light at the end of the tunnel shrank.

'Why do you hate me so much?' she whispered, as her head dropped and fresh tears fell of their own accord, pooling where the top of Caleb's head met her collarbone.

A minute passed and then another, neither able to understand what was upsetting the other, and then Louisa realised she had no other option. Unlocking her phone, she pressed re-dial and called Pete as she'd had to do every day since he'd returned to work. She knew it wasn't fair to keep pestering him there, but she had no other choice. Caleb had been crying for so long that it wasn't healthy to allow it to continue any longer. Pete would just have to come home. He must have been able to see how much she was struggling.

She listened to the dial tone until Pete's voicemail cut in. Hanging up, she hit the redial button, but again the voicemail service cut in before he did.

Maybe he's in a meeting. Or maybe he's left his phone on his desk while he goes to the toilet.

There could be any number of reasons why he wasn't answering his phone, and she tried not to think about the one that terrified her most: he was fed up of her phoning, and simply ignoring her cry for help.

Hanging up the phone, she returned Caleb to his

crib, and raised the side again. His sobs grew louder, even though Louisa wasn't sure how that was possible.

'What do you want from me?' she shouted now, unable to keep her frustration in check. 'I've given you everything, and still you reject me. Why? What is wrong with me?'

She was sobbing silently to herself when she suddenly felt two hands on her shoulders. Had her prayers been answered, and Pete was home?

Looking up, she couldn't understand what her mum was doing there, but didn't question the ghost-like apparition who went immediately to the crib and lifted Caleb out. Nor did she challenge when her mum carried him out of the room, returning a moment later with a bottle of prepared milk from the fridge. Caleb took to the teat like a ravenous zombie, and for the first time in hours, the room fell silent.

'Get yourself off to bed,' Judith told her daughter. 'Grandma's here now to take over.'

Louisa remained still, watching as her mum gently bounced Caleb in her arms as he guzzled at the bottle. It was a miracle of sorts, yet as grateful as Louisa felt to have her mum step in and save the day, it only elevated the throbbing in her heart, and highlighted what was becoming self-apparent: she was a terrible mother. She hadn't inherited any kind of maternal instinct, and in many ways, Caleb would have been better off had she not survived the accident.

And in that moment as she let go of all hope, she pictured herself at her parents' house, throwing a glass vase at Pete's head, narrowly missing him as it crashed against the wall and shattered. Had they been arguing the day of the accident? She saw herself snatching up his car keys from the unit by her parents' front door and stomping across the gravel towards his pride and joy with a feeling of hatred so strong that it made her shiver.

Chapter 23

Abbie – Now

My legs feel week under the strain of the baby and the news that an anonymous source has been feeding Kinga with information that helped her to locate us. Mark's cheeks are flushed and his eyes wide with rage, but doesn't this add credibility to Kinga's story? There are certainly enough newspaper clippings and printed articles suggesting there is more to Kinga's theory about a conspiracy, but it feels so farfetched that I want to laugh at the fact that I'm even considering it.

'You'd better give us more than that,' Mark practically shouts, his frustration echoing off the metal walls of the container.

Kinga glares back at him. 'What is problem? She give me all this information. She tell me to find you. She tell me that not all babies die at these hospitals. She say some were taken and sold to other families. I believe her when she tell me about my son.'

'This is all bullshit!' Mark roars. 'Come on, Abbie, we're going.' He moves towards the door and thumps it open with the palms of both hands, and it clatters against the neighbouring container.

'No, you can't go,' Kinga pleads. 'Your son need you.'

I don't believe she is intentionally lying. Her eyes

are watering, but there is a sincerity to her tone that has me *wanting* to believe her. But if I don't sit down soon, I may collapse. Looking around the enclosed space, there isn't anything adequate I can just rest on. The plastic boxes are too low alone, and too tall if stacked, not that I think either would be able to properly support me anyway. And if I got down on the inflatable mattress, I'm not sure I'd be able to get back up again.

'Mark, can you find me a chair or something. Please?'

The anger in his face dissipates in an instant as he recognises my struggle, and he helps manoeuver me to the side of the room, so I can at least lean against the metal wall. And then he's back out of the door in search of a seat. It gives me the chance to hear what Kinga has to say.

'Can you tell me how this woman first contacted you?'

Kinga strips off the faded leather jacket and drops it onto the mattress. She looks even more petite without that bulk, and the oversized hoodie hangs off her bones. Again, it must be my maternal instinct kicking in, but I feel compelled to offer her my help and support.

'I wasn't lying about call from hospital. At least, I thought it was call from hospital. Lady I speak to say she calling from hospital. She tell me my son's DNA found in ashes after fire.'

The look of hurt and regret cloaking her face now doesn't feel forced.

'I thought was cruel joke. And I tell her, can't be my child because he already dead. She say I am wrong, and that DNA is match to me. I say I only ever have one baby and he die. I ask if I can see body, but she say not possible. She email me DNA results, and it look real, but how would I know?'

I recall the initial shock of her telling me about Josh yesterday and how confusing a message it was to receive, and I want to wrap my arms around Kinga and tell her I understand what she's going through.

'Do you still have the email so I can look at it?' I ask quietly.

She sniffs and wipes her eyes with her wrist, moving to the second box and lifting the lid, extracting another paper wallet and passing it to me. Inside I find a printed email at the back, and in front of it, the ultrasound photographs of what I assume is Kinga's baby, based on the dates of the images.

I read the email which bears the insignia of a hospital in Lancashire. It details the words that Kinga has just shared along with an embedded image of a string of codes relating to the child sample and that of the maternal source, which is listed as Kinga Mutsuraeva. The report claims there is a greater than 99.9% probability of maternity. I've never had a DNA test performed, but the report looks genuine enough, though I'm not sure I'd be able to tell if it was a fake. It looks real.

There is an odd clattering noise approaching from outside the door, suggesting Mark is on his way back.

'Have you reported any of this to the police? I don't know what your experiences in Chechnya were like, but the UK police can be trusted. They're over-stretched and not able to be the protective force we need at times, but they are on the side of good and truth.'

Kinga is shaking her head with every word I utter. 'I have seen police in this country paid money by men who held me. They are not good like you say. If I tell police about my son it will get back to men I escape from, and then they find me. I had to fight to be free. I can't go back. Please, you cannot tell police about me. Men will find out.'

I gulp when I think about last night's conversation with PS Brearton. He didn't strike me as someone who would be mixed up in bribes and corruption. But am I wrong to assume that just because he told me his daughter's expecting his first grandchild that he isn't corrupt?

Or am I naïve to believe Kinga's real motivation for not presenting any of this to the authorities? Is it really because they'd see through the lies and conspiracy and find a scam artist trying to defraud us?

A moment later Mark wheels a flatbed trolley into the entrance of the room.

'Sorry, best I could find,' he tells me, taking my hands and helping me down onto it.

It's so low that my knees are bent awkwardly, and so I swing my legs around and push them flat against the base, resting my back against the cold metal frame. It's far from comfortable but it eases the pain I was feeling in my lower back and the spasms building in my knees.

Mark straightens and looks directly at Kinga. 'I'm sorry I shouted before,' he tells her.

'I swear on my child's grave that I am not lying to

you. My source, she tell me that I not the only mum to lose baby in this way. She tell me about that woman from Wales that you read about. She give me names of other parents who lost babies too. But when she mention you, she say your son not dead. She tell me to find you so that she can give you evidence that he alive.'

Adrenalin heightens every sense. 'Have you spoken to any of the other mums?'

Kinga shakes her head. 'No, you are first. You live closest, and my source insist I find you first.'

I don't know if it's my hormones, but something just doesn't add up in all this. Why would someone entwined in the conspiracy be feeding information about it? And why would she opt for someone disreputable like Kinga, given her background?

Yolanda's words are loud in my ears: *it was all some lame attempt at a con.*

'Did she tell you what evidence she has?' Mark asks, startling me out of my thoughts. 'Right now, this is all hearsay and doesn't prove anything.'

Kinga nods slightly and moves back to her box of folders, before extracting a small phone and switching it on. I'm not sure she'll get a signal inside the container so deep in the warehouse, but she inputs a PIN and flicks the screen until she finds what she's looking for.

She looks back to Mark and me, but when she speaks there is trepidation in her voice. 'In her last message, she says she can provide evidence that your son is still alive, but she can only do it if you pay.'

Yolanda's words fizz through my mind again:

they'll do anything to get the funds for their next fix.

So this was the play all along. I feel sick to the stomach. In fact, I may be about to repeat my vomiting pyrotechnics on this trolley.

'How much?' Mark asks quietly, and my mouth drops.

'She say obtaining evidence is difficult, but will prove beyond doubt that your son alive.'

'How much?' Mark repeats, more assertively this time.

'She say twenty thousand pounds.'

I laugh hysterically at this figure. Does she really think we were born yesterday, and have that kind of money readily available? She should have done her homework better.

'I'm not paying any money until I know what we're getting for that,' he says evenly.

I try to get his attention, but his eyes are fixed firmly on Kinga's, like he's trying some telepathic mind trick.

Kinga sighs and studies the message on her phone again. 'Okay, she say for the money, she will give strand of Josh's hair for you to perform own DNA tests on.'

My mouth hangs open. Such a bold statement, and in fairness to Kinga it would prove one way or another if Josh is still alive, but what happens when we hand over the cash and are presented with a strand of hair from some random child that turns out to not be Josh? I bet Kinga will disappear with the cash just as quickly as she arrived. I'm not buying it.

'Mark, let's just go,' I say reaching out for his hand, hoping he'll help me back up.

'If we can get hold of the money, how do we arrange the exchange?' he asks Kinga.

'I will message her to say we have deal, and then she will supply hair. Once you have had it tested, you pay. That way, no risk to you.'

Kinga's stance and stare hasn't wavered since she produced the phone. Whilst I cannot stop seeing this as a fraudulent con, Mark seems to be buying it.

'If this hair is a match to Abbie and me, I will happily pay the money, but if you're making all of this up, then I swear to God, I will bury you myself.'

Chapter 24

Louisa – Four and a half years ago

The rain hammering against the thin window pane only seemed to heighten the silence in the rest of the office. The invitation to *chat* had been voluntary, yet Louisa couldn't help but feel like she was about to be interrogated. Regardless of what Pete and her mum thought, she'd done nothing wrong.

So why did she feel so guilty?

The ceiling fan whirred its consistent hum in an effort to counter the humidity brought on by the storm outside. It was having little impact on Louisa's overheating body, but she wasn't convinced even a dose of liquid nitrogen direct to the skin would counter her temperature. Maybe they were right: maybe there was something wrong with her.

Dr Patel finished reading her monitor, refreshing her memory on why the appointment had been booked, before spinning slightly in her chair, and fixing Louisa with an empathetic stare. The GP's pale yellow trouser suit did nothing to compliment her skin tone, leaving her looking washed out. Her hair, pinned up in a messy bun, wasn't in keeping with her otherwise perfectly manicured fingernails and well-organised desk.

'Would you like to start by telling me how you are, Mrs Caulfield?'

Louisa hated the formality, but bit her tongue, and simply shrugged.

The GP smiled thinly. 'I'm here to try and help, Mrs Caulfield. You understand that, right? I'm not here to judge or ridicule. But if you won't tell me what's been going on, I don't know how best I can be of service.'

It wasn't my decision to come here, Louisa wanted to say, but unleashing her frustration on the GP was neither fair, nor warranted.

'Perhaps I can start by making an observation?' Dr Patel continued, the skin around her eyes tightening. 'You look exhausted; how are you sleeping?'

'I have a six month-old baby who's teething, so how do you think I'm sleeping?'

Louisa instantly regretted the barb, but hadn't been able to stop herself. It wasn't the first time she'd struggled to keep her emotions in check these last few weeks.

'How many times a night would you say Caleb is getting you up with his teeth?'

The truth was it wasn't the number of times he was waking, more her inability to settle him back down afterwards. And even when she could manage to get him to fall back to sleep, she'd spend the next few hours tossing and turning, waiting for him to erupt again. Her mind wouldn't allow her to settle into deep, restful sleep in case it got disturbed. But it wasn't just Caleb's sorrow that kept her alert during the night. Even when her parents took Caleb at weekends to allow her and Pete to rest properly, she still couldn't remember the last time she'd had more than four hours straight sleep. It was always in the quiet, dark times during the night when her brain engaged most eagerly.

Trying to piece together the flashes of memory about that day was driving her to distraction, and she was now certain that her imagination was just trying to plug holes in her memory, rather than actually recovering images. The flash of her throwing the vase at Pete and narrowly missing him was so vivid, as was the feeling of pure hatred, yet she still had no explanation of what it all meant, and every attempt to discuss it with him was met with avoidance tactics and questioning of her own mental capacity.

'Mrs Caulfield? Caleb's sleeping pattern? Is it just you who gets up when he cries out?'

'My husband works fulltime,' Louisa responded. 'It isn't fair to expect him to get up.'

God knew she wish he would take on some of the burden, but she didn't dare ask. They'd argued about it several months ago, just when she thought she'd reached the point where she couldn't continue. Pete had eventually conceded, and said he'd sort something out, and the next day her mum had popped round and promised to take Caleb at the weekend to give her and Pete time to relax. That hadn't been Louisa's wish, but she'd been given little choice in the matter.

'And you then have Caleb all day on your own?'

'My mum and dad help out when they can.'

'That's good to hear; support networks are hugely important. Have you joined any clubs or support groups for new mums?'

'I wasn't aware there were any,' Louisa lied, thinking about the leaflets her mum kept dropping by.

It wasn't that she didn't appreciate her mum's

efforts to help, but she didn't seem to understand that attending a mother and baby group wouldn't help Louisa feel any less of a fraud. Seeing other mums coping with their new-born's tantrums and the challenge of no sleep wouldn't stop Louisa feeling like an absolute failure.

Dr Patel opened the top drawer of her desk, and shuffled some papers around, until she found what she was looking for, removing three glossy pamphlets, and passing them over.

'There are a variety groups, run by different people most days. Several of the new mums I look after have found attending them helpful. Worth a look?'

Louisa accepted the leaflets and squashed them into her handbag without a second glance.

'Have you noticed any changes to yourself, Mrs Caulfield?'

Apart from the wheelchair, she didn't ask.

'We've briefly touched upon your fatigue, what about diet? How well are you eating?'

'Fine,' Louisa fired back quickly. 'I probably don't get my seven fruits and vegetables every day, but we make an effort to eat healthily.'

Dr Patel seemed pleased by this response, even though Louisa was only now just realising that she hadn't even eaten breakfast that morning.

'And how is your sex life?'

Louisa choked on spittle in her throat, and coughed several times until it settled. 'Since the accident, I … I can't say I've felt the urge to have sex. Plus it's only been six months since Caleb was born.'

Dr Patel looked sad for her. 'I note from your

medical record that you had major surgery on your back injury four months ago. Is the consultant pleased with the progress you're making?'

The only thing that Louisa wasn't failing at was carrying out the twice daily stretching exercises Mr Fitzgerald had recommended.

Not that they seemed to be doing much.

'Would you mind showing me what you can now do?'

Louisa closed her eyes, welcoming the darkness, closing her mind to all stimuli, and focusing on her breathing. Pete never seemed to understand just how much concentration was required. Picturing her legs and how each muscle and nerve connected to her bones, she thought hard about her right foot, groaning with the effort of lifting it half an inch from the paddle it rested on. Exhaling heavily, Louisa opened her eyes again, panting with the strain.

'That's incredible!' Dr Patel exclaimed with too much enthusiasm for such little return. 'You must be so proud.'

Louisa was far from proud at the paltry post-surgery outcome, but Mr Fitzgerald had never promised to *cure* her paralysis.

Dr Patel turned her head back to her monitor for the briefest of moments, before settling her gaze back on Louisa.

'Do you understand why your healthcare visitor asked you to come and speak to me, Mrs Caulfield?'

Because she's an interfering old busybody who spends too much time listening to my mum's paranoia, Louisa thought.

'Do you know what the condition postnatal depression is, Mrs Caulfield?'

Louisa didn't answer, choosing silence over argument.

'Postnatal depression is a depressive illness which affects ten per cent of new mothers to some degree. Mothers can experience a variety of symptoms, which can range from mild to severe, and last anywhere from a couple of weeks to several months. Your healthcare visitor contacted me directly after her last visit, as she was worried you might be experiencing some PND symptoms.'

Louisa blinked back the sting at the corners of her eyes.

'She said that the first couple of times she'd visited – I think your husband had been present at the first, and your mum at the second – everything had seemed well, but when she visited you the last time you were alone, and she was worried enough to make the referral.'

'I'm fine,' Louisa countered. 'Yes, things are tough with Caleb, but nothing I can't handle.'

Dr Patel frowned slightly. 'There's no judgement here, Mrs Caulfield. Mental health is not something we take for granted. Sometimes there is no obvious reason why one mother might suffer these debilitating symptoms, but there are treatments available, and I'd like you to help me determine the best course of action for you. I can see you're tired, but would you say you've become more irritable since Caleb arrived?'

Pete would say she had, but then he wasn't suffering in the same way as her. If anything, she'd argue she'd become more patient of his often selfish attitude to parenthood, but she didn't admit as much to the GP.

'Loss of interest in sex can be another common symptom, as can changes to appetite, negative thoughts, and even intense guilt.' Dr Patel paused, biting her lip momentarily. 'Can you tell me about the claim you made to the healthcare visitor?'

Louisa's gaze misted under the weight of the tears at the floodgates. 'Is that what this is about? Some throwaway comment that I didn't mean? Is that what has you leaping to such extravagant conclusions?'

Louisa's attempt to frighten off Dr Patel by going on the offensive seemingly fell on deaf ears. 'Your healthcare visitor didn't think it was a throwaway comment, and seeing you here now, I don't either. As I keep telling you, Mrs Caulfield, there's no judgement, but you look to me as though you're struggling, and I wouldn't be doing my job if I didn't mention my concerns to you. You're tired, emotional, and I'd say incredibly anxious right now. And it's okay to be all those things and more. God knows you've been through the mill this last year, and nobody is blaming you for what you're experiencing. It isn't your fault, and you shouldn't feel guilty about how you're feeling.'

Dr Patel lifted a box of tissues from the corner of her desk, and held it out for Louisa to take one, as the dam broke.

'You told your healthcare visitor that you didn't think Caleb was your son,' Dr Patel continued, her voice quieter now, almost drowned out by the ceiling fan. 'Can you tell me what you meant?'

Louisa dabbed the tissue against her eyes, relieved

that she hadn't spent hours donning makeup. What could she say? Motherhood certainly hadn't turned out as she'd expected. She knew that it could take time for a baby to settle at home, especially if time had been spent in the neonatal unit, but Caleb's rejection was more than that. He welcomed the embrace of Pete and her mother, but instantly cried when Louisa picked him up. He wanted nothing to do with her, and the only conclusion that made sense in her mind – as unlikely and illogical as it seemed – was that somehow they'd brought the wrong baby home. Yes, Louisa was experiencing several of the symptoms Dr Patel had mentioned, but it wasn't guilt or depression that was telling her that Caleb wasn't her son. A mother knows her child despite everything. She'd felt her baby growing inside of her for nearly nine months; had become used to that movement, but Caleb was like a totally different baby. He didn't curl up and snuggle as her baby had done. He didn't seem to touch her soul when she was feeling sad as her baby had. It was nothing but instinct, but she was certain in her gut that something wasn't right.

She'd delicately tried broaching the subject with Pete and her mum, but neither had seemed willing to consider the prospect that anything was wrong, let alone what was tearing her heart in two.

Dr Patel cleared her throat. 'Okay, if you're not willing to explain what you meant, can you tell me what you were doing with the knife, Mrs Caulfield?'

Louisa's eyes snapped up to the GPs with venom. 'I've already explained that to my husband; it was just a misunderstanding ...'

'Misunderstanding? Mrs Caulfield, you were found hovering beside your baby's crib, holding a kitchen knife.'

Louisa looked away, not wanting to relive the memory, but unable to avoid it. 'I wasn't going to hurt him.'

'Then what were you planning to do?'

Louisa's head snapped back. 'Nothing! I heard a strange noise outside, and I couldn't wake Pete, so I decided to go and investigate. I found that we'd left the lounge window open, and I was worried, so I grabbed a knife from the kitchen for protection, but that's when I heard Caleb crying, so I hurried to his room, and that's when Pete came downstairs, and found me there.'

Dr Patel lowered her eyes for a moment, and when she returned Louisa's stare, her voice was quieter, withdrawn. 'It's not common, thank God, but some mothers suffering with PND, also experience desires to harm their child or themselves. Given what we've discussed and the concerns raised by both your health visitor and your husband, I don't think I have any choice but to refer you on for further counselling, Mrs Caulfield.' She reached out and rested a hand on Louisa's knee. 'We all just want what's best for you.'

Chapter 25

Abbie – Now

Not much more was discussed after Mark's threat – what else could be said? Kinga showed us out of the self-storage centre, and the rain had actually stopped by the time Mark and I returned to the car. Kinga must have disappeared back inside the warehouse, because we didn't see her again.

Mark is the first to speak, 'How are you and the baby doing now? I can only imagine how stressful that must have been. I know it was for me.'

I check the bump, as I can't remember the last time I felt her kick, but all it takes is my touch for a knee or elbow to reassure me that she is okay, if not a little cramped. I almost let slip that *she's* fine, but catch myself at the last second.

'All is fine. I'm glad to be back in a more comfortable seat.'

'I want you to call me the moment Kinga contacts you again. Okay? And if she approaches you when I'm not around, I want you to tell her she's to speak to me. In fact, can you text her my number, and then she can come to me directly?'

I appreciate him wanting to take control and remove any extra pressure from my shoulders, but I don't like the way it feels as though I'm being pushed out. Josh is as much my son as his.

'We'll deal with her together, don't you worry about that,' I tell him, only half-answering his question. 'Do you think Kinga's *source* is real?'

Mark looks over to me. 'To be honest that's the one part of her story I *did* believe. There's no way she could have pulled together all of those articles and clippings on her own. You'd either need a team of legal aids or know exactly what you were looking for to dig it up.'

'Or be a brilliant forger,' I add under my breath.

'What do you mean?'

I let out a long sigh, which does little to ease any of the tension in my back. 'Both you and Yolanda concluded that Kinga's approach was criminally-motivated: a scam or a fraud of some sort. Next second you're offering to pay her the twenty thousand pounds she's demanding. I didn't recognise you in there.'

He starts the car without responding, and negotiates the tight one-way system until we're back out on the main road, and heading north. I can't tell if my words have upset him, or whether he's trying to think of some way to justify his actions. Unless he's been secretly squirrelling away money, we don't have a spare twenty thousand pounds to giveaway. Maybe we could release some equity from our house, but that's going to take time. If we restructured our credit cards, and dipped into our savings pot, then *maybe* we could just about scrape it together, but are we really going to take that risk?

And even if this mythical strand of hair materialises, I don't know the first thing about having it tested to see if the DNA is a match to ours. Short of going on a daytime television show, can ordinary people have DNA tests run? Or would we need to go against Kinga's wishes and involve the police?

Mark clears his throat. 'Do you remember the day we returned from the hospital after … after losing Josh?'

That whole period is more of a blur now because I've spent years repressing it to the Pandora's Box in my brain that I daren't reopen.

'I don't think I've ever felt more depressed,' Mark continues. 'I remember you shutting yourself up in our bedroom, telling me you just wanted to be on your own, but how I could hear your sobs and wails through the ceiling. I kept trying to go up to you and offer comfort, but you kept pushing me away. I wanted to tell you that everything would get better, and that we'd find a way through it, even though I'm not sure I believed those words myself.'

He pauses and switches on the air conditioning as the windscreen starts to steam up at the corners. 'I felt as though I was letting you down; that I'd let you down. When we stood in the registry office and exchanged vows, I swore I would keep you safe, and yet I could feel you slipping away from me, and I felt powerless to stop it. There I was earning good money with my job, paying the mortgage on a nice house in a decent area, but it wasn't enough to keep Josh alive. I'd become complacent, believing that everything would go well for us if I kept working hard and doing the right thing. Suddenly, I was falling and there was no parachute to guide me back.'

I reach for his hand, and give it a gentle squeeze. As uncomfortable as his words are making me, he's never opened up about this stuff before, and I don't know what to say to him.

'The more time you spent shut away, the more I doubted that our marriage would be able to survive the fallout of losing Josh. Suddenly, everything I'd worked so hard for just fell away from my priorities list, and in that moment I would have paid any price to have Josh back. But my credit with God or fate or whoever controls all of this was worthless. I knew no amount of money would bring him back, but suddenly our prayers might be answered. If Kinga told us it would cost us every penny to get Josh back, I'd give it to her. I'd rob a dozen banks and face a life behind bars if it meant our Josh was back with us.'

Those days at home after we left St Philomena's were some of the hardest I faced. I pushed Mark away because I didn't want to drag him into my depression. Tried to muffle my tears and anguish, but I hadn't realised he could still hear them through the floorboards. I too wasn't sure our marriage would survive, but that's because I saw myself as a weight around his shoulders. I'd promised him a loving family, and I'd failed. I felt like he deserved better than me, and in a way I wanted him to leave me and find the wife he deserved: one who could turn him into the brilliant father he would one day be.

'I've never told you this before,' he begins quietly, 'but there was a period where I considered ending it all.'

My head snaps around at this admission, but he

doesn't allow me the chance to interrupt.

'I didn't want to wake up every morning, living with the regret of what we'd lost. It was too painful. It was like someone had shown me a picture of my perfect life, and then snatched it away. It wasn't far and I blamed the world for our pain. I didn't actually attempt to take my own life, but I did get as far as penning a note. I must have written a dozen versions on my laptop where I knew you wouldn't find them until it was too late, but each time I pictured you reading it, it broke my heart. Until that point, I don't think I'd acknowledged just how depressed I was too. Losing Josh broke me, but keeping *you* safe, *made* me. I vowed that day that I would do everything in my power to bring you back from the edge and move us forward as a stronger team. And the day you showed me the positive pregnancy test eight months ago felt like the light at the end of a very long tunnel.'

He switches off the air-conditioning unit. 'It's only money, right? I can always earn more. I'm due to get paid a bonus at the end of the month, which will cover half the cost, and if today's deal goes through, I'll have the rest by next month. I can take a short-term loan from the bank, and pay it off within a few weeks. We can do what is necessary. But,' he pauses, and looks at me, 'we involve PS Brearton. I still don't trust Kinga, and I'm conscious that this could still just be a means of conning us, so I want the police on-board from the outset. I'll speak to Brearton and tell him what Kinga said, and that I intend to cobble the funds together. There may be some way they can track the money once it's transferred, and if this is a con, they'll be able to arrest and punish Kinga and those she's working with.'

'And if it isn't a con? If Josh is still alive out there, how the hell do we find him?'

Mark opens his mouth to reply, but no words emerge. 'I don't have all the answers,' he eventually says. 'Maybe Brearton can investigate St Philomena's? Maybe he can find a list of staff who worked there, track them down and interview them. I don't know.'

Given Brearton's reluctance to help yesterday, I can't say I feel confident that things will change unless I can convince Kinga to speak to Brearton directly. One thing's for certain; I've never felt more convinced that Josh is still alive, and I will do whatever it takes to get him back.

Chapter 26

Louisa – Four years ago

'I can't believe you'd embarrass me like that!' Pete shouted from the top of the stairs.

Louisa craned her neck up so she could see his face, and check whether his statement was intended to mock her hurt. 'Me embarrass you? I can't believe you'd drop a bombshell like that in front of everyone without discussing it with me first.'

His face remained fixed; his eyebrows arching downwards under the strain of disbelief. 'What the hell, Lou? We've talked about it literally dozens of times. We both agreed that Caleb needs to go to the best school if he's to reach his potential.'

She couldn't believe he was trying to twist her words. 'Yes, a *good* school, *not* boarding school!'

He yanked the tie over his head and began to unfasten the buttons of his shirt, dragging it from his torso and hurling it in her direction. She couldn't be sure if he'd specifically targeted her, or was just moving it closer to the washing machine. Either way it fell short of hitting her.

'Lamington was good enough for me; it will be good enough for Caleb.'

'You once told me you used to cry every time your parents dropped you at that school. Why would you want to subject Caleb to that feeling of rejection?'

'I cried *once*, and that was only the first time. But I toughened up, and it was the disciplinary system that made me the man I am today. If you ask me, a bit of discipline and structure is exactly what Caleb needs.'

Conscious that their son was sleeping in the bedroom behind Pete, Louisa bit her tongue and wheeled herself away from the foot of the stairs. She was far from through with the argument, but it wasn't fair to disturb Caleb's sleep. That said, after the way her parents had spoiled him today, he would probably sleep through a thunderstorm and not realise it. He'd been gently snoring in the car on the way home, while she'd quietly seethed, waiting for her chance to question Pete as to why he'd felt the need to tell anyone who'd listen how he'd enrolled Caleb at The Lamington Academy, and that he'd be joining on the eve of his fourth birthday.

Pushing the door open with the foot supports, she wheeled herself to the drinks cabinet and poured a large glass of Pete's scotch, wincing as the liquid burned at the back of her throat, forcing her to cough.

Her parents had offered to host Caleb's first birthday party so they could show off their grandson to their fancy friends. They'd arranged it with Pete, 'in case it was all a bit much for you,' her mother had said over the phone the month before.

'You have enough on your plate, what with your spinal exercises and CBT,' she'd added, taking the chance to remind Louisa that she was in no position to argue as yet another decision was taken out of her hands.

Since Dr Patel had diagnosed the postnatal depression, it felt as though nobody trusted her to make any kind of decision.

You were found hovering beside your baby's crib, holding a kitchen knife.

It didn't seem to matter how many times she told everyone that she'd only grabbed the knife for protection, they seemed to think she was a danger to Caleb. Her doubts about him being hers, but she could never harm him. Whether Caleb subconsciously blamed her for the accident, he was innocent in all of this.

She hadn't argued – there'd been no point – when Dr Patel had prescribed her a mild antidepressant and a course of Cognitive Behavioural Therapy. In fairness, her irritability had eased, and a more normal sleeping pattern had returned, particularly after her mum had temporarily moved in to support during Caleb's teething tantrums. But six months on, even Caleb was now sleeping through the night.

Of course Pete had insisted that Caleb be moved into a room upstairs, almost as if he didn't trust Louisa to be alone with him. And now it was almost like she and Pete were living in different houses. He had the main bedroom, access to the bathroom, Caleb's room, and the guestroom. She had her room, the en suite wet room and kitchen. The lounge-diner was shared territory, but she only ever really saw Pete when he brought Caleb down before going to work, and then when he got home.

She missed the warmth of his body in bed beside her; the feel of his touch. They hadn't made love in nearly eighteen months, and she couldn't remember the last time he'd even kissed her. Deep down, she worried that if Caleb was enrolled at boarding school, she'd see even less of her husband.

And then she'd be all alone.

She'd lost touch with most of her friends after the accident. As Pete frequently reminded her: who'd want a depressed and disabled hanger-on crashing their nights out? They'd all made offers of help and support when she'd first brought Caleb home, but the telephone calls had dried up, and either they hadn't been invited to Caleb's birthday party today, or they'd made their excuses. If it wasn't for her parents' over-protective nature, she might go days without speaking to another person.

Unfortunately, Caleb's grunts and gurns didn't count. She sensed he was getting closer to trying to speak, but most of the time he just pointed at things he wanted. She would say the name of the item each time she'd pass it to him, but so far he hadn't repeated any of them back. Maybe Pete was right and it was the lack of firm structure in his life that was holding Caleb back. At one, he hadn't even started trying to pull himself up to things, choosing to sit on his bottom and cry out if he wanted moving somewhere new.

Whenever she pointed at herself and said the word, 'Mummy,' he looked away, as if he would never bring himself to repeat the lie.

'Oh here you are,' Pete huffed as he pushed open the door, making no effort to close it behind him.

He came across to the table and picked up the scotch she'd poured, assuming it was for him. Again, she didn't argue, almost grateful that she wouldn't have to finish it.

'Have you taken your pills today?' he sneered.

'You know I have; you watch me do it every day, Pete. I took them right before we left for the party, remember?'

He narrowed his eyes, trying to recall the memory, before nodding and dropping into his reclining chair. Louisa remained where she was, waiting for him to re-engage with the battle. But he didn't look at her, instead picking up the remote control and switching on the television.

'Is that it? Aren't we going to discuss Lamington anymore?' she said evenly, desperately trying to keep her growing anger at bay.

'What's to talk about? He's been enrolled, and that's that. I discussed it with your dad, and he agrees that it's probably for the best.'

Her dad; why wasn't she surprised that he'd be lurking nearby?

'I don't want Caleb to go to boarding school,' she said, her voice cracking under the strain.

Pete cocked an eyebrow, as his head turned slowly to meet her gaze. 'I'd have thought you'd jump at the chance to have someone else take responsibility for him.'

She winced at the blow. It wasn't she who insisted her mum move in with them, and it wasn't she who insisted on Caleb spending most weekends at their house.

'Besides, with Caleb at school, you'll have more time to work on building up the strength in your back.'

He paused and took a sip of his drink. 'Show me how much you can move your legs now.'

She knew he was frustrated at the slow progress she'd made since Mr Fitzgerald's surgery, but it wasn't like she wasn't trying to get better.

Wrestling her hands beneath the jogging bottoms, she interlinked her fingers, and lifted the dead weight with all her might, until her foot fell free of the chair's paddle supports, and was resting on the hardwood floor. She then focused her attention on the twinges in her toes, and slowly lifted the foot an inch or so from the floor.

'Is that it? You showed me that last week. It's like you don't want to walk again.

'I'm trying!' she snapped, breathless.

Pete took another sip of his drink, and allowed his eyes to fall back on the television.

She opened her mouth to argue again, but what was the point? She didn't want to fight with Pete. He worked hard to keep a roof over their heads, and it's not like she was contributing financially since the accident.

Maybe all they were missing was a spark to reignite the passion they'd once felt for one another. If she was able she'd go and slip into something more seductive than comfortable joggers and the flower-patterned blouse her mum had picked out for the garden party. But beggars couldn't be choosers. Quickly unfastening the buttons, she separated the material, her arms prickling with bumps as anticipation grew in her gut.

'Pete?' she said quietly, pulling the slip of material away from her bra.

He didn't respond, eyes still on the television.

'Pete?' she tried again, this time cupping her breasts beneath the wire of her bra. 'I want you to come and make love to me.'

This caught his attention, and his lips parted, his snake-like tongue sliding out and wetting them slightly.

'Do you still find me attractive?' she asked, now unfastening the bra from behind her back, pouting slightly as she did. 'It's been so long since you made a move on me, but I'm ready whenever you are. In fact ...' she slipped the bra straps from her shoulders so she was now topless in front of him, and more nervous than she'd anticipated, 'you can do anything you want to me.'

Pete continued to study her face, but she could see the look of disgust slowly fall across his expression as his eyes fell on the plastic tube hanging down to the colostomy bag beside her left leg.

Dr Patel had spoken to her about the complications of intercourse, but had given some pointers to help.

'Just look at my face, and let me ... worry about everything else,' she encouraged

Pete leaned forwards and placed the tumbler of scotch back on the table, before standing, and Louisa held her breath waiting for him to come and kiss her, closing her eyes in anticipation. She only opened them again when she heard the front door slamming closed. A chill blew across her chest, and as her eyes filled, as she slipped the blouse back across her body. His rejection was as bitter as Caleb's, but as the tears threatened to spill, she was suddenly transported back to this very house; in her hands she was holding Pete's phone, staring down at a video of Pete.

A video of Pete and his secretary screwing on his office desk.

Chapter 27

Abbie – Now

Mark is already at work by the time the alarm wakes me, and I make my usual, ache-induced groan as my body creaks into a standing position. That's another part of being pregnant that I probably didn't appreciate the first time around – or maybe it's just because my body is older now – but the ache in every muscle and bone is tiresome in itself. I've been on my feet for only a few minutes, and already I could quite easily climb back into bed for a few hours more sleep. But to be fair, it isn't just the pregnancy that's causing the dark rings beneath my eyes. Last night I had a dream about Josh, and when I woke with a start in the middle of the night, I ended up crying myself back to sleep.

In the dream he was a baby in a pram, and I was pushing him along a leaf-lined street when something caught my attention. I let go of the pram for just a second to look at two baby sparrows fighting over a worm, but when I turned back, a gust of wind had caught the pram, and it was rapidly descending the hill we were suddenly at the peak of. Panic coursed through my body, and I gave chase, but no matter how hard I sprinted, the pram just got further and further away, until I could no longer see it. And that was when I woke. I never looked inside the pram, so I can't even be certain Josh was in there, but I felt in my mind that it was him.

I don't need a degree in psychology to interpret the meaning of that dream.

Showering, I dress and wolf down a banana before driving to the preschool. I'm actually welcoming the chance to put Josh and Kinga out of my head for a few hours and focus on the children in my care. I know I won't be able to be here for them in a few weeks, and I'm going to be sad to miss their continued development. By the time I return from maternity leave, at least half my group will have left to join Year-R, and I'll have a new batch to work with. I've said before it's such a fulfilling role to be able to watch each child develop and grow, but it's tough to let them go.

I think that's why I'm so determined to get to the bottom of what is happening with Toby Orville. I'm almost certain there must be issues at home playing out in his mind, and if I can just get through to him, and give him the reassurance that everything will be okay, I'm sure I can help bring him back out of himself. Mark would say I'm getting too close, and shouldn't embroil myself in other people's lives, but I have a duty of care to Toby, and I feel it is right to try and get to the bottom of it. I don't want him to become just another statistic where the system failed him, because I didn't act.

I spot Gail and Sally's cars in the car park, but that's all, as I'm earlier than usual today. I want to make sure I'm ready for when Toby is dropped so I can try and grab two minutes with his dad. All I'm going to ask is if everything is okay, and to mention that I'm worried about how withdrawn Toby has become over the last few weeks. I won't be judgemental, but I just want to understand what is going on so I'm better placed to help him. Yolanda said Toby's dad Chris is a decent bloke, so hopefully he won't see my intrusion as anything other than in Toby's best interests.

Opening my door, the bitter blast of wind is like a slap across my face, and I pull the extra-large hoodie around my bump, as I lock the car, and move as quickly across the car park as my body will allow. The weather app on my phone said it would be cold today, but this wind is almost arctic. It wouldn't surprise me if the thick blanket of grey overhead didn't result in a bluster of snowflakes later. Hopefully not enough to lay, as my Mini isn't designed for driving on snow and ice. I'm not sure I'd be too up for walking home in snow either. I'm sure Gail or Sally would give me a lift if I asked.

Heading inside, I welcome the warm blast of air as soon as the door is closed. The preschool is essentially a large hall that doubles as a social club at weekends, and the single pane glass windows and rickety roof are not built to withstand poor weather, but the preschool only rents the space and isn't in any financial position to have the windows or roof replaced. At least it's warmer inside than out.

Gail and Sally are clearing up the breakfast club things and don't hear me approach.

'Can I help with anything?' I ask.

I must startle them, as they both look back at me in a state of shock.

'Abbie, what are you doing here?' Gail asks, brushing a silver bang back from the side of her face, and leaving a trail of soap suds in the process.

'I was awake, so I figured I might as well come in early and lend a hand,' I shrug. 'I won't claim for overtime,' I add with a nonchalant laugh.

'How are you?' Sally now interjects, leading me towards the staffroom while Gail continues to wash the crumby plates. 'What did the hospital say?'

'Everything is fine with the baby,' I say, having decided I wouldn't reveal my baby's gender to anyone else before Mark knows. 'They did some blood tests to check my iron levels, and I'm waiting to hear back on the results. Otherwise, I'm in tiptop condition.'

Sally touches my arm gently, and I can see the relief painted on her face. 'That's great to hear, Abbie. You gave us all quite a shock when you tumbled yesterday, but the main thing is both you and the baby are well. You've only a few weeks to go now, right?'

'Just under a month,' I nod.

She takes a step back and considers the size and position of my bump. 'That long? Really? I'd have said you were much closer than that. I mean, you look like you could drop at any minute.'

My brow furrows slightly at Sally's comment. She's always been friendly towards me, and it's not the first time she's asked when I'm due, but I'm sensing an undercurrent to her words now.

'Well, the sonographer did suggest that things might move slightly quicker now, but I don't feel any different today. Mark and I are still planning for a December baby.'

She glances over to Gail, who has her back to us. 'Even so, best not to take any chances, right?'

There's that undercurrent again.

'Of course not,' I concur. 'I'll just need to be more careful when I've been crouched down for a period.'

'Mm,' she hums, 'or there is an alternative.' Another glance towards Gail, who is now wiping her hands on a towel.

'What do you mean?' I ask, already sensing where this conversation is heading.

Sally attempts a passive smile, but I'm not falling for it. 'The thing is, Abbie ... Gail and I were talking last night about what happened, and about you, and ...'

'We thought it might be better for you to move your maternity leave forward,' Gail interjects as she joins us at the staffroom door, practical as ever.

'You want me to move it forwards? We agreed that I would start it as close to the birth as possible so I get more time with the baby after she ... or *he* is born,' I quickly add, hoping neither spotted my slip. 'I figured I'd be here for at least a couple more weeks, or until I get to a point where I feel like I can't cope.'

'But you need to do what's best for you *and* the baby, Abbie,' Gail continues, making no effort to balance her bluntness with the warmth of a smile. 'Yesterday was a shock to all of us, and maybe it was fate's way of intervening.'

I don't like how finality of Gail's tone, particularly as it should be my choice when my maternity leave starts. 'I already told Sally that the doctors said everything is fine with me and the baby,' I say as jovially as my paranoia will allow. 'So there really is nothing for you – for either of you – to worry about. I'm perfectly fine to continue, though I certainly do appreciate your concern.'

Sally's smile loses its lift and droops into a panicked grimace. 'The thing is, Abbie, it's great that no harm came from your fall yesterday, but who knows what might happen if you tumbled again.'

I want to shout out that the fall was as a result of Toby colliding with me, but I'm not sure they'd believe me if I shared that nugget now, and I still can't be certain whether he did it deliberately or by accident.

'If you fell again and it resulted in injury or trauma for you or the baby, and then you sued us, the preschool would go under,' Gail says flatly. 'You know we're reliant on public funding, and don't have the means to fight a civil suit. The business would sink, and all our children would have to find new preschools. It wouldn't be fair on anyone.'

It stings that they think this is what I would do. I have worked hard for them here, and remained loyal, working extra hours and never claiming overtime just because I believe in the service they're offering. I thought we were a team.

'That's not going to happen, Gail.'

'I'm sorry, Abbie, but you can't say that for certain. None of us expected you to slip yesterday, and it isn't fair on the children to see things like that either. Most were excited to see the ambulance and paramedics arrive, but after they took you away, several were worried about what happened to you.'

'Little Bethany even asked me if you'd died,' Sally chimes in, with a grim nod.

'It'll be a relief to many to see you here this morning, but I think you should wait until registration, and then say your goodbyes.' Gail reaches for my hands, but I want to shrink away from her touch. 'You should make the most of the time you have left for yourself. Once the baby arrives, your time will no longer be your own. You'll no longer be able to sleep in till whatever time you want, or take a soak in the bath when the mood strikes.'

'Or binge the latest Netflix series,' Sally pipes up again.

'Once the baby arrives, your every waking second and act will be for them. Once baby is here, you'll no longer be Abbie Friar, instead, you'll be Mum. It's great that you want to stay, and we do appreciate the offer, but you don't need to.'

'But you'll be short-staffed,' I challenge, using the only leverage I feel I have. 'I should at least stay until you can get a replacement lined up.'

It's at that moment I hear footsteps approaching from behind, and when I turn I'm not ready to see the twenty-something with blonde, plaited pigtails wearing the preschool uniform.

'Well, as you know, we've been recruiting for your maternity cover for a few weeks,' Sally says, 'and when we spoke to Claudette last night, she said she was happy to start sooner. So, there really is no need for you to worry about any of that.'

Claudette hangs her coat in the staffroom, and then moves back to the door, ready to greet the first children as they arrive. It seems this little tête-a-tête was never about asking me if I wanted to start my maternity cover early. It was an ambush, and even though I know they can't force me out, I'm not sure I have the mental strength to argue.

A tiny hand grabs at my fingers, and when I look down, I see little Bethany, her water-resistant coat splashed with the spray of rain, staring up at me. 'You're alive!' she declares, and my eyes fill. Sometimes children just know how to cut through all the bullshit we hide behind.

'Yes, I am,' I tell her, my voice breaking.

She releases her grip and hurries back to where Claudette helps her find a peg for her coat.

'We'll let the council pay clerk know that your maternity leave starts from today so they can sort monies out for you,' Gail says, before moving away, the conversation very much over as far as she's concerned.

Sally remains at my side and hands me a tissue for my eyes. 'You'll see it's the right decision,' she whispers gently. 'We just want what's best for you, Abbie. And I'm sure once the baby arrives, you'll appreciate the few weeks of sanity you had before they took control.' She squeezes my hand and moves away, leaving me alone with the regret that I just allowed my world to slip through my fingers.

Toby!

The thought explodes to the front of my mind, and I cut across the middle of the hall, around the tables that Gail and Sally are now setting up, but by the time I reach the entrance, I see Toby is already inside the doors, Claudette kneeling beside him, asking his name and then showing him his peg. Looking out through the rain splashed doors, there's no sign of Toby's dad. I've missed him again.

Chapter 28

Louisa – The day of the accident

Hair dripping from the shower she'd just taken, Louisa padded into her bedroom, tightening the knot at the top of the long towel. It was doing little to blot the water on her legs, the enormous bump providing an almost protective force field around lower half of her body.

Gently patting the towel-covered bump, she allowed herself to smile, picturing the moment when her baby would arrive and she'd hold him or her for the first time. Her skin tingled at the excitement, but she reminded herself that with almost a month to go until due date, there was every chance she could be waiting another six weeks for the big day.

Already worn out by the short walk from the bathroom, she gently lowered herself to the edge of the bed, and reached for her phone on the night stand, surprised to find it missing. She was sure she'd plugged it in there last night, but in truth baby brain meant she couldn't specifically recollect the action from last night. Trying to recall the evening before, she remembered her and Pete were going to watch a movie, but she ended up falling asleep, and headed up to bed before the end. Realising she must have left the phone downstairs, she dried herself with the towel, and dressed in maternity dungarees and a t-shirt, and headed down to retrieve the phone.

She'd never realised how much work a staircase could be when heavily pregnant, and was out of breath before she'd reached the final step. Still at least she wasn't staying at her parents' old manor house, where the staircase to the second and third floors were twice as long. Taking a minute to compose her breathing, she headed into the lounge-diner, checking the coffee tables beside the sofas and then the apothecary table in the centre of the room, frowning when there was no sign of it.

Continuing her search, of the downstairs, she rummaged about in the small guestroom and wet room without success, and then headed into the kitchen. She was about to use the landline to dial the device, when she spotted it plugged into the phone charger in the wall. Pete must have discovered the phone in the lounge before going to work and had plugged it in to his charger for her. Grateful, she typed her PIN into the device, further confusion taking hold when an error message filled the screen.

It was only as she saw the partially transparent image on the lock screen that she realised it wasn't her phone, but Pete's instead.

Glancing over her shoulder and out of the kitchen window, Pete's car definitely wasn't on the drive, which meant he'd either gone to work without his phone, or …

Louisa pressed a hand to her lips as a small smile broke across them. He must have woken and picked up her phone, mistaking it for his, and hadn't realised his mistake before heading to work. She'd warned him it could happen when he'd bought them matching devices.

Swiping at the screen, she decided she'd message her phone and let him know of the mix up. She didn't have any other plans for the day, and could happily drop it over to his office. But when she typed in the digits of their wedding anniversary date, the phone told her the PIN was incorrect. Brow furrowing, she tried again in case she'd mistyped it, but the same error message appeared.

How odd, she thought. She was sure he hadn't mentioned changing his PIN, but her memory was a bit all over the place at the moment, and it was possible he'd mentioned it, and she'd simply forgotten. Trying her date of birth, she struck gold when she typed in his date of birth. Opening the messaging app, she was about to start typing him a message, when the phone buzzed to tell her a new message had been received. He'd probably realised the error of his ways and had messaged to ask if she could bring it in for a swap.

Only when she read the name of the message sender, it wasn't Pete.

'Who's Boring Roger?' she asked rhetorically.

Pete had never mentioned a friend or colleague by the name of Roger, nor why he'd list him as 'Boring'. Perhaps he was an old college friend. Curiosity getting the better of her, Louisa opened the message and gasped when she read the words.

Where are you? I've been waiting for you to come since seven. I'm so wet

> thinking about you that I'm
> touching myself. Hurry.

The phone clunked against the countertop as it slipped from her grasp. There was no denying what such a message meant, and as she dared herself not to believe the ramifications, her mind filled with disappointments. The times Pete had been late home from work and missed dinner; the weekends away when he'd had to meet an international client at the last minute; the fact he hadn't made a pass at her since she fell pregnant.

Lifting the phone again, she scrolled back through the exchange of messages between Pete and 'Boring Roger', each one confirming her worst fears.

> I want you to fuck me on
> your desk.

> I'm thinking about you while
> masturbating.

> If you take me away this
> weekend, I'll let you put it
> anywhere.

Bile bubbled in her throat, and Louisa dropped the phone again as she hurried to the kitchen sink and threw up. How many times had she excused his behaviour? Putting it down to him working so hard when all the times he'd let her down had been so he could screw whoever this other woman was. Assuming Roger was a pseudonym for someone else.

Swilling her mouth with water from the tap, she wiped her lips with the back of her hand and returned to the phone, opening the video gallery, scrolling through the memes and gifs, wanting to retch again when she caught sight of a recorded image of a man and woman on a desk. It appeared the video was a recording of security camera footage on another screen. Although the image was grainy and monotone, the man was wearing a pinstripe shirt and dark socks, his bottom thrusting as the pair of legs wrapped around his waist bobbled with pleasure. It wasn't obviously Pete, but the build was similar enough that he certainly couldn't be ruled out as the thruster.

She swallowed down the urge to retch as she continued to watch, hoping for any sign that this wasn't Pete and that the messages he'd received were one-sided; perhaps a woman he'd met who'd become infatuated, but that he continued to rebuff. She was desperately clinging to hope until the man's head turned slightly and she recognised the profile of Pete's face. It was hardly a smoking gun, but as she scoured the rest of the image for further confirmation, she recognised the surname on the door in the left hand corner of the image.

What had she done wrong to drive him into the arms of this harlot? The fact that the footage of them was clearly captured at work, did that mean she worked with him? Or for him?

Wiping her eyes with a piece of kitchen towel, she selected the 'Boring Roger' profile and dialled the number.

'Oh there you are, big boy,' came the sickly sweet reply. 'You'd better be on your way, or I won't be held accountable for what piece of office furniture I use to get myself off. Are you nearly here?'

Louisa hung up. She knew that voice having heard her making excuses for Pete ever since she'd taken over as his secretary. What a cliché he'd become!

Anger flooded her mind, and picking up her car keys, she drove to his office, determined to catch the pair of them in the act. But the security guard wouldn't allow her through the door, and when she demanded to speak to Pete, he told her that Mr Caulfield had returned home on a personal errand.

It was possible he'd realised he'd forgotten his phone and had returned to collect it, but it was equally possible that he'd gone to his secretary's home instead. Uncertain where to turn, Louisa drove to the one place that had always welcomed her: her mum and dad's.

Pete was already there when she arrived, his Aston Martin glimmering in the early morning sunshine.

He had to have realised the error of his ways, and finding her not at home had determined where she would head next. She hated that he knew her so well. He opened the door as she stalked towards it.

'I don't want to speak to you,' she shouted, as she pushed past him in search of the comfort of a motherly hug.

'We need to talk, Lou.'

'Why? So you can make excuses for why you've been having an affair?' she snapped back, marching from the lounge, to the study, and then into the dining room. Where the hell were her parents?

'They're not here,' Pete said calmly, following her into the room, reading her mind again.

'I told them you'd had a wobble and we'd argued. They said they'd give us space to sort out our problems.'

How could he be so calm? Didn't he realise that a woman scorned was not to be meddled with? Did he really believe he could talk his way out of this? All she could think about was how quickly she could organise a divorce.

'You need to calm down, Lou. This isn't good for the baby.'

Her head burned with frustration and sweat, as she stopped to take a breath, pressing her fingers into the back of one of the antique tall chairs.

Pete stood across the table from her, and held up his hands in a pacifying gesture. 'I know I screwed up, but you need to know she means nothing to me. She was just a bit of excitement. A bit of fun. But I realise that my actions were selfish, and that I've hurt you, and I'm sorry.'

She hated that he was trying to take some kind of moral high ground. Accepting culpability was not the same as meaning it. There'd been too many occasions when he'd told her what he thought she wanted to hear; too many times when he'd manipulated her. He'd forced her to turn her back on her friends and had convinced her that having a baby would make them whole, whilst all the time he was screwing his secretary? No, he couldn't be both prosecutor and defender. He didn't get to choose how this would play out.

She hadn't realised how tightly she was gripping the glass vase until it was flying from her fingers towards him. It narrowly missed his face as he swivelled at the last minute, and made a horrendous crash as it shattered against the wall.

'Are you out of your fucking mind?' Pete glowered.

She didn't hang around to answer, barging past him and out of the room, spotting the keys to the Aston Martin on the unit by the front door, and instantly realising how she could hurt him back once and for all.

***

It was as if someone had penetrated the top of her head with a tin opener and was now pouring in rancid treacle as the holes in her memory filled rapidly. How could she have forgotten everything that led up to the accident? How could she have spent the last twelve months blaming herself for what *he* had caused? And all this time he hadn't once mentioned her discovery of the affair or the fight that had led to her writing off his precious car. She didn't want to explore the memory of the actual crash, but she could recall not wanting to live, and not wanting to bring Pete's offspring into the world. She couldn't be sure if she'd deliberately crashed the car or whether it had been fate's intervention, but none of that mattered right now.

She wouldn't let him leave without confronting him about the lies that had destroyed her life. Unfastening the brake, she wheeled at pace towards the front door, opening it in one swipe, and rolling down the concrete ramp they'd had installed after her release from hospital. Pete was in the Land Rover, staring down at his phone, but his eyes widened when he saw her wheel into the space in front of the car.

'What are you doing?' he yelled from his window. 'I already told you: I don't want to have sex with you.'

She had no idea whether any of their neighbours were out tending to their gardens or walking dogs, but she didn't care whether they overheard what she had to say.

'I know what you did … what you've been doing to me. I-I want a divorce, Pete. Enough is enough.'

She half-expected him to start the engine and drive right through her, but instead he clambered out of his car, and crouched down before her.

'You think you want a divorce?' he said quietly, maybe also concerned who might be able to overhear the confrontation. 'What you don't realise is that nobody else will look twice at you, Lou. You're broken, and the saddest part is you did this to yourself. So I fooled around with my secretary, I wasn't the first and won't be the last. It's not against the law. But what you did: stealing my car and trying to kill our son? That is against the law. And given the PND diagnosis and the antidepressants you're on, one word from me and I could have you locked up in a funny farm. You think your life is bad now?' He smirked. 'You've got no idea how bad I'll make it. Now why don't you head back inside and stop all of this nonsense?'

She blinked several times, unable to see how the tables had turned so easily. He wasn't scared, and as much as she wanted to shout and scream about his infidelity, in her moment of truth, her voice abandoned her.

'You're pathetic, Lou,' he whispered as he straightened. 'I'll deal with you when I get back. It's about time things changed around here. About time you showed me the goddamned respect I deserve!'

Chapter 29

Abbie – Now

I stay for registration, before Gail and Sally formally announce to the children that this is my last day, and that I will be leaving to have my own baby. It is like I'm watching my life play out in front of my eyes, only it is actors I am watching in all the key roles, and I have no control over the script. A bouquet of flowers appears from nowhere, and Gail then invites me to the front of the gathering and hands them to me. She tells the children they can ask me anything, and rather than disappoint them, I face the interrogation, though most of the questions revolve around whether I'm having a boy or girl, and whether I'll name him or her after any of them.

And then as soon as it starts, it's over, and Gail is summoning the children to break in to their usual groups. When my children are gathered around me, Sally brings Claudette over and explains that she will be replacing me, and then I'm ushered to the door by Gail.

'We'll be in touch regarding maternity pay,' Gail tells me again, and then thanks me for my understanding.

Although it feels as though I'm being forced to leave a job I love, I understand why Gail and Sally have made this decision, even if it doesn't make it any easier to swallow. And then I'm outside in the cold, watching as the front door is closed and bolted. I remain there for several minutes, watching through the window to see whether any of my group come to wave goodbye, but they're already lost to the excitement Claudette is delivering. It feels like I've been erased.

In my car, I try and phone Mark to tell him what's happened, hoping for some words of encouragement, but an automated message advises me he's already on a call, and so I leave a brief message asking him to call me back when he has a moment. I manage to keep my tears at bay until the call ends. I'm suddenly a kite with no string holding me back, and it terrifies me where the wind will take me next.

I eventually start the engine, and plot the course for home, but I'm dreading the thought of being stuck there with nothing to do. I have no interest in wallowing and binge-watching Netflix; to do so, would be to admit defeat; to admit that I'm nothing but a baby delivery system now.

I want to put two fingers up at all those who suddenly don't think I'm capable of more, and so as the turning for my road approaches, I kill the indicator and continue straight, not really knowing where I'm going, but enjoying wrenching some level of control back over my flight. I can't say whether it is fate leading me, or something buried deep in my subconscious, but before I know it I'm seeing signs for Stoneclough, and realise exactly where I'm headed.

I haven't been back to St Philomena's Birthing Centre since the day we lost Josh. On some level I haven't wanted to return to a place which invokes such cruel memories. But even though I only came here twice – the first time when Mark was trying to convince me that we could afford the luxury, and the second on the day of inducement – I still know the route, as if it is burned on my soul.

I'm now on a narrow road, lined with thick, evergreens, and beyond them a forest of entangled trunks and branches shutting out the few rays of light trying to break through the blanket of white clouds. I know somewhere beyond the patch of woodland, there is an almost identical lane with traffic heading in the opposite direction, but it does little to relieve the ball of tension in my gut. I'm just grateful there are cars in my rear-view mirror, demonstrating that life does continue beyond the birthing centre.

I seem to recall seeing signs for the venue the last time we were here, but that was five years ago, and if it's no longer in business as Kinga suggested, then it makes sense as to why there are no signposts for it. I don't really know what I'm hoping to achieve by coming this way, maybe it's just a hope that the visual will trigger repressed memories, and help me make sense of the contradiction before me. I've kept these memories buried for so long to ensure my survival, and although I'm not sure if I have the strength to let them out, it appears my body has different ideas.

And then suddenly there is a faded brown sign poking out through the trees, pointing to a dark and narrow turning to the right. Slowing, I can make out enough faded letters to see that this is the enclosed entrance to St Philomena's, and duly turn. Overgrown twigs and leaves squawk as they scratch at the doors and side panels of the Mini, almost sounding like a scream of warning. I try to ignore it and the car rattles as it crosses the cattle grid, and then the tyres crunch over the gravel pathway that curls up through the trees. It isn't too late for me to stop and reverse back out, but I resist the temptation, and climb the incline, the trees eventually separating to reveal the two storey building, surrounded by a moat of wild grass.

The lawn was always well-maintained, and surrounded by the curtain of woodland, the place had resembled a gothic hotel rather than a hospital. It had seemed like something from a horror movie, hidden from the turmoil of urban Manchester and its surrounding towns.

The building before me is now surrounded by a tall wire fence which appears to enclose the entire premises, while wooden boards advertise the property is for sale on a leasehold basis. It doesn't look like anybody has been by for a viewing recently. Following the gravel drive around to the back of the building, I park in one of the marked bays, even though mine is the only car here, and then I clamber out of the Mini for a closer inspection.

Kinga claimed to have been back here and to have broken in with the intention to start a fire, but had found nothing worth burning. I suppose I want to test the validity of that statement. Crossing the gravel to the wire fence, it certainly appears too tall to scale, even for someone as slight as Kinga. There's no obvious way to grip the wire as the circular gaps between the strands aren't large enough for shoes. I continue my circuit of the perimeter, looking for any gaps between the panels large enough for a person to slip between, but the hinges are firm, and there is no give, even when I make it to the enormous padlock keeping the fence's opening tightly closed.

I take several steps back from the fence and take in the building's once white paintwork, but now a dreary grey where upkeep has not been maintained. It's funny, although there is a familiarity about the building, it doesn't quite look as I remembered. I suppose my imagination probably made it appear scarier because of the pain it caused me. Looking at it now in the cold light of day, it looks powerless. How can a place that was once a beacon for bringing life into the world now appear so lifeless?

A vehicle crossing the cattle grid startles me, and as I turn to see what is approaching, several minutes pass as it crunches the gravel like some monster chewing and spitting out bones. But then a dark, saloon car appears out of the trees with the word SECURITY scrawled across the bonnet. A moment later the car is parking beside me, and a young man in a green shirt and tie, with matching baseball cap and unzipped bomber jacket emerges. He can't be much older than twenty, but I don't doubt that he could overpower me if the urge took.

'Can I help you with something?' he asks, keeping one hand tucked behind his back, as if he might have some kind of weapon there.

I wasn't expecting to run into anyone, least of all a private security guard, and I don't really have an adequate explanation for being here.

'Do you need a hospital?' he asks next, spotting my bump and leaping to the wrong conclusion. 'This place isn't operational. If you're in labour, we'll need to get you somewhere to help.'

It's tempting to play along, but I don't want him insisting on escorting me to North Manchester General Hospital.

'No, I'm not due for a few weeks,' I correct, and watch as the relief washes over his face. 'I used to work here,' I say, though I've no idea why I've decided to lie, 'and I just wanted to see what happened to the old place. Do you know how long it's been out of business?'

He shrugs. 'I don't know, I'm sorry. I'm just here to protect the building.'

'Protect from who?' I ask, as it's such an odd thing to say.

'Vandals,' he confirms, extracting his hidden hand, but holding on to the frame of the door, as if he might need to suddenly dive in for his own safety. 'A few months ago, someone broke in and made a mess inside. That's why it's all fenced off now, and why our team was hired to keep watch.'

He nods up to the building and I see now there are small security cameras dotted about the entrance. I see now that my presence probably triggered his arrival. Could Kinga's invasion have been the cause of the added security measures? I certainly can't dispel the possibility.

'Oh, I'm not a vandal,' I clarify, wincing as my daughter kicks out.

'Clearly, but you are trespassing on private

property, so I will need to ask you to leave.'

'Of course,' I concur. 'Do you know what happened to the previous tenants of the building? I'd love to get back in touch with some of my former colleagues.'

He shrugs again, and really does seem to be a black hole of knowledge. It's as he stares back at me that I notice the large sign in the middle of the wild grass welcoming visitors to St Philomena's. It indicates for visitors to sign in at reception, and then lists the resident physicians as Dr Richard Michelson and Sister Theresa Arnott. I make a mental note of the names, and then allow the security guard to escort me back to my car. He warns me that if he sees me on the premises again, he'll have to report the incident to the police, but I assure him I have no intention of returning. I know what I need to do now: find Michelson and Arnott.

***

Back home, I grab my tablet and begin searching for Michelson, but his name isn't unique enough, and thousands of results are returned. Instead, I search for his name and St Philomena's, and find an image of two men in white coats standing beside the very sign I just saw on the overgrown lawn. I shudder when I see his piercing blue eyes, and it's as if the walls around me fade away and I'm back in that delivery room.

My skin is coated in a thin sheen of sweat and dread. The midwife and delivery attendants are panicked, and even though there's a voice at my side promising that everything will be okay, I can almost sense the future. Behind the face mask, all I can see are Michelson's eyes. He's at the back of the room, almost out of sight as they thrust up the curtain above my legs. But I can see the alertness in his eyes. He is in the zone, and his mind is racing through all his medical study and experience for the right solution. Mine and my baby's lives are in his hands.

Mark appears beside me, dressed in scrubs and a face mask of his own. He looks almost like a stranger in such apparel, but I'm grateful to feel the warmth of his hand as it takes mine. His eyes are watering and blotting marks are already appearing at the edges of his mask. I can't hear what he's whispering as I'm trying too hard to hear what Michelson is saying to those hidden behind the curtain. I can't feel anything below my chest, and although I know this is as a result of the lumbar puncture, it is terrifying suddenly not being able to feel the baby moving around inside of me. It is cliché, but it genuinely feels like I've lost a part of me both physically and emotionally. I've lost my connection to my baby, and I am terrified that it's more than just the anaesthetic.

Michelson disappears behind the curtain, and I hear apparatus clanging against the sterilised tray it's being carried on. I have to put my complete trust in the medical professionals working tirelessly between my legs, but this is already the longest two minutes of my life.

I close my eyes and will time to speed up. I want all of this to be over, and just to hold my baby in my arms, and hear him crying for attention. I feel Mark's dry lips press against my cheek, and the warmth of the tear as it escapes my eyes and rolls down to my ear.

I shake myself back into Mark's office as the tablet slips from my fingers and crashes against the carpet. The memory felt so real, but it's the first time I've thought about it since that day. The tension in that delivery suite clearly spelled that something was wrong with Josh, and I suppose that's why when Sister Arnott broke the news, I was so willing to believe it, even though I didn't want to.

'I'm so, so sorry, Abbie, but ... your son didn't survive the birth.'

Arnott's words are so clear and sincere, but did she know that she was lying? If I'm to believe Kinga's version of events, then Josh didn't die and at some point he was taken from that delivery suite by someone and handed over to another family. Was it Michelson? Was it Arnott? They were both present in the delivery suite with me, but so were three or four others whose names I either didn't hear or don't remember. Was it one of them? Were they all involved? To pretend that Josh had died would have taken some level of conspiring.

Nausea washes over me as I sit in Mark's leather chair, and will it to pass. I'll never make it to the bathroom upstairs, and the nearest sink is in the kitchen. I take several deep breaths, trying to focus on any distraction to take my mind off the anger and confusion flooding my mind.

They had to have all been involved. To keep Josh from crying, and to act as though he had passed, only to smuggle him to his new home goes against every oath and moral compass, and defies all logic. As tragic as it was to lose my son, the possibility that he was taken from me is more painful. So, I'm either to accept that six medical professionals conspired against me for some unfathomable reason, or I have to conclude that Kinga and her source are misleading me now.

Yet despite my reasoning, I still *want* to believe that the illogical is more plausible.

I continue reading the hits on the tablet, searching for clues as to where Michelson and Arnott are now. If I can find them, I can ask what really happened, or at least have grounds to challenge Kinga's claims.

And then I see Michelson's obituary and my heart sinks. It is on the site of a local journal from his birthplace in Grimsby. It says he died after a long battle with bowel cancer, after a glittering career in medicine that spanned more than forty years. The obituary is written by his daughter, and acknowledges the vital role he played in saving so many lives.

I lock the tablet as I can't reconcile what I'm reading with the picture my mind wants to paint. I've never felt so confused and alone, and it almost feels like Mark can sense this when he messages me. I wipe my eyes, and open the message, but it isn't checking whether I'm okay. It is blunt and pragmatic: *Meet me at the police station.*

Chapter 30

Louisa – Two years ago

Lying in bed, Louisa held her breath, focusing all her attention on the other sounds in the room; listening for the creak of floorboards in the ceiling above to suggest he was getting dressed; or the telltale sign of his breathing behind the door. He'd mentioned he was going to go into the office at some point today, but he hadn't been specific, and she hadn't dared to ask. She'd been planning her escape for months, and had done her utmost to keep him from catching on. If he even suspected she was plotting behind his back … she didn't want to think about the repercussions.

But what if he'd already gone? Was she wasting valuable time in hiding beneath the duvet *pretending* to still be asleep? If he'd gone in early, then the clock was ticking on when he would return, and her window of opportunity shrinking by the second. The lack of sound – save for the rapid beating of her heart – didn't spell good news.

And then she heard it.

So subtle, yet distinctive: the sound of Pete's knee cracking, and in that moment she knew exactly where he was; standing behind her bedroom door. He had to be listening in, trying to determine if she was awake yet. He wouldn't wait forever, particularly if he was keen to get to and from the office. Since he'd become an at-home worker, he was like her prison guard, always watching and always listening.

Clearing her throat, she made a show of turning over in bed, giving him the cue to unlock the door and enter, without checking if she was ready to be disturbed. Dressed in a suit, shirt and tie for the first time in months, for a moment she forgot all about the last year, momentarily recalling a time when that handsome face and athletic physique had made her swoon at twenty paces.

If only she'd known the monster that lurked behind that chiselled smile.

The only light in the room was coming from behind Pete in the doorway, framing him like some avenging angel. Rubbing her eyes she tried to sit up in bed, manhandling the deadweight of her legs into a sitting position. Pete approached, flattening the duvet at the edge of the bed, before perching there, the glass of water in his hand catching in the light from the doorway.

'Caleb is dressed and ready to come down,' he said quietly. 'I have dozens of things to arrange before his party tomorrow, and I need to collect his cake from the bakery in town, but I'll do that on my way back from the office. You do remember I said I had to go out this morning?'

She took a moment, feigning the attempt to recall the memory, before slowly nodding. The fact that she'd been awake most of the night carefully considering every action she needed to take before he returned home couldn't be betrayed in her actions.

'I'll only be a couple of hours, but I'll leave Caleb in his playroom with plenty of snacks and toys, so he shouldn't need you to do anything. I've told him what's going on, and he understands.'

She kept her eyes on the duvet, terrified that he'd read her mind and decide not to go out. She'd been waiting for a glimmer of light to appear in the tunnel, and now she was ready to charge full steam towards it.

'Are you ready to show me your progress?' he said next, tapping a hand on her right knee.

She didn't respond, because the question was rhetorical. Whether she *wanted* to show him the results of the efforts she'd been making with the strengthening exercises wasn't up for discussion.

Placing the glass of water on her bedside table, he stood, leaning over, and pulling the duvet back to reveal her legs, the draft causing the hairs to stand. She kept still, hoping he hadn't noticed.

'Come on then, show me what you can do.'

Finding the balance between showing him progress and hiding the extent of her progress was becoming a greater battle every day. Too little progress and he'd be angry at her for not trying hard enough; too much progress and he'd realise she'd been holding back for months.

Taking a deep breath, she pulled the nightdress down to cover her knees, surprised she hadn't realised just how far it had ridden up. And then she wiggled the toes of her right foot, and then her left, before sliding her right foot up the mattress, and bending her knee fractionally.

'And now the left leg?'

She lowered her right leg back down as slowly as she'd brought it up, and then focused her attention on her left leg. It wasn't a lie that progress with her left leg had been much slower than with her right.

'Mm,' Pete mused, 'I think we might need to make another appointment with Mr Fitzgerald. There must be something more they can do now. Maybe a second operation to repair more of the damage.'

At least he wasn't questioning her effort this morning.

'We need to shave your legs and find you a nice dress for tomorrow's part; I don't want you showing us up in front of the other parents from The Lamington Academy. I've booked the bouncy castle for the kids, and the clown will be arriving just after three.'

'But, Caleb doesn't …' she began, before biting her lip, and casting her eyes back on her legs.

Caleb had a phobia of clowns and despite being an active toddler, didn't seem particularly interested in climbing and bouncing. Given a choice between haring around and sitting with a picture book, he'd choose the book every time.

Pete checked his watch. 'I need to go,' he said, reaching for the glass of water, and handing it to her.

Reaching into his pocket, he extracted the plastic pill jar, and tipped the day's contents into his palm, handing them to her one at a time. Louisa took a swig of the water, and opened her mouth so he could see inside, before returning the glass of water to him.

'Good, I'll be back in a couple of hours.'

He straightened and kissed the top of her head, and it was all she could do to keep herself from shuddering at his touch. She watched as he left the room, and focused on her breathing, silently counting the seconds, listening for Pete shouting good bye to Caleb, and then the sound of the front door being closed and locked.

Still she didn't move.

It would be just like Pete to double-back and catch her shoving clothes into the backpack beneath her bed. She had to be certain he was gone and wouldn't be returning.

After ten minutes she still couldn't be certain he wouldn't suddenly appear from some corner, but she knew she didn't have a choice but to trust her instincts. Lifting her tongue she spat the two pills into her hand, drying them off on the duvet, and then secreting them in the small jewellery box in the drawer of her bedside table. Then, dragging the wheelchair from the corner, she lifted herself into the seat, securing her feet on the supports, and wheeling herself to the chest of drawers. Opening them, she silently recited the key items she'd need to get her started: underpants, socks, bras, three t-shirts, spare joggers, and a hoodie. Her anorak was hanging on the hook by the front door, and whilst she couldn't reach it down, she'd practiced hooking it with the golfing umbrella Pete kept by the door.

Filling the bag, her body flooded with adrenaline as nervous anxiety took hold. If he caught her in the act, any future chance of escape would be gone. But if she stayed, he'd continue to control every aspect of her life until he'd beaten her into an early grave. Caleb needed her to be strong for the both of them.

Wheeling out of her room, she wasn't surprised to

see Caleb in the wooden pen, head buried in a book. Stopping beside the pen, she wished him good morning, and cuddled him closely when he came over to the side.

'Mummy just needs to grab a few bits from your room, and then we're going to go on an adventure. How does that sound?'

Whilst he still didn't talk much, she was sure he understood a lot more than he could express, and when he smiled, she knew the thought of an adventure excited Caleb as much as it terrified her.

Making her way to the front door, she used the landline to call directory enquiries, and asked to be transferred through to a local mini cab firm. The taxi would arrive in twenty minutes, and she just had to hope Pete hadn't been lying when he'd said he'd be gone for two hours.

And then she faced her final challenge: getting up to Caleb's room to get spare clothes for him. The staircase might as well have been Everest.

During the night, she'd thought about how to scale the stairs, but she had no option but to drag her body up. Her legs were in no condition to support her weight, so walking was out of the question.

Moving the chair to the edge of the bottom step, she carefully applied the brake, and manoeuvred the foot supports out of the way, placing her feet on the hardwood floor. Picturing this moment during the night, she'd imagined hurling herself forwards onto the steps, but now that she was faced with the prospect, the distance between her torso and the carpet seemed too great. The last thing she wanted was to land awkwardly and break a wrist or injure her ribs.

Sliding forwards on the cushioned seat, she leaned as far forward as she could manage without toppling, the sweat quickly pooling at the edge of her hairline.

It wasn't too late to cancel the plan. She could still return the clothes to her drawers and hide the rucksack. That would give her more time to work out how to get the stuff from Caleb's room, but then it could be weeks or months before Pete left her alone again. What if it wasn't for another two years, by which time he'd be marching Caleb off to The Lamington Academy?

No, she had to be strong for Caleb.

With a deep breath, she toppled forwards, the wheelchair scooting away from the steps in reaction to the momentum of her weight shift. But she'd made it, and now she couldn't think of anything but crawling to the top of the stairs, getting Caleb's things and getting away. Each step took so much strength to mount, and when she was halfway up, regret scratched at the edges of her mind, but still she continued, even finding a rhythm as she neared the final step.

It had been almost a year since she'd last been up here, and she didn't want to think about the dirt and grime she was crawling over, and couldn't immediately recall the last time she'd heard Pete using the vacuum cleaner up here. And she certainly hadn't anticipated how tall the chest of drawers in Caleb's room would be. If she was in her chair, she'd be able to reach, but from this low down, the top three drawers would be impossible to access. It would be too much effort to return to the foot of the stairs and drag the chair up, so she rummaged around in the bottom three drawers, only then realising that she'd forgotten to bring the rucksack up with her.

Cursing, she rolled the end of her nightdress into a makeshift basket, and finding pants and socks, she nestled them into the space. She also managed to get hold of a handful of t-shirts, but jumpers and trousers were out of reach. With no other choice, she crawled to the staircase, one arm gripped around the bundle of clothes, and eventually swinging her legs over the precipice.

In her planning, she'd pictured herself being dressed before mounting the stairs, and with the night dress now acting as a temporary holdall, the bristles of the carpet against the skin of her buttocks felt coarse and hard. Sliding down the stairs could result in all kinds of friction burns, but again she had little choice but to try.

Pushing herself off the first step, she winced the moment she crashed against the step, feeling a jar at the base of her spine.

You're doing this for Caleb, she reminded herself. *You're all he has.*

Pushing again, she crashed against the second step, trying to ignore the burning sensation in her bottom. She wasn't wearing her watch, and she couldn't reasonably guess how long it had taken to scale the stairs, but certain that she didn't have any time to spare.

Pushing herself off the edge of the step, she misjudged the amount of force used, and her arm gave way. Suddenly she was slipping forwards, and rather than sliding on her bottom, she was tumbling, limbs flailing as she rolled head over shoulder, feeling every bump and crash, collapsing in a heap at the bottom of the stairs.

And that was the moment she heard keys turning in the front door behind her.

Chapter 31

Abbie – Now

Mark is pacing outside of the entrance to the police station when I arrive. He stamps out the cigarette, and stares guiltily at his feet as I approach, making a half-arsed attempt to waft the smoke away. He knows how I feel about him smoking, and I know he only falls back into the habit when he's particularly stressed. He pops two pieces of gum into his mouth, before kissing my cheek.

'Sorry,' he mutters under his breath, barely slowing his pace.

'What's going on?' I ask. 'Did Brearton find something?'

He shakes his head. 'No, I asked him to meet us.' He finally stops, and tilts his head as he looks at me. 'Are you okay? You look pale as a sheet.' He fumbles his palm to my forehead, before wiping it on the leg of his trousers. 'You're wet through as well. Is everything okay with you and the baby?'

'We're fine,' I tell him, fanning the air near my cheeks with my hand. 'Just hormones.'

The truth is, I haven't been able to relax all day, and now the walk from the car has me overheating; it isn't even that warm out. I just wish all of this would just go away so I can concentrate on the daughter inside me.

'Why did you call a meeting with Brearton?'

Mark looks back at his feet again, ready to spill another secret it would seem. 'I got the money,' he whispers.

'What money?' The words have barely left my lips when I hear Kinga's words in my head: *She say twenty thousand pounds.* 'You want to pay her? But you've said all along you think she's trying to con us.'

'I'm ninety per cent certain she is, which is why I'm not handing over anything without involving the police. If this woman thinks she can steal from us and then disappear, she's got another think coming.'

His eyes are buzzing as he speaks, and explains that he'll ask Brearton to mark the notes in some way, so the payment can be tracked back to those involved in the criminal enterprise and they can be arrested and imprisoned.

'They messed with the wrong family,' he says finally, and I can see now that he's been ruminating on this ever since we left the self-storage depot. I don't doubt that he's been considering his options all night, and has now determined this to be the best and safest avenue to pursue.

'Where did the money come from?' I ask, lacking the strength to argue with him again.

'It doesn't matter where it came from. If Brearton agrees to my proposal, then we should get it all back.'

I'm certain there's more he isn't telling me, but I'm in urgent need of a seat, and I'm keen to know whether Brearton will be able to find anything on Kinga when I give him her full name.

'Let's go in,' I say, nodding towards the automatic

doors.

Mark continues to look at me with concern, but doesn't question my health again. Once inside, the young officer behind the desk listens to Mark speak, and then agrees to phone for PS Brearton to come and meet us. He appears a couple of minutes later, and once we're seated in the same informal interview suite, and he's found me a beaker of tepid water, Mark tells him about last night's rendezvous.

Brearton listens without interruption, his eyes moving from Mark, to me, and then to the piece of paper on the pad on his lap. He has been scribbling some notes on the paper, but his handwriting is unintelligible, and I can't determine which details he finds so salient.

'She must be living there,' Mark concludes, crossing his arms in satisfaction.

Brearton takes a deep breath and slowly exhales, placing the lid on his biro, and finally looking straight at me. There is a sadness to his eyes, like that of a parent disappointed to be reprimanding an errant child.

'I did warn you that money was probably this woman's ultimate motivation,' he says, but there's no malice in the words. 'Are you okay, Mrs Friar? It must have been a shock to hear all those lies about your son. I am so sorry that you've been a victim of such a heinous crime.'

I can feel my brow furrowing as he speaks. Did he miss half of what Mark said about the claim her contact can get hold of one of Josh's hairs to prove a DNA match? Did he only hear the parts he wanted to?

'What if she isn't lying?' I ask the room. 'Just

suppose for a moment that her efforts to locate me are genuine and that all she wants is to reunite us with our son?'

Brearton and Mark exchange a knowing glance that feels like an affront.

'I'm not crazy,' I say to them both. 'You're both so desperate to see deceit and malevolence, and neither is prepared to consider the possibility that all of this could be real.' My neck feels as though a blowtorch is being pressed close to it, and I grab a leaflet from the table and fan myself with it. 'All I'm saying is that I don't know if she's lying or not. One minute I think she is, but the next I can't reconcile it. If you ask me there's a fifty-fifty chance, and how much will we regret it if it turns out you were wrong?'

Brearton sighs again, as he considers his words. 'Nobody is taking your feelings for granted, Mrs Friar, I can assure you of that. But I would be doing you a disservice if I offered you false hope. In my experience, con artists are very good at convincing people that there lies are true. It's what they do. I desperately want this woman's claims to be true – for your sake – but not to the point where I disregard the possibility that a crime is being committed.'

'Which is why we've come in,' Mark pipes up. 'I've got the twenty grand, but I want you to mark it in some way so that we don't lose it. Can you do that?'

He raises his eyebrows, and I can almost hear the wheels turning inside his head. 'Are you paying cash then?'

Mark looks at me momentarily, confusion making the skin around his eyes wrinkle. 'Um … I mean, I assumed she'd want cash. The way her stuff was scattered around that storage unit, I don't imagine she's going to use a bank to wire money internationally.'

'Well – I'd have to check with our fraud team – but it might be possible to make a note of the serial numbers of the notes, and then we'd be able to trace where they reappear in the system. You'd have to sign a disclaimer if you're choosing to risk your own money, as we couldn't be held accountable for what happens to it. But to be honest, I'd rather you tell me where the exchange will be made so that we can surveil it and move in as soon as the money has been handed over. Did she give you any more detail about her *source*?'

Mark shakes his head in my periphery. 'Just that they were someone on the inside.'

'To be fair, there probably isn't a source. It sounds like she might just be using this fictitious figure to exonerate herself of the extortion. By blaming someone else, she'll appear to be on your side, while secretly rubbing her hands together waiting for you to pay up.'

'She said we wouldn't have to pay until we'd verified the hair is a match,' I pipe up to quell their mutual assassination of Kinga's character. 'So if she hands over the hair and we get it verified and it turns out to be a fake, she goes away empty-handed.'

Neither responds at first, but then they share the same glance again, like I'm some naïve child who doesn't understand the workings of the world they live in.

'The promise of the hair is the bait dangled to get you to the exchange with the cash,' Brearton says with disdain. 'Once she has you there, I imagine she'll come up with some excuse as to why she needs the money first – or at least a portion of it – playing on your emotions. With all due respect, Mrs Friar, you strike me as the sort of person who *wants* to see the good in others, and whilst that is admirable, it also makes you a more appealing target for these sorts of people. I don't mean to sound condescending, but I prefer hope for the best, but plan for the worst. It's always served me well in the past.'

'Kinga Mutsuraeva,' I blurt out. 'That's her name. I spotted it on some of the papers she showed me last night. Before you assume that her actions are criminally-motivated, why don't you see what you can find out about her?'

Brearton checks the spelling with me, scribbling it on his pad, and then excuses himself.

'You didn't tell me you caught her full name,' Mark says hurtfully.

'And you didn't tell me you had the power to lay your hands on twenty grand,' I snap back, refusing to meet his stare.

'I borrowed it, okay?'

I frown with disbelief. 'You expect me to believe you managed to get a bank loan in under two hours this morning?'

'No, not a bank loan. I ... I borrowed it from a friend, so no interest expected. Okay? Once I get my bonus, I can pay her back.'

'*Her*?'

His hand moves to his eyes, and he squeezes the bridge of his nose, regretting the slip of the tongue. 'I told Faye what happened, and she offered to lend me the money.'

'In exchange for what …?' I say rhetorically, not sure I want to hear his feeble attempt at an answer.

'Nothing. She just wants to help.'

'Sure she does,' I scoff. 'And I suppose those short skirts are just her way of motivating you men who work for her, right?'

'It isn't like that, Abbie.'

'Oh no?' My head snaps around. 'What is it like then? I saw the two of you coming back in her car yesterday afternoon, all giggly. I can see how she might look more desirable when I'm in this condition, but –'

'Abbie, this is hardly the time and place for this sort of banal conversation. I'm not having an affair with Faye, and actually I'm hurt that you would think I would be capable of something so underhand. She offered me the money and I accepted to get us out of this jam. That is it. End of story.'

I want to believe him, and in truth it isn't him I don't trust; it's *her*. He might think I'm naïve about how the criminal mind works, but I've been around enough women who wouldn't think twice about stabbing a pregnant wife in the back and making a move.

'I'm flattered that you would think another woman might find me attractive,' Mark says, chuckling lightly, in an effort to raise the mood, 'but there's only one woman I want to be with, and that's the Goddess beside me now.'

I look away from him, not ready to let him off the hook so easily.

'In truth, the only reason I agreed to go for a celebratory drink with Faye yesterday is that there's a position coming up in one of the other teams and I want her to put in a good word for me. It's a promotion, but would mean less time on the road, and more working from home. I didn't want to mention it yet, as I didn't want to get your hopes up. She has some sway with her boss, and a recommendation from Faye will go a long way towards securing an interview. You have nothing to worry about.'

Now I'm feeling guilty, so it's a relief when Brearton returns to the room, now carrying an iPad, which has one of those privacy screen covers. He keeps it close to his chest regardless, as he sits.

He clears his throat. 'What I'm about to tell you does not leave this room. Is that clear?'

Mark's face reflects my own confusion, but we both nod.

'I found your Kinga Mutsuraeva, and I think you deserve to know about her mental health issues.'

Chapter 32

Louisa – Two years ago

Pinned to the hard wood floor through fear, exhaustion, and pain. Louisa could only watch on as the front door slowly opened, crashing into the upright wheelchair. And just as she expected to see the looming figure of Pete appear in the gap, relief washed over her as her mum's small face and button nose entered instead.

'Gosh! Louisa, are you okay? What's happened?' The words couldn't tumble quickly enough as Judith's eyes fell on her prone daughter.

Still breathless, and with her heart racing in her chest, Louisa was in no position to explain or concoct a suitable excuse for how she'd wound up outside of her wheelchair, her skin slicked with sweat and pink blotches, the night dress failing to cover her modesty.

'Is Pete outside?' is all she managed, as her brain tried to process what her mum was doing here in the first place.

'Pete? I didn't see him outside. Do you want me to call for him?'

'No, no. You didn't see him? Is his car on the drive?'

Judith peered back out through the front door, before closing it forcefully. 'No, it doesn't look like it's there. Do you want me to call him? If he's out, I'm sure –'

'No!' Louisa quickly interrupted. 'Mum, please, don't call Pete.'

Judith was doing a terrible job of disguising her worry, but she acquiesced, reaching down for Louisa's hand and helping her into a more comfortable sitting position, straightening the nightdress in the process. Collecting Caleb's t-shirts, underpants and socks, she raised her eyebrows.

'I think I know what was going on here,' she said quietly, folding the t-shirts into a pile.'

'You do?' Louisa asked, dread filling her dry mouth.

Judith nodded. 'You're trying to do too much. Correct me if I'm wrong, but you were about to try and carry Caleb's clothes upstairs to put them away. I'm right aren't I?'

Louisa nodded quickly, figuring it was simpler than the truth.

'You mustn't do too much, Louisa. I know you feel useless and trapped down here, but you know Pete or I will deal with simple tasks like putting away Caleb's laundry.'

The only words Louisa heard were: useless, trapped, and simple tasks. It was true that the accident had robbed her of so much, but it was the first time she'd heard the indictment in her mum's voice, and her eyes began to water.

'I'm not sure if I have the strength to get you back into your chair. I think it really would be best if we phoned Pete and –'

Louisa shot out a hand. 'No, Mum, no Pete. Please

just help me onto the stairs, and bring the chair over. I can lift myself in.'

Judith studied her daughter's face for several moments, before sighing and placing her hands beneath Louisa's arms. On the count of three they both used all their strength, shuffling and hustling until a panting Louisa was on the second step of the staircase. Her entire upper body felt like she'd been through the gauntlet, but now all she could picture was the sands of time slipping through the funnel. Pete hadn't returned yet, but that didn't mean he wouldn't soon.

Judith manoeuvred the wheelchair into position, and remained behind it to ensure it wouldn't slip away again. Gripping one handle and the cushion, Louisa took several deep breaths, before lifting and sliding her bottom into place, her arm almost buckling in the process. She'd never been so relieved to be back in the chair: some mobility was better than none.

'Can you watch Caleb for a second while I get dressed?'

Judith rested a cold hand on her daughter's shoulder, and slowly released the brake on the wheels. Ordinarily, Louisa might have complained about anyone taking charge of the chair, but as she allowed the tension in her shoulders to fractionally ease, every bump and bruise throbbed in chorus.

'There's my gorgeous grandson,' Judith called out as they entered the lounge-diner, and he cackled with glee as he saw her too.

'I'll take his clothes,' Louisa said as Judith looked for somewhere to place them as she moved across to the pen to lift Caleb out.

'So long as you're not planning to scale the stairs again,' Judith teased, handing them over.

Louisa didn't laugh, knowing she'd never repeat the mistake. She was lucky to be alive, and even luckier that Pete was oblivious to her actions. Resting the clothes on her lap, she quickly wheeled to the bedroom, and stuffed them into the holdall on the corner of the bed, before lifting herself from the chair to the bed. Part of her just wanted to stay there, the comfort of the duvet offering slight respite to her bruises. But she fought against the temptation, reminding herself that she might never get a better chance to escape.

It took ten minutes to get the night dress off, and the t-shirt and joggers on; ten more minutes bringing Pete closer to home. Collecting toiletries from the wet room, she buried them in the holdall and zipped it up. Satisfied, she now had to worry about how to get rid of her mum, but as she wheeled back into the lounge-diner, she was surprised to find the room empty.

'Mum?' she called out, listening for any sound of movement.

Judith appeared in the doorway a moment later, Caleb in her arms, chewing a toy rabbit's ear.

'I was just fixing us a cup of tea. You looked like you could do with one after your fall.'

'Thanks, but um, actually I'm supposed to be going out, so …'

Judith frowned as she lowered Caleb back into the pen. 'Going out? Where?'

'I'm meeting a friend,' Louisa lied, attempting to pre-empt her mum's next question. 'I've ordered a taxi to collect us, so ...'

The blood drained from Judith's face. 'Oh dear. I hadn't realised ... I may have inadvertently sent your taxi driver away. He knocked at the door while you were getting dressed, but I told him there must have been some mistake.'

Louisa felt a primal scream building in the pit of her stomach, but forced it back into its cage.

'I can give you a lift to see your friend,' Judith piped up. 'Who is it you're meeting?'

'You don't know her,' Louisa snapped, before softening her tone. 'A lift into town would be helpful though.'

'I can watch Caleb for you if you like, so you and your friend aren't disturbed?'

Louisa's eyes widened. Her mum was only trying to be helpful, but seemed to be dropping spanners in the works without realising it.

'Um, actually, she has a son Caleb's age. That's why we're meeting. We thought the boys might become friends.'

'Sounds lovely. Where did the two of you meet?'

The question put Louisa's senses on red alert. It wasn't an unnatural question in the throes of the discussion, and yet it was the way it had been asked. Something felt off.

'We've known each other for years,' Louisa adlibbed, 'and she found me on Facebook and suggested the drink.'

'On Facebook? Are you sure she isn't one of those ... oh what do they call them ... cyber bullies?'

'I think you mean cybercriminal, Mum, and no I'm

pretty sure she isn't a cybercriminal.'

'It's just … When I spoke to Pete he said you'd closed all your social media accounts …'

So that was it: her mum had been talking to Pete. Probably explained the surprise visit this morning; it would be typical of Pete to send someone to watch over his prisoner. But ultimately Judith was *her* mum, and not his. If Judith knew what a bully he'd become she'd be encouraging Louisa to get away.

Louisa looked back at Caleb in his playpen, and then at the clock on the wall. An hour had passed since Pete had left, which meant he could return at any minute. It was now or never.

'I-I'm leaving Pete,' she blurted, and had she had her time over would have softened the blow.

Judith's brow furrowed as if she didn't believe her ears. 'You're what, darling?'

'Please, mum, I'll answer any questions in the car, but we need to go. *Now.*'

'I'm not following, sweetheart.'

Louisa wheeled over to the pen, and lifted Caleb out, despite his flailing protestations. 'You, me, and Caleb need to leave this house now. Pete will be back at any minute, and I need to be gone before that happens. That's why I ordered a taxi; that's why I've packed a bag of our things. Please, Mum, we need to go now.'

Judith made no effort to move. 'Where is all this coming from, Lou-Lou? Pete loves you very much.'

'H-he's a bully,' Louisa countered, the words thick like treacle on her tongue. 'He has been psychologically abusing me for years.'

It was the first time she'd said the words aloud, and it was only now she realised how great a weight they held over her.

'He was having an affair when I was pregnant with Caleb, and that's what led to the accident. He admitted as much last year when my memory started to return, and has been holding me here as prisoner ever since.'

'What do you mean he's holding you as a prisoner? The three of you come over to our house all the time.'

'Exactly! The *three* of us. He only allows me out if he's with me, watching what I say and do. He forces me to take pills every morning to keep me docile and obedient.'

Wrinkles of skin gathered at the edge of Judith's fearful eyes. 'Why have you never mentioned this before?'

'*Because he's always there.* You don't realise what he's like; what he's *really* like. Please, Mum, can we just go, and I'll explain everything on the way.'

Still she didn't budge, her weary mind struggling to process the impact of her daughter's words.

'I can prove it to you,' Louisa said, wheeling herself and Caleb back into her room, returning a moment later carrying the small jewellery box from the back of her bedside table drawer. 'Here you go. Look inside. These are the pills he forces me to take. I've been hiding them under my tongue and then spitting them out. This isn't right, Mum. Can't you see?'

Judith opened the small jewellery box and studied the contents, before closing it, and handing it back.

'Okay, I believe you,' she said quietly. 'We can go. My car is just outside.'

Louisa kept her tears at bay, not speaking as the three of them bundled into her mum's car, and pulled away from the house. Louisa kept her eyes on the wing mirror all the time, expecting the shadow of Pete's Land Rover to appear in the distance; certain he would somehow sense her betrayal.

'Where were you planning to go?' Judith asked as she followed signs to the town centre.

'I-I don't know. I hadn't planned that far ahead. I figured I'd find a B&B somewhere until I could make a proper plan.'

'Then can I suggest you come and stay with me and your dad for a few days? Just while you get things sorted? Rushing off half-cocked is too impulsive, and you have to consider Caleb's health too.'

Louisa flipped down the vanity mirror and looked at Caleb's reflection. He was happily staring out of the window, occasionally pointing at things as if giving an imaginary friend a guided tour. In her desperation to escape, she hadn't properly considered the likely impact on Caleb, nor how much more difficult it would be with him in tow.

'Just for a few days,' Judith repeated, trying to hammer home the point.

'Okay, for a day or two,' Louisa conceded. 'Just until I'm sorted,'

She could see the smile of relief slowly form on her mum's lips, and allowed her eyes to close to regain her composure. When she woke, they were just pulling up at the wrought iron gates at the bottom of the gravel drive up to the manor house. She didn't know why the two of them continued to rattle around the old place, but talk of selling was always avoided.

The gates opened and they proceeded through, but it wasn't until they reached the end of the hedge-lined driveway that Louisa spotted the rear bumper of the Land Rover.

'W-what is Pete doing here? No, Mum, we need to go. Quickly turnaround.'

But Judith didn't respond, continuing until they were parked directly behind the Land Rover. She killed the engine, and slowly turned her head. The pity in her downcast eyes spoke volumes. 'We've asked Pete to move in with us,' she said quietly. '*All* of you to move in with us that is. It isn't fair on him to have to handle all of this in addition to his job, and Caleb.'

Louisa wanted to cover her ears, but kept her hands where they were, trying to think of any way she could get away. Opening the door wouldn't help as her legs weren't ready to bear the strain, and even if she managed to stand, she wouldn't make it more than a metre or so before he caught up.

'Please, Mum, you heard what I said: he's a bully.'

Judith didn't react, simply patting Louisa's leg. 'Pete warned us that you might say something like that. He knows it isn't your fault, but it's because you're off your meds, Lou-Lou. You're lashing out at the one person who's stuck by you all this time. Once the imbalance is fixed, you'll realise how silly all of this is.'

'I'm not crazy, Mum. This is what he does: he manipulates people into believing his stories.'

'Well he won't be able to bully you under our roof will he? Pete is enthusiastic about moving in. He'll be able to concentrate on working from home, allowing you time to rest and recover while your dad and I watch over Caleb. It's a win-win.'

Louisa watched on in horror as Pete emerged from the front of the property, her dad's arm wrapped around his shoulders. That morning she'd dared to dream of escape. Now she had to face the prospect of being trapped forever.

Chapter 33

Abbie – Now

Brearton keeps the tablet angled away from us, and with the privacy screen cover, there's no way we can see what's on the screen, but that only seems to add to the tension in the room, before he begins to speak.

'Kinga Mutsuraeva was arrested on possession of a Class-A substance three years ago, and was sentenced to 12-months in HM Prison Styal in nearby Wilmslow, but she was released six months later.'

He pauses and fiddles with the tablet, before lifting it so we can see the image of the woman on the screen. I gasp when I see the gaunt cheeks and tired eyes I recognise staring back at me. The woman in the image looks younger than the one in the faded leather jacket that I've spent days thinking about, but it's definitely her.

'That's her,' Mark's voice confirms beside me.

Brearton turns the screen away from us again, and nods. 'I was afraid you'd say that.' Another pause. 'For data protection reasons, I'm limited as to what I can tell you about her, and probably I've already said too much. But I think it's important that you understand the person you're dealing with here.

'When she was originally arrested, the interviewing officers were aware of her connections with an

Albanian gang operating in the city, but she refused to admit any connection to them, making bold claims about the cocaine being planted on her by arresting officers. She offered, "No comment," in response to the majority of questions she was asked, even initially refusing to give her name. After a lawful search of her known premises, a passport bearing the name Kinga Mutsuraeva was discovered, and when this was presented to her as evidence, she initially refused to admit that it was hers. She said the passport was a fake; that she didn't own a passport and had been trafficked into the country illegally, but couldn't provide any evidence of her true identity.'

I remember the story Kinga told Yolanda and I about how her brother paid for her to be smuggled out of Chechnya, but how they'd both been betrayed by the traffickers. It had sounded so convincing. Her pitch and heartfelt words had me wanting to believe her, and pitying the journey she'd been on. I don't want to believe that that was just the work of clever deception.

'She later recanted such claims,' Brearton continues, reading through the documents on the tablet. 'After being charged, and prior to trial, she admitted to being Kinga Mutsuraeva, but still refused to roll over on the Albanian gang, and pleaded guilty to the charges. Earned herself a lesser sentence as a result, and has thus far avoided further investigation. Until now. If you're willing to press charges, and help us locate her, then we might just be able to get her off the streets and stop her trying to victimise you further.'

Since she approached me at the shopping centre I've wanted to believe despite the nagging doubt in the back of my mind. Even when we went to the lock-up yesterday, I was convinced by her collection of paper cuttings, and the DNA document that looked so convincing.

Brearton locks the tablet and lowers it to his lap. 'I appreciate that's a lot to take in, but you need to think about the greater good here. Ultimately, the only harm this woman has caused you so far is emotional damage. She's unpicked old wounds and raised your hopes, but her intentions are far worse. And God only knows how many other victims have fallen foul of her games, or *will* fall foul of her lies. You've been brave in not allowing her to manipulate your grief, and in coming forward to report her. It's now about taking the next step.'

'Could we have a few minutes to discuss it?' Mark asks, and Brearton stands, excusing himself, taking the tablet with him.

Once he's gone, it feels like a gulf has been left in his place.

'We did say it seemed farfetched,' Mark says quietly, with no accusation in his tone. Ultimately, he's as much a victim in all of this as I am. And I need to remember that all of his doubt was about protecting me, rather than doubting my assertion. He only has my best interests at heart.

'Sh-She had me convinced,' I struggle to say, as a lump forms in my throat.

'Me too,' he says, taking my hand in his, and gently squeezing it for reassurance. 'If she'd produced a hair, I probably would have handed over the cash without even thinking about checking it.' He sighs, and when he speaks again, I can hear the sob in the back of his throat. 'There isn't a day goes by when I don't imagine how different our life would be had Josh survived. I picture the times I'd have taken him to the park to play on the wings or to kick about a football. I think about you picking the cutest superhero tops for him to wear. I see us on the beach, splashing about in the sea, and then you and me taking it in turns to read him bedtime stories. Every night I go to sleep trying to think of ways we could bring all of that back and live those memories. I wanted to believe Kinga's story as much as you as it gave us a way into that life, but miracles like that don't happen.

'But now we need to do what is right, and see her punished for the heartache she's caused us. Do you agree?'

I think about the tale Kinga weaved: the fear of coming to a new country; being forced to perform sexual acts on strangers; compelled into drug addiction; and then obliged to give up her child. How anyone could have the resilience to overcome such trauma is beyond me, and now it would seem it was beyond Kinga too. As much as I want to believe that Josh is still alive, I can't ignore the overwhelming evidence.

'O-Okay,' I say, opening my bag and removing a tissue to dab my eyes. Ultimately, I don't want anyone else to suffer as we have over the last few days.

Mark stands and moves to the door, finding Brearton waiting patiently outside. The two of them return to the room, and Brearton gives me a moment to compose myself, before speaking again.

'As I said before, I'll need to engage with our detective bureau to check how best to proceed with the proposed exchange. It's going to take a few days to organise, so I'd ask you not to do anything until we're ready to move. Something like this is far more intricate than they make out on the television and in books. God knows I wish it was easier!'

'Sure,' Mark nods, as if he has any idea what is involved. 'If she makes contact again, I'll tell her it's taking longer than anticipated to pull the funds together.'

'Thank you,' Brearton acknowledges. 'There is one more thing you should both be aware of – you in particular Mrs Friar. When she was in prison, Mutsuraeva made several attempts on her own life, but blamed other inmates on instigating it. The warden put it down to troublemaking, and if anything it probably expedited her release in a cruel twist of fate. Off the record, she was prescribed with medication to treat her *disorder*, and when she's not taking them, her paranoia and hallucinations can escalate. Given your current condition, I'd hate for the two of you to be alone.'

'Is she dangerous?' Mark asks, before I can get the words out.

Brearton looks from him to me. 'I don't know, but it would be safest for both of you not to meet with her again until we have things in place. As I said before, I prefer to hope for the best, but prepare for the worst. It's always stood me in good stead.'

Brearton leads us back through the station and promises he'll be in touch in a few days, but warns us to phone him if she makes contact again before he's called. There is a sadness in my heart as Mark walks me back to my car. Whilst I had severe doubts about Kinga when I arrived earlier, now the truth is out, I feel hope has abandoned me, and has left a bitter taste in my mouth.

'Do you want me to drive you home?' Mark offers, but I can see in his eyes that it would be easier if I just allowed him to return to work.

'I'll be fine,' I tell him as I notice the digits on the dashboard clock. 'You should head back to work before Faye thinks you're taking liberties.'

He kisses me, and tells me to phone him if Kinga calls or visits, and I promise I will. I wait until he's pulled away in his car, before, strapping myself in. Toby Orville is due to be collected at 12:30 today, which gives me fifteen minutes to get across town to the school and intercept his father.

Chapter 34

Louisa – One year ago

'I don't know if we can just leave her like this,' Louisa heard her mum whisper through the darkness of the room.

'What choice do we have? The appointment is in half an hour,' her dad replied softly. 'She'll be fine here for a few hours.'

'What about Caleb? What if …?'

'We can't always assume the worst is going to happen. She's his mother, and at some point we're going to have to trust her to do the right thing by him.'

Louisa remained still in the bed, her eyes closed; her breathing steady despite the rise in her pulse.

'But we promised Pete we wouldn't. It was the only reason he agreed to go on his business trip.'

'Come on, Judith, since she moved back home, have you seen anything in her behaviour to suggest that she's a threat to Caleb?'

Judith didn't answer, but Louisa could picture the look of concern on her mother's face.

'I'd feel better if we took him with us. I know he's had enough of hospitals, but –'

'Fine, we'll take him with us if it will make you feel better. Maybe you can take him for a slice of cake while I'm having my treatment.'

Louisa felt her shoulders tense at this. What *treatment* was he having, and why was this the first she'd heard it mentioned?

'Lou-Lou,' Judith now cooed gently, her face so close that Louisa could smell the lavender moisturising cream she applied every morning. 'Your dad and I are going out for a bit. We won't be long. Are you awake? Can you hear me?'

Louisa moaned in acknowledgement.

'We'll be back by lunchtime. I've left your breakfast on your tray just outside the door as usual. I'll administer your medication when I get back. A couple of hours delay shouldn't cause any issues.'

Louisa groaned again, and rolled over in bed, channelling her inner petulant teenager, and counting the seconds until they'd close the front door.

It had been 337 days since she'd tried to flee Pete only to be trapped by her mother's betrayal. And those first days were the worst. She'd pleaded and begged both her parents – separately and together – to set her free, but each time their grim faces delivered the same response: 'you're not well, Louisa. Let us help you.'

Pete's saintly act only served to make her seem crazier, yet she knew deep down that she hadn't imagined his threats, and the way he'd forced her to shun her friends and former colleagues. And worst of all, he'd manipulated the two people who should have been fighting for her into acting as his wardens.

She'd refused to take the prescribed medication, but the more she'd fought, the harder they'd insisted, until they'd given her no choice but to try and play along. Naively, she'd told herself that if she could show them she wasn't fighting that they'd slowly loosen her constriction. What she hadn't accounted for was Pete arranging for her dosage to be increased. Soon she found herself little more than a zombie. She'd wake, be fed and tended to, and then returned to bed. She'd become little more than a vegetable, and was powerless to stop her life slipping through her fingers.

Things had changed last weekend when they'd all suffered with a viral bug. It had wiped out all but Caleb, who somehow hadn't suffered any symptoms, even though he had to have been the one who brought the germs into the house. Unable to keep any food down, Louisa had suffered as much as the rest of them, but having brought up her medication, she'd had a light thrown at her, and she'd seen her means of escape. She'd been deliberately bringing up her breakfast and meds every day since, just to regain some level of semblance. Of course, she'd continued to act a zombie for their sake while she'd waited for her chance.

Judith kissed her daughter's head, and closed the door as she exited the bedroom. Louisa waited until the front door was closed and locked, and instantly pushed the duvet back. Wiggling her toes, she lifted both her legs up and over the edge of the bed. Still not enough strength to walk unaided, the Zimmer frame her mum helped her use had become a friend. But for now, she would rely on her wheelchair. Sliding into it, she raced out of the room, pausing only once at the sound of the Jaguar's engine starting, before racing towards the locked office door.

With Pete away on a business trip, there was no danger he'd disturb her. And she was certain he would have locked her passport inside the office where she couldn't get to it. If it hadn't been for the gastroenteritis she wouldn't have been cognoscente enough to have seen him secrete the office key inside the small pot on the mantel piece in the lounge.

Parking the chair beside the oak mantelpiece over the fireplace, she stretched up and reached for the pot, almost dropping it as the sleeve of her pyjama top caught on the corner of the wooden frame. Lowering the pot to her lap, she gasped when she opened it and found just a handful of pocket change, until she pushed the copper coins with her finger, and recovered the key from beneath the pile.

The bubble of excitement in her gut was tempered by the disappointment at having to go behind the backs of everyone who should have been looking out for her. Without hesitation, she primed the key between thumb and forefinger, and slipped it into the keyhole, twisting open the lock with a satisfying clunk.

Dust danced in the beam of light pouring through the large window to the left of the door as she entered. Cobwebs in the upper corners of the small room reminded her of adventure stories she'd read as a child where daring explorers would break into crypts to discover treasures. The bubble of excitement expanded.

Moving to the side of Pete's mahogany desk, she pushed his leather chair away, and slipped in behind, now facing the open door, and with both sets of drawers within easy reach either side of her. The screen on the desk was covered by a dust sleeve, but what she was after was not on his computer.

Reaching down to the left, she yanked at the handle of the top drawer, unsurprised when it wouldn't budge. She yanked it a second time to test the strength of the locking mechanism, but brute force wouldn't be enough. Running her hands across the top of the desk, she checked under papers, beneath the wireless keyboard, and in the desk tidy of pens beneath the screen, but there was no sign of a key. This was the first time she'd been in this room since Pete had taken it for his work from home office, but for all she knew, he kept the key to the drawers on his person.

Leaning back in her chair, she allowed her eyes to wander around the room, searching for anything that he might use to hide the key. Pete was a creature of habit, so if he'd hidden the door key in a pot, there was every chance he'd followed a similar practice with the drawer keys.

The left wall was lined with a floor to ceiling bookcase, a remnant from when her dad had maintained the room as his study. A drinks trolley also remained beside the open doorway, the decanter of whiskey half-full, a lidded ice bucket, and four tumblers glimmering in the sunlight from the window to the right of the room. Beneath the window, a large radiator stretched from wall to wall, but no obvious vessels for hiding keys.

Glancing back over her shoulder, the plain wall held nothing but a picture of her and Pete on their wedding day. Still no hiding place.

Scattering the pages on the desk again, she found a shatterproof ruler and attempted to jimmy it into the gap between the drawer and the desktop, but there wasn't enough gap.

Something sparked in the back of her mind.

The ice bucket beside the decanter.

She raised her eyes from the drawer to the drinks trolley

If Pete was using the bucket for ice, it would be melted, which probably meant it served another purpose.

Heading to the trolley, she lifted the lid and whooped as she spotted three keys on a small keyring staring back at her. Returning to her position beneath the desktop, she unlocked the drawers to the left. The top drawer contained pads of blank paper; the second drawer was deeper and contained various folders, which seemed to relate to client information, presumably work-related. No sign of her passport or building society savings book.

Turning to the drawers on the right, the top drawer was a mess. Lifting out the loose pages, she rummaged around inside, locating hers and Caleb's passports, as well as her building society book. Opening it, the balance wasn't as high as she'd hoped, but it was more than she had trapped inside this house. It would just about be enough to escape and lay low with Caleb until she came up with a new plan. Squeezing all three items between her thighs, it felt good to feel them held there firmly.

Reaching for the loose pages, she was about to return them to the drawer when something caught her eye. An envelope with her name written on it. Definitely not Pete's or either of her parents' handwriting. There was no address or stamp on the envelope suggesting it had been hand-delivered by someone. Pete hadn't mentioned any of her former friends trying to get in touch. The seal was already torn open, so Louisa slipped the folded page from it, and studied the words.

I KNOW WHAT YOU DID.

I KNOW CALEB IS NOT YOUR SON.

I WILL EXPOSE YOUR LIES.

The letter wasn't signed or dated, but instinctively Louisa believed the threat. It was as if the blindfold had been ripped from her eyes, and the truth poured over her like a bucket of ice water. Yet it couldn't be true. Even in the heyday of her doubts about her bond with Caleb, never in her wildest dreams did she actually suspect that Pete could have conspired to cover up a switched at birth scenario.

What made it worse was whoever had sent the threat had addressed it to her.

It didn't matter. She finally had the proof that Pete had been lying: The PND diagnosis was wrong.

Squashing the envelope between her legs, she reached for the pages again, finding an invoice to a Private Investigator on the top. Lifting it to her eye line, she studied the invoice. It was for a thousand pounds for "investigative works", which was about as generic as an item of work could be.

Why would Pete pay a thousand pounds to a private investigator? What else is he covering up?

Chapter 35

Abbie – Now

Roadworks and a diversion mean I don't make it to the school by 12:30, but as I park on the road, I realise I am directly in front of Chris Orville's work van, advertising his business, with the slogan, "No job is too small".

The rear-view mirror shows me nobody is inside the front of the van, which suggests they've yet to return, which means I can wait where I am without an awkward confrontation with Gail and Sally. I still can't believe they've forced me to start my maternity leave early, but I suppose it's my fault for not telling them about Toby's collision with me causing the fall yesterday.

As I replay the scene in my mind, I'm sure there was contact – malicious or not – and it was that which sent me tumbling and not just the blood rushing to my head. But maybe that's more reason for me not to still be working. Who's to say that another child not looking where they're going isn't going to crash into me again? The last thing I want is to endanger my daughter's safety.

A smile creeps across my face at this thought. I'm having a daughter! I can almost picture the years whizzing past and the two of us hosting tea parties for her dolls and teddies; me plaiting her hair ahead of a ballet recital; then how proud I'll be when she graduates university summa cum laude. And I think Mark was born to be the father to a daughter. He'll love reading her stories of knights and princesses and castles and dragons. I can picture her snuggling under his arm as he puts on dramatic voices. She'll hero worship him, and he'll bask in the glory of it all.

All this recent talk of Josh returning has distracted me from the very fact that in under a month I should be cradling my little girl in my arms, trying to learn what each gurn or cry means, and slowly watching her grow into a beautiful and independent person. We'll have to tell her about Josh one day, and how he would have made a great big brother for her, and how he's probably watching over her from beyond the grave.

My eyes mist slightly, and I take a deep breath because I don't want Toby and his dad to see me in an emotional state. I need to stay strong for Toby's sake. I need to find out what's going on at home, and whether Chris's outburst at the preschool yesterday was a one-off, or far more common. I have a duty of care towards Toby regardless of whether Gail and Sally think I'm up to it.

I've been sitting here for five minutes and they still haven't returned to his vehicle. I can't imagine that Toby's been kept behind, unless he's been involved in another incident today. I open the door, but then allow it to close as doubt peeks through at the edges of my mind. Should I go down there and tell them what I witnessed? If Toby has been violent to another child, Gail and Sally need to know that it's being driven by his own suffering at home. And if they question why I didn't come forward sooner, I'll tell them that I was waiting for the right moment.

Mind made up, I push my door open again, and squeeze out of the car. Waiting for a bus to pass, I cross the road in the direction of the preschool, but freeze as I near and realise that Toby is sitting inside the fenced playground beside the preschool, where Kinga approached me yesterday. He's alone on the bench, despite the fact that nobody else is using any of the equipment. He could be on the swings, slide or climbing frames, but instead, his shoulders are slumped, and his head bowed low. The only sign that he's even alive is his feet swinging where his legs aren't long enough to reach the ground.

I can't see his dad at first, but as I round the edge of the bushes, I see he is standing adjacent to the swings, the other side of the fence on the large sports field where local dog walkers train their pets. But he isn't alone. He appears to be talking to someone, but I can't quite see her face, just the edges of her billowing dress when the wind whips it from out of his shadow. Perhaps it's his wife, but it doesn't explain why neither seem to have noticed how sad and lonely their son is looking.

If I approach them from the opposite side of the field, there's no way Gail or Sally will be able to spot me from the preschool, so I can avoid them becoming involved. Hurrying as best I can along the line of bushes, I'm soon exhausted and have to take several moments to compose myself before rounding the edge and appearing on the far side of the field. I freeze when

I realise who Toby's dad is talking to.

What is Yolanda doing here?

I duck just behind the line of bushes so I can watch them through where the branches are thinner, so they won't see me. I'm not close enough to hear what they're saying, but I can see how animated she looks as her hands grip air and bounce as her arms wave. It's too difficult to see her facial expression, but my guess is she's either excited or angry. Toby's dad is just standing there, occasionally attempting to interrupt, and the breath catches in my throat when I see his arm move into the air, and for a second I'm convinced he's going to slap her, but he quickly lowers it, and I'm able to breathe again.

When I told Yolanda about the incident with Toby and his dad, she said that her partner Tyrese had done some work with Chris Orville a few years back, and that she'd thought the family had left the area. She asked me if it was okay if she told Tyrese they were back, and I'd only agreed as I figured she'd tell him anyway. So, I shouldn't be surprised to see them speaking if they know one another, but there's something off about the way they're engaging here. This exchange doesn't feel like that of people who have a mutual acquaintance. It's more intimate than that.

He's reaching for her arm now, trying to calm her down I think, but she brushes his attempt away, and turns to leave, but he reaches for her again, and this time he does place his hands on her arms and steers her back. She didn't say whether she knew Chris and his wife, but she didn't say she didn't either, but then I realise something else she said that stuck in my mind: *Looks a bit like Tom Cruise, only much taller?*

I hadn't picked up on the comment at the time, as it felt like an apt description of Toby's dad, but of all the comparisons she could have made, why did she choose one that I know she's attracted to? The day we met she told me how much she enjoyed his movies, and not just for the plots. I remember telling her that he was old enough to be my father, but this just made her cackle.

I can just about make out Toby still alone on the bench beyond the fence that Yolanda is leaning against for support. He isn't watching them, but I imagine he can hear every word. I want to go to him, to take him by the hand and tell him everything will be okay. I want to encourage him to use the play equipment and seek the joy that only a child can experience as they whizz down the slide or swing through the air, imagining they're flying. He looks like he's carrying the weight of the world on his shoulders, but I haven't got the energy to stalk back along the hedge line to get to him. If I cross the field, Chris and Yolanda will spot me, and probably halt their conversation, and I'll have to explain why I'm spying on them.

I gasp when I see Yolanda slap Chris hard across the cheek. He takes a step forwards, but doesn't retaliate. I immediately emerge from the bushes, and march as quickly as my bump will allow, which isn't fast. I want to go to my friend's aid, but Yolanda is already making her way around the perimeter of the fence and away from me. Neither of them has noticed me approaching, and Yolanda is soon out of sight. Chris looks forlorn, shocked by the slap and whatever conversation pre-empted it. There must be a fifty metre distance between us, but he has no interest in the pregnant woman crossing the field, and hops over the fence where he collects Toby from the bench and leads him out of the park. I'm in no position to catch up with them, and soon they are disappearing behind the edge of the foliage as well. By the time I make it to the playground, I'm panting, and once I've followed the fence back around to the main road, I'm already too late. There's no sign of Yolanda, and Chris's van is gone.

Is it possible Yolanda was confronting Chris about what I told her yesterday? I can imagine her wanting to stand up for me, but I don't understand how she would know he'd be here collecting Toby at this time. All I do know is that I want to check if she's okay, and so as I squash myself back in behind the wheel of my car, there's only one place I want to go: Yolanda's house.

Chapter 36

Louisa – One year ago

The door to Pete's office was now locked, the key safely back in the pot, and Louisa perched on the hard, upright armchair when her parents returned with Caleb. She'd spent the past half an hour thinking through the consequences of exposing Pete's lies. What if her parents still refused to believe her? What if they'd stomached enough of Pete's cool aid to be permanently scarred against her?

And then of course there was the question of how she would explain her discovery. She didn't want them to know that she had been regurgitating her medication for the last week, but hoped they'd just assume the effects had worn off as they hadn't given her the morning's dose. Hopefully they'd now realise that they'd been helping Pete keep her drugged and quiet.

Judith was the first into the room, and looked surprised when she saw Louisa in the chair. 'Oh good, you're up. I was going to fix some tea, would you like a cup?'

Louisa had planned to just bowl out with the truth, but tea would make the shock easier to stomach, so she remained quiet and nodded at her mum, who headed back out to the kitchen, while Caleb toddled into the room, carrying his favourite bunny toy, and a dummy squished between his lips.

Louisa's heart skipped a beat. Knowing now for certain that he wasn't hers made her think of her own child. Was he or she out there somewhere now? And what about Caleb's real parents? Did they know their boy was still alive? She couldn't begin to estimate the complications brought on by Pete's actions.

Caleb stopped and stared at her, a look of puzzlement in his innocent eyes. Did he know? Could he read her mind, or was it just instinctive?

'W-What've you got there?' she asked, the emotion straining her vocal chords.

Caleb pulled out his dummy and held the rabbit up by its ears. 'Bun-bun.'

'Can you come and give me a cuddle?' she asked, opening her arms wide.

Caleb toddled over and rested his head on her lap, allowing her to affectionately run her hands through his hair. She'd never blamed him for their lack of a bond. Despite the PND diagnosis, she'd put it down to the limited physical contact they'd been able to share whilst he'd been in the neo-natal unit, and she'd been recovering from the accident. None of this was his fault.

'I'll do everything in my power to find your real mummy,' she whispered into his ear. 'I promise.'

Caleb looked up at her, and passed her the scraggy bunny. Missing a button eye, the once soft material crackled as she squeezed it between her fingers. If ever a stuffed toy needed a spin in the washing machine and some TLC it was Bun-Bun, but Caleb was very protective of his toy, and had sobbed the last time the toy had been taken for cleaning.

'I think Bun-Bun needs a wash,' Louisa said, but Caleb shook his head, his face angry.

'No wash,' he said, snatching the bunny back and stomping off to the side of his play pen just as Judith returned to the room carrying a tray with two cups of tea, a plate of chocolate digestives, and the container of Louisa's pills.

'Mind there, Caleb, grandma is coming through with hot drinks,' Judith warned him, placing the tray on the table beside Louisa. Turning, she looked over to him. 'Do you want me to put you in your pen, my darling?'

'Um, actually, Mum, no,' Louisa interrupted. 'I was wondering if you and I could have a talk. I thought maybe Dad could take Caleb to the local playground?'

Judith considered her for a moment, her brow fraught with concern, but she nodded. 'Okay. I'll go and ask your dad.'

Taking Caleb's hand, she left the room once more, allowing Louisa to wipe her eyes with the back of her hand and take several breaths to compose herself. She'd hidden hers and Caleb's passports along with the savings book beneath the mattress on her bed. The pages she'd taken from Pete's drawers were stuffed beneath her leg, and as she extracted them now, they were warm to the touch.

The front door closed, and Judith returned eyeing Louisa suspiciously as she lowered herself into the second armchair. 'What's on your mind, sweetheart?'

Louisa looked up and into her mum's eyes as her own filled quickly again. 'I–I found something that I think you should see.'

Louisa began to pass the folded page, but Judith quickly stood. 'I wish you'd said I needed to read something. Hang on, let me find my glasses.'

Louisa kept hold of the page while Judith headed back out of the room, returning several minutes later, glasses case in her hand. 'Sorry about that. Now, what was it you wanted to show me?'

Louisa unfolded the page and held it up, as Judith fumbled with her glasses case and slid the frames onto her face. The case snapping shut startled them both.

'What is this? Where did you find it?'

'It was in Pete's office, but the letter was addressed to me. Do you realise what this means, Mum? I was right all along: Caleb isn't my son. Pete lied to me; to us all.'

The blood drained from Judith's face. 'How long have you had it?'

'I found it this morning; I wanted to show it to you straight away. I figured you'd know what to do. Should we go to the pol–?'

'No,' Judith spat. 'No police. This means nothing. Forget about it.'

Of all the reactions Louisa had anticipated, this wasn't one of them.

'Mum, no, you don't realise what this means: Caleb isn't my son; he isn't *your* grandson. Pete stole him from …. I don't even know where, but that doesn't matter right now. The envelope this came in didn't have an address or postage on it, which means it was handed to Pete. That means whoever sent it either gave it to him on the rare occasion he goes to the office, or brought it here. If they know where we live, we're not safe. What if they come and take Caleb back?'

Judith carefully folded the page, but made no effort to hand it back. Removing her glasses very carefully, she held them outside of their case, before slowly meeting Louisa's stare.

'You're to forget you ever saw this. Do you understand me?'

Louisa's brow furrowed. 'What? Mum, no, we need –'

'If Pete received this threat then he's dealing with it. There's nothing to worry about, and Caleb will be perfectly safe.'

'*Dealing with it*? Pete's paying thousands of pounds to some private investigator; do you think it's connected?'

'Is he? Good. Yes, that's a good decision: find out who sent the letter and eliminate the threat.'

Louisa could feel the howl building in her throat. Why couldn't her mum see the truth? How was she failing to miss the fact that they had somebody else's baby?

'You don't need to worry about anything,' Judith continued, a new calmness to her voice now. 'We will handle this situation. Don't let it bother you. Everything will be okay, and will get back to normal.'

Louisa sat forward and reached for her mum's hands, hoping to pry the page away from her; worried now that her one piece of evidence against Pete was not in her possession. 'Pete's broken God knows how many laws. We need to speak to the police. Caleb doesn't belong here.'

Judith snatched her hands away. 'Says who? He's loved and cherished here, and has everything he'll ever need or want. What does a silly bit of paper matter anyway?'

Louisa's mind slowly connected the dots, the blood in her veins cooling as realisation dawned. 'You knew all along.'

Judith stood and cut across the room, stopping at the window into the garden.

'Mum? Tell me you didn't know about any of this. Please?'

Judith remained resolute in her stance.

'Mum? Please?'

When Judith spoke, her shoulders were back, her head held high. 'What do you expect? My own flesh and blood was barely clinging to life in the hospital. The medical staff did all that they could to save your son, but the damage sustained during the accident was too great. My heart shattered into a million pieces. I couldn't stand the prospect of losing a child and grandchild on the same day. But then, we spoke to the doctor and he presented a solution if we could afford the price. I didn't blink when he told us the sum it would cost to take away all the pain, and give you hope for the future. I'd have paid double to see you recover, and for you not to hold yourself accountable for the death of your baby.'

Louisa couldn't move, frozen by the fear that her whole family had been conspiring against her for far longer than she'd ever realised. And despite knowing that there was a reason Louisa couldn't bond with Caleb, her mother had encouraged the PND diagnosis and regime of medication to keep her from discovering the truth.

'Y-You're a m-monster,' Louisa whispered, the words sticking to her gums.

Judith spun around and looked her in the eye. 'No, I'm a mother. Don't you realise there isn't anything I wouldn't do to keep you safe, Lou-Lou.'

'He isn't ours to keep, Mum.'

'Why not? I have loved that boy since the first moment I laid eyes on him. He *is* my grandson. He is *your* son too, Louisa. If you'd just allow yourself to try and love him, you'd realise that it doesn't matter that different blood flows through our veins. There hasn't been a single day when I've regretted the decision I made, and I would do it again in a heartbeat.

There was no point in arguing with her any longer, but that didn't mean Louisa would give up on getting her and Caleb free; he was as much a prisoner in the old manor as she was.

'Does Dad know too?'

Judith mused on the question. 'Your father is aware that there were complications at the hospital, and that we spent a considerable sum. I don't want you to discuss this with him, and I will give you a good reason why. Your dad's health is … we went to the hospital this morning, and he has coronary issues. They are going to try and treat it with blood thinners, however, what he doesn't need is any undue stress. Do you hear me? If you start talking freely about any of this, you will drive him into an early grave. I don't think you need any more blood on your hands, do you, Louisa?'

It was a cruel blow, and undeserved, but Louisa

couldn't answer the hard stare now being fired her way.

'I need you to promise me that you won't tell your father, Louisa.'

Louisa ground her teeth together, angry that she'd been left out of the loop about her dad's ill health, and now having it used as a threat against her exposing the house of lies.

'Promise me, Louisa.'

'I don't want to upset, Dad.'

'Good,' Judith said breezily. 'Now be a good girl and take your pills, and we'll say no more about it.'

Chapter 37

Abbie – Now

I'm physically shaking as I near Yolanda's three storey townhouse, still picturing the moment she slapped Toby's dad. Although I was some distance away, I heard the clap as skin collided, and saw the venom in the ferocity of the action. I don't understand what could have driven my friend to have acted so rashly, but regardless, I want to be there for her.

I take several deep breaths to steady my trembling, before ringing the doorbell. I'm just trying to rehearse what I'm going to say in my head when the door is thrust open, and I see Yolanda's crazed glare staring back at me. Her eyes are wide and filled with anguish, but it's the way she's gripping the glass decanter – as if she intends to throw it at me – that causes my sharp intake of breath.

Half-ducking I stretch out a hand towards her. 'Yolanda? Is everything okay?'

She doesn't answer, still glaring, but it's like she's in a trance and can't even see me standing on the doorstep. Perhaps she's picturing Toby's dad.

'Yolanda?' I try again, louder this time, hoping to snap her out of it. 'Yolanda?'

She blinks several times, and finally sees me, lowering the decanter, and wrapping a second hand around it so the glass doesn't slip.

'Abbie, what are you doing here?'

I want to tell her what I witnessed at the park and that I've come to check she's okay, but I don't want her to think I'm prying. She's been a lifeline to me during this pregnancy, reassuring me about the twinges and aches that I'm always so uncertain about, and she deserves my support.

'I was just passing,' I say, stepping forwards, 'and thought I'd stop and see if you fancied a cuppa.'

She's still not fully responsive, and so I gently place my hands on her forearms and steer her back into the house. She doesn't resist. Closing the door behind me, I continue to escort her into the kitchen, and lean her against the countertop. Filling the kettle from the tap, I locate mugs and teabags.

'Should I take that?' I ask, prising the decanter from her grasp. She withstands my efforts at first, but eventually collaborates and allows me to place the heavy glass on the counter. I assume the honey-coloured liquid inside is whisky, but I can't see any glasses, so maybe she hadn't got around to pouring a drink.

'I–I had a bit of a shock,' she says, looking at the decanter. 'Some bad news.'

I'm not judging her. If anything it just echoes the gravity of what I witnessed in the park.

'I'm sorry to hear that,' I say, hoping for an in. 'Do you want to talk about it?'

Her lips part before she thinks better of it and closes her mouth, shaking her head in the process.

'Not bad news about the baby, I hope?' I try again.

She shakes her head again.

'It's not about Tyrese?'

This time a frown, followed by a slower shake of the head. Whatever is going on with Toby's dad Chris, she doesn't want to talk about it; at least not with me.

'Well, strong, sweet tea is good for shock,' I say, switching her tea bag for a caffeinated version, and then reaching for the sugar bowl. 'Is it something to do with work?'

She looks confused, until realising I'm still fishing for information about her shock news. 'No, not work … Look, do you mind if we talk about something else? I could do with taking my mind off it.'

She crosses the room to the sink and fills a glass from the draining board with water and takes a long drink. Once again, everything in Yolanda's kitchen is so well-organised. If this was my kitchen, she'd find plates from last night's dinner and this morning's breakfast stacked beside the sink, with yesterday's washing-up still on the drainer. Even the trainers that had so neatly lined the hallway when I was here yesterday have been put away.

She spins and snaps her fingers, the doubt and anxiety quickly dissipating from her face. 'Tell me, is there any news about your stalker? Has Kinga tried to contact you again?'

There's a part of me that doesn't want to tell her as she's so unwilling to share her own secret, but who else can I talk to about it? At least Yolanda will hear me out before offering her opinion.

'She took Mark and me to a storage depot last night and showed us newspaper clippings and articles downloaded from the internet about her conspiracy. She claimed that the private hospital we both delivered in has been stealing and selling people's babies all over the country. She reckoned they set up in a new town, operate for a couple of years before declaring bankruptcy and starting again under a new name in a town where none of the rumours have surfaced.'

Yolanda pouts with intrigue as the kettle reaches its crescendo, and she takes over making the drinks, handing me the mug with the decaf tea bag, though I now wish I'd swapped mine too. The stress of the day is taking its toll and I feel a nap coming on.

'Do you believe her?' Yolanda asks.

'There was certainly enough paperwork to suggest there's more going on than anyone else realises, but she also claimed to have a source who'd supplied her with most of the detail.'

'A source?'

'That's how she described her. Maybe someone inside the operation? I'm not sure.'

'Have you told the police?'

I nod. 'Mark and I spoke to PS Brearton a few hours ago, and he shared details from Kinga's past with us. Quite the chequered history, but in keeping with what she told us at the restaurant when we first met. Mark wants the police to arrest and prosecute her. Brearton is going to discuss it with his colleagues and is hoping to set up some sort of sting operation.'

'And how do *you* feel about that?'

I shrug.

'It's just ... yesterday you seemed so convinced that she was telling the truth, but now you don't seem so sure.'

I take a sip of tea and let out the sigh that's been building since I left the police station. 'To be honest, I don't know what to believe. One minute I'm certain Kinga's telling the truth, and the next I'm convinced that Mark is right and I'm being conned. I'm sure my pregnancy hormones aren't helping, but I've never felt so indecisive about anything in all my life.'

She tilts her head in a show of empathy. 'Mark only wants what's best for you. We all do.'

'I know, but to make matters worse, when I got to work today, Gail and Sally ambushed me, and told me they want me to start my maternity leave early. As in now. They sent me home, like I have no choice in the matter.'

Yolanda crosses her arms. 'They can't do that; not legally anyway.'

'That's what I thought, but I think they're worried that if I stumbled again, I'd try and sue and then the preschool would go under. Frustratingly, if I was in their shoes I'd probably make the same decision, but that doesn't make it any easier to swallow. You know?'

'Well they're overseen by the local council, right? You could contact the council and complain. Force them to let you come back.'

The thought of confronting Gail and Sally in that way fills me with dread, but maybe I should kick up more of a fuss.

'But do you really want to go back?' Yolanda continues. 'Believe me, if I could afford to stop working now I would. It's hard enough running after two boys while in this state, but juggling work as well, and then there's Tyrese too; he's like my third son at times.'

It's a fair point, and I'm sure Mark would concur. It totally slipped my mind when I saw him at the police station, and he didn't seem to realise that I was able to get to him when I should have been working.

Yolanda picks up both mugs and carries them through to the living room. For once her laptop isn't open and on the table, and the usual pile of papers is nowhere in sight. If I didn't know better, I'd say she hasn't been working today anyway. I sit in the hard backed chair, and it's a relief to take the pressure off my swollen ankles. The midwife has assured me that they'll return to a more elegant curve once the baby has arrived, but right now they resemble small tree trunks.

'I can help you find a number if you want?' Yolanda offers, reaching for her phone, and then scowling at the display.

'Thanks, I appreciate the offer, but I don't think I have the energy for a fight right now. Besides, they've already appointed my replacement.'

Yolanda's mouth drops.

'Her name is Claudette, and she's newly qualified, so they wouldn't have space for me if I returned now anyway.' I pause, as a thought stirs in my mind. 'It's the children I feel sorriest for. Some of them need more attention than the others, and I had to work hard to build up the level of confidence required for them to trust me.' I deliberately pause again. 'Take Toby Orville for instance ...'

Yolanda's shoulders tense at mention of the name, and she involuntarily glances at her phone again.

'I know there's something eating away at him, and I was getting closer to figuring it out. I hadn't even mentioned my concerns to Gail and Sally, so Claudette will have no clue what's going on with him, or realise he's struggling.'

Her eyes are back on the phone, and I am now thinking that maybe Chris has been trying to contact her since the slap.

'I was thinking about trying to speak to Toby's parents away from the preschool. Maybe pay them a visit at home. I don't suppose you happen to know where they're living do –'

'No,' she snaps, cutting me off. 'I mean I didn't even know they were back until you mentioned it yesterday, so how could I know where they are?'

Hearing the deceit in her voice is hurtful, but I don't flutter an eyelid.

'Did you mention their return to Tyrese yet? I wonder if he might be able to find out where they're living.'

'What? Um, no … I mean I didn't mention it to him. Listen, I'm sorry, but I'm going to need to get back to work. Sorry, can we continue our catch up at another time? Maybe tomorrow we could meet for a tea in town.'

I know there's something she's holding back, and no amount of gentle cajoling is going to be enough to get it out of her. I came here to check that she was okay, and overall I'd say she's calmer now than when I arrived, so at least my visit has paid off in that respect. Whatever was going on with Chris is obviously something she's not willing to share yet.

Taking a final slurp of tea, I stand and follow her to the door. Before I leave, I hug her and thank her for listening to my problems, and remind her that I'm only a phone call away if she ever needs a shoulder to cry on. She remains mute, and I stay in my car for a while, trying to figure out if I could have asked her anything else about what happened, but in the end, it's not really any of my business. Driving home, I'm not ready when I see the police car parked in my space on the driveway.

Chapter 38

Louisa – One year ago

In the days since Louisa had discovered the threat in Pete's office, Judith hadn't let her daughter out of her sight. With Pete still away on his business trip, Louisa had hoped the pressure of taking care of Caleb would have distracted her mum long enough for her to grab five minutes with her dad alone. Despite the warning about his poor health, Louisa was in need of an ally, and she was certain her dad wouldn't be happy knowing he'd been lied to for as long as Louisa had.

But every time it seemed like an opportunity would present itself, Judith would seem to develop a sudden headache and require her husband to run an errand: collecting Caleb from the childminder; popping to town for a missing ingredient; or collecting a prescription from the chemist.

Louisa tried to keep her disappointment hidden from sight, taking her pills on command, and only regurgitating them when she was certain her mother was out of earshot. The passports and savings book remained hidden beneath the mattress, and Louisa had made a point of checking them twice a day to be certain.

Now all she needed was an ally who wouldn't think twice about taking her and Caleb into town so she could slip away.

Hearing the shower start upstairs, Louisa decided to make her first play. Heading into the kitchen, she discovered her father with his hands in a bowlful of bubbles, cleaning the breakfast crockery, belting out a Bryan Adams' song at the top of his voice in time to the radio.

He started when he heard her apply the brake to the wheels. 'Oh, it's you sweetheart. You almost gave me a heart attack,' he grinned at the exaggeration. 'Sorry was my singing disturbing you?'

She smiled back, despite the anxiety playing havoc with her gut. The shower could end at any second, so there wasn't time to expose the lie here, plus she didn't want to induce an actual heart attack. Whilst it wouldn't have surprised Louisa to learn that her mother had made far more of his condition to guilt trip her into silence, she couldn't chance it.

'I was thinking you and me could take Caleb to the playground. It's been forever since you and I had some time away together, and it isn't supposed to rain until after lunch.'

He glanced subconsciously towards the staircase, maybe equally concerned at how Judith might react to the suggestion.

'We could wait until your mum is dressed and then all go together if you fancy?'

'No, Dad. I thought it would be nice if it was just the three of us ... It would give Mum a deserved rest too. She does so much for Caleb and me, and she never gets any time to herself.'

He didn't disagree, and Louisa didn't add that she

had no say in her mum's determination to not allow her to help more.

David extracted his soap-covered hands from the washing-up bowl, and dried them on the towel hanging from the radiator. 'Very well then. Can you collect Caleb from his pen while I fetch my shoes?'

The shower continued to echo against the ceiling as Louisa moved swiftly to the pen and helped Caleb to climb out. 'We're going to the park with Grandad,' she told him as he gave her a puzzled look. 'Would you like that? Grandad can push you on the swings.'

His face lit up, and he handed her his bunny. 'Yes, Bun-Bun can come too,' she promised, lifting him onto her lap, and steering them back towards the front door, as her dad came down the stairs.

'I went up to tell your mum where we're going, but she's still in the shower,' he said.

Louisa helped Caleb into his anorak, conscious that the shower could stop and they'd be caught red-handed. Her dad had just opened the front door when Judith appeared on the landing.

'Um, where are you three going?'

'I thought I'd walk them to the playground,' David announced apologetically.

'Give me five minutes and I'll come with you.'

'No, no, you stay and rest. There's a fresh cup of tea in the kitchen for you. We won't be long.'

Judith opened her mouth to argue, but didn't speak, instead firing a glare of warning at her daughter.

Louisa looked away, trying to disguise her fear as David moved to the back of the chair and pushed them out of the house. It was much cooler outside than

Louisa had anticipated, but the stiff breeze on her cheeks for the first time in months was almost as exciting as picturing her mum's anxiety at what might be discussed on the short trip to the playground. The narrow road leading to the village was lined with sodden, brown leaves as the early stages of autumn took hold.

'This reminds me of when I used to take you to the local park,' David mused quietly behind the chair. 'You used to go mad for the roundabout. All the other children would be clamouring for the slide or the swings, but not you. You'd lie down on your back and beg me to spin you as fast as I could. You'd squeal with delight as the clouds span round and round before your eyes until you'd be so dizzy you couldn't walk in a straight line. Do you remember?'

She had a vague recollection of holding her dad's warm hand as they'd walk along this lane, the promise of fun not far away.

'Whereas this young man is definitely a fan of the swings,' her dad continued. 'Of course all the equipment has been replaced since you were a child. The whole place is surrounded by what looks like gym equipment, though most of the kids seem to use it as climbing frames.'

The playground was far busier than either had anticipated when they arrived, but rather than rushing towards the swings, Caleb hopped from Louisa's lap and planted himself at the edge of the sandpit, examining each trowel and bucket before selecting the two that he would play with. David parked his daughter beside a bench, and perched next to her.

She'd pictured this moment a dozen times, what she would say, how she'd broach the subject about Caleb's true origin. Yet now that they were together, and alone, she couldn't remember the script. With the written threat in her mum's possession, it was a case of her word against Judith's, and she was pretty sure which side he'd choose in such a battle.

'I'm glad you suggested we come together,' David said, while she was composing her thoughts. 'There's something I've been meaning to tell you, but I just haven't found the right time.' He paused, staring out at the horizon, beyond the thicket of evergreen trees that enclosed the area. 'The doctors are worried about my heart.'

He quickly took her hand, his tone consoling. 'It's nothing that you need to worry about. They've been running some tests and they're concerned about one of my pipes. All those bad cheeses I've spent my life devouring no doubt. There's no reason to assume that you need to start writing my eulogy just yet, but I thought you should know that I might have one or two more appointments at the hospital whilst they determine the best course of action.'

So Judith's statement hadn't been a cruel way to emotionally blackmail her into silence? In many ways it was a relief to learn Judith hadn't stooped so low, and yet that also meant the reality was that her dad's heart couldn't necessarily stand the strain of a sudden shock.

'I know it can't be easy to hear,' he continued, 'so if you want to ask me any questions, I'll be as honest with you as I can. I don't have all the answers yet, but

I'm being looked after by the best in the business, so if they can't help me, then I'm beyond redemption.'

Louisa wanted to offer her sympathy, but the lump in her throat was blocking back any speech. Instead, she looked away and wiped her eyes.

David put his arm around her shoulders. 'I'm sorry, I didn't mean to upset you; I don't want to ruin our little trip out together, I don't know about you, but just being here is bringing memories flooding back. I remember one time when you must have been about six. You'd climbed to the top of the slide – which was much bigger than the one that's here now – but when you reached the top you were too scared to slide down it. You couldn't climb back down the ladder as there was a queue of other children behind you. I tried to encourage you to slide down, and that everything would be okay, but you outright refused. In the end, I had to climb up the slide and carry you down.'

She pressed her head into his shoulder, not certain she did recall such an event.

'You wouldn't stop crying until I promised to buy you a 99 with a flake in it. So what do you say – for old time's sake – I go and buy us a couple of ice creams from that van over there? I'm pretty sure Caleb won't say no, even if it is still early.'

He didn't wait for her answer, standing, and stretching before crossing the playground in the direction of the stationary ice cream van. Caleb flicked sand as he filled and emptied the bucket on a loop. Louisa extracted her phone and unlocked it, snapping a picture of him: a good profile shot showing his face and dark hair, wondering whether his real mum would see something in his face to realise he was hers.

The phone vibrated in her hands as an email arrived in her inbox. Opening the app, she almost dropped the phone when she read the words from an unknown sender:

I WILL EXPOSE ALL OF YOUR LIES.

CALEB ISN'T YOURS.

COME CLEAN BEFORE IT'S TOO LATE.

Her dad had just made it to the ice cream van when she looked up. It was too big a risk to tell him, and yet if the sender knew her email address as well as their personal address, didn't that mean they were all in danger? Whether she'd been an unwitting party to it all, the messages were targeting her specifically. For all she knew the sender could be sitting in this very park watching.

Her dad was now crossing the playground carrying three ice creams. She had to tell him, but at least now she had the evidence to back up her claim.

'Here you go,' he said handing her one of the cones, and calling Caleb to collect his. 'Are you alright, Lou-Lou? You look like you've seen a ghost.'

Swallowing hard, she kept the ice cream in her left hand, yet to take a lick. 'I have to show you something,' she said quietly. 'I need you to sit down, and to remain calm.'

His eyes seemed to sink back into his skull as confusion took hold. 'What is it?'

She waited until he was seated before handing him the phone.

'What's this supposed to be?'

'Just read it, Dad.'

'Read what? Your empty inbox?'

She snatched the phone back. 'What? It was here just a ...'

She checked the trash folder in case one of them had accidentally deleted the message, but the folder was empty. She flicked to check all messages, but it wasn't there.

'But I saw ...'

A thought chilled her like a shadow crossing her soul: somebody with access to her email account had to have deleted the message and wiped all traces of it. Her first thought was Judith, but her mum had never been particularly technology competent. Which only left ... Pete.

'What's going on, Lou-Lou? What is it you wanted me to read?'

How many other messages had Pete been keeping from her for all these years? How many times had he deleted messages from old friends reaching out and offering support? As she quickly covered her tracks, and told her dad that she'd made a mistake, a plan was formulating in her head: a plan to escape once and for all.

Chapter 39

Abbie – Now

Instinct takes over in this situation; that and paranoia. What are the police doing at my house? Is it Mark? Has there been an accident, and they're here to break the news? He was angry when I last spoke to him at the police station, but does that mean he was distracted when he was returning to work? Come to think of it, he hasn't messaged me all day, but it didn't even cross my mind that an absence of communication could spell trouble. The fact that Mark's car isn't parked in his usual space only adds to my alarm.

What if the police being here has something to do with Kinga? When she approached me in the park near preschool yesterday, I feared that she might have been following me, and if that was the case then maybe she knows where we live. What if she came here with the intention of hurting me or Mark? There's no sign of an officer inside the patrol car, which means they must already be inside the house. But how can they be if Mark isn't here? Unless there was a break-in that one of our nosey neighbours reported. Did Kinga come here to try and claim her twenty grand reward early?

I'm sweating and panting as I hurry to the door, but when I insert my key, it catches something, and won't engage the lock. I jiggle it, and attempt to depress the handle but there's no give. What is going on?

Let me in to my house! I need to know what's happened to Mark! I can't do this without him. Our daughter needs a father.

I hammer against the door, until I hear a clicking inside, and the handle lowers as the door opens a crack. I gasp as I see Mark standing inside, and instantly throw my arms around him.

'Whoa there, Abbie, what's going on? You look like you've seen a ghost.'

I can't answer him as my eyes fill, and my head drops into his chest, and I dampen his shirt with my tears of fear, happiness and frustration. He doesn't speak, instead rubbing his palms across my shoulders and back. It feels so good having his warm touch on my body, and it reminds me of what I feared I came so close to losing. I feel his cheek press against the top of my head, and then he kisses my hair.

'Everything's going to be okay,' he whispers, and it's the reassurance that I needed.

Looking back at the front door as he closes it now, I see his keys poking out of the lock on this side, which is why my keys wouldn't operate the lock. It seems so obvious that this is the reason why I couldn't get in.

'Your car …?' I begin to say, but my breathing has yet to return to a steady level.

'Brearton's here,' Mark says, prising me away from him. 'He was already parked in your space when I got back, so I parked around the corner so you'd be able to use my space; I didn't want you having to walk further than necessary.'

It still all feels like an intense nightmare that I'm yet

to fully wake from. Part of me believes that if I just lie down and close my eyes I'll wake in my maternity nightgown in bed.

'He has an update about Kinga,' Mark adds. 'We should go through so he can tell us together.'

I don't argue, and allow him to lead me through to the living room, which feels more cramped than usual with Brearton on one of the couches and another uniformed officer with her back to us, lurking by the curtains.

'Mrs Friar,' Brearton says, standing and nodding in my direction, retaking his seat when I'm perched beside Mark. 'Is everything okay? Forgive me for saying, but you … you look peaky. Would you like me to fetch you a glass of water?'

Mark studies my face again, and scrapes my sweaty fringe away from my forehead. 'Is it …? Are you in labour?'

I try to steady my breathing, and slowly shake my head. 'Just a bit of a shock seeing a police car in the driveway. I guess my imagination got the better of me.'

I try to smile to reassure them both, but I guess the blood hasn't returned to my face yet. I should really excuse myself and go to the bathroom to freshen up, but my curiosity keeps me pinned where I am.

Mark stands and disappears out of the door, returning a moment later with a dripping glass of water, which he hands to me, and waits until I've taken a few sips before returning his gaze to Brearton.

'Sorry, do either you or your colleague want a drink?'

Brearton waves his hand with an appreciative

glance at me. 'No, we don't want to keep you any longer than is necessary. Are you sure you're okay, Mrs Friar?'

I take another sip of the water, and will my pulse to settle as the adrenalin continues to spike every nerve ending. 'I'm fine.'

Brearton claps his hands together as if calling an imaginary court to order. 'Okay, well, as I explained to you, Mr Friar, after you left the station earlier, I spoke to the head of the fraud team about your situation, and under his advice we entered Apex Self Storage and carried out a search for Kinga Mutsuraeva.'

He pauses, and my head snaps around to Mark to see if he's as shocked by this statement as I am, but his face remains passive.

'Um, how did you know about Apex Self Storage?' I ask looking back at Brearton just as he's about to speak again. 'We never told you the address of where we met her ...' my words trail off as Brearton looks at Mark, and I feel my husband's shoulders sag.

'I gave it to them,' Mark says under his breath. 'I was worried that she might come after you again, and as that was the last place we saw her, I hoped they might be able to find or follow her from there. I'm surprised you managed to get a search warrant so quickly.'

Brearton smiles at this. 'It helps to be on first name terms with the local magistracy. Ultimately, it was a waste of time: she wasn't there. We went to the storage locker that you indicated, Mr Friar, but it was empty. No lock on the door, and inside no sign of the bed, boxes, or paperwork that you observed.'

'Wait, what? No,' I stammer. 'What do you mean she wasn't there? It was pretty clear last night that she'd been sleeping there for some time.'

'Or she wanted you to believe that she'd been sleeping there for some time. With all due respect, Mrs Friar, this is precisely what these confidence tricksters do. They're professional in their approach. Think of them as magicians creating an illusion. For the con to be successful they need to convince you beyond all reasonable doubt that what they're presenting is fact. Meantime, they're using sleight of hand to pull off the trick. Tell me: seeing the newspaper cuttings and printed documents, did that convince you more or less about the story she was presenting?'

I picture the files of stories similar to our own, and the level of detail tracked.

'And when you saw that she had been sleeping on an airbed in that confined space, did that make you question her motives for helping you, or only intensify your desire to help *her*?'

I bite down as I remember considering inviting her back here for a wash and good night's sleep.

'You shouldn't feel bad, Mrs Friar. They can be very convincing, and they play on their victims' emotions to obtain what they want. You're not the first to be duped, and I'm sure you won't be the last. It wouldn't surprise me if she hadn't set up that scenario for you yesterday. Often these people work in groups, and Mutsuraeva will just be one part of the chain. The reams of research you witnessed were probably forged by another member of the team. And as for who targeted the two of you as a couple ...' he shrugs empathetically. 'Given you're a financial trader, Mr Friar that could have been their motivation: assuming you'd be able to lay your hands on funds at a quick pace. I don't know, I'm hypothesising here.'

I can hear what he's saying, but it doesn't reconcile in my head. Kinga gave no reason for me to doubt her situation with the Albanians, and how she too had suffered as we had, but was that all part of her plan to reel me in? If Mark was the ultimate target was I used as bait to hook him too? I feel physically sick.

'So you haven't arrested her yet?' Mark asks, and I can hear the anxiety in his tone.

'I'm afraid not, but I want you to rest assured that her name and description have been shared with our patrols and if she is spotted, we will act.'

'What about protection? What if she realises you're on to her and comes looking for revenge. Given Abbie's condition, I …'

'Nobody takes your fears for granted, Mr Friar, least of all me. If we could provide you with personal protection we would, but at present there is no immediate threat to life.'

'How can you say that?' Mark snaps. 'She's already come after Abbie twice.'

Brearton grimaces. 'Forgive me, what I meant was: Mutsuraeva doesn't have a history of violence, and she hasn't threatened either of you to date; not from what you've said. Criminals like this are only there for the score; as soon as the window shuts, they scarper. There's a strong possibility you'll never hear from her or them again, however, if you do, you have my number, and I will come immediately and intercept.

And failing that, you can call 999 and quote the case number I gave you.'

Kinga was so adamant that we shouldn't involve the police, and that she would bolt if she felt their presence nearby. What if she's now taken off with the truth about Josh because we didn't follow her rules?

'What if you're wrong?' I ask quietly, before repeating the question. 'Have you stopped to consider the prospect that she could be telling the truth? She said she was worried that the Albanians were watching her? What if that's the reason she's taken off? It could be *her* life that's in danger.'

Brearton and Mark exchange knowing glances that show me they're not going to humour me anymore. But it's Mark who breaks the news.

Adjusting his position, I feel his knees knock against mine, and then he clasps my hands in his. 'Abbie, Josh is dead. We saw his body at the hospital, and we had his body cremated. I know how much you want to believe that he's still out there, but my love, continuing to hope and dream is not helping. You need to let go now, and focus on our imminent arrival. Please? I love you so much, and it kills me that you can't see how much you're hurting yourself by clinging on to this hope. I'd hoped that when you heard what PS Brearton said about her criminal past that you'd see this woman for who she really is.'

My eyes fill with tears again, because I can see the pain etched across his face.

'We should go,' Brearton says, standing, and indicating for his colleague to follow. 'I'm sorry it wasn't better news, and please do call if Mutsuraeva attempts any kind of contact again. And best of luck with your delivery. We thought my daughter had gone into labour last night, but it turned out to be Braxton Hicks. Have you had those yet?'

I shake my head, and a tear rolls down my cheek.

He half-smiles, half-grimaces with empathy. 'We'll show ourselves out.'

When they're gone, I'm too exhausted to cook, so Mark orders takeout, but I don't really have much of an appetite, and pick at the Szechuan chicken. I feel like I haven't rested all day, and now my daughter is punishing me for it. I tell Mark about the enforced maternity leave, and he reveals he's pleased that I'll be taking more of a rest in the run up to the due date. He massages my swollen feet and ankles, and it's only when he wakes me that I realise I've fallen asleep on the couch. He helps me up to bed while he heads downstairs to check through his work emails. I cry myself to sleep with the realisation that I'll never get to set eyes on my boy again.

Chapter 40

Louisa – Six months ago

'I can handle it, Mum,' Louisa repeated, as abstractedly as the giddy excitement in her gut would allow.

She turned a page of the magazine on the breakfast bar before her, not that she was reading it, but it gave her an excuse not to meet Judith's stare.

'I'm not sure …' Judith mused, absent-mindedly chewing on one of her nails.

Louisa lifted a spoonful of cereal out of her bowl and placed it in her mouth, chewing as she spoke, 'It's only for a couple of hours. You can give me my meds when you get back. Come on, you deserve a few hours to yourself with everything that's been going on with dad, and Caleb's troubles at school. Let me help you.'

'Don't speak with your mouth full,' Judith nipped with irritation.

Louisa tried not to smile at the deliberate attempt to irk her mother. Caleb's inability to settle at Lamington was taboo in the house, as was the fact that he hadn't returned to school since the holidays.

'Dad has his appointment at the hospital, but he'll be back by lunchtime. Your hair appointment isn't until 10:30, so really it's barely two hours of me looking after Caleb on my own. What could go wrong in that time? He'll probably spend the entire time reading one of his books or drawing a picture. I can cope.'

Judith still hadn't bought the line.

Six months of planning; six months of playing the dutiful daughter and wife; six months of doing as she was told; and six months of taking her medication without complaint; six months of secretly withdrawing savings from the building society whenever she was taken into town shopping. All leading up to this moment. Louisa had worked hard for this, but still required Judith's agreement.

What if something went wrong? What if they figured out her plan? What if all her effort had been wasted?

No, you've put too much effort into this, Louisa silently reminded herself, taking deep breaths to alleviate the tension in her shoulders.

'Please, Mum, you're going to have to learn to trust me at some point.'

'Give her a chance,' David spoke up, winking at his daughter as he lowered his dish into the washing-up bowl.

'Fine,' Judith huffed, shaking her head to concede the battle. 'And Lou-Lou, I do trust you.'

David smiled at this, even if neither woman believed the statement.

Louisa continued to eat her bowl of corn flakes, feigning interest in the magazine while her parents hurried around her, washing and dressing ahead of their different appointments. Louisa took control of Caleb, dressing him in waterproof trousers, a t-shirt, and fleece top, asking him if he wanted to go to the playground with her.

'Will there be ice cream?' he asked excitedly.

Louisa doubted there would be an ice cream van at the playground in the middle of March, but nodded excitedly. Then, as her dad was preparing to leave the house, Louisa came forward.

'Caleb wants me to take him to the playground. Is that okay?'

'Of course it is,' her father replied, without thinking.

'Is this true?' Judith asked Caleb, who was hovering beside Louisa's chair.

He shrugged with indifference.

'How about I take you when I'm back from the salon?'

'No, want Mummy to take me now.' He screwed his face into a scowl on cue, and Louisa could have high-fived him for the performance.

'Very well, but Louisa I want you to take your phone with you. If you have any difficulty, you're to phone me or Pete immediately. Agreed?'

Louisa lifted the phone from her lap and used it to salute the command.

'And you'd both better wear jackets in case it rains.'

David lifted their coats down from the coat hooks, before kissing Judith goodbye and heading out of the door.

Louisa helped Caleb into his coat, and then pulled on her own.

'Don't let me down,' Judith warned, as she kissed her daughter's cheek, and then held the front door open for them to leave.

The thick blanket of grey cloud indicated rain could fall at any minute, and Louisa willed the rain to stay away until they'd at least made it off the driveway and into the little lane. Part one of the plan had passed, but that didn't mean Judith couldn't swing her wrecking ball at the rest of it.

Caleb walked silently beside her as they entered the lane, once more lost in his own world, oblivious to the adventure she was about to take him on. The passports and wad of cash were hidden beneath the cushion on the seat, and had either of her parents demanded a search before they'd left, she'd have had no answer to their accusations.

Louisa stopped, reaching for Caleb, and pulling him close, a finger to her lips. She was certain she'd heard footsteps approaching from behind, but now there was only the howl of the wind in the branches lining the lane. Glancing over her shoulder, she couldn't escape the feeling that she was being watched, but there was nobody else in sight.

Checking her watch, she started moving onwards again, and as they reached the entrance to the playground, she was relieved to see the tail lights of the waiting Uber. Tapping on the window with her knuckle, she indicated she'd need the driver's help collapsing and putting the wheelchair in the boot. He climbed out and held the chair while she lifted herself into the back seat, grabbing the wallet of cash and passports as she did. Strapping Caleb into the seat, it broke her heart to see the disappointment in his eyes.

'I thought we were going to the park?'

'Not today, Caleb. I wanted it to be a surprise, but today we're going to go on an aeroplane. You've never been on one, have you?'

The disappointment remained. 'But what about the ice cream?'

'I promise I'll buy you an ice cream when we get to the airport. You can choose whatever one you want.'

With the wheelchair safely stored in the boot, the driver returned to his seat. 'Manchester Terminal 1 is it?'

Louisa nodded, her breathing unsteady as she waited for something to stir her from the dream.

***

The taxi journey passed without incident. Caleb kept asking where they were going on the plane, and all Louisa would tell him was it was a surprise. She'd been relieved the taxi driver hadn't asked where her luggage was, and presumably had assumed she was going to meet someone at Arrivals. It was a crazy move to snatch Caleb like this without packing clothes, but she couldn't risk either Pete or her parents becoming suspicious. Her plan from hereon in was simple: buy tickets, fly, and head to the British embassy when they reached their destination.

What she'd yet to decide was where they'd fly to. And that depended on availability and cost as much as it did location. The funds withdrawn from her savings would likely be enough for two single tickets, but the funds wouldn't last indefinitely, and she'd yet to truly consider how easy it would be to find a hotel and apparel once they got there.

Releasing the brake on her wheels, she invited Caleb to clamber onto her lap, and moved them through the automated doors, and towards the Departures board, skim-reading the options.

'I want an ice cream,' Caleb whispered into her ear.

'In a minute, sweetie. Let me just figure out where we're going and I'll get you one.'

'When's Daddy getting here?'

'Daddy's not coming with us, sweetie.'

'What about Grandma and Grandpa?'

'No, they're not coming either. It's just you and me. Is that okay?'

He shrugged.

Louisa studied the screen. She ruled out flights to London, Belfast and Glasgow as too close to home, while Malta, Budapest, and Abu Dhabi were too far. But any of Amsterdam, Paris, or Brussels would work. As large European cities, they were all bound to have embassies or consulates she could contact on arrival.

Her mum's name appearing on the screen of her phone wasn't what she'd expected. Deciding it was better to avoid an awkward conversation than giveaway any hint of what she was doing, Louisa ignored the call, and carried Caleb to the WH Smith and allowed him to choose an ice cream.

'I wanted a 99,' he moaned, and despite Louisa's efforts to convince him to go for a Cornetto, he outright refused. It was only when she threatened to leave the shop without buying him anything that he relented and opted for a tropical lolly. Paying for the treat, she loaded him back onto her lap and headed for the ticketing booth.

There were only five people in the queue ahead of her, but the wait was unbearable. She listened to the voicemail her mum had left.

'Lou-Lou, it's Mum. I spoke to the salon and they said they can fit you in for a wash and trim immediately after me, so I thought we could go together and take it in turns to watch Caleb. Can you call me back so I know you've heard this? I'll come to meet you at the playground now.'

Louisa deleted the message. Even if her mum made it to the playground, there was no reason to suspect that she'd figure out they'd come to the airport, and even if she did, hopefully it would be too late to stop them.

The queue finally moved forwards. The woman behind the counter wearing a turquoise jacket and matching neck scarf smiled at the two of them and asked for their tickets or reservation number.

'I haven't booked anything yet. Apologies, this is all a bit last minute. I want two single tickets to Paris on the next available flight.'

'Okay,' the woman replied breezily, 'I'll just check what's available.'

Louisa slid their passports onto the counter, her phone ringing again, but she cancelled the call. Judith must have made it to the playground and discovered Louisa wasn't there.

'Right,' the woman behind the counter said, drawing out the vowel, 'Today's flight to Paris is fully booked I'm afraid. I can get you tickets on tomorrow's flight which leaves at 10:50, if that helps?'

Louisa ground her teeth. 'How about to Brussels

today?'

The woman behind the counter frowned with confusion. 'I can check Brussels instead for you, but I don't think you'll be able to get a connecting flight from Brussels to Paris. I could book you a flight to London and then maybe something on to Paris, if that would …?'

'No, no that's fine. Please just check if I can fly to Brussels today.'

The woman's gaze returned to her screen. 'Um, okay, yes I do have two seats on the 11:05 flight to Brussels if you'd like me to –'

'Yes, please book those seats.'

The woman tapped her keyboard and took the passports from the counter, opening and scanning each one. 'Have you any luggage to check-in?'

Louisa shook her head. My husband already went on ahead with the luggage. He's in Paris today, but is due to be in Brussels tomorrow, so we'll just arrive a day early and catch-up with him then.'

The woman didn't look like she was fully buying the story.

'My husband is travelling through Europe on business,' Louisa added.

The woman froze and glanced nervously down at Louisa. 'Could you just wait here a moment; I need to double-check something with my supervisor.'

She didn't wait for an answer, slinking out of Louisa's view and through a small door in the wall behind her.

It's nothing to worry about, Louisa told herself, sweat pooling at the edge of her hairline.

Minutes passed, and still the woman didn't return.

Somebody behind Louisa cleared her throat, and when she looked around and caught sight of the moustachioed security guard, her heart sank.

'Mrs Caulfield, would you mind accompanying me to the guards' station, please? There appears to be a problem with your passport.'

***

An hour alone in a quiet and bare-walled room left Louisa in no doubt about what had happened. And when Pete was brought into the room, Caleb was ushered out to a waiting and pale Judith in the corridor. Pete closed the door behind him, and unfastened the button on his blazer.

'Did you really think I wouldn't notice yours and Caleb's passports missing?' he said, without a greeting. 'I've known for months that you might try something like this. Your mum almost had me convinced that you'd come around for the sake of your dad, but I knew better. I had an alert added to his passport in case you tried to do a bunk. Child abduction is a serious crime in this country.'

'It isn't child abduction when he's my own son.'

Pete smiled at the irony of the statement. 'Your mum told me you'd learned the truth about Caleb, but before you try and take the moral high ground, know this: we've saved him a life of pain and tragedy. His real mum died in childbirth. That's why the doctor offered to help us. If we hadn't taken on Caleb, then he'd have ended up in Child Protective Services and in foster home after foster home. We did a good thing, Lou, and if you stop to think about it you'll see I'm right.'

'You're a thief and a liar!'

'Well, that seems a little two-faced when you look at which of us is facing criminal prosecution.'

She snorted; he wouldn't dare.

'But I don't want to see Caleb lose a second mother, so I'm willing to forgive and forget if you are.' He paused. 'The alternative is that the police will arrest you now and take you in for questioning. And before you start spouting conspiracy theories to them, bear in mind they're fully aware of your mental health history. It's up to you how this ends.'

Louisa couldn't bear to look at him for another second, because she knew she had no choice but to comply. She couldn't leave Caleb alone with him for a second longer.

Chapter 41

Abbie – Now

I'm alone when I wake in bed, and judging by the lack of heat in the mug of tea he left for me on my bedside table, Mark's been gone for some time. I have no recollection of any dreams or whether my sleep pattern was disturbed last night. A squashed bladder has become the norm, and as I lumber towards the bathroom, I receive a morning nudge and stroke my bump. I should make the most of this affectionate contact, as it won't be long until she's no longer this close to me. God knows I never made the most of this intimacy when Josh was in her place.

Washing in the basin, I drag up maternity jeans, and a loose top and head down to the kitchen. The house is so quiet at this time of the day. Again, I know I should make the most of the peace, but it just feels like something is missing; *someone* is missing.

I make a fresh mug of decaffeinated tea, but the smell of the milk makes my stomach turn, and I soon abandon it for a glass of fresh water instead. And then I sit down at the breakfast bar and consider my options for the day: no work to attend; Mark probably in meetings all day; not due to see the midwife until next week. I'm at a loose end, and I have no idea how I'm going to fill the silence until Mark returns.

I locate the enormous pile of books that I've purchased over the years because the cover or description has caught my eye, but I can't concentrate as I make a go of the first one, and soon give up. The television fails to capture my attention as well, and soon I have my tablet on, and find I'm searching for information on St Philomena's and Dr Michelson and Sister Arnott.

Kinga had printed copies of online articles that must exist somewhere. There's a part of me that thinks if I could just locate the online versions of those articles, I could take them to PS Brearton and show him that he was wrong. I realise that if the articles were mocked up that the fake versions might also be online and therefore prove nothing, but surely the police cyber team would be able to determine that? Worst case scenario, they'd prove that the articles aren't real, but they might be able to trace who created them, or the IP address of where they were uploaded from.

I feel cheated right now. To have had a dream offered and then snatched away isn't fair, and if Brearton is right about Kinga, then I want her punished for taking advantage of me.

My searching is fruitless, and within the hour the words on the screen are blurring and the warmth of the tablet on my lap is causing my thighs to overheat and itch. Returning to the kitchen, I boil the kettle, and this time opt for a raspberry tea pouch, inhaling the sweet smell as the leaves come alive in the cauldron of steam. Beyond the front window, I watch as the slim, headphone-wearing, post lady darts from one house to the next, delivering letters and small packages, and so am not alarmed when I later hear a knocking at my own door. But it isn't the woman in the red polo shirt I'm expecting.

'You need let me in,' Kinga says, jamming her scuffed trainer in the gap before I have chance to slam the door in her face.

'No, you need to leave,' I say as firmly as my trepidation will allow, but my pressing against the inside of the door is doing little to overcome her resistance.

This is precisely what Mark was afraid of. She's tracked us down, and maybe Brearton was wrong to assume she wouldn't become violent just because she had no history of it. After all, I've never received a speeding fine, but that's only because I've never been caught.

My hands instinctively cover my bump, not that they'll offer my unborn daughter much protection, if Kinga does become violent.

'You need to go,' I shout around the side of the door. 'You shouldn't have come here.'

'Abbie, let me in.'

I scan the immediate vicinity for any kind of weapon, but the best that's on offer is a pair of feather-covered sliders on the staircase. I left my phone on charge in the kitchen, but if I go for it, Kinga will be in and able to get at me before I've even had chance to unplug it. I could try screaming for help, but I've not seen any sign of my neighbours since waking, so I doubt anyone would hear and come to my rescue. The letters on the doormat indicate that the post has already been delivered so the post lady is unlikely to hear my screams either.

'I'll phone the police if I have to,' I call out again, feeling my feet sliding across the carpet; I'm losing this battle, and need to think faster.

'No, no police. You want son back or not?'

I freeze. Why does she have to go straight for the heart? What mother wouldn't cave at such a question? I know what Brearton said, and how Mark feels, but they don't feel what I do inside; they don't know the empty hole that was left when Josh was taken from us; a hole that has never been filled.

I slowly relent and straighten, allowing the door to open wide enough for her to dip through, and then I swiftly close the door, grabbing my mobile from its charger as we head into the kitchen. Pressing my thumb against the screen, I unlock it, and locate Brearton's number.

'You have five minutes,' I say, showing her the screen.

Her eyes drop with betrayal as she reads Brearton's rank on the screen. 'I tell you no police.'

'I know what you said, but when a stranger demands twenty thousand pounds for information about a lost child, we'd have to be pretty naïve not to call them. They told us about you, Kinga; about your past.'

She slumps against the sink, her faded leather jacket seemingly hanging from her shoulders as though it's trying to swallow her gaunt frame whole. The heavy metal t-shirt is the same one she wore the first time I saw her, and I'd swear her hair is no cleaner.

'I know you're not the refugee you claimed to be,' I say with slightly more confidence than I'm feeling. 'I know that you admitted to drug possession, and tried to take your own life in prison. The police say you're a con artist, trying to defraud Mark and me by using our loss against us. You ought to be ashamed of yourself.'

She straightens suddenly as if her energy has been renewed, and I take an uncertain step backwards, but she remains where she is.

'What wrong with you?' she shouts, and I start at the outburst. 'Why you not fight for son? If was me and I told my boy is alive, I would do everything in power to find him. You not love your son?'

'You're lying to me,' I say, the words catching in my throat. 'My son died five years ago,' I add, summoning Mark's words.

'You wrong. He not dead. Why not believe me?'

'Because you're a liar and a criminal. The police told me who you are and why you're targeting us.'

This time she does step forward, and I tense expecting her to lash out, but instead she waves a finger in my face. 'You don't deserve to get your son back. You are coward, and your boy better off where he is.'

She storms from the kitchen, but I keep my thumb hovering over the green phone icon, ready to dial Brearton as soon as the door is closed. But she stops at the door, keeping her back to me.

'My name is not Mutsuraeva,' she says quietly. 'Is Dudayeva. I didn't lie to you. Mutsuraeva is name the Albanians give me when I am arrested. They not want police to know about trafficking, so give false identity. I try to tell police is not me; that I am refugee, but they no believe. I tell you there is same corruption in this country as mine. Police call me liar, and then Albanians threaten my brother in Chechnya if I not agree. They show me photographs of him at work and at home, and say that if I not agree they torture and kill him. I had no choice.'

Is this all part of her plan to continue to manipulate me? Should I just phone Brearton and be done with it? Maybe I should message him secretly, tell him she's here and try to keep her long enough for him to come and arrest her.

'In prison, Albanians try to have me killed to stop me talking. I never try to take own life. Other prisoners they try to kill me. They force me to take pills. They try to hang me from rope. They cut my skin with razors. For some reason, I not die. I think maybe God want me alive to work for him; to help you.'

I switch to the message app, and type: *K HERE. COME NOW.*

'But maybe I make mistake and you not deserve to find son.'

She reaches for the door handle, and I know I need to say something to keep her here, as I haven't yet sent the message to Brearton. I'm tempted just to send it, but if I do and she takes off, I'll have wasted his time.

I cough to catch her attention. 'Wait, please? You must understand how difficult it is for us to believe what you claim about Josh. Losing him broke our hearts and we've had to battle to move on with our lives, learning to deal with our grief. We saw his shrivelled body, but now you're claiming that we were lied to.'

She releases the handle, and turns back to face me.

'Is not *claim*; is truth.'

'Then *convince* me you're telling the truth, Kinga. Help me to convince Mark *and* the police that this isn't just a trick to extort money.'

Kinga reaches into the inside pocket of her jacket, and I gasp as I imagine her fishing out a small pistol or knife, but instead she extracts a folded brown paper envelope. She offers it out to me, and against my better judgement, I take a step forward, and accept it.

'You want proof? There your proof.'

I lower my phone to the counter, unfold the envelope and lift the flap. Inside I find a small, transparent, plastic, sealed pouch. Holding it up to the light, my eyes widen when I see the dark strand of hair inside it.

Chapter 42

Louisa – Three months ago

Louisa lifted the phone into the air in her left hand, and angled the screen so that her face filled it, and then she pressed the red record button.

'To whomever finds this video, I ask that you take it to the police so that they'll know why I chose to do what I'm about to do. I have been held prisoner in my own home for the last five years, forced to take medication for a condition that I do not suffer with. My gaolers will tell you I suffered with anxiety and depression. They'll say this violent act was because I've not been taking my pills. But what they won't tell you is how spaced out those drugs make me feel. I spend most of the day asleep, and barely recognise myself. This is the real reason I'm doing *this* now: it's the only way I can escape.'

She thought back to her call to the police a month ago when she pleaded for someone to call by the house and save her and Caleb, but the officers who eventually turned up bought the lie about her being unhinged, and by the time they came to speak to her, she'd had the pills forcefully shoved down her throat by Pete, and was practically comatose.

She thought back to the messages she'd sent to former friends, begging for help, but her messages went unanswered, save for one who simply responded, 'Why would you think anyone would help you after what you said?'

Louisa had had no idea what she was talking about until the realisation slowly dawned on her: *she* hadn't said anything spiteful, but that didn't mean Pete hadn't. If he had access to her emails, then she was almost certain he probably had access to her social media account. Maybe he'd even sent messages direct from her phone when she was out of it on the sedatives.

No friends, nobody to turn to; she was on her own, and that left her with only one way out.

Lowering her arm, she tried to keep the camera steady as she squeezed the edges of the plastic cap and twisted until it snapped and began to spin in her hand. Dropping the lid to the carpet, she switched the camera from selfie to normal, and zoomed in on the hazard notice on the side of the large green, plastic canister.

'Found these in Dad's garage,' she said aloud for the benefit of the recording. Petrol I assume from the smell. And also some paint thinners. I never did like this old house. It's just too bad that the three of you won't be here to see it burn to the ground.'

Securing the canister between her legs, she moved slowly out of her room, making her way around the living room, sloshing petrol over the armchairs where she'd learned of her mother's betrayal, over the mantel piece, the settees, the curtains, the bookcases and the drinks cabinet. Keeping the camera angled, she continued through to the hallway, and filmed herself pouring accelerant over furniture in the drawing room, dining room, kitchen, and two guestrooms. The solvent in the liquid was so strong she felt almost giddy as the smell filled the entire downstairs of the property. Not a single room was left clean. She wanted the whole place to crash and burn, serving as a beacon to those who'd turned a blind eye.

She stopped when she got to the staircase, and lifted herself into the stair lift. Grabbing her bag from the wheelchair, she placed it between her legs, unscrewing the lid of the second canister, and held it at an angle. Reconnecting the battery to the stair lift, as she'd seen Pete do dozens of times, the motor whirred to life and she began to rise. Petrol splashed onto the hard tiles, forming a makeshift waterfall as she neared the top.

The spare wheelchair was waiting for her at the top of the stairs, and she slipped awkwardly onto it, before continuing her journey. She targeted Pete's room first, laughing manically as she tore his suits from the wardrobe and splashed petrol over them on the double bed. Locating his shoe drawer, she began to pull them out one at a time, hurling them towards the forty inch television hanging in the corner of the room. On the fifth effort, the screen smashed as the loafer made contact.

She moved to her parents' room and splashed fuel over the bed, her mum's dressing table where her jewellery boxes stood gathering dust. How could two people, who should have been trying to protect her, have allowed Pete to dominate her life as well as their own? She thought about asking the question to the video, but decided not to. Instead, she moved to the guest rooms, making light work of dousing each of them.

And then she arrived at Caleb's room. She paused, and took a deep breath, craving fresh air, but knowing how important this next step was. Discarding the green canister, she reached into her bag and withdrew the transparent bottle of white spirit.

Reaching for the door handle, she quietly cracked the door open, and pushed herself inside. Caleb was fast asleep. He'd spent the day at a theme park with Pete, and had fallen asleep before his bedtime. Rolling to the bed, she pressed a hand against his forehead, relieved when he didn't wake.

Unscrewing the lid of the bottle in her hand, she videoed herself splashing liquid around his still body, careful not to wet and wake him. The bottle crackled as she squeezed, and sprayed his toy boxes, desk and poster with the liquid.

Finally she lifted the phone back into the air, so her face once again filled the screen. Holding the bottle in her other hand, she allowed the remaining liquid to splash over her head, the liquid tickling as it dripped down the sides of her face. It splashed against her thighs, dripping from the edge of the cushion, pooling on the carpet around her. Satisfied that she was soaked through, she discarded the bottle and examined her dripping hair on the screen.

'You made me do this, Pete. And when they find our bodies, I hope your conscience eats you alive.'

With that, she reached the box of matches from the bag, and removed one. Her fingers trembled as she struck it against the rough edge of the box. The orange flame fizzed to life.

'I'll see you in hell you son of a bitch.'

Chapter 43

Abbie – Now

My mouth drops open, but no words emerge as my brain can't process what I'm seeing.

'Is this …?' I eventually manage.

'My source say this hair belong to your son. All you do now is test with sample of own hair, and you will have your proof.'

I grip the edge of the counter to stop myself floating away.

This isn't real, I tell myself, willing my imagination not to run away.

I try to recall Brearton's warnings, but it's like someone has dropped a whisk into my brain and mixed all of my thoughts. I allow my eyes to close and focus on breathing deeply, trying to settle my rapidly racing pulse.

This strand of hair could belong to anyone. It could be one of Kinga's own that she plucked before coming in here. Or it could be taken from any random child.

I open my eyes and look back at the transparent pouch in case I've just imagined what was there, but the hair strand remains where it was, curved like a crescent moon; the truth of what I'm holding similarly blurred just out of sight.

'H-How did you get the hair?' I ask, studying

Kinga's face as she reacts to the question.

I'm no body language expert, but I'm aware that eye movement, vague responses, and self-grooming are all cues that someone is being deceitful.

'My source give me.'

An image of the sign outside St Philomena's suddenly fills my mind and I see the names of Michelson and Sister Arnott. Could she be the insider behind all this?

'Your source? You said before you'd never met her?' I say, eager to find out as much as I can before I send the message to Brearton.

She shakes her head. 'No not meet. She send me.'

'She sent it to you? But how, you don't have an address. The police went to Apex Storage, and your stuff was gone.'

She continues to shake her head. 'No. We have place. How you say …? Postal box?'

'A PO Box?' I clarify, and she clicks her fingers together in acknowledgement.

'Source post messages that I collect. That how I get other evidence.'

I so desperately want to believe that Kinga is part of Sister Arnott's efforts to get the truth about places like St Philomena's out in the public domain, but if there really is a conspiracy surrounding all of this why wouldn't the source just go to the police or the press? Why use an untrustworthy patsy like Kinga?

Brearton's words echo in my mind: *she was prescribed with medication to treat her disorder, and when she's not taking them, her paranoia and hallucinations can escalate.*

I step back further into the kitchen, glancing towards the draining board in the hope I've left a sharp knife near the sink that I could use for protection. The cutlery tin is empty, because we had takeout last night.

I close the message app without sending it, and show the screen to Kinga. 'I need to phone Mark and tell him about –'

She suddenly closes the gap between us, and I'm now very conscious of just how vulnerable I am here, and that I should never have let her inside my house. Why didn't I just phone Brearton when I had the chance?

'Not husband. He bring police. You want to find son, it just you and me.'

'Mark only contacted the police because he was worried about me,' I try to say without sounding as anxious as I feel. 'He thought you were trying to con us, but when he sees the hair, and we have it tested, he'll see then that you're telling us the truth.'

I start when she snatches the phone from my hand. 'You phone him, I go and not come back. If you want son, you do what I say. Yes?'

She isn't leaving me much choice, and I nod vigorously, terrified of how she might act if she thinks I'm resisting. Right now, all I can think about is keeping my baby safe. I want Mark here, but I don't want to anger Kinga either. A new idea jumps to the front of the queue.

'Mark's the one who has your money, so I'll have to tell him we've got the hair. What if I phone him – letting you listen on the speaker – and ask him to come home? Then, once he's here, we can show him the hair, get it tested and persuade him that the police can't help.'

She doesn't answer initially, and I cross my fingers behind my back in the hope that she's actually considering the suggestion, but she makes no effort to return my phone to me.

'No husband. No trust him. Just you and me. Your choice.'

Brearton's words are in my head again: *given your current condition, I'd hate for the two of you to be alone.*

But again she's leaving me no choice. If I let her walk out of our lives, the possibility of finding Josh vanishes too.

'Okay, just you and me,' I say, lifting the transparent pouch up to the light again. 'How do we get this tested?'

'There are companies that will do DNA tests. Look online.'

I reach for my tablet and run a search. There are far more companies offering DNA testing services than I'd anticipated. It isn't a factor of the cost, but I want the results as quickly as possible. I click on a link offering instant results, but when it opens I see it's a kit that can be ordered but requires blood samples, and the reviews of the product are more negative than positive, and I quickly refine my search. I'm hoping to find some kind of clinic or lab where I can drop this hair with a sample of my own DNA and wait for the results, but quickly learn that that's not how these things work. If I could take the samples to Brearton, there might be a possibility that he could get them analysed by whoever the force use for DNA profiling, but something tells me that Kinga won't be so keen on that idea.

I eventually find one company who offer to send a pack out for paternity testing, which I'd need to return, and then they'd send the results within 72 hours. It's not ideal, but I show Kinga the screen.

'Three days is too long,' she says dismissively. 'Source need money today.'

I'm lost for words. 'B-But you said you'd give us the hair and wouldn't need the money until we had the results.'

She shrugs empathetically. 'Source say money needed now.'

I shake my head. 'I'm sorry, but no. Forgive my doubt, but for all I know you plucked this hair out of your own head. I only have your word that it belongs to Josh. I'm not going to hand over twenty thousand pounds just because you say it is his.'

She reaches into her inside jacket pocket, and I tense, but this time she extracts a folded piece of paper and hands it to me.

'W-What's this?'

'Read.'

I unfold the sheet and my eyes glaze over as I read the name on the letterhead. It's printed by a company called 'Gene Assurance' and lists details of a DNA sample comparison, confirming that there is a 99.9% likelihood that applicant-1 and applicant-2 are related.

I look back at Kinga. 'I don't understand.'

'On day we first met, I take sample of your hair and run test with other hair of your son. These are results.'

I think back to that moment when she bumped in to me on my way to the toilets, and then how she was when we invited her to join us in the café. I don't recall her plucking any of my hair.

'When you be sick and go to bathroom, I find one of your hairs on table, and take it with me. I wanted to be sure that my source right, and so I have test done. This prove hair belong to your child.'

I look at the letter again, desperately wanting to believe her, but again I only have her word to rely on, and given her background it isn't enough.

But what if I'm wrong to doubt her? What if what I'm holding is the proof that Josh didn't die and is still out there? Why am I not falling over myself to find him as quickly as possible? This could be everything I've wished for since that horrific day when the midwife broke the news. He could be out there with no idea that he was stolen from us and that he is about to become a big brother.

My knees go from under me, and it's all I can do to grab on to the counter to keep myself from collapsing. Kinga catches my elbow, and helps steer me back towards the stool beside the breakfast bar. She makes sure I'm able to hold myself up, before finding a mug hanging from the wall and filling it from the tap. She passes me the water and encourages me to drink

'I promise you I not lie. I take your hair and second hair that source give me and have test run. I swear on my own son's grave that this is truth. Your son is alive, Abbie.'

I study her eyes, and all I see is the empathy of a mother who understands the journey I've been on. I'm ready to believe her when I hear Brearton's voice in my head again: *I imagine she'll come up with some excuse as to why she needs the money first ... playing on your emotions.*

'My source is risking so much to help you,' Kinga says, as if reading my mind. 'She need the money to be safe.'

'I-I told you, Mark has the money. I'd need to speak to him to get it for you.'

'You still not believe me, Abbie?'

'No, no, no, I *do* believe you, Kinga, but the money is in Mark's account. If you let me phone him, I'm sure we can convince him and then ...'

My words trail off as she reaches into the inside pocket of her jacket once again, and extracts another folded sheet of paper. This time she unfolds it, and holds it up for me to see. A hand shoots up to my mouth as I recognise Mark's deep-set eyes and dark hair, and my own jawline and dimples. I already know what I'm looking at before Kinga confirms it.

'I not supposed to show you this until you pay money, but this is your son, Abbie.'

The portrait image is the kind taken at infant's school, with a blue background. The child dressed in a white polo shirt, his hair neatly parted to one side, and his baby teeth poking out through his smile. My eyes fill as I take in every contour of his face. I have no doubt that the original photograph that this has been copied from is genuine, and not something manipulated using graphics software. Somewhere in the world, this young boy is living his life, not realising he has the wrong parents.

'He look like you,' Kinga adds, placing an arm around my shoulders. 'He is very handsome boy. Now what will you do to get him back before too late?'

I wipe my eyes with my fingers and force myself from the stool without another word. Heading through the living room, I duck into Mark's office and switch on his computer, opening the URL for his internet banking and typing in his username and password. I find the twenty thousand pounds sitting in his online savings account, and instigate a transfer to our joint building society account. I'm more than aware that my actions are tantamount to theft, but I'm also aware that I have no choice if I ever want to get Josh back.

Chapter 44

Louisa – Three months ago

With the camera recording over, Louisa watched as the flame burned towards the end of the match wondering if it wouldn't just be easier to actually go through with it; drop the match and wait for death to take her. A gentle knock on the door, was followed by Louisa's dad poking his head around.

'All done?' he mouthed.

Louisa nodded, shaking her hand until the flame extinguished, and then allowed it to drop to the carpet, knowing the water she'd poured would kill any lingering heat.

'You look just like when I used to collect you from the swimming baths,' her dad said, offering a smile in an effort to lighten the mood, but she could see how much he was still struggling to come to terms with what she'd told him.

His face disappeared, returning a moment later with a warm towel from the airing cupboard. Moving around behind her, he draped it over her head and slowly massaged her hair and scalp. They didn't really have time to try and rebuild a connection, but given it was the last time they'd see each other, she allowed him to continue.

'I really am so sorry, Lou-Lou,' she heard him

whisper through the towel, the emotion scratching at his words.

She knew how much he regretted how their lives had turned out, but his actions were speaking louder than his words. This plan to escape had been of his making.

The day after the police had responded to her desperate call, he'd come into her room and asked her to tell him the truth. He'd said he'd sensed there was something Pete and Judith weren't telling him, and he was fed up of being kept out of the loop. Despite Judith's warnings about the impact a shock could have on his heart, she came clean and told him *everything*.

He'd listened attentively, his facial expressions switching from disbelief, to shock, to heartbreak, and finally to regret. He'd held her as they'd both cried, but she'd never anticipated exactly how he would react. They didn't speak about it again as the days passed, until the following week when Judith was at Pilates and Pete had taken Caleb to school.

'You need to go and never come back,' he'd told her.

'I've tried,' she said, telling him about Pete stopping her at the airport, but he'd simply shaken his head.

'No, I mean *properly* escape. Pete will never stop looking for you unless … unless there's nothing to look for.'

And that's when he'd told her how they'd do it. She'd never realised how resourceful he could be.

'We'd better get going, he said to her now, lowering the towel, and dropping it on her lap so she could dab the water off her jeans. 'I've got a bag of new clothes to get you both started, and plenty of cash. You'll have to stay in the UK to begin with, but there are plenty of places you can start afresh.' He paused, and sighed, the end drawing nearer. 'I'll carry Caleb down to the car, and then I'll return for you.'

She moved backwards so he could get access to the bed, and then she watched him lift Caleb into his arms, and snuggle him close as they departed the room. He hadn't said whether he'd come to terms with the fact that Caleb wasn't his actual grandson or not; after all Pete and Judith had had years to get comfortable with the idea. Yet something told her that he would miss him more than the other two.

Reaching into her bag, she pulled out the small bundle of tissue, and unrolled it on the mattress. Three of Caleb's teeth – reclaimed from the tooth fairy – and some strands of hair she'd recovered from his comb. Hopefully they would withstand the fire long enough to be recoverable from the ashes of the house. She then took hold of a section of her own hair, and pulled hard, broken strands coming away in her balled fist. She scattered these liberally around the room too.

Her dad pushed open the door as she reached into her bag for the final object. 'Do you want me to do that? It might be easier.'

Louisa turned the pliers over in her hands, feeling the weight of them, and the freedom they offered. 'No, I need to do it, but could you fetch the hand mirror from the bathroom and hold it for me?'

He nodded silently, returning with the dainty mirror that she'd given her mother as a birthday present before all of this. Opening her mouth, she ran her tongue across her teeth, before pressing the cool metal clamp into her mouth, and selecting one from her upper left gum. The pliers tasted of oil and grime, but she tried to put it out of her mind. Any escape came at a price, and this was hers.

Chapter 45

Abbie – Now

The air conditioning is doing little to take the edge off my body overheating as morning sunshine streams through the windscreen. In normal circumstances, I'd be the first stripping down and sunbathing in the garden, but right now I'd just give anything to be in an ice bath. Carrying an eight month-old baby is only making the temperature even more constricting. Of course it isn't helped by the fact that I know I've stolen twenty thousand pounds from Mark, and he hasn't stopped phoning me since Kinga and I left home.

Kinga still has my phone in case I change my mind and decide to tell Mark what we're doing. Despite her reservations, I'm sure if I could just speak to him I could make him understand how important it is for us to go along with Kinga and her source. My brain is telling me to question everything she says or does, but it's my heart I'm listening to. That image she showed me of the five year-old in his school uniform is now ingrained on my brain, and every time my eyes close, he's all I see.

When we first conceived, I vowed I would fight until my last breath to protect my child, and I have no intention of giving up when he needs me most.

The car park in town is busier than I'm expecting,

and clearly the brilliant sunshine has encouraged more to flock to the shops. I can hear my phone vibrating in Kinga's hand again, but she makes no effort to check the display, just allowing it to ring out. Parking the car, I lift my bag, and clutch it close to my chest as we climb out. We both know that the building society book inside the bag is the key to the money, but I don't want Kinga to snatch it away and prove my heart wrong.

Kinga walks close beside me, and it's only when I catch our reflection in the shiny window of a dress shop that I realise how odd a pair we make. Me heavily pregnant and melting under the oppressive heat, wincing as I walk; the guilt an additional burden to carry. It's almost like my unborn daughter senses it too as she's more active than usual, poking and kicking at me from inside. Kinga, on the other hand looks calm and collected, and there isn't a bead of sweat penetrating her heavily made-up face, despite the thick leather jacket. She's a good foot shorter than me, and her dark hair is in stark contrast to my own honey-coloured locks. Nobody we've passed seems to have picked up on the odd vibe we must be giving off, but I hope the staff inside the building society aren't more observant.

The smell of fresh bread and sweetened cakes drifts out of the bakery we pass, and my stomach grumbles as my daughter reminds me that we haven't eaten today. If the queue for the bakery wasn't out the door, I'd insist we stop to grab something to eat. I wince again at another nasty knock from inside, and nearly drop my handbag. It slips from my grasp, but my hand catches it just in time.

Kinga narrows her eyes as she looks at me. 'You are okay?'

I strain a smile. 'Yeah, I'm fine. Just a bit hot.'

She offers me her arm, which I'm reluctant to take at first, but relent, and am relieved as we step into the building society, and am hit by a wave of cool air from the ceiling. I'd forgotten the building was so well air conditioned, and if I had my way, I'd happily spend the rest of the day in here.

Kinga waits beside me in the small queue, until I'm the next to be served, at which point she crosses the room and sits in a chair by the front door. A position opens at the window, and I take a deep breath, before heading over, and placing my book in the metal tray below the glass.

'I w-want to withdraw some money,' I stammer, feeling as though all eyes have suddenly turned on me.

Do they know I stole Mark's money? Are the police here and observing what's unfolding? Will Brearton and his colleagues leap out the second the crime has been commissioned?

Kelly, the girl behind the counter who barely looks old enough to be out of school, offers a welcoming smile, and as she does, I see her teeth are wired with braces. She brushes the orange fringe from her eyes, and opens my book, pressing it flat and then sticking it into the printer below her monitor.

'Certainly. I'll just check the account is updated, and then I can arrange the withdrawal for you.'

I let out the breath I've been holding since I approached the window, and will the time to pass quicker. I glance over to Kinga who is attempting to look inconspicuous, by studying a glossy pamphlet about annuities, but she sticks out like a sore thumb.

'I see you transferred some money into the account this morning,' Kelly says pleasantly, 'so we'll just get that updated, and then we can arrange your withdrawal. Have you got any plans for the rest of this beautiful day?'

'W-What?'

The question throws me. What does she mean do I have any plans? What's it to her?'

She leans closer to the window as the printer buzzes between us. 'I wish I wasn't stuck in here to be honest,' she whispers, 'but hopefully it will still be warm enough for a walk beside the river after work.'

I nod because I don't know what else to say. I don't want to tell her that my only plans are to hand this money over and to try and find my missing son.

'When's your baby due?' Kelly asks next.

'A few weeks now,' I reply, biting down on one of my nails.

Why is this taking so long? And why is she taking such an interest in me? Are these just delaying tactics while the police get into position?

'Right that's all done now. So how much were you looking to withdraw?'

The man at the desk to my left has bright white hair, thick-rimmed spectacles, and is wearing beige trousers and a pea soup green coloured jumper. He appears to be chatting quite jovially with the woman behind the window. The young man to my right looks about Kelly's age, is at least half a metre taller than me, with no fat on his short and t-shirt clad body. I don't know who either of them are, whether they're part of the police sting operation, or whether they might try and jump me if they realise how much money I'll be carrying in my bag.

I lean so close to the small microphone that my sweaty forehead leaves an impression on the window.

'Twenty thousand pounds,' I whisper, watching the two men in my periphery.

'Was that twenty thousand?' Kelly asks with no discretion.

'Yes,' I reply through gritted teeth.

Concern replaces the affable exterior, and she looks off at something to her right.

'Is there a problem?' I ask, a bead of sweat tickling as it rolls the length of my spine.

'We have a ten thousand pound withdrawal limit,' she says awkwardly, 'unless you've given advanced notice of the larger amount.'

'But it's my money, so if I want to withdraw it there shouldn't be a problem.'

Kelly holds her hands up in a passive manner, which feels over the top given my lack of aggression. 'Of course it is, and we understand that, but we only hold a certain amount of cash on site, which is why we have the limit in place. If you don't need the funds today, we can have it ready for you tomorrow –'

'No, I need it today,' I interrupt, before catching my raised voice, and quickly apologising. 'Is there nothing you can do to help me?'

'Do you mind me asking what the money's for?'

It's none of your business, I want to shout back, but

resist the urge.

'W-We've been having some renovation done at the house ... before the b-baby arrives ... and I need to settle the bill.'

She doesn't question the lie, but asks me to wait to one side while she goes to speak to her manager. I head away from the window, and wait where she's indicated, and Kinga soon joins me.

'What problem?'

My body is still overheating despite the cool air being pumped out overhead. I'm sure dehydration will be next given the amount of fluid I've lost in stress and sweat already today.

'What time is it?' I ask her, and she lifts my phone up so I can see the numbers on the display.

It's just after ten, but more importantly I can see I've missed a dozen calls from Mark and he's just messaged checking if everything is okay, and asking me to call him back. He's probably now panicking that I've either gone into labour, or that Kinga has made her move. I want to reply that everything is okay, but right now I'm not sure if it is. If the building society refuse to give me the twenty thousand then Kinga's source won't tell me where Josh is, and Mark won't allow me to get at the rest of the money tomorrow.

A closed door buzzes behind us, and a woman with her arm in a cast and sling appears. 'Mrs Friar?'

I nod, and follow her into the room while Kinga returns to her seat by the window. The woman returns to her side of the desk and urges me to sit in either of the two bright red tub chairs across from her. I feel my back straining as I try to lower myself in to the closest one, and wince as the baby jabs at me again.

'Are you okay?' the woman asks, her face reflecting my own pain.

'I-I'm fine,' I manage, trying to focus on my breathing. The air conditioning isn't nearly as strong inside this box room.

'I'm Cynthia Gregg, the branch manager. I don't think we've met before have we?'

I recall speaking with her some years before when Mark and I first opened the savings account, but I don't correct her.

'And I understand from Kelly that you wanted to withdraw twenty thousand pounds this morning for renovation work on your home?'

I nod at the lie, grateful that Kelly has done some of the leg work for me.

'As I'm sure Kelly explained, it isn't branch policy to exceed the stated ten thousand pounds limit apart from in exceptional circumstances or when we've received advanced notice.'

'I-I understand that,' I stammer as shortness of breath gets the better of me, 'but is there … any way you can make an exception?'

She doesn't immediately respond, studying me instead. It's quite off-putting, and I can't help feeling like she's trying to read my mind, so I force myself to think about the imaginary refurbishments to the house.

'Is everything okay, Mrs Friar? Would you like me to get you something to drink? You look quite peaky.'

'It's just this heat,' I say and then use my hands to frame the bump. 'This little one isn't appreciating it either.'

She fixes me with a hard stare. 'Are you sure?' A pause. 'The woman you arrived with today isn't threatening you in some way?'

My shoulders tense at the realisation that they're aware of Kinga's presence here too.

'No, she isn't threatening me,' I say, but not even I'm convinced by my tone.

'Just give me some kind of sign and I can have the police called,' she says, her voice lower now.

'I promise she isn't threatening me. She's ... she's my sister-in-law actually. She was worried about me coming here alone today and said she'd tag along. That's all.'

Cynthia continues to study my face, and I wish she'd stop as I'm struggling to maintain this false calmness.

'I'm going to ask one more time, Mrs Friar: are you *okay*?'

'I'll be fine as soon as I have my money and can get home for a lie down and rest,' I say, making no attempt to hide my frustration.

Cynthia types something in to her computer, and then pushes herself away from the desk. 'On this occasion, I'm going to authorise the full payment to you, but I'd ask in future that you give us some warning about such large withdrawal amounts.'

It's music to my ears, and I feel my eyes begin to fill, but blink them back. She moves to the door, and promises that she'll have Kelly prepare the money and place it in a padded brown envelope for discretion. I remain in her office until Kelly arrives, and counts the money on Cynthia's desk, before handing it over to me in the envelope. I secure it in my bag, and thank them both for their understanding, welcoming the relief of the air conditioning in the main body of the building before Kinga and I exit out to the even hotter street.

We've barely made it more than a metre when a voice calls from behind us. 'Yoo-hoo, Abbie?'

I half glance back, but panic when I see Yolanda crossing the road in our direction.

'We need to go,' I say to Kinga quickly, and she doesn't stop to ask why.

Ordinarily, nothing would please me more than having Yolanda at my side with what I'm facing, but she's made no secret of her suspicions about Kinga, and the last thing I need now is further obstacle. The end is in sight and I need to get there as swiftly as possible. Josh needs me.

Ducking down an alleyway, I lead Kinga through a maze of parked cars until we're back at mine. Once inside, I spot Yolanda emerge from the alleyway, searching for us, but she won't be able to pick us out from there.

'Did you get it all?' Kinga asks, eyeing my white knuckles gripping the bag.

'I-I did,' I pant, 'but I'm not giving it to you. If your source wants this money, you tell her to come and meet us. I will only hand it over to her when she tells me where Josh is.'

Chapter 46

Louisa – Today

The sound of birds chirping outside the window caught Louisa's attention first. She'd been awake for more than an hour, not that she'd had much sleep prior to that anyway; she never did anymore.

Each night she ran through the same checklist once she'd settled Caleb into bed and read him a story. Bag packed in case they needed to leave quickly. An envelope with the manager's name written on it, beside the television and containing the night's room cost. Mobile phone fully charged and checked for any messages from the only person who had the number. Whilst they'd agreed it would only be used for emergencies, part of her had hoped to have heard from her dad.

In the three months since he'd helped her escape the old manor house, she'd thought about him often. Would he be able to keep his nerve and not let her secret out? Would he crack under police interrogation and admit it had been his idea to burn down the house? How was his heart coping with the added burden of her secret?

She left the phone on for twenty minutes every morning, and every evening once Caleb was asleep. If he'd phoned in between, he hadn't left a message. A different B&B every night in a different town or village. The money her dad had given her would allow her to maintain this pattern for at least a year, but she wasn't ready to relax yet.

She'd tried to follow the aftermath of the fire in a local newspaper that had covered the destruction of the old place, but there'd been no mention of further police investigation. She'd sent her suicide video message to Pete before they'd driven from the engulfed house, tossing the phone into the flames for good riddance, but she hadn't managed to find out whether the police had completed their search for remains in the collapsed hull.

It was possible Pete hadn't bought the video and was still actively searching for her, and that's what terrified her the most. He'd used a private investigator to try and track the blackmailer, and what if he'd hired them again to try and find his wife and daughter? There were only so many places she could hide; only so many B&Bs she could stay in.

Caleb stirred in the bed beside her. It hadn't been easy explaining to him why they'd had to leave. He was just about buying the lie that they were on holiday, but it would become more difficult when he didn't return to school in September. He missed his father and grandparents, although he was trying to put a brave face on it.

Not for the first time, she wondered whether her actions had been selfish. Despite the trauma Pete had put her through, she'd never witnessed him show Caleb anything but love.

Sitting up, she lifted her legs to the thin carpet, and

wiggled her toes in the pile. There was a time she never thought she'd be able to feel the tickle of the fibres, let alone be able to stand and walk. Although she could only move short distances, and not without the aid of her walking stick, she'd made great progress in the years she'd been a prisoner. With a deep breath, and reaching out for the bedside table to steady herself, she rose, allowing a second for the feeling to return, before shuffling slowly to the bathroom, careful not to disturb the bed too much. Inside, she applied toothpaste to her toothbrush, before flicking on the light. She grimaced as she caught sight of the shaved head of her reflection. She still wasn't used to having so little hair, but if Pete's people were looking for a woman in a wheelchair with long flowing, blond hair, they wouldn't look twice at her. At least that's what she hoped.

Rinsing her mouth with water, she hobbled back into the main room, putting on her hoodie, before sitting back on the bed where she planned to wait until Caleb woke. She wanted to treat him to a cooked breakfast this morning, rather than the cereal bars and long-life brioche rolls she kept stocked up for ease. One day she hoped they'd be able to stop running, but until she managed to find his real parents, their journey wouldn't end. Her online searches so far had thrown up no beneficial information, and she'd since learned that St Philomena's had gone out of business less than a year after she'd been admitted. Whether any records of deliveries there still existed was beyond her.

She started at the low hum on the bedspread. Looking down at the screen, she didn't recognise the number that was calling, but she did know the area code. Picking it up, she carried it back to the bathroom, closing the door so Caleb wouldn't be disturbed.

'Hello?' she said quietly into the receiver, hear heart racing, waiting to hear the low grumble of her dad's voice.

But her mouth dropped open when she heard her mum's voice instead. 'Lou-Lou? Is that you? I'm calling from the hospital, sweetheart. It's about your dad.'

Chapter 47

Abbie – Now

Kinga has been messaging her source since we left the car park, but it's only after we've driving around without direction for twenty minutes that she finally directs me to a specific location.

'Where are we going?' I ask on more than one occasion. The first couple of times she doesn't answer.

'Will tell you when there,' she eventually responds, but it doesn't instil any confidence.

Brearton's words are in my head again: *given your current condition, I'd hate for the two of you to be alone.*

'I need to phone Mark,' I tell her as I leave the roundabout at the third exit, as she has instructed. 'He's not stopped phoning, and is clearly worried about me. I know what he's like: if he thinks I'm in danger, he'll contact the police. If I could just phone –'

'Yes, is fine, you can phone when we get there.'

I'm surprised she's caved, but then I really don't know how to judge her change of heart. What does she know that I don't? Where exactly are we going?

She was prescribed with medication to treat her disorder, and when she's not taking them, her paranoia and hallucinations can escalate.

I scream out at the sting of another internal jab, and the car jars as I temporarily lose control of the wheel. That was the most painful one yet, and Kinga is looking at me suspiciously.

'Just the baby,' I pant, struggling to adjust my sitting position behind the constraint of the seatbelt. She's clearly not happy being restricted in this manner.

Wiping my forehead with the back of my hand, I fiddle with the car's air conditioning, and adjust the vent so it's pointing at my face. It provides scant relief. What I really need is a cold drink, and a stretch of my legs, but for all I know we could have hours until we reach our destination.

Why didn't I insist on speaking to Mark? Kinga threatened to leave if I did, but would she have really? If Brearton is right and her source is fictional then Kinga doesn't strike me as someone who would walk away from the promise of twenty thousand pounds. But then her entire appearance could have been designed to appeal to certain aspects of my personality.

'End of road, turn left, and park,' she says, studying the directions on her phone.

I follow the command, and am surprised by the horizon of green I see beyond the low wooden fence that borders the edge of the rough track. There are football pitches as far as the eye can see both sides of the track, and a small concrete car park at the end, which I now enter and locate a space near the exit. There are only four other cars parked, but space for twenty or so more. I can't see anyone sitting in any of the stationary vehicles, so if Kinga's source is planning to meet us, she isn't here yet.

'Here phone,' she says, resting it in my lap. 'You can message husband, but make sure no police. My source risking everything for you.'

I'm almost in tears at another jab to my abdomen, and have to take several breaths to compose myself.

'I need to stretch,' I tell her, collecting the phone and opening the door. I manage to clamber out at the third attempt, but I hadn't realised how much discomfort I've been dealing with. My legs don't feel like they can support me, and so I grip the frame of the car and door, until the blood begins to flow back to my legs.

'You not look good,' Kinga tells me from her seat, which really isn't the criticism I need right now.

Holding out the phone, I listen to Mark's messages on speaker phone, feeling obliged to allow Kinga to hear how much trouble this morning's rendezvous has caused.

Hi Abbie, just checking in with you. How are you doing today? Give me a call when you get this, will you?

I delete the message and the second begins to play.

Abbie, I still haven't heard back from you. What's going on? Is everything okay? Starting to worry a bit. Call me back, please?

I delete it again, but I can hear from his voice that panic is already starting to set in.

You need to call me back, Abbie. I just spoke to Yolanda who said she saw you in town with that Kinga woman. She said the two of you were emerging from the building society, and I've just checked and someone transferred the twenty thousand out of my account this morning. Are you with her now? DO NOT HAND OVER ANY MONEY! Tell me where you are and I'll get the police to you. Please, Abbie, I need to know you and the baby are safe.

I look at Kinga for permission to call him back, but she shakes her head. 'Tell him you are okay, and fighting for your son. If he'd fought harder maybe you not be in position now.'

I type out a message to Mark telling him that I'm okay, that I am with Kinga, but that she's taken me to meet her source. I promise I'll call as soon as I can, and then I hand her back the phone.

In the distance I can hear high-pitched screams, and although none of the football pitches are in use, I now see there is a children's playground just beyond the car park. More importantly there is an ice cream van idling on the grass near the playground.

'I need some water,' I tell Kinga, pointing at the ice cream van. 'Do you want anything?'

She is studying her phone again, and shakes her head.

Taking several deep breaths, I push myself away from the frame of the car, relieved when muscle memory kicks in, and I'm able to place one foot in front of the other. The grass is cool and tickles my toes through my flip-flops. I can't get over how restless the baby has been today, but she can probably sense how conflicted I am by this morning's events. I know it wasn't fair to take the money without discussing it with Mark first, but if Kinga's source leads us to Josh, he'll forgive me and realise I had no other choice.

Passing the small playground I catch sight of a girl at the top of the slide calling for her mother's attention. The mother in question is sitting on a park bench nearby, but is too engrossed in her phone to hear the girl's cries. I pause and lean against the railings, offering the girl an encouraging smile and thumbs up. Satisfied that someone will witness her bravery, she waves at me, and then prepares her descent. She shrieks as she slides down at great speed, and looks back at me as soon as she's at the bottom, awaiting my acknowledgement. I silently applaud as she hurries back to the ladder and begins to climb again.

There's a little boy on the roundabout, and another being pushed on the swings by someone I'm presuming is his grandfather, given his age. My eyes widen as a steamroller of a thought slaps me sideways: what if Josh is in this playground now? What if that's why Kinga's source brought us here?

Gripping the railing, I look at the boy on the swings, but he doesn't look like the boy in the school photograph Kinga showed me. Then I look at the boy on the roundabout, but his head is bent low, as he clings on for dear life, and it takes several rotations, before I rule him out too. The third boy is on the far side of the playground, waiting patiently beside a pushchair while his mother focuses on the toddler inside it. The boy has his back to me, but is the right sort of height for a five year-old; his hair isn't quite as dark as the photograph suggested, but then it is a bright day. Could it be …?

The woman grabs his hand, and then they are on the move, away from me, towards the exit to the playground.

'No wait,' I gasp, though not nearly loud enough for them to hear me.

I need to be certain, and keep my gaze focused on them as I move across the uneven grass, practically hugging the railing to prevent myself from stumbling. They're already through the gate, and I don't feel like I'm gaining, but then they turn left instead of right and suddenly I've got every chance of intercepting them.

The boy is walking to the right of the woman and the pushchair, so I'm still no closer to seeing his face, but I attempt to increase my pace, which the baby reacts to, almost knocking the wind from me. I have to stop to draw breath and grimace at the sharp pain. When I look back up, I'm relieved to see the woman has stopped beside the ice cream van, giving me precious seconds to regain my composure before approaching them.

The woman is talking to the man through the window in the side of the van, and then asking the boy what he wants. I can see he is bouncing with excitement, but the handles of the pushchair are distorting my view.

The pain in my abdomen subsides, and I drag myself forwards, towards them, thrilled when there's only a couple of metres between us as she hands the boy an orange lolly. For the briefest second I see my Josh there, but then I blink and realise that this little boy is not the one in the school photo. He's wearing glasses, his chin is pointy, and his cheeks still chubby with baby fat. Despite his height, this boy can't be much older than four, if that.

'Can I help you with something?' his mother asks, clearly not happy with the interest I'm showing in her son.

I continue to watch him for a moment, in case it's just my mind playing tricks on me, but I can now see that this is not my son.

'I-I'm sorry,' I say quickly. 'I just need to get some water.'

She eyes me with suspicion, before reaching for her son's free hand, and leading him away from me and the van, glancing back at me over her shoulder several times until she's satisfied I'm not following.

'Just a water, is it?' the man asks through the window, and I nod.

He places a dripping bottle of water on the counter, and I willingly hand over the extortionate two pound fee. Cracking off the lid, I take a long drink from the bottle, savouring the cool relief on my throat, and then placing it against my forehead.

'Are you all right, love?' the man asks. 'Do you want me to phone for an ambulance?'

I straighten, still breathless. 'No I'm fine, thanks,' I tell him.

He doesn't look convinced, frowning at me. 'You sure? Coz if you ask me, you look like you're in labour.'

I scoff at this; like I wouldn't know if I was …

'I'm not due for a few weeks yet,' I correct him, but

I'm not sure whose benefit the statement is for.

The jabs I've been feeling, I assumed were from the baby, but what if …?

I try to recall what labour was like with Josh, but my racing mind can't concentrate for long enough.

Probably just Braxton Hicks, I tell myself, remembering Brearton's reference to them yesterday. Lots of mother's experience the echo of labour pains in the days or weeks leading up to the actual start of labour, like it's the body's dress rehearsal for the big day. That's all it is.

It must be.

Reassuring him again, I tighten my grip on the bottle, and begin to cross the grass back towards the car, as it suddenly dawns on me that I left the bag of money in the footwell of the seat, and for all I know Kinga's grabbed it and scarpered. I try to increase my pace, but it's tough, and I'm relieved when the car comes back into sight, and I see that she's still in the passenger seat. I can't believe I was so stupid to just leave it there.

'Where's your source?' I ask her when I'm back in the car, and I subtly run my hand inside the bag to check the envelope is still inside. I also grab my phone which has been left in the bottle holder behind the handbrake. Mark hasn't responded to my message yet.

'On way,' she replies, but I can hear the agitation in her tone.

A car arrives and circles the car park, but as it passes us, I see it's a woman in a brightly-coloured head scarf but she doesn't park beside us, and my shoulders sag.

Brearton's voice is in my head again: *sounds like*

she might just be using this fictitious figure to exonerate herself of the extortion.

I'm about to ask her to call her source so I can hear his voice when the woman in the headscarf appears just outside my window. She's looking in at us, but as she opens her mouth to speak, something catches her attention and she looks away towards whatever it is. Just beyond the windscreen, another car has skidded to a halt, and the passenger in the back is yelling something at the woman beside us.

Chapter 48

Louisa – Today

Louisa didn't speak, unable to compute how she could be talking to the woman who'd betrayed her, when she'd made the ultimate sacrifice to escape that life. Bile filled her mouth, and if it hadn't been for fear of waking Caleb on the other side of the paper thin wall, she would have retched into the toilet bowl.

'Lou-Lou. Are you there? Please, sweetheart, I just want to hear your voice.'

Louisa remained silent, not prepared to give anything away, her mind now racing with the prospect that if her mother and Pete had this number that could also mean they knew where she was.

'Your dad has told me *everything*,' Judith continued, and it was the kick to the gut that Louisa didn't need.

Reaching out for the countertop, she just about managed to grip it for long enough before her legs turned to jelly, and gave way. Her bottom bore the brunt of the fall, landing on top of the closed toilet lid with a crash.

He'd sworn he would do what he could to help her, but maybe she'd been wrong to trust him. How could everyone she loved betray her so easily?

'I returned last night and found him collapsed in the

doorway of our hotel room. Paramedics were already there and treating him for a mild myocardial infarction.' Her voice strained under the emotion. 'I thought I was going to lose him.'

Louisa felt sympathy for her despite everything she'd put her through. Ultimately, Judith and David Kinghorn had once been so in love they'd chosen to marry and start a family. Nothing would ever take that away from them. And even if they'd rarely shown affection towards one another when Louisa was around, those weren't feelings that could simply be switched off like a tap on a sink.

'They're giving him oxygen, and monitoring his heart rate, but they're hopeful he should pull through, but it's what caused the attack that now has he me more worried. The hotel manager said other guests had complained about shouting coming from the room, and your dad told me he was arguing with Pete. That's when he told me the rest.

'I am so sorry, Lou-Lou, but I really had no idea things were as bad as you felt. I only ever wanted to help you and Pete, and help you recover from your depression and anxiety.'

Louisa listened, desperate to interrupt and counter every lie with a home truth. How could she think that forcing her to take antidepressants and mild sedatives would help? Why did she choose not to see what was really going on?

'Your dad told me about Pete's controlling behaviour and how you confided in him when you reached the end of the line. He told me that burning down the house was his idea to help you escape. He had hoped the police would find the video and your DNA in the property and you'd be free. He had no idea their investigation would prove inconclusive. He'd assumed the DNA samples from the teeth would be enough to support the video you sent to Pete, but they didn't find any bones in the hull of the old building so couldn't prove for certain that anyone had died.

'Pete placed the obituary in the newspaper to try and draw out the blackmailer, and it worked. She got in touch with him directly, but he had no intention of negotiating with her. He's been using a private investigator to track her, and according to your dad he now knows where she is.'

She?

Since first discovering the letter in Pete's office, Louisa was embarrassed to admit that she'd assumed it would be a man threatening to expose the truth about Caleb. Maybe on some level it was unconscious bias to assume a woman couldn't be just as capable of something so cruel.

'Your dad gave me this number and he wanted me to call you. We want to do whatever we can to help you get Pete out of our lives once and for all. You don't need to keep running, Lou-Lou. You and Caleb can come home and we'll sort this mess out together.'

A thought rippled through Louisa's head, slowly chilling every blood cell in her body: this could all be a trap. She only had Judith's word that any of what she'd said was true. What if Pete had threatened them, and that was what had made her dad betray the truth?

'W–What's her name?' Louisa stammered into the phone.

'Lou-Lou? Is that you? You are alive?'

'What's the woman's name? The blackmailer?'

'Um, hold on, I wrote it down.' A pause. 'Michelson? Dr Elizabeth Michelson. Wait, why does that name sound so familiar?'

Louisa pictured the white-haired old man at St Philomena's.

'Where is she?' Louisa demanded next. 'If he knows where she is, she could be in danger. Pete doesn't negotiate with problems.'

'I-I don't know. Your dad didn't say, but we can worry about that when you're safe.'

Louisa almost dropped the phone. 'What do you mean *when I'm safe*?'

'Didn't I make that clear? That's what your dad and Pete were arguing about. He knows where you are, Lou-Lou. His private investigator has been tracking you too. You need to come home so we can go to the police together.'

Louisa hung up the phone without another word, and switched it off. She'd been so careful, always watching over her shoulder when she and Caleb weren't behind closed doors. They couldn't have found her, could they? But then she was no expert in counter-espionage, so was it really surprising that trained professionals had found her?

Stumbling towards the bedroom, she willed her legs to work quicker than they were used to, reaching for the holdall, and shaking Caleb awake.

'We need to go. I need you to put on your.'

He rubbed his eyes, but made no effort to get out of bed.

'Caleb, please? I need you to listen to Mummy, and get up. We have to go. It's an emergency. Like we practiced, yeah? Come on, quick as you can.'

She scooped his trainers from the floor and placed them on top of the bedspread, shuffling to the window and looking outside for Pete's car, relieved when she didn't see him staring back up at her from the street. But that didn't mean he wasn't on his way.

Zipping up Caleb's anorak, she promised him food once they were in a taxi, grabbing all of their things, and hurrying to the staircase. Stairs still weren't easy for her untrained legs, so sitting down on the top one, she scooped Caleb onto her lap, and the two of them slid down, landing in a heap at the bottom, much to the bemusement of the B&B's owner who was carrying a tray of toast through to the dining area.

The woman delivered the toast, before returning and helping Louisa to her feet. Louisa handed her the envelope of money, and asked her to call for a taxi. When it arrived, she bundled Caleb inside with a cereal bar, and told the driver just to drive. She had a B&B booked for that evening in a town five miles away, but if Pete knew where she was now, he might also know where she was headed next.

And that's when she made a decision that would alter her life forever. Switching the phone back on, she opened an internet page and searched for the name Dr Elizabeth Michelson. If there was one person who could finally prove what a monster Pete was, then Michelson might just be the answer to all her problems. The question was whether she could get to her before Pete did.

Chapter 49

Abbie – Now

It's like watching a movie playing in slow motion. The woman in the headscarf, whose face is pale and gaunt turns towards the taxi that has blocked her car in. I can't hear what is being shouted, but I can see the fear in the eyes of the person who is yelling. At first I think it's a young man – the shaved head and hooded sweatshirt reminding me of boys I've seen walking to college – but then I realise the feminine curve of her jawline is proof I'm mistaken.

Lowering my window, I try to listen to what is being said, but Kinga is talking at me, and it's hard to catch a word.

'Who these people?' Kinga says, almost chuckling at the odd scene unfolding.

I'm concerned that whatever is going on between these two strangers might frighten off Kinga's source, and I need them to move on so I can try and spot her. Exiting the car, I move slowly around the front, freezing when I hear the words *danger, kill,* and *Michelson.*

The woman with the shaved head is opening her door and urging the woman to get in the back, and that's when I catch sight of the young man seated beside her. His head is also shaved, and his face is turned away, but my brain floods with questions and possibilities.

Is one of them the source?

The woman in the headscarf turns back to look at me, and there's something in the look that I can't place. Is it recognition? I don't see how it can be as I've no idea who she is, nor that we've ever met. But it's more than that. It's a look I've seen staring back at me in the mirror countless times: fear.

She next stares at Kinga, and it's like something clicks into place, yet when the woman with the shaved head clambers awkwardly out of the taxi, the woman in the headscarf turns deathly pale. It's like she's staring at a ghost, and in that moment I feel like she may just keel over.

'Please, Dr Michelson,' the other woman says, as she wobbles unsteadily on a walking stick. 'It's not safe for you here.'

Now it's my legs that feel unsteady. This isn't the Dr Michelson I remember, but it must be too coincidental for the woman in the headscarf to bear that name. Surely she can't be his wife, daughter perhaps, but then the skin around her face looks so pale and tired that she looks too old to be his daughter. My mind is whirring, and the uppercuts my daughter is delivering are driving me to distraction now. I press my hand against the wing of the car, and lean into it, hoping for a few minutes just to compose myself.

'W-What are you doing here?' Michelson asks the woman with the shaved head. 'I thought you were … dead. I spoke to your husband and he confirmed what I read in the obituary.'

'Pete isn't someone you can trust. He's on his way here now. Please, you must come with me. I know now about Caleb. I didn't realise what they'd done all those years ago, but now I do. I just want to get him back to his real mum.'

My eyes widen at this statement, and I'm certain I've stopped breathing, as if my brain is too busy processing all this new information that it's forgotten basic tasks. I look beyond the two of them, but my view into the back of the taxi is now blocked.

My hands are clammy and my throat so dry that if I did try to speak, the words wouldn't come out. Ever since Kinga approached me in the Trafford Centre I've had visions of the moment I would come face-to-face with my son, not daring to believe they could ever come true. He looks nothing like the boy in the picture that Kinga shared this morning, but then I've not had chance to properly study his face, and for all I know that picture wasn't real.

Whatever is unfolding here, it feels bigger than the two of us. Is one of these women the source Kinga has been in contact with? Or is all of this being carefully played out to pull on my heart strings.

Brearton's warnings are now all I can hear pulsing through my head: *once she has you there, I imagine she'll come up with some excuse as to why she needs the money first – or at least a portion of it – playing on your emotions.*

If this was a confidence trick isn't this exactly how they would play it out? Kinga hooks me, as Brearton described, with the promise of access to Josh if I hand over the money. Now that we've come to the so-say exchange, a woman in obviously poor health ends up in an argument while I'm busily distracted by the child who seems to be deliberately hiding his face from me. For all I know, any minute now, they'll all just take off and leave me standing here empty-handed.

I wish I had told Mark what I was planning and where we are so he could come to my rescue. But I've betrayed him in the worst possible way, and I'm not sure he'll ever be able to forgive me for not listening to his and Brearton's warnings, and stumbling blindly towards the inevitable conclusion of this trick.

'Please, Dr Michelson, Pete could be here any minute. We need to go.'

This is it. This is the moment they'll disappear with my money and leave me heartbroken for a son who I've already lost.

I need to stop them. I take an unsteady step forward, but then there's a splash and my socks are taking on water through my trainers. I look down expecting to see an enormous puddle that I've just trodden in, but despite the newly wet circle of concrete around me, there's no obvious puddle.

It's only when the woman in the headscarf comes to my side and takes my arm that I start to connect the dots.

'I think your water just broke,' she says. 'We need to get you to a hospital.'

'But I'm not due for a few weeks,' I try to argue, but now every twinge and ache from this morning are echoing in my head like a big 'I told you so.'

'Help me get her in the back of my car,' Michelson calls to the other woman.

'It's fine, Kinga can drive me,' I reply, breathless as what I now realise is a contraction stabs at my insides and forces me to bend under the strain.

'Not likely.'

Glancing back at my windscreen I see what she means. Kinga is gone, and with it I expect so has the money.

Chapter 50

Abbie – Now

The next twenty minutes pass in a blur. Elizabeth Michelson – if that really is who she is – drives us in her estate car, with the boy beside her in the front seat so I can't see his face, and the woman with the shaved head in the back with me, supporting my neck, as I am lying down. The contractions are coming every four to five minutes, and lasting for a minute. They are much stronger now, and even if it hadn't been for my waters breaking, I think I would have clocked what was going on.

How could I have been so distracted today that I didn't realise I was in early labour?

The woman with the shaved head introduces herself as Louisa, but that's as far as introductions go, as I'm too busy answering Michelson's slew of questions about my contractions, and being told when to breathe in and out. This is not the Zen trip to the hospital I've been hoping for these last few months.

I need Mark with me.

As soon as I've been admitted to the maternity ward and I've been given gas and air, I try to call him, but his phone goes straight to the messaging service which means he's either switched it off or is on another call. I've missed more than a dozen calls from him since I transferred the money out of his account. It was done with the best of intentions, but maybe if I'd listened to him, and ignored the charade created by Kinga, I wouldn't be in this mess now.

I don't have my maternity bag with me. It's packed and at home, but I didn't think I'd need it when I left the house with Kinga this morning.

There's been no sign of Louisa and Michelson since I was transferred to a wheelchair upon arrival at the hospital. And it wouldn't surprise me if I never see either of them again. If they'd managed to concoct this elaborate ruse to trick me in to handing over twenty grand, of course they'd have known that Michelson was the doctor I dealt with at St Philomena's, and would use the name to keep me playing along until Kinga could abscond with the bag of money. I can't believe I allowed myself to fall for the scam despite Mark's and Brearton's warnings.

I suppose I should phone Brearton and tell him what's happened, but I want to speak to Mark before I do. He deserves my first apology.

Lying in this hospital bed is stirring up memories and with each comes new waves of anxiety. What if I'm unable to deliver my daughter and we lose her in the same way as Josh? I know this is an NHS hospital and I absolutely trust the medical staff to do what's best for me – unlike St Philomena's – but she shouldn't be coming yet. It's too early and that's what terrifies me the most.

I wish Mark was here.

I've left him a breathless voicemail, sent a text message, a message via Facebook, and a WhatsApp.

He hasn't seen any of them. What if something's happened to him? I realise it's my anxiety but what if the gang went after Mark as well? What if one of Kinga's former gaolers attacked him because we went to the police? What have I brought down on us?

'You need to stay as calm as you can,' one of the nurses instructs, handing me the gas and air and encouraging me to suck on the pipe. 'Your pulse is a little higher than we'd like, and baby needs you to be as relaxed as possible.'

They've strapped a heart monitor around my bump, and are keeping checks on my unborn daughter.

Please don't let me mess this up again.

I recall the counselling sessions after we lost Josh, how the psychologists and psychiatrists insisted Josh's passing wasn't my fault, but I never accepted that. It wasn't his fault, and I shouldn't blame the medical staff who delivered him, so who else does that leave? It was my job to bear him, and I failed. I don't want to repeat that mistake.

Another contraction comes and sucks the life out of me. How do some mothers do this over and over again? It's the most pain I've ever experienced, and the moment the contraction ends is such a relief, even though I know the next one is only minutes away.

I start at the knock at the door. I don't immediately recognise the figure in the blue surgical gown, hat and face mask, until I spot the walking stick which appears to be the only thing holding her up.

'Do you mind if we come in?' she asks, telling the young man wearing matching apparel and enormous headphones to sit on the plastic chair in the corner of the room.

I'm in no position to eject them from the room, but would prefer some company even if it's just to stop me driving myself crazy.

'How far apart are the contractions?' Louisa asks as she approaches, and then leans against the end of the bed as if she'll collapse without it.

'Three to four minutes now,' I tell her performing the mental arithmetic.

'Not long to go then. Do you know what you're having?'

'A girl,' I say, grimacing as I remember now that Mark still doesn't know.

Where is he?

'Can I ask you a personal question?'

I nod, inhaling the gas and air as I feel the next contraction starting to build.

'How do you know Elizabeth Michelson?'

'I-I don't.'

'But you were meeting her earlier. Did Pete send you?'

'I don't know who that is. I was there with Kinga.'

'Who, sorry?'

'K-Kinga,' but I can't say more as the contraction takes hold and sends me to hell and back.

'Can I get you anything?' Louisa asks as I choke down the gas and air, but I shake my head. 'Who is Kinga?'

As the contraction passes I recount the last week, from bumping into Kinga at the Trafford Centre to her revelations in the restaurant, the rendezvous at the storage unit, and then this morning's DNA result and meeting at the park.

'You lost a child at St Philomena's?' Louisa questions. 'I did too. At least, I didn't realise I had until recently.' She glances back over her shoulder to check on the boy in the corner, but his face is buried in the game he's playing on his tablet, oblivious to the two of us and the nurse who comes and goes to check on the baby's heart readings.

'How do you know Elizabeth Michelson?' I ask once the next contraction passes.

She then proceeds to tell me how she was in a car accident five years earlier, and lost use of her legs, but left hospital with a baby boy. I can't keep up as she explains her husband and mother made her believe that the child they'd brought home was hers, when in fact they'd paid for someone else's baby. I don't understand how she could raise a child and not realise he wasn't hers, but maybe I'm being unfair.

My mind spins with what Kinga told me about my name being on a scrap of paper with a monetary figure. I concentrate on the memory to help me through the next contraction.

But if this is all part of a confidence trick, why is Louisa still here? The group have their money so why continue to string me along? Unless ...

My gaze flies over to the young man on the seat, my heart aching as I stare at him. Here I am judging Louisa for not realising the boy in her home wasn't hers, and yet I could be staring at Josh and not realise it. When all this started I thought there'd be this moment when our eyes would meet and we'd instantly know, and our hearts would begin to mend, but I'm not feeling it.

Something isn't right.

The next contraction is agony, and I'm close to passing out with the pain this time. My vision blurs as I lie there panting, but I'm sure I see Elizabeth Michelson appear beside Louisa.

'Is Abbie Caleb's real mum?' I hear Louisa ask, and I ache to hear her answer.

The room erupts in a cacophony of bells, and I miss what she says. My head rolls to the side, and I try to see beyond them to the boy.

Are you Josh? Have you come back to us?

The nurse rushes back into the room, and calls out to her colleagues.

'W-What's going on?' I try to ask, but she's not looking at me, pressing a stethoscope to my bump.

I don't need her to confirm that something's wrong with my baby.

No, not again. Mark, where are you?

Chapter 51

Louisa – Now

The hum of chatter echoes off the yellowing walls of the ground floor restaurant within the hospital. Louisa locates a small table in the corner of the room that's just been vacated by an elderly man in a hospital gown, who wheels the IV drip apparatus as he departs. The squeaking wheels grate every nerve in Louisa's head, but she ushers Caleb to sit, and promises him they'll be on their way as soon as they've had a bite to eat and a drink.

Elizabeth Michelson carries a tray with refreshments through the dining area, joining them at the table a moment later. She hands Louisa a packet containing a tuna and cucumber sandwich and a bag of crisps. She rests the plate with the large slice of chocolate cake in front of Caleb, whose eyes widen with excitement.

'He's not allergic is he?' Elizabeth quickly checks, relief flushing her otherwise pale face as Louisa shakes her head, and encourages Caleb to tuck in. 'My son would choose chocolate cake over anything else,' Elizabeth adds, ripping open a sachet of sugar and tipping the contents into the mug of black coffee before her.

'Are you not eating?' Louisa checks, noting the

remaining cup of tea and carton of juice on the tray.

Elizabeth shakes her head. 'I probably should, but the drugs I'm on have a tendency to suppress my appetite. I'll force something down later.'

Louisa studies her thin arms, and gaunt face and frame.

'Leukaemia,' Elizabeth explains noting the intense stare.

'I'm sorry,' Louisa says, suddenly conscious that she's not the only person facing an uphill struggle.

Elizabeth shrugs off the pity. 'I just want to make the most of the time I have left. I've come to terms with what's going to happen, but I have work to do before then.' She pauses, and stares back at Louisa, her eyes creasing with uncertainty. 'I can't believe you're here.'

'You've no idea how long I've been searching for you … well, for answers for Caleb. By the way, he has no idea about any of this, and I'd sooner it stay that way until I can introduce him to his real parents. I wonder how Abbie's getting on upstairs.'

'Abbie *isn't* Caleb's mum.'

It's Louisa's turn to look dumbfounded. 'What do you mean? He must be.'

'I overheard the two of you talking before, but you've leapt to the wrong conclusion,' she says evenly.

'I don't understand. You sent me letters and emails saying that he …' she lowers her voice, 'he wasn't *mine*. Abbie confirmed she was at St Philomena's around the same time as me, and was told her child was taken.'

'You were both at St Philomena's under my father's care, but several months apart. You gave birth in May, but Abbie wasn't admitted until September. Caleb isn't hers.'

Louisa opened the bag of crisps and bit down on one in frustration. 'Then you must be able to tell me where his real parents are. I need to find them. He deserves to meet them.'

'I'm sorry, Louisa, but Caleb's parents ... they're not around anymore. I wish there was something else I could say, but you're all he's got. I thought you were both dead. When you ignored my letters, and then I saw the obituary in the newspaper and read about the fire, I requested to work the evidence in your case.'

Louisa frowns heavily.

'I'm a forensic pathologist who specialises in DNA profile analysis and interpretation. It's what I do.'

'But the fire was three months ago. I found your first letter more than a year ago.

'I knew Caleb wasn't yours before the fire, but the teeth confirmed it for me.'

'But how did you know? I don't understand.'

Elizabeth passed the carton of juice to Caleb, before lifting the tray from the table and resting it on the vacant chair beside her.

'My father was a complicated man. He was my hero for so many years, and I desperately wanted to be just like him: someone who worked hard to help others. That's why I worked so diligently at school and university, and then at medical school. I wanted to make him proud of me.' She pauses and takes a sip of her coffee, the mug shaking as she lowers it back to the table. 'He died two years ago – lung cancer – and it was on his death bed that he revealed the truth about what he'd done at St Philomena's and a string of other private hospitals.

'He said the first time it happened, he was trying to do what was right. A mother died in childbirth, and rather than allowing the child to grow up in the social care system, he made a choice, and swapped the child with that of a stillborn. He said the parents were none the wiser, and he felt that he'd done a good thing, despite the moral and criminal implications. I was so disgusted, but there was worse to come.

'He said it happened a second time when a woman severely injured in a car accident lost her premature son, and her family offered a huge sum of money to his partners and they agreed to the switch.'

Elizabeth doesn't have to confirm she's talking about Louisa, as the silence speaks volumes.

'I-I never knew,' Louisa says. 'Not at first. I struggled to bond with Caleb, and I thought there had to be something wrong with me. He never felt like mine, but my husband and parents said I was imagining it and had me diagnosed with PND.'

'When my father died, I got access to his personal files, and discovered the full extent of his actions. I was horrified, and that's when I discovered your name and the figure paid. I was angry at him and you, which is why I sent the letter threatening to expose the lie. I couldn't believe it when you refused to acknowledge the crime, so I decided I'd do what I could to locate all the bereaved parents and relocate them with their children. It takes up all my free time, but I will continue the fight until they're all reunited, or until the leukaemia defeats me.'

'Abbie said she thought her son had died, but some woman told her he was still alive.'

'He is, and I'm going to do what I can to get them back together, but it isn't easy. There are issues with his new family that I need to pick through first.'

Louisa glances down at Caleb to ensure he isn't listening in, but he's too busy stuffing forkfuls of cake into his mouth, his lips covered in chocolate. 'Can you tell me anything about his original family?'

'I don't have any of my work with me today, but if you give me your number, I promise I will get back in touch and share what I know.'

'You need to be careful. My husband Pete … he's dangerous and he's looking for you.'

'I appreciate the warning, and I'll call the police if I sense him nearby. You look as though you might need to watch your back too.'

Louisa nods, uncertain what her next step should be, and whether her mother's apology this morning could really be trusted. At the very least, she should take Caleb to see his grandfather at the hospital before it is too late.

Chapter 52

Abbie – Now

I don't know how much time has passed when I start to come around after surgery, but the first words I hear are from a voice I don't recognise.

'We need to keep an eye on her; she's not out of the woods yet.'

She.

Internally I'm screaming out for answers.

What is wrong with my daughter? Has my body let me down again? Does Mark know I've failed him for a second time?

I must faze in and out of consciousness several times as the hours pass, and I can't be sure whether the faces of Mark, Michelson, and Louisa are real or imagined.

When I finally manage to keep my eyes open for more than a few seconds, I'm convinced I must still be dreaming until I feel the warmth of Mark's hand in mine, and he asks if I want something to drink.

'You need to build up your strength,' he says softly. 'How are you feeling?'

I don't know how to begin answering such a broad question. I'm exhausted, terrified, sorry, confused, and overjoyed that Mark is by my side despite everything I've put him through.

'I-I'm sorry,' I croak at him, my mouth as dry as the Sahara.

He leans over me and reaches for a beaker of water, placing the straw between my dry and cracked lips.

'Small sips, the nurse said. Once they reduce your painkillers you'll be allowed tea and food. Is there anything you fancy? Given you've abstained from pate and brie for so many months, I feel I should have brought a hamper of food with me. I think there's a Burger King downstairs if you want me to get you a burger or some fries?'

I sip the water, clear my throat, and try again. 'W-Where's our baby?' My eyes fill instantly as I await the news I'm dreading.

Mark releases my hand and moves away from the bed, returning a moment later with a bundle of blankets. It's only when he retakes his seat beside the bed that I see the tiny face inside.

'Here she is,' he says. 'She's been asleep for about half an hour, but I'm sure she must be desperate for a cuddle with her mum.'

If this is a dream then it's the cruellest I've ever known.

I sit up in bed, plumping the cushion behind my back for support, and open my arms out. Mark lowers the tiny bundle into my grasp and kisses the top of my head.

'I suppose we'll have to choose a name for her. The midwife asked me what we'd decided on, but I didn't want to confirm until I'd spoken to you. What do you think she looks like?'

I can't answer as my lips tremble and the tears blur

my vision. I have spent more than five years waiting for a chance to hold my own child, and now that she's arrived, I'm overwhelmed. Warm tears break free of my eyes as I stare at the world's most beautiful baby girl. Her tiny nose curls up slightly at the end like mine, and she has tiny dimples in her cheeks like me.

'She's perfect,' I whisper, not wanting to disturb this sleeping angel in my arms.

Mark leans in and kisses me tenderly on the lips. 'She must take after her perfect mother then.'

'Oh Mark, I'm so sorry about the money. She showed me what I thought was DNA confirmation and a picture that was probably photo-shopped using pictures of us. I was stupid, and –'

'I don't care about any of that right now, Abbie. You're safe, and our baby is safe; that's all that matters.'

'I'm sorry I didn't listen to you.'

'You don't need to apologise to me. I'm sorry that I wasn't more supportive. Losing Josh is the hardest thing I've ever dealt with, and I wasn't ready to consider reopening that scar. I'm sorry. I promise from hereon in everything I do will be for you and this little girl. My family is more important to me than anything else.'

I don't doubt that he means every word.

'So,' he says, beaming from ear to ear, 'what are we going to call her?'

Chapter 53

Abbie – One week later

I don't think I've ever welcomed so many visitors to the house as we've received since I was discharged from hospital. And we can barely move for helium balloons and bouquets of flowers. I've actually had to borrow extra vases from neighbours. I still ache when I stand or twist suddenly – I'm stitched up to the nines down there – but I wouldn't have it any other way. Mark is on paternity leave, and every night when I go to sleep, I realise how lucky I am to have this little family. I'm not sure what contentment is supposed to feel like, but hand-on-heart I've never been happier than I am right now.

It's not all tweeting birds and dancing daffodils though. The night feeds are the worst, especially when she resists my winding technique, but we're getting there. Mark's trying to do his bit, but he clearly isn't cut out for functioning at three in the morning. So the routine we've developed is that he does the night feed at 11, and the first one at six, and I cover in between. She won't be this small and needy forever, and I just want to make the most of every moment she is.

Her eyes seem to light up when I enter the room, and even if those little smiles are just wind, I like to think they're because she's pleased to see me. I used to imagine what it would have been like having these moments with Josh, until it became too painful to focus on what I'd missed out on.

A knock at the front door has Mark charging out of the room on tiptoes, as we've only just got her back down to sleep after we took her to meet Mark's colleagues at his office this morning. He returns a minute later, and I see that Sally is creeping quietly behind him. She smiles as our eyes meet, and she mouths a hello, having been briefed by Mark that Operation Silence is underway.

Sally comes over and beams as she looks into the Moses basket. I slowly stand and follow her out of the room, throwing hand signals at Mark to say and watch the baby. I mime a drinking gesture and he sticks his thumb up. Once the kitchen door is closed, I fill the kettle and select three mugs.

'She's beautiful,' Sally says, still smiling widely.

'Thank you,' I reply stifling a yawn.

'And how are you coping? It's a big change isn't it?'

I nod, and would be quite happy to go for a nap, but a fully caffeinated tea should be enough to snap me out of it. Sally hands me the bunch of chrysanthemums she brought with her, as well as the large gift bag she's holding.

'When we told the children your daughter had arrived, they all asked if they could come and visit you. Gail and I said that wouldn't be possible, but that you might bring her in to meet them when you're ready – no hurry. So, instead they all made you cards, which are in the bag, and some of the parents asked us to pass on a few gifts, which are also in there.'

My hormones must still be out of sync, because my eyes fill, and I have to swallow down the imminent sob.

Sally tears off a strip of kitchen towel and passes it to me while she fills the mugs with boiling water and makes the tea. 'It can be very overwhelming,' she admits. 'I remember when both of mine were born. You want to believe they'll stay that tiny forever, but they grow so quickly, believe me.'

I accept the mug and sit down on one of the stools at the breakfast bar, Sally following suit. 'How is everything at work? Is Claudette settling well?'

Sally pulls a face and rolls her eyes. 'She lasted four days before handing in her notice. Better offer elsewhere apparently. She was only maternity cover, so there's not a lot we can do about it. If I'm honest, some of the children didn't take as well to her as they did with you. I don't think I appreciated just how good you were until you weren't there anymore. As soon as you're ready to return, you're welcome back.'

It's nice to hear that I'm missed, and as frustrated as I was when Gail and Sally insisted I start my maternity leave early, it was just as well they did given the earlier-than-expected birth.

'Toby came to speak to me after you left. He said … He was worried that he was the reason you'd left. I explained to him that it was because you were due to have your baby, but he said he'd pushed you over, and was blaming himself for messing up everything. Is that what happened that day? Did Toby push you?'

My cheeks flush because I know I should have

reported the incident when it happened, but there's no point in denying it now that Toby's admitted wheat he did. 'I'm sorry I didn't say anything at the time. I couldn't be sure whether the collision was deliberate or just an accident. I was hoping to speak to his dad before coming to you and Gail, but I never got the opportunity and then things kind of snowballed. I'm sorry.'

'I spoke to his dad after he came to me last week, and it turns out there are problems at home. His parents are separating and it's clearly having an impact on Toby's stress levels. I've said I'll keep an eye on him, and we'll handle it as needed. Anyway, I told Toby I'd pass on his apologies, so I have now.'

Sally stays for twenty minutes while I open the cards, and spend most of the time crying happy tears. When she leaves, we hug, and I promise I'll bring the baby by to meet the children in the next week or so. As she's walking down the road to her car, I see Yolanda moving slowly towards our house. She's carrying a bottle of prosecco, and a box of Belgian chocolates, and wearing an apologetic frown.

'I hear congratulations are in order,' she says as she hands over the gifts. Can I come in and meet your daughter?'

I nod, and move back from the door, allowing her through. Her bump is enormous, and she almost looks ready to burst, but she doesn't make any fuss as she squeezes past me, and removes her anorak.

'Did the two of you decide on a name?' Yolanda whispers as she stares into the Moses basket.

'Eleanor – after my mother. Mark's grandmother

was also called Eleanor, so it seems a good fit.'

She glances over at Mark who is gently snoring in the armchair beside the basket. 'And how are things with the two of you?'

'Couldn't be better,' I say, smiling.

Eleanor stirs, and opens her eyes, her bottom lip trembling as though she's about to erupt. I pick her up gently and carry her through to the kitchen, her face pressed to my collarbone. Mark deserves his rest, so Yolanda and I settle in the kitchen, and I allow her to cuddle Eleanor. I make more tea, and fill Yolanda in on everything that happened since I last spoke to her.

'So, that's why you didn't stop when I waved at you in town?' she questions.

I nod. 'Yeah, sorry I didn't stop. My head was all over the place, and I believed Kinga was about to take me to Josh. I'm sorry I didn't listen to you when you said she was just trying to con me. Very expensive lesson learned.'

'Did you report the theft to the police?'

I nod again as I take a sip of tea. 'Yes, we told PS Brearton all about it and he's given us a case reference number, but isn't confident we'll ever see justice or get a penny of the twenty grand back.'

'What a bitch!' Yolanda declares. 'Do you have any idea why she targeted you in the first place?'

'No,' I say with a sigh. 'She was so convincing that I did believe she was acting in our best interests.'

Yolanda hands Eleanor back to me as she starts to grizzle. 'There's something I need to tell you as well,' she says. 'You asked me about Chris Orville and I wasn't totally honest with you about how I knew him.

I wasn't lying when I said Chris and Tyrese did a couple of jobs together a few years back, but I should have told you the reason Chris and his wife moved away.'

She looks away for a moment, searching for the right words, and when she meets my gaze, I can see her eyes are tearful.

'Tyrese had an affair with Chris's wife. That's why they left: to start over. I was so angry at Tyrese, but I didn't want his mistake to destroy my family. The boys dote on their dad, and he admitted to what he'd done and was sorry, so I learned to forgive him. It wasn't easy, and if I'm honest I'm not sure I'll ever be able to trust him as I once did, but I can see how much he regrets what happened. That's why I was so surprised to hear that Chris and his wife were back. I went to see him and we ended up having an argument in the park. He told me they're getting divorced, but what annoyed me was him suggesting the two of us should sleep together to get even with Tyrese.'

Suddenly her reaction after the park seems so clear. Whether she would have drunk the whiskey had I not shown up I may never know, but I can see how that kind of a shock would affect someone as far gone as she is.

'I had no idea,' I say, rubbing her arm gently, 'and you'll get no judgement from me. It isn't easy to forgive a partner's duplicity, but I'll support you any way I can.'

She wipes a stray tear from her cheek, and mouths, 'Thank you.'

I swap Eleanor to my other arm. 'I'm glad you

stopped by actually, as there was something I was meaning to ask you. Mark and I aren't particularly religious, but we've decided to have Eleanor christened because we have a lot to be thankful for. I was hoping you might agree to be her Godmother? I can't think of anyone I'd prefer her to go to for guidance.'

Yolanda doesn't answer, moving to my side and hugging us both close. 'I'd be honoured.'

We agree to meet for lunch in a day or two, and as I show her to the door, Mark wakes and collects Eleanor from me for her next change and feed. I'm watching my two loves together when my mobile rings and I see Elizabeth Michelson's name on the screen.

Chapter 54

Abbie – Now

'Thank you for coming,' Elizabeth says, when Louisa and I are gathered in the farmhouse on what must be a couple of acres of green fields.

I didn't spot any animals grazing nearby, and given her slight frame, I don't sense farming is her profession. Louisa has also come unaccompanied, as per Elizabeth's request, but I'm still not sure why she has invited us both to her home. Mark is at home watching over Eleanor, but is aware of where I am and is only a phone call away if I need him. I had to promise I would message him every ten minutes so that he knows I am safe, but I think he may have overestimated the level of threat.

The farmhouse has a warm, cosy feeling to it. We are seated at a large wooden table that looks as though it was handcrafted. The table top is uneven due to the ridges of the planks used, but it also feels sturdy, as if it would take an army to move it. The wall behind me is dominated by a huge AGA and the only appliance that looks new is the washing machine. If there is a refrigerator or freezer in this kitchen, then it's well-hidden.

We haven't been given a tour of the property, but I'd estimate it must have three or four bedrooms, but it does lack modern conveniences such as carpets and double-glazing. It certainly has character, though I imagine it must get pretty cold in winter.

'Given everything you've both been through, I think it's only fair that you both hear what I have to say. Before I continue, there is someone missing from the party, but I'd ask you to stay calm Abbie, and listen to what I have to say before reacting.'

Heat rises to my cheeks at being singled out like a disobedient child, but when Kinga appears at the door behind Elizabeth, I realise why she said it. Kinga is wearing a free-flowing summer dress, and her clean hair is hanging down around her face. She looks far prettier than I ever gave her credit for, and without the faded leather jacket, I would hardly realise it was the same woman. She's obviously made good use of the money she stole.

'How is baby, Abbie?' she asks, sitting down at the table beside Elizabeth and across from Louisa.

When I think of the run-around she's given me this last week, and her betrayal when I finally allowed myself to trust her I don't want to give her the satisfaction of an answer. What I should do is phone Mark and ask him to send Brearton to arrest her, but at Elizabeth's request I bite my lip instead.

'Sh-She is doing well, thank you,' I eventually reply.

Elizabeth reaches into a box on the vacant chair beside her and extracts a padded brown envelope, sliding it across the table to me. I already know what it contains as I recognise the building society's insignia in the left hand corner.

'It's every penny of the money that you left with Kinga. You're welcome to count it to be sure.'

I reach for the envelope, and although my head is telling me it's rude to take her up on the offer, I've seen enough shows to know there could be fake notes hidden. Lifting the flap I empty the wads of notes onto the table, and make a show of thumbing through them. It's not as accurate as running a magic marker over each, but I'm confident that this is the money I left in my car with Kinga. I push the notes back into the envelope and nod my head for Elizabeth to continue.

'Louisa, what I have to say to you isn't easy. When we went for that drink in the hospital restaurant, you asked me whether Abbie was Caleb's mum, and I told you that she wasn't.'

My shoulders tense at this statement, but my mouth is too dry to speak.

'That was the truth, but I did also lie to you that day when you asked me whether I knew who Caleb's real mum was. I said she wasn't around anymore, because I needed to double-check my analysis.' She pauses, and turns slightly so that she's facing Kinga. 'When I first contacted you three months ago, I told you your son had died in a house fire as I believed that to be the case. However, I now know that,' she looks directly at Louisa, 'he survived that fire. Louisa, Kinga is Caleb's real mum.'

Neither Kinga nor Louisa speak, each knocked for six by the news.

'Kinga, you should know that Louisa had no involvement in the transaction that saw your son stolen from you. According to my father's notes, the men who brought you to him for the delivery asked that the child be given away to a suitable family. They were adamant that the baby was unwanted, and on the same day Louisa lost her child as a result of her accident. I'm not excusing his behaviour, but I do believe he thought he was acting in both your best interests. His notes say that the money Louisa's family provided was handed over to the men for you, Kinga, but I'm sensing you never saw a penny of it.'

'M-My boy is alive?' Kinga says, a hand shooting up to her mouth. 'He alive?'

Elizabeth slips a page out of the box and I recognise the layout of the DNA Analysis sheet. 'There is a greater than 99.9% probability, yes. Louisa, you were desperate to find Caleb's real family. Here she is.'

Louisa looks close to tears, and Kinga's face is pale as a sheet, as they size one another up.

'We should give the two of you a chance to talk,' Elizabeth says, pushing her chair backwards, and standing. 'Abbie, would you mind coming with me? There's something I'd like to ask for your help with.'

I don't want to move. I've never seen Kinga looking so vulnerable, and I want to offer her my support, but this conversation really is none of my business.

I stand and follow Elizabeth, but press my hand to Kinga's shoulder as I pass, and tell her to call for me if she needs to. Elizabeth shows me through to a larger room, which contains a long settee with a pillow and folded blanket stacked at one end. The rest of the room is taken up with cardboard boxes, stacked in random piles, and not dissimilar to the storage unit Kinga was sleeping in.

'These are all my father's notes,' she says, waving an arm at the boxes. 'Not all to do with his meddling in other families' lives, though some of it is. This has been my life's work for the last two years, but I now know I'm not in a position to finish it. There are at least another half dozen mothers out there who don't know that their children survived the delivery. I need someone to continue my work when the leukaemia catches up with me.'

Suddenly the headscarf and gaunt frame makes sense. Instinctively, I move to her side and hug her. 'I'm sorry. How long do you have left?'

Her body seems to melt into mine, but she weighs next to nothing. 'Weeks; a couple of months if I'm lucky.'

'Can't you share all of this detail with the police? They should be the ones to investigate the crimes committed by your father and his business partners, surely?'

She pulls free of me and moves across the room, facing the window. 'The people responsible for these horrific crimes ought to be strung up from the nearest yard arm, but first these parents and children need to be reunited. That has to be the priority. But it isn't easy tracking people when you only have a name to go on. Do you know how many Abbie Friar's there are in the UK alone? You share your name with two thousand other women, and that doesn't include those who've subsequently married and taken a different surname. It's hard work.'

I feel like she's angling for me to pick up the baton, but with Eleanor and then returning to preschool after maternity leave, I'm in no position to support her efforts. But then something else scratches at the back of my mind.

'How do you know how many Abbie Friars there are? If I'm not Caleb's mum then why would you be searching for me?'

She tenses slightly at the question, but doesn't answer it. 'Do you know why I asked Kinga to demand twenty thousand pounds from you and Mark?'

I'm too confused to answer, given she's just handed it back.

'I wanted to test how resourceful the two of you were, and how far you'd be willing to go to uncover the truth about your son.'

I'm about to ask her what she's talking about when she heads out through a second doorway at the far side of the room. I'm not sure if it's some kind of broom cupboard at first, but when she doesn't reappear, I decide to follow. The door leads to a narrow corridor, and then an old staircase up. She's at the top of the stairs when I reach the first step, and she waves for me to follow.

At the top of the stairs, she puts a finger to her lips, and heads to a closed door. She knocks gently five times, and then repeats the process. The door opens a moment later and when I see the face of the little boy staring back at me, my heart skips a beat, and I almost collapse. It is the same face as in the photograph Kinga showed me last week.

'Josh, this is Abbie, a friend of mine, do you mind if we come in to your room?'

He looks from Elizabeth to me, and then back again

before nodding his head and stepping back. The room is like nothing I've seen before. There are papier-mâché planets hanging from strings in the ceiling. The hard floor has a large red cross dissecting it into quarters. One corner is lined with dry-wipe boards, which are covered in drawings. Another corner has a variety of instruments on the floor ranging from a tambourine and triangle, to maracas and castanets. A third corner is stacked from floor to ceiling with books and comics, and it is here that the boy plonks himself on a beanbag and returns to reading the open comic beside it.

'Josh is a very special boy, Abbie,' she tells me. 'This is his sensory room where he gets to explore what he's interested in. You should feel very privileged that he's allowed you to come in even though you've only just met. He's not always so welcoming to strangers'

I can't speak. This can't be real. I pinch at my skin and bite down on the inside of my cheek as I try to wake myself, yet I remain in the sensory room, staring down at the little boy who I instantly know is my son.

'Josh is autistic,' Elizabeth continues. 'A very intelligent boy, but he needs to be cared for with a certain amount of attention. He has difficulty ordering his emotions, and as desperate as I'm sure you are to hug him, it needs to be on his terms. He loves reading and drawing, as you'll see, but he's also absolutely fascinated by space and other planets, aren't you Josh?'

He doesn't answer, lost in his comic.

'His favourite film is ET, and I wouldn't put it past him to be the first autistic astronaut in space.'

I open my mouth to speak, but I can't form the string of questions and exclamations vying for my attention.

'It's probably best if we go back downstairs for now,' Elizabeth urges. 'It'll be lunchtime soon, Josh. I'll call you when it's ready.'

He doesn't acknowledge us as we depart the room, but Elizabeth closes his door and leads us back down the narrow staircase. I collapse on the settee as soon as I reach it, burying my head in my hands.

Elizabeth joins me, but when she speaks there is a sadness to her tone that is heart-breaking. 'When my dad brought Josh home that first day, he told me that Josh's parents had put him up for adoption, and he asked me if I would step in and raise him as my own. I fell in love with his eyes the moment I saw him, and was only too willing to give him a second chance at life. It wasn't easy raising him as a single mother, but we found a way, and when his autism was diagnosed, it felt like the angels had brought me to him in his hour of need. I had no idea about any of my dad's work until he was on his death bed. He admitted to me that Josh's real parents hadn't known he'd been taken, and when my leukaemia was diagnosed I knew that I had to prioritise finding you. I never anticipated it would take as long as it did, but I'm so relieved the battle was worth it.'

I keep my face buried to stop the room from spinning. 'Why did you send Kinga to tell me rather than come yourself?'

'Josh is a very special boy, and I wouldn't feel happy just handing him over to anyone. I know I have no right to say this, but I wanted to check you were worthy enough to take on the responsibility.'

My mouth drops along with my hands.

'No that wasn't exactly what I meant,' she retreats. 'I love Josh as my own, and I wanted to make sure that when I'm no longer around, he would receive the enhanced care he needs. I had to be sure that you would give him everything he needs. I'm sorry.'

I'm angry, but try to put myself in her shoes: if I learned I had to give up Eleanor, wouldn't I do absolutely everything in my power to make sure that her future was secured and she would be properly looked after?

'Did we pass your test?' I ask glibly.

'I wouldn't have introduced you to him if I had any lingering doubts.'

'Does he know?'

'That he's adopted? No. I didn't want to put him through and further unnecessary emotional turmoil.'

'What about your illness? Does he know about that?'

'I had to explain to him that I was ill when all my hair started falling out because of the treatment. He knows I have leukaemia, but I don't believe he truly realises what that means for him in terms of the future. As I said, he's very bright, and understands what a terminal illness is, but I don't think he's applied that knowledge to his own situation. It's going to take time to explain to him, and I think you should also be involved in those conversations.'

This is far more than I was expecting when she phoned this morning, and I'm suddenly conscious that I haven't messaged Mark to reassure him that I'm okay. I mean, I'm not okay – I'm an emotional wreck – but he needs to know I'm not in danger. I have no idea how I'm going to break this news to him.

'I appreciate this is a lot to take in, but there's something else you need to know. I plan to leave this house and land to Josh in my will. This is the only house he's known, and I'd like it if you and your family moved in during the transition. It's going to be hard enough for him to come to terms with me going and you taking him on without changing his home as well. He's in a school that caters for his needs, and it's only ten minutes down the road. He knows the staff and children there, and they understand what he needs.

Of course, you're welcome to choose a new school for him when term restarts, but there aren't many finer places for him. I'll leave stipulation in my will in the form of a trust to cover the costs of his full education, so you won't face a financial burden. And I know it's a lot to ask, but if you and your family move in sooner rather than later, I think it will really help Josh. I don't expect you to answer now, but would ask that you and your husband talk about it and let me know as soon as possible.

'If you decide that you can't take on Josh's needs then –'

I raise my hand and cut her off. 'There is no question about whether Mark and I are prepared to support our son. I've spent five years waiting to be his mum, and I don't want to waste another second of not being in his life.'

Her lips curve up at this and her eyes fill. 'You have no idea how happy I am to hear that. I should warn you that it won't always be easy.'

'Whatever it takes, right?'

The tears flow freely down her cheeks, and I embrace her because I don't know what else to do. After all this time, I've found my son.

***

Louisa and Kinga are talking when we return to the kitchen, and Louisa is showing her pictures of Caleb on her phone.

'He's with my parents at the moment,' Louisa says, 'but I think you should meet him as soon as possible.'

Kinga still looks overwhelmed, though the colour is slowly returning to her cheeks. I sit down next to her, and check that she's okay. She nods, and I can see from her smeared makeup that she too has been crying, but she looks happier than I've seen her before. She seems to be sitting taller somehow.

A fresh thought pops into my head, and it's spilling from my lips before I've even had the chance to properly process it.

'Are you still looking for a place to stay?' I ask Kinga.

She nods.

'Elizabeth was just telling me that she needs someone to help her locate the remaining families impacted by all of this, and I was just thinking that maybe *you* could pick up the reins. All the paperwork is here, and I imagine there must be a guestroom you could sleep in?' I look to Elizabeth and she nods, her smile widening.

'I think that would be a brilliant idea,' Elizabeth concurs. 'You're nothing if not resourceful, Kinga. I could show you the ropes, and then ... when the time comes ... I'll know it's in good hands.'

I pull out my phone ready to message Mark and ask him to come and meet me, but my phone doesn't have a good signal. I stand, ready to go outside to try for better coverage, as Louisa and Kinga decide they're going to go and see Caleb. We all make it to the front door as there is a knock. Louisa opens the door as she is at the front, but she recoils in horror at the figure looming in the doorway.

'Pete,' I hear her gasp.

He isn't the ogre I was expecting based on how she described him in the hospital, but then I know appearances can be deceptive. He looks like an overweight, substitute geography teacher I once had. Whatever he's done to Louisa, I can see the power he has over her. He doesn't seem the least bit interested in her presence here, and is oblivious to the morning's revelations.

He's about to speak when Kinga steps forwards, pushing herself onto tiptoes to try and bridge the gap in their heights, but it's like watching a modern reworking of David and Goliath.

'This is man you tell me about? This is man who threaten you?' she asks Louisa, who nods grimly.

Kinga runs her eyes from his face to his feet, taking him in.

'Hello man, with small willy,' she says, before winding her arm in and sending a fist flying at his face. She connects with his nose and he instantly shrinks before us, doubling over as his hands shoot to his face.

'I eat men like you for breakfast,' she continues, stepping out of the house, and brushing past him on the way to the taxi that Louisa must have called. 'You will leave Louisa and her family alone now. Oh, and she want divorce.'

Pete is howling as he rummages in his pocket for a handkerchief, and when he straightens, he looks like he wants to say something, but he retreats when he sees Kinga glaring at him, and is soon hurrying back to his mud-spattered Land Rover.

I step out of the house, and put the phone to my ear, listening to the rings as I try to compose what I'm going to say to Mark.

He answers on the fourth ring. 'Thank God, I was about to summon a search party. Is everything okay?'

I want to tell him everything I'm feeling. How our prayers have finally been answered, and how Eleanor is about to get the best big brother she deserves, but I can't put into words the joy and excitement that is coursing through every nerve in body. It's almost as if I can feel my broken heart being stitched back together.

'Abbie, are you still there?' Mark says.

I take a deep breath. 'I found him.'

The End

AUTHOR MESSAGE

Thank you for taking the time to read **THE PRODIGAL MOTHER**. If you enjoyed it, please post a review and share the story with your friends. If a book is written to entertain, then the reader is the target audience, and I feel honoured that you chose one of my books to read.

Please don't be afraid to contact me via Facebook or Twitter to let me know what you thought of the story. There's nothing more joyful for an author than hearing from a reader who loved one of their books (believe me!). I really do respond to *every* message.

If you'd like to keep up-to-date with all my latest releases, you can join my mailing list via my website. Your email address will never be shared and you can unsubscribe at any time.

Thank you again for reading my book. I hope to hear from you soon.

Stephen

Website: www.stephenedger.com
Facebook: www.facebook.com/AuthorStephenEdger
Twitter: www.twitter.com/stephenedger

ACKNOWLEDGEMENTS

I'd like to say special thanks to the following people, without whom ***THE PRODIGAL MOTHER*** wouldn't be in existence today:

Dr Parashar Ramanuj, my best friend for more than twenty years and my first port of call whenever I have strange questions about medical procedures and body parts. His knowledge of psychological illness was essential for this story, and any errors are my misinterpretation of what he explained.

Joanne Taylor who has been reading and providing feedback on my novels since the beginning. Thank you to Alex Shaw and Paul Grzegorzek – authors and dear friends – who are happy to listen to me moan and whinge about the pitfalls of the publishing industry, offering words of encouragement along the way.

Away from publishing, I wouldn't be a writer if it wasn't for my beautiful and always supportive wife Hannah. She keeps all the 'behind the scenes' stuff of my life in order and our children's lives would be far greyer if I was left in sole charge. I'd also like to thank my mother-in-law Marina for all the championing of my books she does on social media.

And final thanks must go to YOU for picking up and

reading ***THE PRODIGAL MOTHER***. You are the reason I wake up ridiculously early to write every day, and why every free moment is spent devising plot twists. I feel truly honoured to call myself a writer, and it thrills me to know that other people are being entertained by the weird and wonderful visions my imagination creates. I love getting lost in my imagination and the more people who read and enjoy my stories, the more I can do it.

Printed in Great Britain
by Amazon